recovering apollo 8 and Other Stories

Kristine Kathryn Rusch

GOLDEN GRYPHON PRESS • 2010

Contents

To Dean, without whom these stories would
not have been written.

❖ ❖ ❖

Introduction

WHEN I CAME INTO THIS BUSINESS IN THE LATE 1980s, there were "good" anthologies and "bad" anthologies. The "good" anthologies were "original" anthologies that published a variety of stories, usually without a theme. The "good" anthologies were also edited by the premier editors in the business (we all knew who they were). Occasionally someone could sneak into that category of premier editor by editing an anthology (or series of anthologies) that received excellent reviews.

That's how I became one of the premier editors in the field at the ripe old age of twenty-nine. I edited *Pulphouse: The Hardback Magazine*, it got excellent reviews, and suddenly, I was the hottest editor in the business.

Most editors aren't so lucky. They edit anthologies that never get reviewed. Back in the late 1980s, those anthologies were "theme" anthologies—a group of stories written around the same idea (say, pirates or vampires). Everyone in the field understood that these anthologies weren't very good, because no story written to demand could be anything other than mediocre. Of course, the people who made these judgments rarely (never) read the theme anthologies.

Times change. During the 1990s, Mike Resnick did a series of award-winning critically acclaimed theme anthologies. Then the premier editors ran into a stumbling block: Publishers didn't want hodgepodge anthologies. They only wanted theme anthologies. Theme anthologies, believe it or not, are easier to sell.

So the premier editors started editing theme anthologies. But because the premier editors put the anthologies together, they had to be good, right?

Slowly, the distinction between "good" anthologies and "bad" anthologies became blurred. The die-hards continued to argue that theme anthologies in general were bad, but an occasional theme anthology by a premier editor was just fine. Those die-hards continued to make their judgments without reading the theme anthologies by unknown or "non-premier" editors.

When people read the theme anthologies, they discovered something: the same percentage of good to mediocre stories occurred in those anthologies as in the anthologies edited by the premier editors.

Why? Because theme anthologies work. At their very best, they stretch writers to try something new, something the writer has never tried before.

I have written for theme anthologies since 1991, when Ed Gorman asked me into an anthology called *Invitation to Murder*. Back in those dark days, I had no idea there were such things as "good" anthologies and "bad" anthologies. All I knew were two things: 1) Ed Gorman was a hell of a writer; and 2) he liked my work well enough to ask me into an invitation-only anthology.

That story led to more than a hundred others, all written for theme anthologies. All of those stories stretched me as a writer. Not once had I considered the topic to be easy or to be something I would have approached on my own.

Some of those stories are in this volume. When Joe Haldeman asked me to participate in his anthology, *Future Weapons of War*, I accepted. Then I looked at the topic. I didn't want to write a story that might inspire someone to create a new and more deadly weapon.

I struggled with that ethical conflict for days. I almost left the anthology, something I have never ever done. Then I decided to try.

What I wrote came out of that ethical conflict. The story, "Craters," garnered some of the best reviews of my career. It also was reprinted in *The Year's Best Science Fiction Twenty-Five*, edited by Gardner Dozois.

I can guarantee I would never ever have gone to the dark places that "Craters" took me without the request for a story from Joe Haldeman.

Five of the nine stories in this volume came about because of an invitation into a theme anthology. All five are either award winners or have been reprinted in year's best collections. Two are award winners that also appeared in year's best collections.

Three of the remaining four stories are award-winners. These stories appeared in the science fiction magazines. Two of them were cover stories. I adore the SF magazines—after all, I used to edit one. I try to write at least one story per magazine per year, which is, in my own way, my own private attempt at a theme anthology.

Because science fiction stretches me as well. When I attended Clarion Writers Workshop in 1985, my fellow workshoppers told me to give up writing science fiction and to only write fantasy. According to them, I didn't have the background to write true science fiction, and I couldn't get that background without going back for an advanced degree in one of the sciences, something I didn't want to do.

Those voices haunt me every time I sit down to write science fiction. As so many young writers are at the first major workshops they attend, I was quite vulnerable and ready to believe every negative thing everyone told me. The flip side to that is that the vulnerable young writer (in this case, me) refuses to believe all the good things that she gets told.

So the fact that Damon Knight and Kate Wilhelm (and Joe Haldeman, Michael Bishop, Algis Budrys, and Elizabeth A. Lynn) told me I was on the right path and I should keep writing what I was writing meant a lot less than the negative comments from my peers.

However, those positive comments from the professional writers kept me writing science fiction. Thank heavens. Many other young writers quit when they receive the kinds of criticism I received twenty-four years ago.

But the negative comments did serve one purpose. They make me even more rigorous with my science fiction than I might have been if I hadn't attended Clarion in 1985. Two of the three novellas in this volume, "Recovering Apollo 8," and "Diving into the Wreck," combine some hard science with extrapolation. I consulted friends, scientists, and texts to make sure I got the details right.

Those stories have received great critical and popular acclaim. Both won the *Asimov's* Readers Choice award—an award I value highly because the readers of the magazine vote based on which story they like, not on who edited the volume or who their friends are.

That reader acclaim means a lot to me because it gets to the core of science fiction writing. Heck, it gets to the core of all fiction writing.

It doesn't matter if the anthologies are "good" or "bad" based on some weird critical bias. It doesn't matter if the magazines are "genre" or "literary."

What matters is whether or not the readers have enjoyed the work. Did the story take them away from their daily worries, even for an hour? Did the story make them want to read another? Will they remember the story?

I strive for these things every time I write a story because I appreciate them as a reader. I love short fiction and I'm proud to be a short fiction writer.

I have included nine of my best stories from the past eleven years. I hope they give you hours of reading pleasure.

And for those of you who like to know how stories came about, I've included an afterword with a little bit about each story. It surprises me how many came about because an editor said, "Hey, Kris, write me a story about this particular topic."

I did. And here they are.

Enjoy.

—Kristine Kathryn Rusch
February 2009

Recovering Apollo 8 and Other Stories

Recovering Apollo 8

Part One
2007

*R*ICHARD REMEMBERED IT WRONG. HE REMEM-bered it as if it were a painting, and he were observing it, instead of a living, breathing memory that he had a part of.

The image was so vivid, in fact, that he had had it painted with the first of what would become obscene profits from his business, and placed the painting in his office—each version of his office, the latter ones growing so big that he had to find a special way to display the painting, a way to help it remain the center of his vision.

The false memory—and the painting—went like this.

He stands in his backyard. To his left, there is the swing set; to his right, clothes lines running forward like railroad tracks.

He is eight, small for his age, very blond, his features unformed. His face is turned toward the night sky, the Moon larger than it ever is. It illuminates his face like a halo from a medieval religious painting; its whiteness so vivid that it seems more alive than he does.

He, however, is not looking at the Moon. He is looking beyond it where a small, cone-shaped ship heads toward the darkness. The ship is almost invisible, except for one edge that catches the Moon's reflected light. A shimmer comes off the ship, just enough to make it seem as if the ship is expending its last bit of energy in a desperate attempt to save itself, an attempt even he—at eight—knows will fail.

Someone once asked him why he had a painting about loss as the focus of his office.

He was stunned.

He did not think of the painting, or the memory for that matter, as something that represented loss.

Instead, it represented hope. That last, desperate attempt would not have happened without the hope that it might work.

That's what he used to say.

What he thought was that the hope resided in the boy, in his memory, and in his desire to change one of the most significant moments of his past.

The real memory was prosaic:

The kitchen was painted bright yellow and small, although it didn't seem small then. Behind his chair were the counters, cupboards, and a deep sink with a small window above it, a window that overlooked the sidewalk to the garage. To his left, two more windows overlooked the large yard and the rest of the block. The stove was directly across from him. He always pictured his mother standing at it, even though she had a chair at the table as well. His father's chair was to his left, beneath the windows.

The radio sat on top of the refrigerator, which wasn't too far from the stove. But the center of the room, to his right and almost behind him, was the television, which remained on constantly.

His father could read at the table, but Richard could not. His mother tried to converse with him, but by his late childhood, the gaps in their IQs had started to show.

She was a smart woman, but he was off the charts. His father, who could at least comprehend some of what his son was saying, remained silent in the face of his son's genius. Silent and proud. They shared a name: Richard J. Johansenn, the J. standing for Jacob, after the same man, the family patriarch, his father's father— the man who had come to this country with his parents at the age of eight, hoping for—and discovering—a better world.

That night, December 24, 1968, the house was decorated for Christmas. Pine boughs on the dining room table, Christmas cards in a sleigh on top of the living room's television set. Candles at the kitchen table, which his father complained about every time he opened his newspaper. The scent of pine, of candle wax, of cookies.

His mother baked her way to the holiday and beyond; it was a wonder, with all those sweets surrounding him, that he never became fat. That night, however, they would have a regular dinner since Christmas Eve was not their holiday; their celebration happened Christmas Day.

Yet he was excited. He loved the season—the food, the music, the lights against the dark night sky. Even the snow, something he usually abhorred, seemed beautiful. He would stand on its icy crust and look up, searching for constellations or just staring at the Moon herself, wondering how something like that could be so distant and so cold.

That night, his mother called him in for dinner. He had been staring at the Moon through the telescope that his father gave him for his eighth birthday in July. He'd hoped to see Apollo 8 on its way to the lunar orbit.

On its way to history.

Instead, he came inside and sat down to a roast beef (or meatloaf or corned beef and cabbage) dinner, turning his chair slightly so that he could see the television. Walter Cronkite—the epitome, Richard thought, of the reliable adult male—reported from Mission Control, looking serious and boyish at the same time.

Cronkite loved the adventure of space almost as much as Richard did. And Cronkite got to be as close to it as a man could and not be part of it.

What Richard didn't like were the simulated pictures. It was impossible to film Apollo 8 on its voyage, so some poor SOB drew images.

At the time, Richard, like the rest of the country, had focused on the LOS zone—the Loss Of Signal zone on the dark side of the Moon. If the astronauts reached that, they were part of the lunar orbit, sixty-nine miles from the lunar surface. But the great American unwashed wouldn't know they had succeeded until they came out of the LOS zone.

The LOS zone scared everyone. Even Richard's father, who rarely admitted being scared.

Richard's father, the high school math and science teacher, who sat down with his son on Saturday, December 21—the day Apollo 8 lifted off—and explained, as best he could, orbital mechanics. He showed Richard the equations, and tried to explain the risk the astronauts were taking.

One error in the math, one slight miscalculation—even if it were accidental—a wobble in the space craft's burn as it left Earth orbit, a miss of a few seconds—could send the astronauts on a wider orbit around the Moon, or a wider Earth orbit. Or, God forbid, a straight trajectory away from Earth, away from the Moon, and into the great unknown, never to return.

Richard's mother thought her husband was helping his son with homework. When she discovered his true purpose, she dragged him into their bedroom for one of their whisper fights.

What do you think you're doing? she asked. *He's eight.*

He needs to understand, his father said.

No, he doesn't, she said. *He'll be frightened for days.*

And if they miss? His father said. *I'll have to explain it then.*

Her voice had a tightness as she said, *They won't miss.*

But they did.

They missed.

Mission Control had a hunch during the LOS, but they didn't confirm the hunch with the astronauts, not right away. They asked for a few things, another controlled burn, hoping that the ship might move back on track, a few more reports than usual just to get the men's voices on tape while they were still calm (apparently), but nothing they did changed the tragic fact that the astronauts would not return to Earth.

They would float forever in the darkness of space.

And for a while, they didn't know. The ship itself had limited control and almost no telemetry. The astronauts had to rely on Mission Control for all of their orbital information—in fact, for most of their critical information.

Later, it came out that the astronauts deduced the problem almost immediately, and tried to come up with solutions on their own.

Of course, there were none.

Which was why Cronkite looked so tense that Christmas Eve, sitting in the area cleared for broadcasters in Mission Control. Cronkite had known that the three astronauts were still alive, would remain alive for days as their little capsule headed into the vast beyond. They stayed in radio contact for longer than anyone felt comfortable with, and because they were heroes, they never complained.

They spoke of the plainness of the Moon, and the beauty of the Earth viewed from beyond. Apparently, on a closed circuit, they spoke to their wives and children one final time. They belonged to the Earth, as long as the radio signal held. As long as their oxygen held. As long as their hope held.

That was what Richard remembered: he remembered the hope.

No one played the tape any longer of Lovell, Borman, and Anders, talking about the future. The future had come and gone. What reporters and documentarians and historians played nowadays were the good-byes, or, if they were more charitable, the descriptions of Earth—how beautiful it looked; how small; how united.

It's hard to believe, Lovell said in what would become his most famous quote, *that such a beautiful place can house so many angry people. From a distance, it looks like the entire planet is at peace.*

Of course it wasn't.

But that didn't concern Richard then.

What worried him—what frightened him—was that this failure of the space program would end the program.

It worried the astronauts as well. They made a joint appeal with what would be damn close to their last breath.

This is not a failure. We're proud to be the first humans to venture beyond the Moon. Please continue the space program. Get us to the Moon. Get a base on the Moon. Send another group to explore the solar system—one who can report back to you. Do it in our name, and with our blessing.

Merry Christmas to all.

And to all, a good night.

That broadcast brought Richard's mother to tears. Richard's father put a strong hand on Richard's shoulder. And Walter Cronkite, that stalwart adult, removed his glasses, rubbed his eyes for a moment, and gathered himself, much as he had done five years earlier when a president died unexpectedly.

Cronkite did not say much more. He did not play the radio reports from the bitter end. He let Lovell, Borman, and Anders's desired last statement *be* their last statement.

He did not speculate on the means of their deaths, nor did he focus on the failure.

He focused on the future.

He focused on the hope.

And so did Richard—

At least, he tried.

But while he worked toward the conquest of space, while he studied his physics and astronomy, he remained in great physical condition so that he could become an astronaut at a moment's notice, and he would look through his telescope into the darkness beyond the Moon—and wonder:

What had they seen in those last hours?

What had they felt?
And where were they now?

Nearly forty years later, they were coming home.

Or as close to home as they could get with a dead ship and a dead crew, and no one heading out to greet them.

Apollo 8 had ended up in an elliptical orbit around the sun, much as the experts predicted might happen. The orbit took just over sixteen months to complete, but kept the small craft far above the plane of the Earth's orbit most of the time. The first time Apollo 8 had come home, or at least close to home, it had been just over eighteen years.

That first time they were discovered almost by accident. Sunlight, glinting off the capsule, drew the attention of amateur astronomers all over the world. Something small, something insignificant, reflecting light in an unusual way.

People speculated about what it was, what it might be. Giant telescopes from the Lowell Observatory to the new orbiting telescope began tracking it, and pictures came in, pictures showing a familiar conical shape.

It couldn't be, the experts said.

But it was.

Everyone hoped it was.

Richard spent those heady days begging his friends at the University of Wisconsin's observatory to turn their telescope toward it—ruining research, he was sure, and he didn't care. He wasn't even an astronomy student any longer. He had done his post-grad studies in aeronautics and engineering and had just started the company that would make him the country's first billionaire.

But in those days, he was still a student, with little power and even less control.

In the end, he had to go to the outskirts of town, away from the light, and try to see the capsule for himself. He stood in the deep cold, the ankle-deep snow, and stared for hours.

Finally, he convinced himself that he saw a wink of light, that it wasn't space dust or the space station the U.S. was building in Earth orbit, or even some of the satellites that had been launched in the last few years.

No, he convinced himself he saw the ship, and that fueled his obsession even more.

Perhaps that, more than the incorrect memory of the original loss, caused the wink of light on the capsule in his painting.

Perhaps that was the catalyst for it all.

Or maybe it was, as his mother claimed, his overactive imagination, held in place by his first experience of—his first real understanding of—death.

Only this didn't seem like death to Richard. It never had. In his mind, there was always a chance that the three men had lived. Maybe they had gone on, as their ship had gone on, exploring the solar system, seeing things that no man had ever seen up close. Or maybe they had encountered aliens, and those aliens, benign like the ones in the *Star Trek* shows of Richard's childhood, had saved them.

He knew such things were improbable. He had been inside an Apollo capsule in the museum in Huntsville, Alabama, and he had been shocked at how small those capsules were. Human beings were not meant to live in such small places.

He also knew how fragile the capsules were. The fact that the capsule had survived for so many years was a miracle. He knew that. He also knew that his thoughts of the men's survival were a remnant of his childhood self, the one who didn't want to believe that heroes died.

All his plans, all his hopes, for the next eighteen years after that first sighting were based on the theory (the certainty) that the astronauts were dead. And that Apollo 8 would survive again and return.

The ships he had built, the missions he had planned during those years, were based on the idea that he was going after a death ship, a bit of history. He was going to recover Apollo 8, the way an archeologist would resurrect a tomb from the sand or a deep-sea explorer would record the remains of famous ships like the *Titanic*.

Richard had spent much of his fortune and most of his life finding ways to greet Apollo 8 on its next near-Earth return.

And now that the ship had been spotted on its odd elliptical orbit—on schedule, just like the scientists said it would be—he was ready.

And he was terrified.

Some nights he'd wake up in a cold sweat, wondering if a man should ever achieve the dreams of his childhood.

Then he'd remember that he hadn't yet achieved the dream. He'd only created the opportunity.

And sometimes he'd wonder why that wasn't enough.

*   *   *

The ship, which he had had primed and ready since the beginning of the year, was named the *Carpathia* after the ship that had rescued most of the survivors of the *Titanic*. He liked the metaphor, even though he knew deep down that there would be no survivors of Apollo 8. The command module itself was the survivor; a manned ship that had gone farther and longer than any other man-made vehicle and had returned.

Mankind had sent craft almost everywhere in the system, from rovers on Mars to probes to Venus, and had greater knowledge of the solar system than ever. NASA planned to send more craft even farther out, hoping to go beyond the bounds of the solar system and see the rest of the galaxy.

Government funding was there—it had always been there—for space travel. The latter part of the twentieth century and the first part of the twenty-first were called the Epoch of Space Travel.

Richard liked to believe humankind would look back on it all, and call it the Beginning of Space Travel. He hated to think that satellites and a large, fully equipped space station in orbit, a small base on the Moon, and some commercial traffic would be all that there was to space travel.

He wanted to see human beings on Mars; humans—not un-manned craft—exploring the far reaches of the solar system; humans boldly going, as his favorite childhood show used to say, where no one had gone before.

And that was why he started Johansenn Interplanetary, all those years ago. With a broader version of that speech, with a great marketing strategy, and with the best minds in the country helping him create the space vehicles, the prototype bases on Mars and beyond, and finally, just last year, the artificial gravity technology that would take mankind to the stars.

Much of this technology, primitive as it was, had military applications, so Richard got his money. His was the first private firm that specialized in space travel, even though he didn't achieve space travel for another few decades after his funding. Instead, he created subcorporations to handle the other scientific developments. Artificial gravity was just one component. He also corralled computer scientists to help him make computers small, so that the spacecraft wouldn't need bulky on-board computers. And one of his computer visionaries, a man named Gates, had proposed selling those smaller computers to the business market.

That idea alone had made Richard a billionaire.

Others, from the freeze-dried food to the lighter-than-air space suits, simply added to his fortune.

Everyone thought he was the visionary, when really, all he wanted to do was the very thing he'd been too young to do in 1968.

Rescue Apollo 8.

So that was how he found himself wearing one of his own space-suits, standing on the docking platform outside the *Carpathia*, look-ing up at its streamlined design. Up close, he couldn't see the scaled-back wings, which allowed the ship to glide when necessary. Nor could he see most of the portals installed for the passengers, since this thing had been designed as both research vehicle and luxury liner.

He could see the outline of the bomb bays underneath, added so that this ship design, like so many others, could be sold to the U.S. military for applications he wasn't sure he wanted to think about.

That the *Carpathia* had the bomb bays as well he attributed to the paranoia of his chief designer, a man named Bremmer, who, when he learned what Richard really wanted to use this ship for, said, "You don't know what you'll encounter. Let's make sure this is a fully functional military vehicle as well."

Which meant that they had to have a military unit on board, astronauts who knew how to use the guns and the bombs and the defensive technology that Richard only understood in theory. There was the military unit and the research team—real archeologists, excited that they got to practice at least part of their craft in space; a handful of space historians and some medical personnel, in case something horrible came into the *Carpathia* through Apollo 8. Then there were the investors, the "tourists" as the real astronauts called them. Richard liked to call them "observers," partly because he was one, no matter how much he liked to pretend he wasn't.

The non-astronauts had trained to the best of their abilities. They were in the best physical shape of their lives; they could all handle zero-g like pros; and they'd even survived multiple simulated space walks without screwing up.

Richard could do all those things and more. He'd had astronaut training in the 1970s, but never went into space because his busi-ness had taken off. Besides, he had hated NASA's regulations, many of them designed after the Apollo 1 and 8 tragedies. He had a hunch the regulations would become even more restrictive after more tragedies, and he left before they could.

Even so, his hunch had been prescient. After Apollo 20's spectacular crash into the Moon's surface, the regulations for astronauts had become so restrictive, it was a wonder anyone signed up for the program. Particularly as the private sector began to make its own advances.

Despite his retreat from the NASA program, Richard kept up his training. He was always a bit too thin. He trained on various exercise equipment for more than two hours daily—six on weekends. He became a marathoner. And, as the technology became available, he began to sleep in an oxygen deprivation tent, so that his lungs learned to be efficient with minimal oxygen.

He wasn't the most in-shape person on this mission—after all, he was nearly fifty—but he was the most in-shape observer. He could outrun two of the astronauts, and he could certainly outperform all of the researchers.

Still, he felt nervous on the docking platform of the ship he'd helped design. He'd been in and out of these ships hundreds of times over the years. He'd even been in low Earth orbit for several trips, so standing on the platform in a space suit wasn't new.

What was new was this sense of awe, this moment of surrealism: he had envisioned going into space on a rescue mission for almost forty years, and now here he stood.

He was crossing into new territory.

When Richard had mentioned this to Bremmer, Bremmer had laughed. *You've been in new territory all your life, boss*, Bremmer had said.

But it was imagined territory, not just by him, but also by his specialists.

This, this was new—to all of them.

And no matter how much he justified it, no matter how similar he claimed it was to recovering wrecks of historic ships or finding the tombs of the pharaohs, he knew it wasn't.

When he entered the *Carpathia*, he was becoming one of the first humans to recover a space-vessel. He was someone who both captured and created history at the same time.

Instead of being a billionaire or an inventor or a crazed eccentric—all of those media portrayals that haunted him even now—he'd become what he always dreamed of.

He'd be an adventurer.

For the first time, he felt as if he were stepping into his own life.

*   *   *

The *Carpathia* was roomy. She was designed for longer trips with comfort in mind. While her cabins were small, the fact that she had them at all separated her from other ships. Her public areas were large and comfortable—a lounge, two research rooms, which could double as equipment rooms or extra sleeping berths, and it had a cargo bay, which had its own separate environmental system, designed—ostensibly—to bring back things found on the Moon. Richard had watched over the specs himself. He made sure that the cargo bay was also large enough to carry one 1960s Apollo capsule, with plenty of margin for error.

Even though the ship's captain tried to give him the largest space, Richard insisted on the smallest berth. He also insisted on privacy—even though he had delegated as much as possible, he still had to conduct some business. And he had always been a loner. The idea of being in close quarters with a dozen people he barely knew made him shaky. He needed some privacy, a place where he could close the door and not see anyone else. This mission was of indeterminate length; he had to have a place that would keep him sane.

Before he left, Richard tried not to watch the press coverage, but he absorbed it anyway: Richard Johansenn's vanity project, which would probably get him killed; Richard Johansenn's pipe dream; Richard Johansenn's dream.

Columnists accused him of grave robbing or worse. The scientifically illiterate among them felt that he was taking money from the mouths of children for his little space adventure, not realizing that even if he didn't recover the capsule, he—and the country—would learn what happened to vessels that spent almost forty years in space just from the photographs he got of the ship.

He tried not to have expectations of his own. He tried not to imagine—any more than he already had—what he would find.

Instead, he downloaded old memoirs from the Apollo and Gemini missions as well as contemporaneous newspaper accounts and books written about those missions. He also scanned interviews with those crews, watching them, seeing what they had to say.

He barely paid attention to the ride into orbit; he'd done that so many times that it felt like old hat. Two of the archeologists had clung to their couches, looking terrified. The rest of the newbies had watched with great fascination as the *Carpathia* passed through the atmosphere and settled into an elliptical orbit that in three times around would swing them away from the Earth and on a path to match course and speed with Apollo 8.

Below, Earth was, as she always seemed, placid and calm—a deep blue planet with a bit of green, lots of cloud cover, the most beautiful thing in this solar system—maybe even in the universe.

It was home; oddly, it felt like home even as he rode above its surface. It felt like home the way going back to Wisconsin felt like home, the way snow on a clear, moonlit night felt like home, the way pulling into his driveway felt like home.

Sometimes, when he was feeling spiritual and not scientific at all, he wondered if this sensation of home was inbred even when looking at the planet from space. Did the feeling come from knowledge that he had sprung from this place? Or did it come from something more innate, something bred into every creature born on that blue-green surface? Had the astronauts of Apollo 8 felt it as they pulled away from Earth? Or as they soared away from the Moon? Had they looked back, somehow, and reflected on their own folly? Or had they felt like explorers, finally getting a chance to escape?

Richard mostly stayed in his cabin for the twenty hours it would take them to reach Apollo 8. He was nervous. He was worried. He tried to sleep, couldn't.

He wanted answers, and he wanted them now. Yet at the same time, he was afraid of the answers, afraid of what he would find. Finally, he had dozed, coming awake instantly with a call from Susan Kirmatsu.

Most of the flying was automatic; still, he had hired Susan, one of the best pilots ever for this mission.

He quickly made his way to the cockpit, standing behind Susan to watch. She wore her black hair in a buzz cut that accented her shapely skull. The console dwarfed her small form, yet she controlled the ship as surely as he controlled himself. She watched the read-outs on the screen, ignoring the double-sheets of clear pane plastic windows that he had built into the nose of the ship.

Instead, he was the one watching the darkness ahead. Earth now had shrunk to the size of a large grapefruit. He had never been out so far before.

The co-pilot, Robbie Hamilton, sat at another console and also watched the instrumentation. Two more pilots in seats behind him followed the flow of information on their handheld screens as well, ready to jump in at a moment's notice.

"We have her," Susan said. "She's coming in on the proper trajectory."

Their plan sounded simple: They'd match Apollo 8's path, grab the ship, and pull her into the cargo bay.

They'd done this type of thing before; such maneuvers were old hat for the astronauts on board now. Two of them had helped build the space station. Another had gathered dying satellites as part of his work for one of Richard's companies. And Susan had flown half a dozen practice missions, bringing in everything from satellite pieces to bits of rock, just to make sure that Hawk-class designs like the *Carpathia* could handle this bit of trickery.

"Can I see her?" Richard asked.

"Over here." Robbie ran his fingers along his smooth console, and then, on the screen in front of him, a new picture appeared. Something small and cone-shaped appeared in the upper left.

Richard squinted. "Can we magnify?"

Robbie slid his fingers across the console again, and this time the ship appeared close. And it was tumbling slightly. That had been another worry of his. If it had been tumbling hard and fast, they would have had to try to slow that down first.

Apollo 8 looked worn. Its exterior had dark streaks and lighter streaks, which Richard did not remember from any of the photographs. The nose cone itself seemed dented, but that might have been a trick of the light.

"How bad is she damaged?" he asked.

"Dunno," Robbie said. "We'll find out soon enough."

Soon enough would be hours from now. It would take that long to match the speed and path of Apollo 8. Richard wasn't sure he could stand waiting in the cockpit.

He went back to the lounge.

The scientists were peering out the windows. The observers had dialed up the exterior view on one of the large screens and watched the changes the way someone would watch television.

Richard couldn't stand that either, so he went back to his cabin. The bed took up most of the floor space. He had strapped his clothing bag into its little compartment, but he hadn't needed to. Unless something happened with the artificial gravity, everything would stay where he placed it.

He was too restless to lie down, so he closed the door again and reentered the hall. For a man who planned everything down to the smallest detail, he was stunned that he hadn't thought through these last few hours, that he hadn't planned some sort of activity to keep his mind awake, active, and off the rendezvous.

He returned to the lounge, with a vague idea of reviewing the plans, but instead just sat silently in the corner, thinking about what he was about to do.

Or not do, as the case might be.

As the large screen showed a looming Apollo 8, Richard went back to the cockpit. He listened as Susan gave terse instructions, and watched through the windows he had designed as his ship—his ship—lined up with a ship he had only seen in his dreams.

Apollo 8 looked larger than he expected and appeared formidable in a rockets-and-rivets kind of way.

The capsule wasn't streaked, like he had thought at first; it was damaged with tiny holes blasted along its sides. The cone's nose was dented—something had hit it hard—but hadn't burst open. The small round portals had clouded over and appeared to be scratched.

Susan reported damage near the engines that had malfunctioned—flaring too early and too hard, was the speculation, but no one knew exactly what had gone wrong. Once his team had the capsule, they might be able to figure that out and solve that old puzzle.

Richard was shaking. He threaded his fingers together as the ship lined up next to the slowly tumbling capsule. The first thing they would do would be to stop the tumbling.

He came to himself long enough to make certain the live feed back to Earth had actually started. It had. One of the other astronauts and one of the observers were giving a play-by-play as they watched through a different portal.

Alicia Kensington, the modern day Walter Cronkite, had asked Richard to do the play-by-play, but he had known he would be too nervous. Yes, he was the celebrity, but he hadn't wanted to be at this moment.

At this moment, he needed privacy.

Eventually, as they worked to carefully slow the tumble, he made his way to the back to the entrance of the hatch, watching on small screens as he passed. The tumbling stopped, and next the grappler's metal fingers found purchase near Apollo 8's hatch.

He stood still as that happened, terrified. One of his greatest worries, one of the scientist's great worries as well, was that the old ship would disintegrate when touched. It had been through a lot, the theory went, and it might have been held together by next to nothing. A push from the grappler, a touch of the hooks, the grate of metal against metal, might cause the capsule to come apart.

And then his great adventure would be over.

But the capsule didn't come apart. It held. In fact, it looked sturdier than the grappler.

He turned toward the live feed, watching from one of the outside cameras, struck at the fact that the older ship looked so much stronger than the *Carpathia*. The *Carpathia* was built of lightweight materials, designed for maximum efficiency, both in space and in the atmosphere.

Apollo 8 had a thick sturdiness he associated with his childhood, the sense he'd learned from every adult back then from his teachers to his parents, that if something was overbuilt, it was better, it could survive more, it would be the best it possibly could be.

He smiled for the first time that day.

They had been right.

He stood outside the bay doors with Patricia Mattos, the chief archeologist. Her team waited behind them, shifting from foot to foot, obviously as nervous as he felt. They all wore their space suits, just in case there was a problem with the environmental systems when they went into the cargo bay, but at the moment, everyone held their bubble helmets. A few tucked their helmets under their arms, the way that the first astronauts used to as they walked to the rockets that would blast them into space.

No one spoke.

They watched the nearby screen, and listened to the scraping sounds within.

The scrapes did not go onto the live feed. Neither did the conversation of the astronauts out there working the grappler—the grunts, the single-sentence acknowledgements, the occasional curse. Live feeds with live astronauts were NASA's purview. No matter what Alicia Kensington wanted, Richard was determined to keep some privacy here, some mystery.

The entire world could watch if it wanted to as Apollo 8 got loaded into the cargo bay. They just couldn't hear the discussions as the astronauts got it into position.

Susan had activated the cameras inside the bay as well, and started a second feed. The first came from outside the ship, showing Apollo 8 as it looked to the *Carpathia*. The second came from inside, showing, at the moment, the bay, and the backs of the astronauts, looking small against the vastness.

The cargo bay was spacious and empty. Even though it had its own environmental system, it had few other controls—just an extra door and an airlock for smaller items, and a series of overrides near the back of the room, in case something malfunctioned with the bay doors.

At the moment, the doors were open. The two astronauts, guiding Apollo 8 inside, wore their space suits and gravity boots. They looked like slimmed down versions of the men who had first walked on the Moon. Their bubble helmets were smaller and more efficient, their suits form-fitting for ease of movement, the gloves less bulky. Even the oxygen units were different, threaded into the suit itself instead of hanging off the back like a pack a child would wear to school.

Accidents could still happen with the suits—the astronauts had to stay clear of the capsule and the grappler's metal fingers as much as possible—but they were less likely. Most people who died in space now did so because of their own carelessness, not because their suits ripped or malfunctioned.

Still, Richard watched this part nervously. This was the most dangerous part of the mission. One small bump, a mishandling of the grappler, a momentary klutziness on the part of an astronaut, could result in disaster.

He would never admit to the others that for him, a disaster would be the loss of the capsule somehow, not the loss of life. He'd be willing to lose his own life to bring this thing in; he hoped the astronauts would too.

A darkness filled the doorway, and then the astronauts moved away. The view on the outside camera made it seem as if Apollo 8 had pointed herself into the *Carpathia* and gotten stuck. The view on the inside was a sort of darkness that could, when he squinted, resolve itself into the cone of the capsule.

The astronauts, moving near the doors, gave it all a bit of perspective, but everything seemed large and a little out of control.

Richard held his breath.

Next to him, Patricia Mattos was biting her lower lip. Her second for this part of the mission, Heidi Vogt, watched with wide eyes. Her forehead was dotted with perspiration much as Richard's had been earlier.

Anticipation made them all nervous.

He turned away from them and watched the screen. The scrapings from inside grew even louder—that unbearable squeal of metal against metal.

"I hope nothing's getting ruined," Heidi muttered, and one of

the other scientists, someone whose name Richard couldn't con-
jure, nodded.

Finally, the capsule disappeared from the view of the outside
cameras. Two of the inside cameras only showed the capsule herself. The other two cameras had partial views of the bay doors,
which were easing shut.

Richard's heart started to pound. He still had fifteen minutes
before he could enter the bay—fifteen minutes for the environmental systems to reestablish the artificial gravity. The temperature
would remain low, and the atmosphere would remain a special mix
to preserve everything. Richard's biggest fear was that they'd thaw
out the craft and the bodies it held too fast.

He didn't want three famous—legendary—astronauts to explo-
sively decompress on a live feed heading back to Earth. He was
already in trouble in some circles for messing with a grave; he didn't
want to be responsible for one of the most disgusting mistakes ever
made.

He had promised America and, by extension, the rest of the
world, that he would treat these men with respect.

He planned to honor that.

But first, he planned to free them from their decades' old prison.

He planned to be the first to greet Commanders Borman,
Lovell, and Anders on the last part of their journey home.

Susan gave them five minutes warning before she opened the cargo
bay entrance. Richard and his team of scientists put on their bubble
helmets, turned on the oxygen in their suits, and started the small
heaters to keep their own bodies warm.

If he hadn't done this before, he would have protested the use of
the heaters. He was hot enough at the moment; nervousness had
made him sweat again. But he knew once inside the bay, he had
only a few hours before the deep cold would permeate his space
suit. He wanted as much time with the capsule as he could get.

He helped Heidi strap on her helmet, then checked Patricia's.
He gave the other three scientists a cursory glance, but they seemed
more competent with the equipment than the archeologists, which
made sense. Archeologists usually didn't have to wear space suits to
look at remains. They simply dug into the ground.

Here, they'd be opening a cold ship, preserving the scene, and
beginning an intellectual voyage of discovery, one that could, hope-
fully, retrace everything that Apollo 8 had seen.

He could hear the rasp of his own breathing, and that reminded him to turn on the audio chips outside the helmet. The audio chips were an addition for this mission. Most of the time, astronauts didn't need the external sound sensors.

But he'd had them added to all of the helmets. Even though the team would use their internal communications equipment to keep track of each other, he figured they all wanted to hear this process as well as see it.

He wanted as many of his senses engaged as possible.

Once everyone was suited up, and Susan gave the all clear, he opened the single door leading into the back of the cargo bay.

The bay looked different, smaller, with the capsule inside. It was also darker since the capsule blocked much of the light from the center of the room. The two astronauts stood near the side of the capsule. They weren't going to be active in this part of the mission, but he knew they wanted to be here, to see everything.

He handed one of them a video camera. Even though there were cameras inside the bay, and at least two of the scientists were filming the entry, Richard figured he couldn't have enough film of this historic moment.

He straightened his shoulders and smiled at the team, even though they couldn't see his face. "Let's go," he said.

It was, all-in-all, a belated command. The archeologists were already filming, taking samples from the exterior, finding ways to preserve as much of the stuff surrounding the ship as possible.

As excited as he was, Richard knew this was important, just like he knew that proceeding methodically was important.

He had little to do in this early stage, so he walked around the capsule slowly, taking it in.

The dent in the cone was uneven, almost like something larger had hit it with a glancing blow. The area around the dent was worn, and the metal looked fragile. If he had to guess—and that was all he could do at this point—he would have thought that the damage there was quite old.

What he had originally thought were streaks were tiny holes all along one side. The holes were very close together, almost as if the capsule had been pelted with gravel. Only Richard knew that gravel would have done much more damage; more likely, it had gone through some sort of rock belt as fine as sand.

His stomach lurched—excitement now, not nervousness. The capsule had quite a story to tell. All these little details, the burn marks near the engine, the long score against the metal on one side as if someone had run a car key against it, the little holes and dents and divots, were records of everything that happened to this capsule.

In some of those dents and digs might be dust from civilizations long gone. Evidence of life from some other planet, or a bit of ore that no one had believed existed this far out. There might be as-yet-undiscovered chemicals, minerals, biological matter, things that boggled the human imagination.

They could all be on this capsule, smaller than anything he could see through the reflective plastic of his helmet, more important than anything he could imagine.

Finally, he rounded the capsule and stopped by the small hatch. He and his team on Earth had discussed the hatch several times. They had studied the specs from the various capsules and had even visited the two that were in museums.

Since the fire on Apollo 1, which killed three astronauts, the capsule hatch opened outward. But they were designed so that in space they were sealed shut.

Richard and his team knew that they'd have to cut the hatch open, and they needed to do so in a way that would cause the least amount of damage. But, they agreed, he would try to open it by hand first.

The scientists had photographed and then cleared an area around the hatch. Richard's stomach lurched again—he was so glad he hadn't eaten anything—and he tried not to look at the light from one of the cameras that someone was pointing at his face. He knew they could only see him in profile, and even then they couldn't get a clear reading through the plastic in his helmet.

No one would know how close to tears he was.

He had waited a lifetime for this.

He wished the internal mikes were off. He wanted to whisper, "Welcome home, gentlemen," but he was afraid that not only would his team hear him, but so would everyone who watched on Earth.

Instead, he gripped the handle, and yanked.

To his surprise, the hatch moved. Just a little, but it moved all the same.

Some dust and particles fell off the capsule's frame.

He caught himself before he cursed.

He looked at the others and thought he saw surprise through their helmets. They pushed closer to him. The light from the camera was on his superfine white glove.

He braced his other hand on the capsule's side and then pulled again.

The whole capsule shook, but the hatch moved enough that he could see its outline on the frame.

"My heavens," one of the women said. "We aren't going to have to cut it."

Her voice held a mixture of shock, awe, and relief, precisely the same emotions that Richard was feeling.

He pulled with all his strength.

This time, the hatch fell open, banging against the capsule with a loud clang. Richard stumbled backward, freeing his hand at the last minute, narrowly avoiding being part of that bang of metal against metal.

He hoped he hadn't destroyed anything near the hatch.

The interior was shrouded in darkness.

The team, bless them, didn't move forward, but instead waited for him to get his feet beneath him. He stood upright, still feeling slightly off balance from loosening the hatch, and then headed for the capsule.

He had to remind himself to breathe.

He might find anything in there, from skeletons (depending on how long the environmental systems survived) to carcasses exploded in their environmental suits to body parts strewn throughout the interior because the capsule had somehow gone through explosive decompression.

He had ordered that no one film the interior until he gave the signal. He now hoped that the astronaut he'd given the camera to remembered that instruction.

Richard took a small flashlight one of the archeologists handed to him, then leaned through the hatch.

The interior was dark and, for a moment, his breath stopped in his throat. He couldn't see the astronauts. He braced himself, figuring he'd find parts of them all over the equipment and the metal interior.

He tried to keep his breathing regular, so that anyone listening wouldn't think something was wrong. He shined the light, saw frost on the panel displays, wondered how it got there, then remembered there had to be a lot of biological material in here, and that material had had some time—he wasn't sure how much—to grow.

He hoped some of what he was looking at wasn't the astronauts themselves.

Then he shown the light past the couches to the so-called computer display to the flight equipment. He saw bags against the side, the pee-tube curled up against one side, and a crumpled food container near one of the storage units.

He stared at all that for a moment, knowing something was wrong, feeling that something was wrong. His subconscious saw it, but his conscious brain hadn't caught up.

He shone the light one more time, registering how small the space was; he wondered how grown men could have survived in this small environment for even a few days, let alone the rest of their lives.

Something had been braced under one of the couches, wrapped in some kind of metallic heat blanket.

Something had been placed there.

Then his conscious caught up. He saw no evidence of explosive decompression. He saw no evidence of any kind of traumatic sudden end to Apollo 8's mission.

But he saw no evidence of a slow death either, aside from the food container and whatever it was stored under that couch. His hands were shaking, making the light shake.

He examined the interior one last time.

Nothing.

No men, no space suits, no evidence—except those bags and that food wrapper—that anyone had ever been inside this capsule.

"What do you see?" Susan asked from her vantage in the cockpit. The scientists, apparently, could wait him out, but the pilot couldn't.

"Nothing," he blurted.

"Nothing?" she asked. "What do you mean 'nothing'?"

"I mean," he said, "they're gone."

The theories came in from all over. The scientific illiterates, the ones he called Flat Earthers, were convinced that friendly aliens had arrived and taken the crew somewhere special. Borman, Lovell, and Anders were now enjoying a new life on some unnamed planet or back on Earth in secret (and unknown) identities at Area 51. Or, Susan had stated sarcastically, they were in that zoo in *The Twilight Zone*.

Others believed that Richard was too hasty—that they had died in the capsule and he just hadn't seen it. Some wag suggested (and it got credence on the 24-hour news channels for a while) that the astronauts had moved to another dimension, just like in some *Star Trek* episode.

In fact, much of the chatter that filtered to the *Carpathia* focused on old science fiction scripts, either from shows like the *Outer Limits* or *Time Tunnel* or *Land of the Giants*. Apparently some of the most renowned scientists of the day were spouting off on the cable channels, and so were some of the better-known science fiction writers.

Richard ignored the chatter. Susan followed it as if it could give her the truth of her experience in space by filtering it through the talking heads on Earth.

The scientists spent days checking the interior for evidence of explosive decompression and found none of it. They did find the mission's carefully protected garbage, which included the feces that they hadn't discarded into space—clean to the last ("from that," Patricia said, "we can determine how long they lived").

The scientists found evidence of vomit ("someone had gotten space sick," Heidi said. "Probably Anders," Richard said. "It was his first experience with zero g.").

But they didn't find much else; certainly not brain matter or blood or bits of bone.

They also didn't find evidence of alien arrival—"If it came," someone said, "it came in a form we don't recognize as living matter."

What they did find, carefully wrapped in a blanket and as much heat shielding material as possible, was the Hasselblad camera the astronauts had taken with them, plus rolls and rolls of film.

Richard would have the film carefully developed and preserved if possible, but he knew, even without the scientists saying much of anything, that the chances of photographs surviving intact for so very long in the radiation and the extreme conditions were next to none.

The astronauts themselves had probably known that and had done what they could to protect it. Along with it were some letters to the families written on the few sheets of fireproof paper the astronauts had brought along. The flight plan was also wrapped with the camera, and on the back of that paper was careful handwriting.

Richard recognized the quote. It was from Genesis:

In the beginning, God created the heaven and the earth; and the earth was without form and void, and darkness was upon the face of the deep; and the spirit of God moved upon the face of the waters.

And God said, "Let there be light," and there was light.
And God saw the light, that it was good.
And God divided the light from the darkness.
And God called the light Day and the darkness He called Night.
And the evening and the morning were the first day . . .

It went on, quoting the entire passage. Whoever had copied it had done so in a clean hand. Although, looking at it, Richard wasn't sure it was copied. He wondered if someone had written it from memory.

He stared at it a lot as the scientists worked, his gaze always falling on the last few lines:

. . . And God called the dry land Earth, and the gathering together of the waters called He Seas.
And God saw that it was good.

And then a hasty scrawl:

God bless all of you, all of you on the good earth.

Richard was the one who finally told the scientists what happened. He figured it out using four pieces of evidence: the scrawls on the back of the flight plan—"A goodbye note," he said—the missing space suits, the missing bodies, and the unlatched hatch.

He gathered the entire team into the cargo bay and stood as close to the capsule as he could get. By now, days later, the temperature had returned to normal. The capsule had been scraped and examined and reviewed; most everything that had to be stored had been.

The crew still wore breathing masks—they had to, in case something in the particles caused allergic reactions or other kinds of reactions (and, the scientists insisted) to keep the particulate matter on a flat surface, so that it could be removed.

Richard held the flight plan, wrapped as it was in protective plastic, and stared at it before he even spoke to the team. When he did, he explained his thinking.

"They wrapped up everything they considered important."

Or maybe, he thought to himself, the last person alive had done that. Probably Borman as captain of the mission; old nautical traditions died hard. Richard had seen Borman's handwriting and had a hunch it had been Borman who had written the passage from Genesis on the back of the flight plan.

"Then," Richard continued, "they put on their space suits, unlatched the hatch, and evacked."

"What?" Heidi said. They weren't being filmed now. The live feed to Earth had ended days ago. "Why would anyone do that?"

Richard glanced at the capsule. "They knew they were going to die."

"You think it was a blaze of glory?" Susan said.

He shook his head. "I don't think they were being dramatic. They were astronauts, for heavens' sake. They had a choice between dying in a tin can and dying in the freedom of the great unknown."

"They climbed out and pushed off into space?" Patricia asked. "Is that sane?"

"Does it matter?" Richard asked. "They had only two choices of how to die. They took the one they considered to be the best."

"But that took out all possibility of a rescue," one of the younger scientists said.

Everyone looked at him as if he were crazy.

"They knew they couldn't be rescued," Richard said. "Not with 1968 technology."

He thought of all the movies made in the 1970s, movies about astronauts being rescued from the Moon, astronauts being rescued from deep space, astronauts being rescued from orbit. The entire country—the entire world—had been haunted by their loss, never realizing that the men had taken the choice away from the rescuers' and their imaginations long ago.

"So they drifted into nothingness," Heidi said.

Susan smiled at her. "It's not nothing," she said quietly. "It's the greatest adventure of all."

Great adventure or not, Richard now knew that the *Carpathia*'s mission was over. One of the archeologists asked him if the ship would go after the bodies, and he had stared at her, trying to remember her specialty was ancient societies, not modern ones.

"Finding the capsule was a miracle," he said. "All three of them will be in different orbits. if they still exist. Finding a body in the vastness of space is like finding a needle in a haystack."

Maybe a needle in a galaxy's worth of haystacks.

Still, his own answer echoed in his head. And while his scientists grew excited about new discoveries made every day on the *Carpathia*, bits and pieces of the Apollo 8 puzzle, he had already gone beyond that.

He needed to figure out how to find three needles.

How did a man search a galaxy's worth of haystacks?

And more to the point, how did he succeed?

Part Two
2018

"We have something," the researcher said.

Richard pulled up a chair, letting the movement hide his irritation. Of course they had something. If they hadn't had something, he wouldn't have flown halfway across the continent to get here.

But he didn't say anything. The researchers in this wing of the Asteroid Collision Project knew that Richard wasn't really looking for asteroids on a collision path with Earth. He was looking for three bodies, jettisoned into space beyond the Moon sometime between December 27 and December 31, 1968.

This wing of the project—the secret wing—had its own equipment. The rumor in the ACP was that this wing, called ACP-Special (ACP-S), had military and spy satellite connections. The regular ACP employees figured that the ACP-S was searching for bombs or weapons or materiel that other countries had launched into space.

ACP did have a military arm; it needed one, in case one of the asteroids on a collision course with Earth was large enough to threaten human life or was small but on a trajectory that might harm the transports to the Moon Base.

It had been a long time since he had been in this room. He hadn't been to the ACP since it was built nine years before. This room, and the equipment inside, had layers of security protocols just to reach the interior.

As he arrived that morning, he had felt as if he were going into one of those *Dr. Strangelove* bunkers that he used to see on television as a child; it made him wonder just how paranoid he really was.

The young researcher sitting next to him was, according to his nametag, David Tolemy. Richard found his gaze going to that nametag over and over again. He'd heard the researcher's name mentioned several times in the last twenty-four hours, but somehow he'd always expected the spelling to mimic the Pharaoh's—Ptolmey.

The researcher looked nothing like a pharaoh. He looked like a barely thirty-something man who spent most of his time behind dozens of sets of locked doors, staring through layers of equipment that led him to space. Tolemy had a special cart next to his equipment. It contained both a small refrigerator and a tiny gourmet coffee maker (although Richard's generation was the only one that called that stuff "gourmet" anymore; most people simply called the variety of drinks with cocoa beans in them "coffee").

As Tolemy's fingers fluttered over his flat-screen control panel, one hand would slip to the cart, grab a large soda/iced coffee container, and sip from the straw. It was an obsessive, unconscious maneuver, which Richard had seen a lot from his indoor techs.

He both hated it and felt powerless to do anything constructive about it. He hired the best minds of all generations, and if he'd learned anything in his decades of running the most creative corporations in the country, it was that the best minds came with more baggage than he'd ever thought possible.

When he'd mentioned it to his closest advisor after a visit to the Gates wing in Seattle, she'd laughed. *You have baggage,* she said. *Isn't that why you never married?*

He'd never married because he didn't have time for small talk, and he didn't feel right vetting women just to see if they were interested in his money. He had no desire to have children. His legacy, he knew, were these corporations and all the discoveries he'd made on his way to fulfilling his childhood dream.

He pulled the chair closer to Tolemy's wide screen, careful to stay away from the cart.

"I was warned not to waste your time," Tolemy was saying, "but I want to lay the foundation. Stop me if you know this."

He launched into a verbal dissertation about evac points and speed, about trajectories and distances in space. Richard did know this; he was the one who designed the program after all, but he listened just the same. He wanted to hear how Tolemy came to his current conclusions.

After twenty-five minutes of illustrated monologue, what Richard learned was this: Tolemy guessed that the astronauts took the last possible evac point. Their ship's oxygen was gone; they only had their suits left. Maybe they had put on the suits, and then realized they wouldn't even be able to see each other's faces as they waited for sleep to overtake them.

That last was Richard's fanciful addition. He'd been in the old suits; Tolemy hadn't. He knew how isolating they felt. Isolating and cramped.

"Add to that being inside a tiny capsule," Tolemy said, "with the windows already clouding, and who can blame them for leaving?"

Who could, besides Richard? And he knew that his blame was simply self-interest—the unwillingness of an obsessed man to lose his original vision, long after it had truly disappeared.

Unlike the other researchers, Tolemy hadn't tried to prove who evacked first. Borman to show it could be done? Or Anders because he was the junior member of the team? Had Lovell gone first because he was more of a cowboy than the rest?

The original researchers had contended that it mattered, that mass, height, and the strength with which the astronaut pushed off determined where the others ended up.

Tolemy claimed that none of that mattered; that they were all weak and dying and that they would have pushed away with little or no strength.

"I figured that the first one would be the easiest to find, and that's what I concentrated on," he said.

He had planned to take the last possible evac point and work backward, after exploring each area from top to bottom. He computed maximum speed and drift; he computed all the possible directions. He developed a region of space where he believed the first evacuee would be, and he searched, painstakingly, for two years.

"I found a lot of possibles," Tolemy said, "but they didn't pan out."

He spoke of months as if they were moments. Richard leaned closer to the screen, feeling a respect for the young researcher that he hadn't felt before. Tolemy shared some of his obsession, whether he admitted it or not, or Tolemy wouldn't have sunken so much time into this, no matter how much he was being paid.

"Then I saw this one." Tolemy used a pointer to touch a small mark on the side of the screen.

He amplified the image, but even at full magnification, Richard couldn't see what Tolemy had. It looked no different than all the other small space debris Richard had looked at over the years, some of it in the early months of this very project.

"Why is this one special?" Richard asked.

"The reflection," Tolemy said as if it were obvious. "Let me show you some time lapse."

He clicked on the image, then clicked on it again. It changed from a light mark against the blackness of space to a slightly brighter mark, but Richard really didn't see the difference.

"I guess I'm not trained well enough," Richard said.

"Okay," Tolemy said, lost in his own excitement. "Let me show you a few other things."

He opened up several more windows, all of them with astronauts building the space station that was completed in orbit at the end of the 1970s. He would click on one astronaut and then shrink the image. When he was done, the astronaut's image looked like the one in the upper corner of the screen.

What Richard wasn't sure of was whether you took an image of a meteor and did the same thing if the meteor would look like the tiny image in the corner either.

He said something to that effect—mumbled it, really, because he was concentrating and not paying attention to stroking the researcher's ego.

"Oh, no," Tolemy said. "They're all different. There are components in those early space suits—particularly the plastic in the helmets—that aren't used any more, and they don't occur naturally that we know of. When light reflects off those, it's distinct."

Richard's expression must have showed his skepticism, because Tolemy grinned.

"My bosses asked the same thing before they called you and so I showed them this."

It was a light spectrum chart, showing how various materials reflected the sun's rays outside of the Earth's atmosphere. According to the chart, the plastic in the helmet, particularly on the visor, did have its own signature. And, somehow, young Tolemy had gotten a reading from the bits of light given off by the image in the upper corner of his screen.

"You have to understand," he said as he explained all of this to Richard, "I worked this out over weeks of study."

"You have to understand," Richard said. "If I take action based on your light spectrum analysis and your speculative equations, I'm going to spend millions of dollars, risk several lives, and take many months of time. You have to be sure of this."

Tolemy took his left hand off the console and pushed the cart away with his right. He turned slightly in his chair.

"I think you were the one who called this searching for a needle in a galaxy full of haystacks," he said.

Richard nodded.

"Well, I found something small and thin and made of metal. You gonna check it out?"

Richard smiled. "When you put it that way," he said, "I think I will."

*   *   *

The trip toward the object that Richard now called the Needle took both more preparation than the trip to the capsule and less. More because, deep down, Richard had never expected to find the astronauts, so he hadn't done some of the basic imaginings he'd done for the capsule trip, and less because modern ships were so much more efficient than they had been eleven years ago.

For one thing, cargo runs from Earth to the Moon base had become common. Trips out of the atmosphere were even more common, with wealthy and upper middle-class tourist opting to stay in orbiting hotels.

The Needle never even approached Earth orbit. He floated out there for fifty years, following a predetermined path of his own. At his closest point to Earth in exactly eight months and one day, he would still be a hundred times the distance from the Earth to the Moon out in space

Richard had ships that could easily go beyond the Earth/Moon run. One of his companies was on the forefront of Mars development. NASA had bought several of his deep space ships (not an accurate name, Richard knew, but NASA liked the sound of it) for their first manned Mars missions, and several other companies had bought more of those ships to scout Mars locations for another base.

Richard had stayed out of most of that planning. He didn't really care about Mars. His interest was still in the needles and the haystacks and space itself, not in colonizing the solar system. He figured someone else could take care of that, and until his meeting with Tolemy at ACP-S, he'd let them.

After that meeting, he'd seen his mistake. The ships his companies had designed were for transport—humans, cargo, materiel—not for maneuvering or quick travel. To get to the Needle and match its orbit, he'd either have to design his own kind of ship or buy one from one of his far-sighted competitors.

And he only had eight months.

So he bought several of his competitors' ships—something that took more middlemen than he had thought it would. His competitors thought he was trying to steal proprietary information or at least copy proprietary technology, and while that might be a side benefit of this trip, it certainly wasn't Richard's intention.

Instead, he tried to make the ships as Richard-friendly as possible.

Deep Space Darts, as these ships were called, were designed for long travel at great speeds. All engines and fuel, little interior room.

The ships accommodations were cut down too much for his tastes. Richard examined half a dozen from various international companies, and worried about how travel would feel—cramped and narrow and uncomfortable, not something he wanted to experience, even though he was an in-shape fifty-eight. He needed some kind of cargo area with a separate environmental system, and a good cabin.

In the end, he bought one of his competitors' largest darts and gave his own team two months to retrofit it. He made certain the ship was supplied with right equipment—a state-of-the art grappler (complete with multiple hand sizes), automatic lifeboat technology, and an up-to-date medical unit. The dart had the cargo bay he needed, but not a large captain's cabin. Nor did it have a relaxation area for the crew.

Richard wasn't bringing a large team this time—just himself, and a few astronauts to help him wrestle the Needle from space. He also brought a biologist and a forensic anthropologist with an interest in space. If he got the body, most of the tests would be conducted on Earth in one of his labs—no need doing the work in cramped conditions—but he'd be able to report a few breakthroughs while still in space.

No live feed this time. There was too big a chance for error. He didn't want to pull up beside the Needle only to discover that it was a bit of mislabeled space debris.

That's what he worried about most: discovering nothing. Some early ACP-S missions led him directly to space debris and fortunately, he hadn't recorded those either. He hadn't been on a trip for an ACP-S identified project in eight years, and he worried about this one. He had other scientists double-check Tolemy's information, but they kept coming up with the same result:

They couldn't verify that it was a Needle. They couldn't guarantee anything.

In the end, he had to trust his own response. Tolemy's information was the first in almost a decade to convince him.

He wanted to give this one a chance.

On the ride out, he spent most of his time doing simulations with the grappler. He wouldn't run the grappler to bring the body in, if indeed what they'd found was a body. But he was going to help the team this time. He couldn't stay away.

His closest advisors had insisted that a single, multimedia reporter with impeccable credentials be included on the flight. If the dart didn't find a Needle, the reporter would write everything up as an experimental trip. She wouldn't know the real mission until it was achieved—if it was achieved.

She came along only with the agreement that she could talk with Richard on the way back. He would give her unlimited, exclusive access.

Any good reporter would jump at that, and one did. Helen Dail, a woman who had three Pulitzers for journalism under her belt, spent most of her time interviewing the crew. She also explored the dart—what little of it she had access to—and lived up to her part of the agreement by not interviewing the astronauts, science team, or Richard.

He could see her storing up questions, though. She was old enough—maybe forty—to make sure she had a paper back-up, but she was also heavily wired. She had digital cameras and PDAs and more notebooks than he'd thought possible. She had met her weight limit for the dart not with clothes or personal items, but with equipment.

She made him nervous. She was good enough to figure out what he was after, even if he never found it, even if no one ever told her what the mission was.

He stayed out of her way as much as he could.

Ten days past the Moon, the dart had reached its target destination. The little ship wasn't equipped with many cameras or long-distance scanning equipment (not that any of it was yet at the level Richard wanted it to be). They were close enough to confirm that something was in the position that Tolemy had predicted, but not close enough to confirm that something was (or had been) human.

"Let's get close," Richard said to the pilot. He was in the cockpit along with the pilot and co-pilot. The science team was in the cargo bay, and the astronauts were suiting up. He would wait to suit up until the last minute.

He didn't want Helen Dail to know he cared enough about whatever this was to suit up.

Over the next long half hour, the pilot took the dart into camera range. The item appeared on the screen, large and whitish gray. It tumbled slowly—a slow spin that seemed like something it had done for a long, long time.

It was long and slender, and could very well have been a human astronaut. But Richard couldn't see a helmet, nothing obvious that told him what they had.

Richard manipulated the external cameras himself, trying to catch all sides of the object.

Finally he saw what he needed—a glint of sunlight off a thick plastic visor.

His breath caught.

"Well?" the pilot asked. "Should we scrub?"

"No," Richard said. "We have a go."

He hurried out of the cockpit, careful to close the door behind himself, wanting to keep Dail out. Then he hurried to the cargo bay where the astronauts waited. They were watching the same image playing over and over again.

"Shouldn't be hard," Mac McFerson said as he watched. "One of our simpler maneuvers, actually."

Richard slid into his space suit, his hands shaking.

"So long as we don't grab the thing too tight," said Greg Yovel. "Don't want to damage it."

"Maybe we should tether, do a walk, and guide it in," McFerson said. He was a bit of a cowboy, which was why Richard wanted him along.

Richard turned, helmet in hand, and looked at the slowly spinning Needle. *Who are you?* he wondered. *Anders? Borman? Lovell?*

His heart was pounding. "Let's just bring it in as we planned and hope for the best."

McFerson made a small disapproving noise in the back of his throat.

They'd follow the procedures Richard had established with the capsule—keeping the bay cold once the body was inside, making sure that nothing in the process damaged the body outside of what had already occurred in space.

"Greg," Richard said, "you run the grappler."

"You and I will handle the door," he said to McFerson. "Magnetize."

Everyone pressed a button near the wrists of their suits to magnetize their boots. He felt a sharp tug on the bottom of his feet, tried to lift one, and felt the magnetic pull.

"It's a go," he said to the pilot.

The dart vented atmosphere from the cargo bay—away from the Needle, so as not to push him off course.

Greg slipped his hands into the net that ran the grappler, his body tense. Richard stood behind him, watching the imagery on the screen.

First, Greg had to stop the Needle from spinning. Then he had to wrap the grappler's long fingers around the center of the Needle and slowly bring him toward the bay doors.

Once the Needle was close, the doors would open and Richard, along with McFerson, would grab the Needle and bring it inside.

The first part went according to plan. Greg managed to slow the spin—not stop it entirely, but bank it enough so that the Needle wouldn't turn hard and damage itself against the grappler's fingers.

Then he grabbed the Needle around what should have been its waist.

"It feels like this thing is going to slip," he muttered, the words coming through everyone's helmets. Rachel Saunders, the forensic anthropologist, walked toward the screen, but the other scientist pulled her back.

Richard wanted to go there too—he wanted to slide his hands into the gloves that operated the grappler from a distance—but he knew he couldn't compensate for any errors.

The Needle—if indeed that's what it was—did look slippery and unstable. The slipperiness came from its absolute rigidity; the unstable part from its tiny size. Richard never seen anything so small in the grappler before.

Greg leaned into the gloves, his body as rigid as the Needle's. Richard could feel the fear coming off him in waves.

"Positions," McFerson said.

Richard jumped. He had forgotten to give that order. Rachel and the other scientist moved to the edge of the bay, grabbing onto the handles just in case. Richard took his spot near the door, holding a handle as well. It felt cold through his thick glove, but he knew that was just his imagination; he couldn't really feel anything except the sweat on his palms.

"Open the door," Greg said, his voice taut.

McFerson hit the controls before Richard could reach them. Or maybe the pilot had done so from inside the cockpit. He wasn't sure.

The bay doors slid open, and there it was—the grappler—long bits of metal curving out toward the edges of the solar system, unfiltered sunlight reflecting off them, so bright that he wanted to look away.

But he didn't. Because in the center was something whitish gray. Whitish gray and long, like a man's body would be, only the knees were slightly bent and so were the arms.

Richard let out a small breath and it sounded like a sigh of relief. Or maybe he'd heard the sigh through his communications equipment, coming from someone else.

The grappler's arms came closer to the door than he would like. Richard swung out, like he'd been trained to do, keeping his magnetized boots on the floor and one hand on the handle. McFerson did the same from the other side.

The suit had pockmarks and one large hole that went through the middle of one leg, but it was mostly intact. It faced away from them. Richard recognized the oxygen equipment, so bulky it made the original astronauts look like they were about to topple over backward.

"Wow," McFerson said.

Richard didn't say anything. He had to be cautious as well. He was less worried about himself—he knew if he lost his grip and his magnetization, he would tumble into space, but someone would get him—than he was about breaking the Needle.

Someone, at the beginning of this mission, had called the Needle a corpsicle, and while Richard vehemently objected to the characterization, it had some truth. This body was breakable the way ice was breakable. Grab it wrong, and a part would snap off.

Richard reached inside the grappler and slid a hand underneath the arm closest to him. Then he gently pulled backward. McFerson did the same.

The grappler moved with them—Greg was letting them control the speed. It reached the mouth of the doorway when McFerson said, "Lift up."

There wasn't really an up—only an imagined up—but Richard didn't question. He'd done simulations and he knew in this case, up meant toward the top part of the door.

He lifted just in time to get the Needle's bent feet past the lip of the dart.

"God," Richard breathed. "That was close."

McFerson said nothing. He used both hands to hold the Needle. Richard did the same, keeping one hand on the Needle's chest bracing him, and the other under the Needle's arm.

"Got him," McFerson said, even though Richard hadn't given him a go-ahead.

The grappler fingers loosened, and Richard held fast, using only his boots for balance.

The grappler slid out of the bay.

"Close doors," McFerson said, and he didn't sound as calm as he had before.

The doors eased shut, and they were inside the bay, holding a man, frozen in position fifty years ago.

Rachel hurried over, awkward in her magnetized boots.

She joined them, bracing the body, and helping them move it toward the center of the bay. Richard could hear her breathe. She was frightened—or maybe awed—he couldn't tell.

He couldn't tell how he felt either, except that somewhere in the middle of this mess, the object he had called the Needle had become a body.

He was holding one of the astronauts from Apollo 8. His theory had been right.

They had evacked.

And he still had two more to find.

But this one entranced him.

It had a name, sewn onto the exterior of the space suit. Lovell. That made sense to Richard. Everyone else expected the first one out of the capsule to be the lowest ranking astronaut on the mission, but Richard knew better.

Borman wouldn't have gone first. He would have stayed with his vessel as long as possible. Lovell, the daredevil former test pilot, who saw himself at equal rank with Borman, would go first to show it could be done.

To show all three that fear could be conquered.

It wouldn't have been right to send the rookie out first.

The bubble-shaped helmet was intact. That was the first thing Richard looked for as he, Rachel, and McFerson eased the body away from the bay doors. The helmet was intact and the body inside had mummified.

It looked like the mummies that came from Egyptian tombs— after the poor things had been unwrapped. The face was hard and leathery, the eyes gone, the mouth open in some kind of rictus.

But worse than that, this one was burned.

Richard had been told to expect radiation burns, but he wasn't sure how they'd show up. They showed up in patches, holes in the skin.

"Good thing we got him," Rachel said. "I don't know how many more decades these suits would hold up."

Richard didn't respond. The suits would hold up as long as they remained intact. Obviously, the hole in the leg of this one came so late that there was no more oxygen, no more environment inside it.

When they reached the far wall and had the body face down over the examination table that would hold it, he said, "Now we can have gravity. Bring it up slowly."

"Roger," the pilot said.

Then Richard felt a buoyancy he hadn't even realized he had vanish. He was heavier, and his ankles ached from the boots. The body in his hands slowly settled onto the table, face down, the large backpack upward.

"Let's get him recorded," Richard said.

Recorded. Saved for posterity.

It was time to call in Dail.

Richard told the pilot to have Dail watch from the screens outside the cargo bay.

The recording and cataloguing was mostly a job for the scientists, and once Richard stepped back from the body, he would let them go at it. But he made some notes of his own.

The way the boots shone in the bay's lights. The still-bent limbs. The face, unrecognizable. And the suit, as familiar as the one he wore, because he used to stare at the ones in the Smithsonian.

Puffy and bulky, unbelievably difficult to maneuver, this suit had somehow protected Jim Lovell's body for half a century. The gloves made his hands look almost small.

The helmet with its thick plastic built to resemble glass. The old American flag on the arm, with only fifty stars—no Puerto Rico yet—making this seem like a suit lost to time.

And yet so real.

Richard could feel the suit's solidness through his own gloves, knew that some of that came from the frozen corpse inside.

He thought of the outcries on the original mission, the fact that they were desecrating a grave. No one felt that way any more. He doubted anyone much thought of the Apollo 8 astronauts any more.

Yet here was one, big as life. They would think about them once again, at least for a while.

Richard hadn't carried Jim Lovell, still alive, from the capsule. Nor had he brought the man into the dart with a fireman's carry, hoping to retrieve a long lost soul.

But he'd done the best he could.

Maybe the only thing he could.

*   *   *

The buoyancy Richard had felt just before the gravity had turned back on never completely vanished. He felt buoyant still, as if something lifted him ever upward.

When they brought the dart back, and he'd finished all the interviews (*How had you known where the astronaut was, Mr. Johansenn? Is it worth the expense, bringing a long dead man to Earth? Why didn't you consult the families?*), he went back to ACP-S to consult with Tolemy.

"How hard do you think it'll be to find the other two?" Richard asked.

Tolemy shrugged. He looked a bit more haggard than he had before the mission. He'd had a lot at stake on the mission's success, but it didn't look like the success had helped him. If anything it seemed to have depressed him.

"I've been thinking about it a lot," Tolemy said. "I'm pretty sure it'll be harder."

"Harder?" Richard hadn't expected that answer. He'd thought Tolemy would tell him it would be easier now that they knew what to look for. "In addition to the orbit we mapped for the capsule, you have two more points—the place where we found Lovell and the place where we found the capsule. You can make some kind of grid. We'll know in general what region of space the other two will be in."

"I've already done that," Tolemy said.

He ran his fingers along his console, brought up a new screen with the Moon and Mars and the rest of the solar system. An entire area between Venus and Mars was colored in red.

"That's the probably zone," he said. "But here's the problem."

He overlaid a green bubble, even larger, on top of the red.

"We made some assumptions to find Lovell. We assumed that we were getting the first astronaut at the last possible evac point. We assumed that they waited until the very end to evac. But what if Lovell waited until the end? What if the other two went days ahead of him? What if he planned to stay in the capsule and changed his mind at the last minute?"

Richard shook his head. "He wouldn't do that."

"You don't know it," Tolemy said. "Any more than I know which direction the astronauts went when they stepped out of the capsule. More than likely, it was tumbling slightly. They could have gone in any direction, with any kind of speed. If anything, the search area is now bigger. We'll defeat ourselves if we only look in the red part."

"It can't be bigger," Richard said. "We know some of the path now. That narrows it."

Tolemy shook his head. "I watched the vids you made of the rescue. You were worried about losing Lovell, of sending him off the small path you'd charted for him just by venting atmosphere from your cargo bay. Imagine if some other ship had done that. Or if a small rock had hit with enough force to push him in a completely different direction without making a hole in his suit. Or if he had vented oxygen on purpose, propelling himself in a particular direction to give himself a sense of control? We don't know. I don't think we'll ever know."

Richard leaned over and shut off the map on Tolemy's screen. This was not the man he'd seen before the mission. That man had been certain of his numbers, worried that he'd made the wrong assumptions, but sure enough of himself to insist that his bosses bring in Richard.

"What's changed?" Richard asked gently. He tried to control his impatience. He didn't like interpersonal relations—he'd never been that good at them. He usually let his staff handle that.

Tolemy glanced at him, about to say "nothing," in fact, the word had formed in his lips, when something in Richard's face must have stopped him.

"It was just luck," Tolemy said. "Finding Lovell. It was luck."

Like the press had been saying. Like Tolemy's boss had said when the mission came back, mostly because he couldn't take credit for a mission he hadn't approved of.

"You said it," Tolemy said. "We found a needle in a galaxy full of haystacks."

"Because we looked," Richard said. "Most people would hear the odds and give up. But we looked."

Tolemy gave him a frightened glance. "It took ten years of round-the-clock work by some of the best minds, and it was me that found him. The new kid."

"The new kid who worked harder than everyone else," Richard said. "The kid who believed in himself."

Tolemy shook his head. "That's the thing. After the mission left, I didn't believe any more. I was so convinced that all you would find was space debris that I nearly fell apart. If someone had died up there—"

"It would have been on my head," Richard said, "Not yours."

Tolemy nodded, but Richard could tell the young man didn't believe him. Tolemy wasn't willing to accept his success.

Richard stood, his patience nearly gone. He started to turn away, and then he stopped as an idea hit him.

"This has been part of your imagination for a long time, hasn't it?" he asked.

Tolemy looked up at him. Richard hadn't noticed before, but Tolemy was balding right at his crown. He didn't look quite so young any more.

"What has?" Tolemy asked.

"Finding one of the astronauts. You'd imagined it, you dreamed of it, you just didn't expect to do it."

Tolemy bit his lower lip, then shrugged one shoulder. "I guess I didn't."

Richard patted that shoulder. "Neither did I. And yet we did it, didn't we?"

Tolemy frowned, as if the idea were new to him. Richard walked away, hoping that little talk would be enough. Tolemy had a gift, whether he realized it or not. That imagination, that way of looking at the solar system, at the small details, was unique.

Richard doubted he could find that combination again.

Part Three
2020

And he didn't, at least not in the next two years. Tolemy tried to find Anders and Borman, but flamed out quickly. Six months after the success of the Lovell mission, as the press called it, Tolemy took an extended leave. Then he quit, citing personal reasons.

His staff asked Richard if he would talk to the young man. Tolemy had quite a talent, they said. It would be a shame to let him go.

But Richard knew better than to keep him.

Some men couldn't handle achieving their dreams. Tolemy was one of them.

Even men like Richard, who could handle it, had a difficult time. No one had ever told him that success—real personal success—carried its own stresses.

He'd always thought he'd understood that. After all, he'd bootstrapped himself into one of the richest men in the world. But those successes meant nothing to him. They were side issues on the way to his real goal—finding Apollo 8.

That success had been bittersweet. He'd found the capsule and not the men, and yet he had done what he had set out to do.

Just like he had done with Lovell.

Two successes. Two important successes.

But maybe he was insulated against those successes like he had been insulated against the earlier ones. Maybe he wouldn't have the same problem Tolemy had until he discovered Borman and Anders.

If he could even find Borman and Anders.

The remaining researchers at ACP-S worked the grids that Tolemy had left and found nothing. A few worked outside those grids and found nothing.

They hadn't even found anything that was possible.

Richard was thinking of firing the entire team and installing a new one, when he got a personal phone call from the Chinese ambassador to the United States.

"Mr. Johansenn," the man said in perfect accented English, "we have some information we would like to trade."

His advisors told him to set up the meeting through the United States government, that going around them to the country that former President Rockefeller had once called the most dangerous nation on Earth might get Richard into legal trouble. If he ended up making an unapproved trade with them for secret technology, he might even be charged with espionage.

Richard didn't see China as the most dangerous nation on Earth. They were merely a larger and politically more repressive nation. He also knew that when the Soviet Union collapsed in 1979, the United States had substituted China for the U.S.S.R. in its foreign policy. The big, evil superpower now was China, and nothing Richard did or the Chinese did would change that.

He told only his chief of staff that he was going to the embassy in Washington D.C. He decided to meet the ambassador there to prove to his own government (should they inquire) that he had nothing to hide. He could always say, with utter truth, that they had called him; he was just curious enough to go.

The Chinese Embassy looked no different than the other embassies on Embassy Row. They were all stately buildings, with armed guards and formidable security. The only differences were the flags and the uniforms. The Chinese had its large red flag, which would have seemed festive if Richard hadn't seen so many movies in which the flag had featured menacingly. The guards wore austere greenish uniforms that made him think of robots in early 1940s movies. They also wore small caps that hid the shape of their skulls, and they carried AK-47s over their shoulders in a display of force.

Richard had to go through three levels of security just to get into the building. Even then, he seemed to have acquired three guards all to himself.

He wasn't even carrying a briefcase. There was nowhere to hide weaponry on his person, and besides, they'd searched him enough to find even the smallest bomb.

The interior made him feel as if he'd entered another land. The furniture was ornate and mostly wood, all of it antique from various dynasties. Expensive vases were filled with cherry blossoms. Tapestries hung on the wall behind the vases.

Richard had been raised with the impoverished—and austere— Soviets as the Evil Empire. He wasn't used to the Chinese mixture of ancient beauty and hidden power within the embassy itself.

He was taken to a third floor reception room, and offered tea and little cakes. He accepted them with a small bow, feeling out of his element. He knew that diplomacy required a detailed understanding of a particular country. He didn't even know if the Chinese had a tea ritual that he might be violating, the way the Japanese did.

He'd been to most countries in the world, but somehow he had missed China.

After a few moments alone with the guards, a door nearly hidden in flowery wallpaper opened. A short man wearing a military cut jacket over dark blue trousers entered. He nodded at Richard, who stood.

They shook hands. The man introduced himself as the ambassador, and Richard introduced himself as well, just to be polite.

"Forgive my pre-emptive invitation," the ambassador said. "It is just that I know your interest in the Apollo 8 astronauts."

Richard smiled. "The whole world knows of my interest, Ambassador."

"Yes." The man bowed slightly. He folded his hands together. "It is my understanding that your interest supersedes your government's."

"I wouldn't say that," Richard said. "We lost a lot of good men and women going into space. We couldn't afford to rescue them all."

"But these were the first lost in actual space travel, is that not correct? At least in America."

Richard nodded.

"I remember that time," the ambassador said. "I was but a boy. My country rejoiced in the failure of yours, but I asked my father why we celebrated when brave men died. He had no answer."

Richard set his teacup down. The ambassador hadn't touched his tea or the cakes.

"But you understand now," Richard said.

"I acknowledge the impulse to find joy in another's defeat. I still do not understand why the loss of brave men is a cause for celebration."

The ambassador's language was formal, his face unsmiling, but Richard had a sense that the man was sincere. Richard had to remind himself that a diplomat's job was to seem sincere, even when lying for his government.

But Richard wasn't sure what the ambassador had to lie about.

"I have been instructed to inform your government of our discovery. I am to ask for several things in trade in regards to the whereabouts, things I know your government will not grant. It is a propaganda ploy on the part of my government. They can go to the media in both of our countries, claim criminal disinterest on the part of the United States, and say that your country is unwilling to bargain with the Chinese even when something valuable is at stake."

Richard threaded his hands together, mimicking the ambassador's position. "The location, while a curiosity, isn't of value to my government."

"You and I both know this, and so does my government, but our people do not. The propaganda ploy would work in our favor."

Richard nodded. He could see that.

"I have come to you, *ex parte*, to see if you can make a real and valuable trade to my government for this information. A bit of technology, perhaps, or permission to study the blueprints of one of your larger ships. We would give you the coordinates of the lost astronaut and, should our governments agree, we would send one of our own people with you, to learn with you."

Richard felt unusually warm. His staff had been right and he had been wrong.

"Ambassador," Richard said, "I must clear any such trade through my government."

"They will deny you permission."

"Yes, I know. I'm not even supposed to discuss business with your people. We have no formal trade agreement."

The ambassador nodded. "We can keep this between us."

"We can't," Richard said. "Particularly if one of your people joins us on the mission."

"Perhaps we can drop that point," the ambassador said. "And work through mutual friends."

Mutual friends. Richard had heard of that kind of approach before. Working with a neutral country that would negotiate the deal on both sides.

"Why weren't you willing to take this to my government?" Richard said. "They could have contacted me."

"Ah," the ambassador said. "But I did. I went to the government first and asked them to contact you, claiming time is of the essence. At first they refused. Then they promised they would take care of things. When I did not hear from you within the week, I called you directly."

A drop of sweat ran down the side of Richard's face. "Whom did you contact?"

The ambassador named names.

"I'll see if they contacted me and somehow I did not get the message."

The ambassador smiled. "There is no need to save face for your government. We do not trust each other. I doubt they contacted you."

"Still," Richard said. "I'd like to check. I'd also like to work through official channels wherever possible."

"Do what you must," the ambassador said. "But we know where your man is now. We cannot guarantee knowledge of where he'll be six months from now. We have no real interest in tracking him."

"I understand," Richard said.

Time was of the essence. The ambassador had not lied.

Of course no one had called any of Richard's companies or had contacted his own personal staff. But then, Richard had only the ambassador's word that the man had even contacted the U.S. government. And while Richard had believed the ambassador about his memories, he was not willing to believe him in business.

Richard had an assistant track down whom the embassy had contacted within the U.S. Government. She was able to confirm that the contact had occurred and been ignored. She asked him if he wanted to make an appointment with the State Department Undersecretary who had handled (or at least received) the contact.

"No," Richard said. "Make me an appointment with the President."

The President wouldn't see him. She had pressing business elsewhere, probably aware of the fact that he hadn't contributed as much to her campaign as he had to her predecessor's.

Still, he was the richest man in the country. He couldn't be ignored.

So the next day, he sat in the office of the Secretary of State. The National Security Advisor sat to his left. The head of NASA to his right.

Richard told all three about his meeting with the Chinese ambassador, and after hearing the expected rigmarole about protocol, they got to the heart of the matter.

"I am going to retrieve this astronaut," Richard said. "The question is whether or not I'll do it with your approval."

They had already jousted over the Espionage Act and the Favored Nations Agreements. Richard hadn't budged from his position.

The Secretary of State, a slender woman of Japanese-American descent, pretended sympathy. The National Security Advisor, a tough older woman with a touch of Margaret Thatcher in her bearing, had already decided Richard was an enemy of the state. And the head of NASA, a thin former astronaut who helped build the Moon Base was, surprisingly, on Richard's side.

"What can you give them that's not proprietary?" he asked.

Richard shrugged. "They hadn't really made a specific request. I figured they would on my next visit."

"You can't give them any space-related technologies," the National Security Advisor said. "And you most certainly can't have one of their people on board your ship."

"Even if they have the specs for that ship?" Richard asked. "What else could they learn?"

"Have you given them the specs for the ship?" she snapped.

Richard turned his chair slightly so that he wouldn't have to look at her. Instead, he focused on the Secretary of State.

"I'm not a diplomat," he said, "but the ambassador seemed sincere when he approached me. He—"

"They always do, Mr. Johansenn. That's their job," the National Security Advisor had a way of sounding extremely condescending.

He ignored her. "The ambassador said he had a memory of the

day those astronauts were lost. He seemed intrigued by what I was doing. Maybe they have some astronauts of their own to retrieve?"

"They do," the NASA head said. "They lost several astronauts in the early 1980s, after they acquired the Soviet Union's technology and scientists at bargain rates. But they didn't have the trained astronauts and they lost a lot."

"How come we haven't heard of this?" the Secretary of State said.

"We did," the NASA head said. "It was in reports at the time, but it never hit the media. You know how secretive the Chinese can be."

Suddenly the National Security Advisor was interested. She moved her chair forward. "How many did they lose?"

The NASA head shrugged. "I can get the exact figures for you later. But I'd wager they lost two or three dozen astronauts in those early years."

"Because they wouldn't ask for help." The Secretary of State tapped one long, painted fingernail against her lips. "Do you think they're trying something new now?"

"The space race is, for all intents and purposes, over," Richard said. "They can buy their way onto our ships. They lost the Moon to us, and have to cooperate with us to get to Mars. They have their own program, but it's not as advanced as Europe's. Theoretically, China's is only designed for asteroid mining."

"I thought it was for defense," the National Security Advisor said.

"I said theoretically," Richard said. "That's what they claim. But yes, it's for defense."

"Rumors throughout the scientific community say they're planning their own Moon Base. They doubt we can stop them. We're not geared for a war on the Moon," the NASA head said.

Richard nearly sighed, but managed to control himself at the last minute. "What if what they want is as simple as it sounds? What if they want to see how we're recovering our own people?"

"If they've lost so many," The Secretary of State asked, "how do they know this is one of ours?"

"The suits are different," the NASA chief said. "They'd reflect differently."

"Or," Richard said, "they've already got a recovery program, and they've seen him up close."

"I wonder," the Secretary of State said slowly, a twinkle in her eye, "if they can bring him to us."

*   *   *

Richard argued against it. He wanted to be on the ship that recovered the next astronaut. But he had set the events into motion by being above-board.

When he left the White House, the Secretary of State had already called for a closed-door meeting with the congressional leadership to see if they could have a space-trade agreement with the Chinese, a short-term exchange of information that would allow space scientists to share as much knowledge as possible.

The National Security Advisor loathed the idea; she said the Chinese would get a lot more out of it than the Americans would. But the head of NASA wasn't so sure. His program had stagnated with the rise of private enterprise in space. NASA needed new ideas. Besides, he wanted to know if all the rumors about the various Chinese programs were true.

Richard didn't care about any of that. He had an astronaut to rescue, and he wasn't going to do it from a distance. He left the White House, and went to the Chinese Embassy alone.

The ambassador met him immediately. This time, they went to a more formal room, with red silk wallpaper and delicate carved chairs. No guards stood inside the room, and no one brought tea.

"I had heard you were on Capitol Hill," the ambassador said.

"I saw the Secretary of State," Richard said. "They don't want me talking to you."

"And yet you are here," the ambassador said.

"I realized something while talking to them," Richard said. "I never asked how you knew where our astronaut was."

The ambassador smiled slowly. "They put you up to this."

"Believe me, they did not," Richard said. "If all goes according to their plans, someone will work with you on recovering that body. Only I won't be able to go along."

"And you feel you must go along," the ambassador said.

Richard nodded.

"So we are back where we began."

"Yes," Richard said. "What would you like in trade for the information about where our astronaut is?"

The ambassador smiled slowly. "This information is very important to you."

That was obvious. Richard had lost any negotiating point on that by returning so quickly.

"Yes, it's important," he said, "and time *is* of the essence."

*   *   *

It wasn't one of his better negotiations. Usually Richard was a shrewd businessman and a champion negotiator, but he was in new waters here. Not in dealing with the Chinese—he'd dealt with representatives of cultures he didn't entirely understand before—but because he really and truly wanted something.

In the past, he'd always had the ability to walk away.

This time, he could not.

He sold the Chinese government two of his own dartlike ships, the kind he designed after the Lovell mission, along with the specs. He didn't care if the U.S. government came after him for doing so. He had already informed his lawyers that he had chosen not to take the Secretary of State's advice. If the U.S. government wanted to try him under the Espionage Act or fine him for violating various Fair Trade Agreements, fine. He just wanted the time to get to the astronaut and back.

The lawyers had to tie the government up in court.

Then Richard put his P.R. people on the deal. They talked to the media, and suddenly he was the next world-class diplomat, a man who could negotiate with the difficult Chinese and walk away with what he wanted. He broke the story through Helen Dail, promising her another exclusive on his trip to find the second astronaut.

Through it all, he finally understood how Tolemy felt. He hadn't even asked for proof. The great negotiator had missed one of the essential rules of negotiation: he should have made certain the item he desired was what he desired.

If the Chinese were lying—if this wasn't the second astronaut—they were playing him for a fool. They probably thought he was one already. He had given them proprietary technology. If the astronaut—the whatever they had found—wasn't from Apollo 8, they would have won.

From the moment he accepted the agreement, he had a knot in his stomach. He wasn't even looking forward to the trip, and the past two times he had.

On those trips he felt that even failure would be a success: at least he tried.

He didn't feel that way this time. Just scared and a little sick.

His mood colored the entire trip.

He took the same team that he had two years before. The Chinese gave him the coordinates when he was in orbit, knowing that he would inform the U.S. government when he had them. The

Chinese were in a sector of space they shouldn't have been in if their technology was designed for asteroid mining or defense.

Something else was going on, something the astronauts on his ship speculated about.

But Richard didn't. He'd felt a little relieved, able to give the U.S. government something in exchange for this mission. He should have been even more relieved. His lawyers informed him that the Chinese had vehicles similar to the dart on their drawing board, meaning they had either gotten his or his competitors' proprietary information through some illegal back channel, but that didn't make him feel better.

He hadn't realized until this mission how truly single-minded he'd been. How great his focus was on these astronauts. It wasn't healthy.

He was no longer even sure it was right.

They were dead. Really and truly dead. There was no rescuing them, and what little he'd learned from Lovell and the capsule hadn't really made up for the effort he'd expended over decades to find them.

He wondered what they would have thought of him, these men who had launched themselves into space on a rocket, protected only by a tin can. Would they have thought he was foolish? Or would they have applauded his audacity?

He used to think they'd understand, but not even he understood any more.

Fifty years was a long time to focus on one thing. Maybe it was time to focus on something else.

They discovered the object not far from the coordinates the Chinese had given him. That was a surprise, given the amount of time it had taken to get here. Clearly, the object was moving very slowly.

The reflection was right; the build was right; the position was familiar. It took Richard one look through the viewscreen and he knew that the Chinese had played fair with him.

He had another Apollo 8 astronaut.

The team cheered, and he cheered with them. He slid into the rescue as if he'd done it a thousand times before instead of just once.

This time, he braced himself properly as he guided the body into the bay. He smiled for Dail's camera—he'd allowed her to suit up and come inside as well—and he'd carefully moved the frozen astronaut to the back of the bay to a berth designed for him.

McFerson hadn't complained about not operating the grappler. He'd laughed, as if he were having the time of his life. None of them were scared this time. Even if they damaged this corpse, they succeeded. They already had brought one intact astronaut to Earth.

This one was just a bonus.

Richard hated how his thoughts ran. Even as he held the man's arm in his gloved hands, he wasn't thinking of this astronaut as a person, as someone to be rescued, but as an item, as a commodity.

And wasn't that what he'd been? Something to be haggled over, an item for trade? Something that might cause a great loss or a great win?

Certainly not a human being, not any longer.

He tried to keep these feelings to himself—and managed to lose them only briefly, when he learned this one's identity. The name etched along the suit was almost gone, but he could still see its shape, and the first three letters. *B. o. r.*

Borman. The commander.

McFerson speculated about the order of evac, just like Richard had the last time, but Richard wasn't playing that game any longer. Borman was in a part of space that wasn't on Tolemy's map—not in the red section or the green section.

It was as Tolemy had said—impossible to predict where these men would be.

Borman was here, in a place that had no logic at all that Richard could see. And he doubted that anything on Borman's suit would give them real clues about how he got here.

Someone would try to map the trajectory. Someone would make semi-educated guesses, but it wouldn't be Richard.

He was, for all intents and purposes, done.

He didn't say that of course. In public, he sounded the mantra: they still had one astronaut to find—the junior man on the mission, Bill Anders.

Anders family got involved. They asked to help in the search. Publicity stunts—the Anders family looking through telescopes, viewing star charts—abounded. Newspapers carried headlines *Family Still Hopes Missing Astronaut Will Come Home*, and the twenty-four-hour news channels did specials. Websites appeared as amateur astronomers tried to figure out, based on all the points that Richard had discovered, where Anders would be.

Richard supported all of this and more. He kept ACP-S running, and he made sure that anyone with information about the last astronaut should feel free to come to him. He kept the best minds in the business searching, and he even tried to get Tolemy out of retirement.

But Tolemy's heart wasn't in it, and neither was Richard's. Something had changed for him at the last. Maybe he was afraid of success too—or afraid to complete the project. Maybe all that self-examination was just a way to prevent himself from finishing the job.

Because, if he found Bill Anders, what else would drive him? The entire crew of Apollo 8 would be home. The capsule was already here and on display in the Smithsonian, with his private company credited for the donation. Children climbed in and out of the couches where, essentially, three men had died.

After a few years, he stopped monitoring the program. He actually got what most people called a real life. He married for the first time to a woman half his age, a woman who could keep up with him in conversation. They had three children—a daughter and twin boys—and while he found fatherhood interesting, it was not all-consuming the way most people claimed it would be.

His wife said that was because he was not most people. Others he mentioned this to told him it was because he had nannies and assistants who took some of the burden off the childrearing.

But that wasn't what he meant. He had expected raising children to be as focused an activity as searching for Apollo 8 had been. He expected to think about them each waking minute, get lost in their smallest deeds, praise their greatest accomplishments.

And while he paid attention, he did not think about them every waking minute. He barely thought of them at all. Once he learned who they were—how their personalities were forming—he treated them like he treated most people, with a casual coolness that he couldn't quite help.

His wife claimed she expected it, but he could see disappointment in her eyes. His children always sought his approval for everything they did, and yet when he praised them, it wasn't enough.

"They don't want your approval," his wife finally told him. "They want your love."

He thought about that. He wondered if he had ever loved anything. Really loved it.

And eventually he came to the realization that he loved the dream of space. The dream that he had absorbed as a child—the one painted in the picture in his office—of possibilities and fears and greatness unknown.

That had been what he'd been pursuing with Apollo 8. Not a rescue, so much as a hope. A hope that the universe out there would be different than the world in here.

The realization calmed him, and he went back to work, much to his family's dismay. Once again, he checked on ACP-S, not because he had any hopes of finding Anders—he didn't, not really—but because that was part of what he did in the same way that he checked on all of his various projects the world over.

He grew older and he watched as the dreams of his youth—the dream of space flight and far-ranging exploration, of colonizing the solar system, and humankind moving beyond the confines of Earth—slowly came true.

He marveled at the way things went, and he was proud of his part in them.

Part Four
2068

Which was how he came to be on the starliner *Martian Princess* on its maiden voyage from the Moon to the newly opened Mars colony. The colony had existed on Mars for nearly thirty years, but it had expanded and now had a small resort for adventurous travelers who wanted to inspect the area before they bought homes in Mars's second colony, which was under construction.

Richard had a stake in both colonies. He owned the resort. And he owned the *Martian Princess*. The starliners made him proud—not because they were passenger ships like the old luxury liners that used to cross the ocean—but because they were really fast. And that ever-increasing speed was pulling in the outer system with each increase, making things seem closer, more possible.

People still had to commit upward of three months of their life to the journey, depending on where Mars was in relationship to Earth, but that was nothing like the years for a there-and-back journey in the 2030s.

He had the V.I.P. cabin near the front of the ship, but he made a point of visiting all the decks, being seen in the restaurants and the shops and even in the educational wing, where he conspicuously took lessons in Mandarin.

He moved slowly now. Even with all the advancements in medical science, his life had taken its toll on his health. He was 108 and frail. He had to be careful of his old bones. His daughter Delia, who was also on the trip, insisted on bringing a retinue of doctors in case Richard fell ill or tripped and hit his head.

If he had known that the girl was going to be this protective, he never would have made her head of most of his companies. He would have stuck with assistants. Although no assistant had half the intelligence and drive that his daughter had. At forty-two she reminded him of himself at the same age—focused, edgy, and successful in spite of herself.

The resorts were more her dreams than his. She could see past the solar system. She wanted to get to a time when human beings traveled the galaxy the way that they now traveled around the Earth.

That was a bit far for him. Even Mars seemed far for him. This would be his first trip to the red planet, even though he'd had property there for decades. He never wanted to commit to the trip.

He wasn't sure what had made him commit this time either.

He suspected it had a lot to do with the conversation he'd had with his sons, when he told them they needed to be adventurers. They didn't understand him, and he realized that they hadn't seen him in his adventurous years—going through astronaut training, all that risky travel into orbit and beyond, his rescues of Apollo 8 and the two crew members.

His boys knew of that, of course—this was all part of their father's lore—but they hadn't seen it. And they were their mother's children. While bright, they didn't understand what they couldn't see.

They weren't dreamers the way his daughter was. They did strive, though, and they handled themselves well, unlike many children of the rich. They started charities with his excessive fortune, and were working to change the Earth, something he had never even thought of.

He had a hunch they did it as a rebuke to him, but he was proud of them for it. They had seen a gap and filled it, and while they weren't quite what he expected, they were good men with good hearts—a tribute to the woman who had raised them.

Certainly not a tribute to him. When he realized how limited they were, he focused on his daughter. She was his child one-hundred percent, and that fascinated him. She reflected his good and bad qualities—his single-mindedness, his coldness, and his casual way of coming up with a viable idea that somehow made millions.

Yet she was dedicated to him, more dedicated than he had been to his own parents in their declining years. He wasn't sure if that was socialization, a difference in the culture, or if she had a slightly softer side than he had.

He wasn't going to figure that out, either. He was going to enjoy it, as he enjoyed her company when she gave it.

Mostly she spent the trip in her two cabins—the other V.I.P. suite, and the secondary suite she'd commandeered to keep the corporations running. She ran from place to place, like he used to do, frustrated by the slowness of interplanetary communications, and worried that she was going to miss something by being so far away.

He tried to tell her that sometimes being far away was exactly what an entrepreneur needed, but she'd looked at him as if he'd insulted her intelligence, and he vowed to stop giving advice at that moment.

Instead, he retired to his own cabin, which he loved.

He always insisted on luxury. The luxury suites on the *Martian Princess* were spectacular, but the V.I.P. suites took that one step farther. He had his own living room, a dining room, and two bedrooms on the second story, not that he needed both, one of which he turned into an office. The bathroom had every luxury, and the functioning kitchen could cook some foods itself.

But what he loved the most was what the brochures called the backyard—the deck outside the cabin with a floor-to-ceiling view into space. The material that the windows were made out of was so clear that it looked to Richard like space had looked through the open door of the cargo bay on the dart.

Someone had furnished the yard like a formal living room. When he examined the suite the week before the *Martian Princess* left, he had the formal furniture replaced with chaise lounges and wooden tables—the lawn furniture of his youth. The lights, scattered around the yard, looked like tiki torches. All that he needed was some green grass and some fireflies, and he would be at home.

He spent most of his time on the deck, reading or listening to music. He didn't watch any programming or have holo performances on the yard because he didn't want to get lost in them. He never invited anyone into his cabin. If he saw people, he saw them on the decks or in the restaurants.

The view was enough.

And it was the view that caught him, two days out from Mars. He was standing in the middle of the lawn, transfixed by the way the darkness of space wasn't really dark. There were hints of light in it. Sunlight went everywhere. The all-powerful star that was the center of this solar system had a greater reach than any human being ever could.

He tilted his head up, and saw a reflection in the distance, a flash of light off something white ahead of the ship. He blinked, certain he'd imagined that. But it came again, larger now, as if the object were spinning ever so slowly.

He went to the cabin, used the on-deck telescope for his particular suite, and turned the exterior lens on the object.

The very powerful telescope had an automatic computer tracking function and he set it on the object.

His breath caught when he looked.

An astronaut in an old-fashioned suit.

His heart started to pound.

Anders. Could it be?

Richard wiped his hands on his pants, thought for a moment, and knew how everyone would react. They didn't treat him like a doddering old man—that kind of treatment disappeared as aging became a way of life for so many people—but people who had passed 100 still had achieved a milestone that made the younger generations dismiss him.

He wasn't in his prime any more physically—that was obvious— and so many people thought that meant he wasn't in his prime mentally either.

The ship would be past the object in less than a minute. He had to act, and act quickly.

His hand shook as he pressed the comm link. "Delia," he said to his daughter, "come here please. Now. Quickly!"

Then he called the bridge. "I need your best pilot, with a few changes of clothes, to meet me in ten minutes."

"May I ask why, sir?" the Captain asked.

"No."

Richard shut down the comm link, then grabbed some of his own clothes, stuffed them inside a bag, and put the bag over his shoulder.

The door to his room glided open and his daughter entered, looking worried. She was trim and athletic with her mother's dark hair and eyes.

"I want you to see something," he said before she could speak.

He indicated the telescope. "Look quickly. It's more than likely almost out of sight."

She started to object and he held up his hand. "Quickly."

She sighed and walked over. She wrapped one hand around the viewer, and peered through the lens, then gasped. "This has to be some kind of joke."

"Possibly," he said. "But I'm still going after it, joke or not."

He knew that the liner couldn't just turn like a ship in the ocean. This ship was turning around only after it reached Mars orbit. And by the time they got there, Anders would be again lost.

The last astronaut. The last part of Richard's dream.

He had just passed it.

But he had no intention of losing it.

"Dad, what are you thinking?" Delia asked as she walked with him from his suite and headed down the hall.

"I'm going to go get him."

Delia looked at him as if he had suddenly lost his mind. "Daddy, there isn't any way to pick him up. We're already far, far past him."

"Not that far," he said. "I'll take one of the lifeboats. It's designed with more than enough range."

He'd insisted on the old-fashioned term when he'd approved the design of the starliner. He worried that such a large, grand ship would suffer the fate of the *Titanic*—that some sort of disaster would hit it, and hundreds of people would die because he hadn't prepared. He'd insisted on smaller ships, most of them two-man sized, a few a bit larger, all of them with enough power and supplies to last a year with a dozen people on board.

"They don't have grapplers," she said.

Richard gave her a surprised look.

"I studied your space rescues, Dad," she said. "They were miracles of efficiency."

They hadn't seemed like it at the time.

"I don't need a grappler," he said. "I need a lifeboat, a spacesuit, and a pilot."

"Daddy," Delia said, "this is crazy."

He ran a hand along her face, then smiled at her with the most affection he'd ever felt.

"Yes," he said, "it is."

The pilot was a small woman named Star. He thought the name a good omen. Before she was hired as a tertiary co-pilot for this mission, she'd been with the U.S. military, flying orbital defense missions around the Moon colony. He looked up her record, saw the reprimands in the file for a bit too much cockiness, for a tad too much recklessness, and decided she was exactly what he needed.

He could have flown the ship himself—the controls were so simple that a child could fly it (he'd insisted on that too)—but he chose not to. He needed the help.

The lifeboat didn't have a cargo bay like the ones he was used to—no separate environmental system, no real storage area—but it did have two doors, one inside, and one with an airlock out the side. That was all he needed. And it had six small cabins. He could put Anders in one and shut off the environmental systems to that cabin to keep him frozen.

"I'm going with you," Delia said as they reached the lifeboat entrance. Star had already gone on board and had the ship coming to life.

"No," he said. "You have to pull every string you can pull to get back here and pick me up, with a ship equipped to handle what I'm going to go get, and then get us all back to Earth."

He then kissed her on the forehead and stepped aboard, closing the hatch behind him.

Star got the lifeboat slowed to a stop within six hours, and had them back to the area of the Anders's position in another eight hours. The entire time Richard sat in the copilot's chair and stared ahead into the emptiness of space. And every hour he had to calm Delia, tell her he was fine. He had no idea his daughter worried so much. That made him feel wanted, and he liked that feeling.

The old ships that Richard had used on the first three missions never had this kind of speed or maneuverability. In fact, at the speed the liner was moving when they left it, the old ships wouldn't have even had the power to slow and stop, let alone go back.

It took surprisingly little searching to find Anders. The newer equipment on the ships also made that easier.

Star matched Anders's course and pulled in close beside him. The body was barely turning. It seemed to just float there.

"You take the controls," Star said, "and I'll get him."

"No," Richard said. "I will."

She gave him a sideways look.

"I'll be all right," he said.

It took him a little longer to climb into the new space suits. They looked more like a white tuxedo than an actual space suit, and the helmets were close-fitting and light. Everyone on the liner had been trained to put them on, but they still didn't feel right, as if he wasn't wearing enough to protect him from the cold he was about to step into.

He climbed into the airlock and magnetized his boots. Then he vented the atmosphere.

He felt stronger than he had in years.

The tricky part, he knew, would be reaching for Anders. Star had gotten the lifeboat to a point where it nearly touched the man, but Richard had little to support him. He used the tether inside the airlock, and wrapped it around his waist, securing it tightly.

Then he opened the outer door.

Unfiltered light hit him, reflecting off the lifeboat's silver sides. He blinked in the glare.

Then his eyes adjusted.

Anders floated near him, just an arms-reach away.

Looking free. Almost as if he didn't want to be rescued.

For the first time, Richard understood the impulse that had led to the Apollo 8 astronauts evacuating their small ship. Why stay inside a tin can when the entire universe waited? What would Anders have said if he knew that his body would be found so very close to Mars? How would he have felt to know that he had spent a hundred years gazing blindly on the entire solar system?

Richard reached forward and grabbed Anders's cold, stiff arm.

It would be so easy to lock elbows and step into the darkness.

It would be so easy to chose this death. Eventually, he would just go to sleep. He would be unencumbered by anything, gazing at the vastness of space and of the future.

Yet he had no reason to step out. He still had years yet. Years of adventures.

He was going to Mars where he already had businesses. He had been traveling on a starliner, for heaven's sake, something that the original Apollo astronauts could only dream of.

Their sacrifices had brought him here.

Their courage, their loss, their dreams.

He had an obligation to keep living the future they always wanted, to continue to make their dreams of the stars even more possible for succeeding generations.

Part of that was bringing Anders in, letting scientists see what happened one hundred years out. To learn, as they had from Borman and Lovell, about the adventures these men had had, even after death.

"You okay?" Star asked.

"Fine," Richard said.

It took only a gentle tug to bring Anders to the door. Richard wrapped his arms around the hundred-year-old adventurer and pulled him gently so that his booted feet didn't hit the door's lip. Then Richard eased the body inside.

As he reached for the mechanism to close the outer door, he saw the vastness of the stars, as mysterious as the Moon used to be when Richard was a boy.

All his life, people accused him of pursing death.

But he hadn't been. He'd been exploring possibilities, reaching toward a future he could only see in his imagination.

He went after these men because they inspired him. But he never rescued them.

They were the ones who had been the heroes.

They were the ones who had always—always—rescued him.

The Taste of Miracles

*H*AYES STARED AT THE VASTNESS OF SPACE through the freighter's window. He swiveled slightly in the pilot's chair, wincing as he banged his knees on the control panel. No matter how many times he did this run, the sight fascinated him. Even the blackness looked crisp, and the points of light appeared sharp. Thousands of stars. Thousands of possibilities.

Trish brushed his shoulder. He turned, and she handed him a steaming mug. "Cocoa," she said.

He took it, feeling the heat through the durable plastic. "I didn't know we had chocolate aboard."

She smiled and eased in the chair next to his. She was as slim and battered as the freighter, her skin lined with the effort from all the years of hauling, lifting, and loading. He had called her scrappy until he had seen her in a fight with one of the ore miners in the bar at the ass-end of the Moon base. After that, Hayes decided, "tough" was too wimpy a word for Trish.

"Needed a little something special tonight," she said, then blew gently at the steam.

He glanced at her, her small, strong hands wrapped around the mug as if it would give her warmth. "Didn't think you celebrated holidays."

Her grin was tiny. She didn't look at him. "Don't. Not really, anyway. But I kinda like this run on Christmas."

Earth to the Moon and back. One of the easiest runs on the freight line. He preferred Earth to Mars because he liked Mars better. It stirred his imagination in a way the Moon never did. "I like it too," he said. "Pays triple."

"No. I don't care about that." She slurped. The entire area smelled of hot chocolate. "You celebrate Christmas, Hayes?"

"I'm not religious," he said.

"I mean as a kid. You get to celebrate? Tree and tinsel and toys?"

"Shoppers Mecca," he said, remembering the tree from his twelfth year. His mom shelled out for a Grow-Your-Own, the only way to get real trees then. It had been enormous, decorated with popcorn and ornaments generations old. The lights were miniature candles that appeared to be burning, and his parents had bought so many presents that the packages spilled across the living room floor.

"Was it fun?" She huddled in the chair, her legs drawn up to her chest, mug balanced on one knee.

He shrugged and thought. It had been so long since he had done the holiday thing. He was usually on some run or another, earning extra cash. "The anticipation was great," he said after a moment. "All month. The tree, the lights, the packages filled with surprises. The feeling that something magic could happen. That was fun."

She was staring at the stars, like he had, only her scarred features had a touch of wistfulness. "Never had any of that. The Shoppers Mecca or the religious stuff."

"Never? Not even as a kid?" He regretted the question the minute he asked it. She had spoken of her childhood enough—in the program from the age of eleven, bounced at sixteen when she became too hard to handle after her grandmother's death, running freight ever since because she was strong and one of the best damn pilots in the business.

"Not the shopping. Not the religion." She finished her cocoa and set the mug on the floor beside her seat. "Christmas Eve, my gram would fill a thermos with hot cocoa, then she would bundle me up, take me outside, and when we were all snug in the snow, drinking our cocoa, she'd point to the stars. She'd tell me this story about how, when she was a girl, they had this race to get to the Moon, and how, one Christmas Eve, those astronauts orbited the Moon for the first time, and they sent holiday wishes to Earth."

"Apollo 8," Hayes said. "Borman, Lovell, and Anders."

"You know it?" she asked.

"Space history is a hobby of mine."

She nodded, still staring at the blackness. "Anyway, Gram thought it was a miracle. A real miracle. So every year, she went outside and pretended she could see them up there, circling."

"So that's why you do this," Hayes said.

She looked at him for the first time, her nut-brown eyes bright. He could almost see the little girl, bundled against the cold, holding her grandmother's hand and staring at the night-darkened sky.

"No," she said, her flat voice shattering the illusion. "We were born too late to be cowboys, Hayes, and there's no such thing as miracles any more."

She picked up her mug and straightened out her legs, then pushed out of the seat. Space was as dark as ever, the stars bright beacons of the future, waiting for him. But he would never go farther than Mars. He was a pilot who shuttled ore, equipment, and people from place to place. Not even allowed the glamour title "astronaut" any more.

She had stopped behind his chair. He could see her reflection against the window as if she were standing in space, unsupported by the freighter.

"That's why I like this run on Christmas," she said. "I need to remember that once upon a time, this was the stuff of dreams."

She touched his shoulder, a fleeting warmth, a moment, dreamer to dreamer. Then she let go.

"More cocoa?" she asked.

"Yeah," he said, glad she had brought it along.

Before handing her his mug, he took one last sip. He stared at the stars, swirling the chocolate on his tongue, and savored the taste of miracles.

The Strangeness of the Day

*J*UST ONCE, SHE THOUGHT, JUST ONCE, SHE would like a little magic in her life. She believed magic was possible, on days when the sun shown through the clouds, on afternoons when rainbows dotted the countryside, on mornings when the light was so sharp it looked as if everything had been freshly made.

Not on a day like this. On a day like this, all she wanted was someone to come home to, a man to cook her meals and rub her feet, and laugh at the sheer strangeness of the day.

That was what she was thinking about as she exited the elevator into the bowels of the parking structure below her office building. The concrete structure smelled like gas fumes, and the lighting, even in the middle of the day, was a gray florescent that made her think of rain.

She rounded a corner, her heels clicking on the concrete, and saw a man sitting on the back of a 1974 Lincoln, holding a cigarette lighter in one hand, and a snake in the other.

The snake was alive, and twisting.

She swallowed, uncertain whether or not to keep walking. The man was gorgeous: long black hair, brown eyes, smooth skin the color of toffee. He wore a shimmery gray silk suit that accented his broad shoulders and long legs, and on his feet he wore cowboy boots trimmed with real silver.

Nora pulled her purse tight against her side. She would walk around the car and continue toward hers as if she saw nothing wrong.

"Who'zat?" A nasal male voice demanded.

"Probably someone on the way to her car." The responding voice was deep and smooth, soft and in control. Even without clear eyesight, Nora knew who spoke second.

A tiny man stood on the bumper of the Lincoln. The first man had slid across the hood to make room for the small guy. The little guy was perfectly proportioned, square with a pugnacious face, a nose that obviously had been broken several times, and powerful arms. He wore dark blue jeans and a T-shirt with a pack of cigarettes rolled up in the sleeves.

"It'd be nice to have a woman," the tiny man said.

His companion smiled. The snake wrapped itself around his wrist. "Things are a bit different now," he said. "You can't just have any woman."

As he said that last, his gaze met Nora's. His brown eyes sparkled as if they shared a joke.

She wasn't in the mood to share anything, no matter how gorgeous he was. She had a video deposition to take, a lunch to grab on the run, and a court appearance at two. She didn't have time for any of this.

"Excuse me," she said, and tried to hurry past them. The little man scurried along the bumper until he could extend his small arm in front of her.

"Who are you?" he asked in his annoying nasal voice.

She had had enough of their strangeness. She rose to her full five feet four inches (in heels) and said, "Nora Barr. I'm a lawyer." She added that last so that they wouldn't screw with her.

The tall man raised his eyebrows and looked at the little man. The little man shrugged. "Told you we needed a woman," he said.

So that was how she found herself back in her office, the two men seated across from her, looking at her degrees and framed prints cluttering the fake wood paneling on the wall. She had sent her assistant Charlene to do the video deposition, rationalizing that Charlene needed the experience, knowing that she would regret this action should that particular case go to trial. But she really didn't want to leave Charlene alone with these two—Nora wasn't sure she wanted to be alone with them either—but she felt compelled to listen to their case.

The little man sat like an overgrown child in her green metal office chair. His stubby legs extended over the seat, and didn't even pretend to try for the ground. Like a little boy, he put his hands on the armrests as if he were trying to hold himself in place. He watched her every move, and she wasn't sure she liked that.

The other man slid into the remaining chair as if it were built for him. He had pushed the chair back so that he could extend his long legs. His booted feet still hit the metal edge of her desk, rattling it. The snake had disappeared, probably hiding in his suit, and he had also hidden the cigarette lighter.

"All right," she said, leaning forward and folding her hands together in what she hoped was a business-like position. "What can I do for you?"

"Can you have someone tested for a witch?" the little man asked.

"That never worked," the other man growled.

"Exactly," the little man said.

Nora glanced at her watch. "I have to be in court in less than ninety minutes."

"Right," the gorgeous man said. "I—"

"If she can't have her tested for a witch, perhaps tarred and feathered—?"

"Wrong century."

"Hung from a tree until she's dead?"

"Wrong century."

"Boiled in oil?"

"You know no one did that."

Nora slapped her hands on her desk and stood. "I do appreciate the comedy routine, but I also bill by the hour, and so far you gentlemen have taken up nearly fifteen minutes of your free session. So unless there's a *realistic* way I can help you—"

"I'm sorry." The good-looking man stood too. "I get so preoccupied I forget that the rest of the world doesn't work the way I do." He extended his hand. "I'm Blackstone."

"*The* Blackstone?" she asked with just a trace of sarcasm in her voice.

"Well, actually, yes, but not the one you're thinking of. He, in fact, was the imposter, but that's a long story that ended rather nastily for all concerned. He—"

"Blackstone," she said, sinking down to her desk. This would be a long interview. "Is that a first or last name?"

"It's a surname," he said, sitting too. "My given name is Aethelstan."

"Aethelstan?" Whatever she had expected, it wasn't that.

He shrugged prettily. "It was in style once."

"A long, *long* time ago," the little man added.

"And you are?" she asked him.

"Let's just call me Panza," the little man said. "Sancho Panza."

She shook her head. "If you want me to do something for you in a court of law, I'll need your legal name."

The little guy shrugged. "It's not me you're helping," he said. "It's Blackstone."

She sighed. Why did she feel as if she had been taken, and she hadn't known what for? "All right, Mr. Blackstone," she said, "what can I help you with?"

"You charge what?" he asked. The question sounded rude. As he spoke, the snake stuck its head out of his shirt and looked at her as if it too expected an answer.

"Two hundred dollars an hour, plus a—" she almost quoted her regular rate, then decided to double it because these two were proving to be so much trouble— "plus a thousand dollar retainer."

"A thousand dollar—?" the little man said, strangling on the last word. "In my day, you could run a country on a thousand dollars."

"In your day, there was no such thing as dollars," Blackstone muttered.

"As I told you in the parking garage, the first hour of the consultation is free." She glanced at her watch. "However, you're rapidly running out of time."

"What do you prefer?" Blackstone asked. "A check or cash?"

"Or gold?" the little man added. She would be damned if she would think of him as Sancho Panza.

"A check is fine," she said. No sense taking currency. With these two, it could just as easily be forged, and then where would she be? The worst thing a check could do was bounce.

Blackstone put a hand inside his suit coat and brought out a checkbook. A pen appeared in his other hand. She hadn't seen him take it from anywhere. He poised it over the paper. "To you or the law firm?"

She was still nonplused by the appearance of the pen. "Um," she said, wishing she could gather herself more quickly in this man's presence. "The law firm."

He wrote the check, signed it with a flourish, then handed it to her. She glanced at it, noting his name in bold and only a post office box for an address. It was time, she thought, to get serious.

She pulled out a legal pad and took her pen out of its holder. "Let's get your exact address and phone, starting with you, Mr. Blackstone, and then going with your friend here."

"You don't need me," the little man said. "I already told you."

"Then I'll have to ask you to leave," she said.

"I don't mind him staying," Blackstone said, leaning back as he said so.

"I do," she said.

Blackstone raised an eyebrow. The little man scowled. "You got books in the waiting area."

"Law books," Nora said.

"Good enough," he said, and let himself out.

The room felt three times larger without him. She wasn't certain how a person that tiny could fill such a big space.

"Mr. Blackstone," she said, not missing a beat, "street address and phone number?"

He gave her both with an ease that made her uncomfortable. She wasn't sure why it did; most people could recite their addresses in their sleep. But everything about him seemed strange.

"So," she said again. "How can I help you?"

To her surprise, a flush covered his cheeks. He threaded his hands together, glanced nervously at the door, and then said, "A—dear friend of mine—has been in a—coma—for—some time. Her—guardian—won't let me near her, and although I've fought for that right for—some time—, I haven't made any progress."

"And you want me to—what? Contact the guardian?"

"Isn't there anything legal you can do?" he asked.

"Depends," she said. "What's your exact relationship?"

His flush grew deeper. She sighed inwardly. Girlfriend. Right. But then, she had a rule about getting involved with clients anyway.

"She's—ah—someone special to me."

God, she hated clients like this. They wanted her to fix whatever it was, but they weren't forthcoming right from the start. Her favorite second year law professor had warned them all about this, but she had thought he was exaggerating until she hung out her shingle and began to interact with the great unwashed.

"Special." She let her tone go dry. "As in fiancé? Lover?"

"No," he said. "But she will be."

She closed her eyes. Will be. He had hopes, but the woman probably didn't. Which meant he was a stalker. Why were all the gorgeous ones also crazy? She opened her eyes. He was watching her, looking puzzled.

"Look, Mr. Blackstone," she said. "I can't help you in any legal way unless the woman in question is in some way a relative. I'm sorry, but that's just the law. You'll have to accept the situation for what it is and move on."

She pushed his check back toward him.

"You can't help me?" he asked, sounding a bit astounded.

She shook her head. "Not me, not any lawyer. You have no rights with someone who is just a friend. The guardian has legal control."

The snake stuck its head out farther and hissed softly. Its long, forked tongue curled as it did so. He shushed it, and pushed it back inside his coat.

"This is becoming untenable," he said.

"I'm sorry." Her heart had started pounding hard. He had made her nervous from the beginning, but she had thought his strangeness harmless. Now she wasn't sure.

He took the check, stood, and held out his hand. "Sorry to take all of your time," he said.

"The first hour's free," she said lightly. But it had cost her a good deposition.

"Nonetheless," he said. "I appreciate your candor." And then he slipped out the door and out, she hoped, of her life. Still, as a precaution, she made notes of the entire strange meeting. Her secretary had been complaining about the dullness of the routine lately; she would get a kick out of this.

Nora didn't think of Blackstone again. She had chalked up the interview to one of those weird experiences that attorneys sometimes had, and she had moved on. So, two weeks later, as she was leaving the courthouse after a particularly successful trial, she was surprised to receive a call from her secretary, saying that Blackstone had requested her presence immediately at an address that put him squarely in the center of the westside suburbs. Nora protested: she had told him she wouldn't be his attorney, but her secretary insisted.

"I think he's in some kind of trouble," she said.

It took Nora ten minutes on the freeway to get to the neighborhood Blackstone had indicated. As she got closer, she watched a cloud of inky black smoke loom over that section of town. Fire equipment and ambulances screamed by her, slowing her trip. Each time she pulled to the side of the road, she cursed slightly, and she wondered what she was getting herself into.

The exit was jammed with milling people, emergency vehicles, and baffled on-lookers. The inky black smoke was rising from an area two blocks over. It looked serious.

A roadblock greeted her halfway down the street. A cop she didn't recognize rapped on her window. As she rolled it down, she said, "I'm Mr. Blackstone's attorney. He just called me."

The cop waved her through.

As she drove past the roadblock, she felt as if she had entered a nightmare. Burning bits of wood littered the road, and she had to constantly swerve around them. Several homes were on fire, their residents outside, holding hoses on them or weeping. A couple of cars parked alongside the street had large holes through their roofs and sides, as if someone—or something—had punched through the metal. The air was filled with ash, and the smell of smoke was so overpowering, she continually sneezed.

The address her secretary had given her was right in the middle of the devastation. Police cars blocked the entire road. She couldn't drive any farther. She really didn't want to get out, but she felt she had no choice.

She sighed, grabbed her tennis shoes from their spot beneath the passenger seat, and removed her lucky Ferragamos. She shoved her nylon covered feet into the tennies, and got out of the car.

It was worse outside. The stench permeated everything. Bits of charred wood and flame floated down with the ash. The sky was so dark, it seemed as if a severe storm were about to break overhead. Her eyes watered. People were sobbing, police band radios were crackling voices and static, and firemen were yelling directions at each other. She stepped over hoses and blackened debris, not quite sure where she was going, but knowing she'd recognize it when she saw it.

And she did. The five policemen were standing around Blackstone. He was on a green lawn, untouched by flames, its flowers an obscene reminder of what the neighborhood had been just hours before. A woman was sprawled on the driveway face down; her position was unnatural, the turn of her head, the clawed tension in her fingers all confirmed what Nora feared.

The woman was dead.

A shiver ran through Nora despite the dry heat from nearby flames. She didn't do criminal work. She was a civil attorney; this was way out of her league.

She rounded a 1970s brown and orange VW microbus, and headed toward the police. No one tried to stop her. The microbus rocked slightly, and as she looked up, she could have sworn she saw Sancho Panza or whoever the hell he was moving behind the window. Then, when she blinked, he was gone.

She swallowed against the smoke-ravaged dryness of her throat. She had to stay focused. She had to somehow get through these next few moments and then get out of here.

Blackstone's face softened when he saw her. It had been hard lines and angles before. Now it was gentle, rounded, as if someone had changed the lighting or he had become a different person somehow. She felt the transition as much as saw it, and remembered suddenly, uncomfortably, of the transition people said Ted Bundy's face went through when he was angry.

She was in much too deep. At least she knew it.

She stopped beside one of the police officers, a middle-aged man whose soft stomach edged over his belt. His face was soot-streaked, and his eyes were red.

"I'm Mr. Blackstone's attorney," Nora said in her best don't-screw-with-me-voice. "What's going on here?"

"Nora," Blackstone said, his voice warm. "Get my partner. We're going to need your help."

"What's going on?" she asked again.

The cop looked around as if what she saw explained everything. "Your client destroyed this neighborhood." Then he nodded at the dead woman. "We're not sure what happened there. All we know is that folks placed her as alive not fifteen minutes ago."

"What are you charging him with?"

"What aren't we charging him with? Carrying incendiary devices. Arson. Murder and attempted murder, I would say."

"Nora," Blackstone said again. "Get Sancho. We need to secure the glass case and we don't have much time."

"You shouldn't be talking," Nora said. "Listen, I'll meet you at the jail. And if possible, I'll have a criminal defense attorney there as well. We'll get you out—"

"I'm not worried about me," he said. "Get Sancho—"

"You coming with us, lady?" the police officer asked.

"Where are you taking him?"

"Downtown," the officer said. "This one goes right to the jail. We're not taking no chances."

"Nora—"

She pointed a finger at Blackstone. He flinched visibly. "I don't want to hear another word from you. You will not speak again until you are in the presence of an attorney. Is that clear?"

He nodded. She had no idea if they had already Mirandized him, but she wasn't taking any chances.

The cops led him away. He looked over his shoulder once and mouthed "Remember." She wouldn't forget. Even though she wanted to.

She brushed a strand of hair out of her face. The smoke was making her woozy. She didn't want to think about what he had done to destroy this neighborhood. She didn't want to think about that feeling she had gotten earlier, when she had first met with him, when she felt that he was a stalker. She wondered how much she had seen at that moment, and how much she had missed.

Well, it wouldn't be her problem for long. She would turn it over to someone else, and that would be it. Except that he wanted her to do something, something with a glass case.

She passed the VW microbus and as she did, the passenger window rolled down a crack. A tiny face pressed against it. "I'm going to your office," a voice whispered.

Sancho. She suppressed a sigh and didn't even nod as she passed him. The last thing she wanted was for the cops to investigate the microbus. Who knew what they would find inside? She couldn't believe they hadn't cordoned it off already as part of the crime scene.

She climbed over hoses, and returned to her own car. It was covered in a film of ash. As she settled into the driver's side, she turned on the wipers. The ash smeared all over the glass.

He had destroyed a neighborhood and maybe killed a woman. Was this because Nora hadn't helped him? Or was something else going on here, something she didn't entirely understand?

She started the car, and executed a series of small Y-turns in the tiny space, careful not to run over any hoses. The situation looked grim. Houses were still burning. She wondered how many would be gone by nightfall.

If she had to lay a bet, she would bet on all of them.

She was shaking as she drove back to her office. Shaking and slightly woozy from the smoke. Her nylons were ripped and she didn't know how she had done that, and her best suit was covered in soot and ash. She smelled like charred wood, and she doubted that smell would ever come off.

Traffic was horrible—backed up for miles as people gawked at the smoke, and pulled over for the occasional ambulance. When she got herself together enough to speak, she called her secretary and had a conference call with Max Raichelson, the best defense attorney in the city, maybe in the entire state. She and Max had been close in law school—she had even hoped he would ask her out—but nothing had come of it. After graduation, they had gone their own ways.

He agreed to meet Blackstone ("You're kidding, right?" Max asked) at the police station.

The problem was no longer hers. Except she didn't tell Max about Sancho. And she didn't want to think about him either. She wanted simply to get on with her life as if nothing happened. She knew that would be impossible, but in the spirit of pretense, she flicked on the radio to get her mind on something else.

Instantly a shrill female voice, filtered through a phone line, grated on her nerves. She was about to flip away, when a professional radio voice broke in and clearly hung up on the caller.

"Crackpots," the announcer said. "We have a situation and all we get are crank calls."

"Several dozen of them, though, Dave," said a professional female voice. "Don't you think we should pay attention to them?"

"No," Dave said. "To recap, there's been an incident—"

He started to describe the neighborhood she had just left, adding nothing to what she already knew. Fortunately he didn't have Blackstone's name and he didn't seem to know about the dead woman. At that moment, the radio was reporting that no one had died.

"—another caller from the neighborhood," the woman announcer was saying. "And this one we both happen to know. It's Rick Ayers, our morning news announcer. Rick?"

"Stefanie." Rick's voice crackled over the phone lines and through Nora's radio. She had turned off the main highway, but traffic was still backed up. It was dark as night around her. The smoke had settled over the valley. "Even though Dave thinks the other callers are cranks, they aren't."

"Come on, Rick. Two people fighting with fire? It gets out of control? A big, wild fireball battle like something out of Tolkien? We're supposed to believe that?"

Now they really had her attention. Nora glanced at the radio as if she could gauge its truthfulness just by looking at it. She was still shaking.

" 'Fraid so," Rick said. "I was across the street. I got the kids out and down the block as fast as possible. There were two people involved—a man and a woman. The man had been coming out of the woman's garage. He had a glass case in front of him, and it appeared to be full. That's what got my attention. He wasn't carrying the glass case. It was floating in front of him."

"And what were you drinking this afternoon?" Dave asked. It didn't sound like banter.

"I wasn't. He put it in an orange and brown VW microbus when the woman comes out of her house and lobs a ball of fire at him. He deflects it, and it lands on a neighbor's house. That's when I got the kids and sent them down the block, knocking on doors. I think we got the place evacuated by the time the fire fight started in earnest."

"You mean to tell me . . . ?"

Nora pulled into the underground parking lot beneath her building and momentarily lost the signal. Instead of regaining it, she shut off the radio, not really wanting to think about what she had just learned.

She had wished for magic. She simply didn't like the form it was taking.

She pulled into her normal parking space, opened her door, and heard a clang. She frowned, wondering if she had hit the car next to her.

Only it wasn't a car. It was a brown and orange VW microbus.

Sancho or whatever the hell his name was crawled from under her door. "Man am I going to have a headache," he said, one hand cradling the side of his face.

"What's going on?" she asked again.

"You don't want to know."

"I'm supposed to know," she said. "I'm supposed to help you."

"Let's go to your office," Sancho said.

She sighed and grabbed her briefcase. She decided she was enough of a mess to forgo the heels. Indeed, when she got to her floor and exited, wandering down the hall, Sancho behind her, her secretary squealed.

"Are you all right, Ms. Barr?"

"Fine," she said. "Although I could use a couple of bottles of water, pronto. I don't think I've ever been this thirsty."

Then she showed the little man into her office, and closed the door. He headed toward the chair he had used before. She didn't know how he had managed to stay soot-free from all the smoke and fire, nor how the microbus had gotten to the garage ahead of her.

"I won't do anything for you," she said, crossing around to her desk and placing her briefcase on it, "until I know your real name."

He placed a birth certificate, a social security card, a passport, and a driver's license on her blotter. They all showed his name to be Sancho Panza, and the driver's license and passport photos confirmed that the name belonged to him.

She shoved them back at him, more angrily than she would have liked. "I don't deal in fake I.D.," she said.

"Neither do I," he said.

She glanced at it again. The driver's license had the supposedly unduplicatable holographic sticker just under the photo. The passport was old with several stamps already inside. If it had passed customs, it was good enough for her.

"I still don't believe it," she said.

"You don't have to." He settled in his chair. "Just help us."

"I already got a defense attorney for Blackstone."

"Fine," Panza said, as if he didn't care. "The most important thing is the glass case."

"Yes," Nora said. She took a recorder out of her briefcase, then closed the case, and set it on the floor. "I understand that he levitated it out of someone's garage."

"How he got it isn't your concern," Panza said. "Helping him with it is."

"I don't deal in stolen property," she said.

"It's not stolen," Panza said. There was a knock on her door.

"Come in," Nora said. Her secretary brought in four cold bottles of water.

"Need a glass?" her secretary asked.

Nora shook her head. "Thanks."

Her secretary left. Nora offered one bottle to Panza, but he declined.

"I really don't want to be involved," she said.

"You're already involved. You identified yourself as Blackstone's attorney. People will come to you."

It was a weak argument, as arguments went. She opened a bottle of water, and took a long, long drink from it. The coolness felt good against her parched throat. The smoke and heat had dehydrated her.

"Why did Blackstone destroy that neighborhood?"

"He didn't," Panza said.

"Someone did," she said.

"Don't worry about it," Panza said.

"I have to worry about it." She ran a hand over her face, felt the soot flake off. "People make jokes about lawyers having no ethics, but that's not true. I can't help him and stay true to myself if I know he destroyed that neighborhood."

Panza clenched a fist, hit the arm of the chair, and then shook his head. "What if I told you everything will be fixed?"

She laughed, and felt its bitterness. "That can't be fixed. Not in the way I would want."

"And that is?"

"To make it seem as if today never happened. But people don't forget. Even if everything were made better, people would remember and—"

"Say no more." Panza stood in the chair. She was constantly amazed at how small he was. "We can do that."

"Sure," she said. "And pigs fly."

"Not without help," he said, and he seemed perfectly serious. "Now. Assist us."

He wouldn't go away. And no matter how ethical she got, the images wouldn't go away. She might as well see what they wanted. "Tell me what you need," she said.

"I need you to store our microbus," he said.

"You can do that."

He shook his head. "We can't know where it is. Only you can know. You'll store it for us, and then when we come and get it, everything will be safe."

"It doesn't sound legal."

"It is. All you have to do is find a garage, rent it, and keep the microbus there. We might not come for it for years."

"Years?" Nora asked.

"Years." He reached into the breast pocket of his shirt and removed an envelope. The envelope was four times the size of the pocket. "This should cover rent for the next twenty years, plus your fees and time, based on the estimate you gave Blackstone when you first met. If it takes us longer to get the microbus, we will send more money."

She took the envelope. It was too thin to be holding cash. Instead she found a very ornate check for a very lot of money. It was issued by Quixotic, Inc. and signed by Sancho Panza. "I'll have to verify the funds," she said.

"Of course."

She took the envelope, stood, and walked to the front office. There she had her secretary call and verify the check. It was good.

She came back in, tapping the envelope against her hand. The little man was still standing in the chair. He was watching her. She closed the door and leaned on it.

"Here's what I'm willing to do," she said. "I will take your money, and put it in a special account. I will have the rental for the garage removed from that account, and my monthly fee. I will keep the keys here, but I will not inspect the microbus. I will not touch the microbus after I take it to the garage, and I will not relinquish the keys to anyone but you or Mr. Blackstone—*ever*. Is that clear?"

"Will the account bear interest?" Panza asked.

"Yes," she said.

"And who gets the interest?"

"Probably the person who owns the garage, when you don't come back in twenty years," she said.

The little man smiled. "I like you," he said. "If Blackstone's heart weren't imprisoned, I bet he would too."

After Panza left, she dictated the necessary instructions to her secretary. Then she went home, showered, changed into jeans and a sweatshirt and drank another gallon of water. Her eyes were still red. The smoke cloud remained over the city. Even though she had cleared her own lungs, the smell of smoke went everywhere with her. She shut off the radio because she couldn't stand the constant jabber about the "Battle of the Wizards" as one of the stations had dubbed the day's events.

She found a brand-new garage complex on the edge of town, and signed a year's lease with an option for renewal. Then she drove back, got the microbus, and took it to the garage. It drove like a VW Bug—an old VW Bug—that was about to explode. Something weighed the back down, and made corners difficult. But she didn't look. She didn't want to.

She parked the microbus in the garage, pulled down the door, and locked it with a brand new lock that required a combination and a key. Then she took a cab back to her office.

It was getting dark, and she could no longer see the smoke.

As she was walking in the door, her phone rang. Her secretary was long gone. The main room was dark. She stumbled against a chair as she reached for the desk, and managed a shaky hello, just as she realized she should have let the service get the call.

"Nora?"

It took her a moment to recognize the voice. "Max? How did it go with Blackstone?"

"Buy me a drink," Max said. "No. Buy me fifteen drinks, and pour me into a cab. I really don't want to go home."

That bad. It was that bad. And she had already helped him. She had already implicated herself by taking care of the microbus.

"All right," she said. "Where?"

"Grady's."

Grady's. It had been the law school's watering hole. She hadn't been there since she graduated. At least she was dressed for it. She grabbed her purse and took her car down to campus.

It wasn't hard to find Max. He was the only man over thirty in the place. Even if he weren't, the silk suit in a bar filled with jeans, T-shirts, and tattoos would have been a dead giveaway.

He sat in a booth in the back, and looked as if he had already had a few drinks. She slid in across from him, and a tired smile crossed his lined face. She had liked Max more than she cared to admit. He had made quite a name for himself. They had always exchanged pleasantries when they passed in the courthouse, but they hadn't had time for much else.

She had missed him. She hadn't realized how much.

A waitress with studs in her eyebrows, cheeks, and nose made her way to the table. Nora ordered a beer, and found that she had to choose a microbrew instead. Finally Max ordered for her—and paid for it.

When she protested, he grinned. "You got me the case."

"You asked me to buy," she said.

"I've just made more money for doing nothing than I've ever made for doing something," he said.

She frowned.

"I cashed one very large check on the way back from the jail this afternoon," he said, "and I verified the funds before I did. It's good. I'm supposed to give some to you. Finder's fee."

He slid a check across the table. She gasped at the amount. "Max—"

"No," he said. "Don't argue. After what I saw today. Don't argue."

She rubbed her eyes. "What did you see?"

"I saw police forget a crime was committed. I saw a dead body get up and walk. Your friend Blackstone promises me I'll remember all this, but he says no one else will. No one else—except you."

"Tell me," she said.

And so he did.

"The coroner's office is in the basement of the main police station," Max started.

"I know," Nora said.

"Well, I wasn't sure," he said. "You never know what civil attorneys know about the criminal system. I got to the station at the same time the corpse of that woman did, and as I was walking to the elevator, the ambulance had pulled up in front of the double doors." The attendants opened up the ambulance doors, and were starting to remove the body when it sat up.

Everyone jumped and then one of the attendants said, "Well, that happens sometimes."

But what didn't happen was the body unhooking itself from the straps and getting off the gurney. Max was already in the elevator. The woman joined him.

She was like nothing he had ever seen before, long dark hair with a streak of white along the side, a black robe untouched by the smoke and long curved fingernails, almost like talons. The doors closed as the attendants came running forward. Max huddled in the side of the elevator, planning to get off on any floor.

The doors opened on his floor and he hurried off. The woman hurried behind him. Max veered toward the sergeant in charge. Several police officers tried to restrain the woman. The attendants were running up the stairs, yelling.

Max asked to see his client, and was led into an interview room. Blackstone was leaning against a chair, feet out. He smiled. "You must be the attorney Nora sent," he said. "Sorry to have wasted your time."

"Are they going to let you out?" Max asked.

"You'll see," Blackstone said.

At that moment, the woman somehow burst through the locked door. "Where is she?" the woman shouted.

Blackstone shrugged.

"I know you know," she said.

"Actually, I don't." He seemed very calm. "You think after a thousand years this would grow old, Millicent."

"I will not let you have her."

"You won't let anyone experience true love," he said. "But she's somewhere even I can't find her."

The woman crossed the room, and before Max or anyone could stop her, she grabbed Blackstone's head. She held it with one hand and sparks flew all around. She frowned at him, as if she were trying to pull every thought from his head. Then she cursed and shoved him away.

"You won't get away with this," the woman said. "I will find her."

"You have fifteen years, Millicent, and then she's on her own."

"She's too young."

"She's too beautiful. Women leave home well before they turn one thousand. You're just jealous."

The woman narrowed her eyes, and waved an arm and disappeared.

Blackstone stood and took Max's arm. "There's going to be chaos in a moment," he said. "Just follow my lead."

Then a police detective came into the room. "Max!" he said. "What are you doing here?"

"Showing me around," Blackstone said before Max could answer. "I hope you don't mind."

Max was stunned. This was a man who had been under arrest a moment before, and no one seemed to notice. In fact, at that point, Max checked Blackstone's wrists for cuffs and saw none.

And then Blackstone calmly led the two of them out of the precinct and into the parking garage. The ambulance attendants were sitting on the edge of the ambulance, looking winded.

"You didn't call for an ambulance did you?" one of them asked Max.

"No," he said.

"I don't get it," the attendant said to his companion. "How did we end up here?"

Then Blackstone led Max to his car, and gave him the check "for his time and services" instructing him to split it with Nora. "I'm sorry you had to see this," he said. "You can't forget because you were in my presence when everything reverted. And Nora can't forget because then—well, then I'd be, as your generation so quaintly puts it, screwed. But we did as she asked and put everything back the way it was."

"What's going on here?" Max asked.

"You don't want to know," Blackstone said.

"But I do," Max said.

"All right," Blackstone said. "But it's not my fault if you fail to believe me."

"Well?" Nora asked. "What was going on?"

"You know," Max said, leaning over his fourth beer. His words were becoming slurred. "When I drove here, there wasn't any smoke. And no one said a word about anything on the radio. It was strange. So I swung over to the neighborhood. It looks fine. No burned houses. No ashes. Just flowers and porches and electric lights."

"Max," she said, worrying that he might lose complete control before he got to the point. "What did he tell you?"

"He said that fairy tales are true. Sort of."

"Great," Nora said, leaning back.

"And we got in the middle of Snow White and the Seven Dwarves. Only there was only one dwarf. And she didn't bite into a poison apple. It was a spell. But the glass case was correct—"

"Max." A chill ran down Nora's back. "From the beginning."

"Blackstone is a wizard." Max ran a hand over his face as if he were trying to hide the words. "Over a thousand years ago he fell in love with a witch's daughter. Only the witch didn't want anyone near her daughter, so she hid the daughter with her assistant, a magical dwarf named—"

"Sancho Panza."

Max looked at her strangely. "Merlin, actually. After the great Merlin of old. But the dwarf was a good friend of Blackstone's, and he managed to get Blackstone and the girl together. What they didn't know was that the witch had put a curse on them so when they kissed, the girl passed out. Merlin knew the girl would die if she didn't get back to the witch to remove the spell, but Blackstone outsmarted the witch. He put the girl in a glass coffin. She would remain as she was, not alive and not dead, until the spell was removed. Merlin knew the witch's spell would wear off after fifteen years if the witch didn't know where the girl was. But before they could hide the coffin, the witch stole it. Over the centuries, Blackstone has stolen it back. But he's never been able to hide it from the witch. She's telepathic. She's always been able to pull the information from him. Until now. As long as he doesn't know where the coffin is the witch won't either."

"Shit," Nora said.

"You know, don't you?" Max asked.

"I have a hunch," Nora said.

Max held up his hand. "Well don't tell me. I don't want to be any more involved than I already am." He got up and swayed once. "I told you what I know. Now I'm leaving."

"Max, we have to investigate."

He shook his head, then caught the table to hold himself in place. "It would raise too many questions," he said. "Like, if there is a woman in a glass coffin in your possession, is she dead? And if so, are you an accessory after the fact? And if she isn't, what then? Do we believe she's been alive but asleep for a thousand years? And isn't that Sleeping Beauty? Doesn't the prince get to wake her with a kiss? Where did this going to sleep with a kiss come from? It seems all wrong to me."

He stumbled forward. "I am going home to pretend this was all a drunken fantasy."

"And the money?" Nora asked.

"I'll pretend I defended a mobster and it was so traumatic I forgot all about it." He wandered out, clutching the back of booths for support.

She sat there, trembling. He was right. She had said she wouldn't investigate what was in that microbus. But now, it seemed, she had no choice.

She had to go to her office first to get the key to the lock she had put on the garage. As she drove, she noted a full moon over the town. The air smelled fresh, with the trace of night flowers. She paused before making the turn-off to her office, then drove down the freeway to the neighborhood.

Streetlights were on the entire way, and the roads were clear of debris and emergency vehicles. As she pulled onto the residential streets, she saw the silhouettes of houses trailing off into the distance. Some had lights on. Many, by this time, had their lights off. Vehicles were parked in the street as if they belonged there.

She pulled over to the curb, parking between the two houses where she thought, but wasn't certain, the microbus had been parked earlier. She got out and wandered to the lawn, recognizing its greenery and its flowers from the afternoon. This was the place. She would bet her practice on it. And yet the neighborhood stood around it. Nothing was destroyed.

A porch light came on at the house behind her. She frowned. That house probably belonged to the radio personality. He had seemed like the nosy type. She slipped back into her car and drove away.

A feeling of disorientation that had nothing to do with the beer swept through her. Maybe when she got back to her office, she wouldn't even find a key. Maybe in the morning, Max would deny having this conversation with her. Maybe none of this had happened.

Maybe.

But it felt as if it had.

She pulled into the parking garage beneath her building and got out of her car. As she walked, she passed a 1974 Lincoln. A little man stood on its fender, and a tall man leaned against its hood. He wore a shimmery gray silk suit that accented his broad shoulders and long legs, and on his feet he wore cowboy boots trimmed with real silver. A snake peeked its head out of his sleeve.

"You know," he said in that rich, warm voice of his, "if you get the key and go to the microbus, I'll simply have to follow you. And if I follow you all of this will be for naught."

"Max tells me there's a woman in that glass case."

"And she's alive," Blackstone said. "She's been asleep for a thousand years. If you help us, she'll sleep for fifteen more."

"Why can't your friend get the information out of my brain?"

"Because it's not there," Blackstone said. "Right now, all you have is supposition. She could probe, but her powers won't let her unearth supposition. They'll only unearth fact."

"The fact is I have your microbus. She'll know that."

"You have *my* microbus," the little man said. "Sancho Panza's microbus."

"And we all know that's not your name," Nora snapped.

"No," the little man said. "You *suspect* that's not my name. You *know* that I have all the legal documentation to prove that it is."

She smoothed a hand over her hair, and took a deep breath. "This afternoon," she said. "I saw a destroyed neighborhood and a dead woman. I saw the police lead you away in cuffs."

"Yes," Blackstone said.

"But you're here, and the neighborhood's back the way it was, and Max says the woman's not dead."

Blackstone's smile was small. "We live differently from you, Sancho and I. And we don't really die."

"So you're saying what I saw was real."

"For that moment," he said. "But you asked us to fix it, to put it back. So we did."

"For the record," the little man said. "*She* was the one who destroyed everything, not us."

"What if she's the one who is in the right?" Nora asked.

"You don't even know what the battle's about," Blackstone said.

Nora crossed her arms. "Enlighten me."

"Love," Blackstone said. "It's about love."

"Seems to me it's about possession," Nora said. "There's a woman who has been asleep for a thousand years because her family and her boyfriend are fighting over her. Seems to me that she has no say in this matter."

The little man put his face in his hands. Blackstone frowned. The snake hissed at her.

"What happens if I raise the coffin lid?" Nora asked. "Will I wake her up?"

Blackstone shook his head. "You'll destroy my spell, but not the death spell. If you open that coffin, she'll die."

"Lovely," Nora said. She started for the elevators. Midway there, she stopped. "If all of this happens in fifteen years, why did you pay me for twenty?"

Blackstone hadn't moved. The snake had wrapped itself around his arm. The little man had disappeared along the side of the Lincoln. "I didn't pay you," Blackstone said.

"Why did your friend, then?"

Blackstone raised his beautiful silver eyes to hers. "The world has changed," he said. "She's been sleeping for a thousand years. It'll take her time to adjust, time to find herself again. She'll need to make decisions, need to make choices, and she can't make good choices when she first wakes up. Five years may not be enough. You might get a renewal after that."

"You expect me to babysit?" Nora asked.

"I expect nothing," he said. "But my friend here expects you to find competent help for any problem that might arise during your service to him. If that's too much to ask, tell us now. We'll find someone else."

Nora pushed a strand of hair off her face. The hair still smelled faintly of smoke. "The battle between you and this woman, this witch, is over?"

"It will be," he said, "if she can't find what she's looking for."

"And she won't find it," Nora said, "as long as I help your friend."

"You could say that." Blackstone lifted an edge of his sleeve. The snake crawled inside.

"That's giving me a lot of control over something that's important to you," Nora said.

"Yes." Blackstone stood. He seemed taller than he had before.
"Why?" she asked. "Why me?"

"Because," he said. "You believe just enough to take a chance."

"Believe," she muttered. Could he hear thoughts too? Had he known what she had been thinking the day she met him? She shook her head. She couldn't believe that. It was one thing too many. "What happens to you?"

But her words echoed in the empty garage. Blackstone, the snake, the little man and the Lincoln were gone. She rested a hand on a rusted Beamer, more to hold herself up than anything else.

"I guess that answers my question," she said. She stared at the elevator, and thought about the key on the wall in her office. The key with the combination taped to it.

She could look now and satisfy her curiosity. Or she could do what she was supposed to do, and let things alone. She believed that a neighborhood burned down. She knew the neighborhood was fine now. She had seen it. Just like she had seen it burn this afternoon.

And that was the secret: she could no longer trust her senses. What if she went inside that VW microbus and found a glass coffin? And what if a woman were inside? And what if she opened it and ruined the spell? She wouldn't know how to find Blackstone or his little friend Sancho. She wouldn't know how to make everything better again.

Her own car keys were digging into the skin of her right hand. She started back to her car. She wasn't going to go. And it wasn't because of true love. Or fear that she might ruin a spell.

She had been given a strange gift these last two weeks. Someone had shown her that magic could exist. What if she went to that microbus and there was no glass coffin inside? There was no woman? Would she have to question everything she had seen? Would she want to?

When she reached her car, she got inside, and picked up the phone. Before she even knew what she was doing, she asked directory assistance to dial Max's home number. The phone rang six times. She was about to hang up when Max answered.

"Max?" she asked.

"You looked," he said.

And in that response she felt a deep and profound relief. She hadn't imagined any of this. Or if she had, Max was suffering the same delusion.

"No," she said. "But I'd realized we had skipped dinner. You want to go?"

"Now?" he asked.

"Yes," she said.

"Is this . . . a date?"

There was enough hesitation in his voice to make her hesitate too. But dating Max was something she had wanted to do since college. And she had never taken the initiative before. "Yes," she said.

He laughed. "Who'd've thought—after a day like this—well, maybe wishes do come true."

"Max?" she said.

"Sorry," he said. "Muttering. I'd love dinner. I think I'm a little more sober than I was before."

"I'll pick you up," she said. "In ten minutes."

She hung up before he could say no. And then she realized he wouldn't. Two shy people, finally getting their wish. She wondered if that was part of Blackstone's payment, and then decided she wouldn't think about Blackstone any more.

She leaned her head against the steering wheel and giggled. She was the one who wanted a little magic in her life, just once. And she had gotten more than a little. She had gotten too much.

Be careful what you wish for, her grandmother used to say.

Well, Nora's wish that day two weeks before had been a two-fold wish. She turned the key in the ignition. Max wasn't going to cook, and he probably wasn't going to rub her feet unless things moved faster than she expected. But he would certainly discuss the strangeness of the day with her, and that would be enough.

For now.

Substitutions

SILAS SAT AT THE BLACKJACK TABLE, A PLASTIC
glass of whiskey in his left hand, and a small pile of hundred
dollar chips in his right. His banjo rested against his boot, the
embroidered strap wrapped around his calf. He had a pair of aces to
the dealer's six, so he split them—a thousand dollars riding on each
—and watched as she covered them with the expected tens.

He couldn't lose. He'd been trying to all night.

The casino was empty except for five gambling addicts hunkered
over the blackjack table, one old woman playing slots with the
rhythm of an assembly worker, and one young man in black leather
who was getting drunk at the casino's sorry excuse for a bar. The
employees showed no sign of holiday cheer: no happy holiday pins,
no little Santa hats, only the stark black and white of their uniforms
against the casino's fading glitter.

He had chosen the Paradise because it was one of the few
remaining fifties-style casinos in Nevada, still thick with flocked
wallpaper and cigarette smoke, craps tables worn by dice and elbows, and the roulette wheel creaking with age. It was also only a
few hours from Reno, and in thirty hours, he would have to make
the tortuous drive up there. Along the way, he would visit an old
man who had a bad heart; a young girl who would cross the road at

the wrong time and meet an on-coming semi; and a baby boy who was born with his lungs not yet fully formed. Silas also suspected a few surprises along the way; nothing was ever as it seemed any longer. Life was moving too fast, even for him.

But he had Christmas Eve and Christmas Day off, the two days he had chosen when he had been picked to work Nevada 150 years before. In those days, he would go home for Christmas, see his friends, spend time with his family. His parents welcomed him, even though they didn't see him for most of the year. He felt like a boy again, like someone cherished and loved, instead of the drifter he had become.

All of that stopped in 1878. December 26th, 1878. He wasn't yet sophisticated enough to know that the day was a holiday in England. Boxing Day. Not quite appropriate, but close.

He had to take his father that day. The old man had looked pale and tired throughout the holiday, but no one thought it serious. When he took to his bed Christmas night, everyone had simply thought him tired from the festivities.

It was only after midnight, when Silas got his orders, that he knew what was coming next. He begged off—something he had never tried before (he wasn't even sure who he had been begging with)—but had received the feeling (that was all he ever got: a firm feeling, so strong he couldn't avoid it) that if he didn't do it, death would come another way—from Idaho or California or New Mexico. It would come another way, his father would be in agony for days, and the end, when it came, would be uglier than it had to be.

Silas had taken his banjo to the old man's room. His mother slept on her side, like she always had, her back to his father. His father's eyes had opened, and he knew. Somehow he knew.

They always did.

Silas couldn't remember what he said. Something—a bit of an apology, maybe, or just an explanation: *You always wanted to know what I did.* And then, the moment. First he touched his father's forehead, clammy with the illness that would claim him, and then Silas said, "You wanted to know why I carry the banjo," and strummed.

But the sound did not soothe his father like it had so many before him. As his spirit rose, his body struggled to hold it, and he looked at Silas with such a mix of fear and betrayal that Silas still saw it whenever he thought of his father.

The old man died, but not quickly and not easily, and Silas tried to resign, only to get sent to the place that passed for headquarters, a small shack that resembled an out-of-the-way railroad terminal. There, a man who looked no more than thirty but who had to be three hundred or more, told him the more that he complained, the longer his service would last.

Silas never complained again, and he had been on the job for 150 years. Almost 55,000 days spent in the service of Death, with only Christmas Eve and Christmas off, tainted holidays for a man in a tainted position.

He scooped up his winnings, piled them on his already-high stack of chips, and then placed his next bet. The dealer had just given him a queen and a jack when a boy sat down beside him.

"Boy" wasn't entirely accurate. He was old enough to get into the casino. But he had rain on his cheap jacket, and hair that hadn't been cut in a long time. I-Pod headphones stuck out of his breast pocket, and he had a cell phone against his hip the way that old sheriffs used to wear their guns.

His hands were callused and the nails had dirt beneath them. He looked tired, and a little frightened.

He watched as the dealer busted, then set chips in front of Silas and the four remaining players. Silas swept the chips into his stack, grabbed five of the hundred dollar chips, and placed the bet.

The dealer swept her hand along the semi-circle, silently asking the players to place their bets.

"You Silas?" the boy asked. He hadn't put any money on the table or placed any chips before him.

Silas sighed. Only once before had someone interrupted his Christmas festivities—if festivities was what the last century plus could be called.

The dealer peered at the boy. "You gonna play?"

The boy looked at her, startled. He didn't seem to know what to say.

"I got it." Silas put twenty dollars in chips in front of the boy.

"I don't know . . ."

"Just do what I tell you," Silas said.

The woman dealt, face-up. Silas got an ace. The boy, an eight. The woman dealt herself a ten. Then she went around again. Silas got his twenty-one—his weird holiday luck holding—but the boy got another eight.

"Split them," Silas said.

The boy looked at him, his fear almost palpable.

Silas sighed again, then grabbed another twenty in chips, and placed it next to the boy's first twenty.

"Jeez, mister, that's a lot of money," the boy whispered.

"Splitting," Silas said to the dealer.

She separated the cards and placed the bets behind them. Then she dealt the boy two cards—a ten and another eight.

The boy looked at Silas. Looked like the boy had peculiar luck as well.

"Split again," Silas said, more to the dealer than to the boy. He added the bet, let her separate the cards, and watched as she dealt the boy two more tens. Three eighteens. Not quite as good as Silas's twenties to twenty-ones, but just as statistically uncomfortable.

The dealer finished her round, then dealt herself a three, then a nine, busting again. She paid in order. When she reached the boy, she set sixty dollars in chips before him, each in its own twenty dollar pile.

"Take it," Silas said.

"It's yours," the boy said, barely speaking above a whisper.

"I gave it to you."

"I don't gamble," the boy said.

"Well, for someone who doesn't gamble, you did pretty well. Take your winnings."

The boy looked at them as if they'd bite him. "I . . ."

"Are you leaving them for the next round?" the dealer asked.

The boy's eyes widened. He was clearly horrified at the very thought. With shaking fingers, he collected the chips, then leaned into Silas. The boy smelled of sweat and wet wool.

"Can I talk to you?" he whispered.

Silas nodded, then cashed in his chips. He'd racked up ten thousand dollars in three hours. He wasn't even having fun at it any more. He liked losing, felt that it was appropriate—part of the game, part of his life—but the losses had become fewer and farther between the more he played.

The more he lived. A hundred years ago, there were women and a few adopted children. But watching them grow old, helping three of them die, had taken the desire out of that too.

"Mr. Silas," the boy whispered.

"If you're not going to bet," the dealer said, "please move so someone can have your seats."

People had gathered behind Silas, and he hadn't even noticed. He really didn't care tonight. Normally, he would have noticed anyone around him—noticed who they were, how and when they would die.

"Come on," he said, gathering the bills the dealer had given him. The boy's eyes went to the money like a hungry man's went to food. His one-hundred-and-twenty dollars remained on the table, and Silas had to remind him to pick it up.

The boy used a forefinger and a thumb to carry it, as if it would burn him.

"At least put it in your pocket," Silas snapped.

"But it's yours," the boy said.

"It's a damn gift. Appreciate it."

The boy blinked, then stuffed the money into the front of his unwashed jeans. Silas led him around banks and banks of slot machines, all pinging and ponging and making little musical come-ons, to the steakhouse in the back.

The steakhouse was the reason Silas came back year after year. The place opened at five, closed at three A.M., and served the best steaks in Vegas. They weren't arty or too small. One big slab of meat, expensive cut, charred on the outside and red as Christmas on the inside. Beside the steak they served french-fried onions, and sides that no self-respecting Strip restaurant would prepare—creamed corn, au gratin potatoes, popovers—the kind of stuff that Silas always associated with the modern Las Vegas—modern, to him, meaning 1950s-1960s Vegas. Sin city. A place for grown-ups to gamble and smoke and drink and have affairs. The Vegas of Sinatra and the mob, not the Vegas of Steve Wynn and his ilk, who prettified everything and made it all seem upscale and oh-so-right.

Silas still worked Vegas a lot more than any other Nevada city, which made sense, considering how many millions of people lived there now, but millions of people lived all over. Even sparsely populated Nevada, one of the least populated states in the Union, had ten full-time Death employees. They tried to unionize a few years ago, but Silas, with the most seniority, refused to join. Then they tried to limit the routes—one would get Reno, another Sparks, another Elko and that region, and a few would split Vegas—but Silas wouldn't agree to that either.

He loved the travel part of the job. It was the only part he still liked, the ability to go from place to place to place, see the changes, understand how time affected everything.

Everything except him.

The maitre d' sat them in the back, probably because of the boy.

Even in this modern era, where people wore blue jeans to funerals, this steakhouse preferred its customers in a suit and tie.

The booth was made of wood and rose so high that Silas couldn't see anything but the boy and the table across from them. A single lamp reflected against the wall, revealing cloth napkins and real silver utensils.

The boy stared at them with the same kind of fear he had shown at the blackjack table. "I can't—"

The maitre d' gave them leather bound menus, said something about a special, and then handed Silas a wine list. Silas ordered a bottle of burgundy. He didn't know a lot about wines, just that the more expensive ones tasted a lot better than the rest of them. So he ordered the most expensive burgundy on the menu.

The maitre d' nodded crisply, almost militarily, and then left. The boy leaned forward.

"I can't stay. I'm your substitute."

Silas smiled. A waiter came by with a bread basket—hard rolls, still warm—and relish trays filled with sliced carrots, celery, and radishes, and candied beets, things people now would call old-fashioned.

Modern, to him. Just as modern as always.

The boy squirmed, his jeans squeaking on the leather booth.

"I know," Silas said. "You'll be fine."

"I got—"

"A big one, probably," Silas said. "It's Christmas Eve. Traffic, right? A shooting in a church? Too many suicides?"

"No," the boy said, distressed. "Not like that."

"When's it scheduled for?" Silas asked. He really wanted his dinner, and he didn't mind sharing it. The boy looked like he needed a good meal.

"Tonight," the boy said. "No specific time. See?"

He put a crumpled piece of paper between them, but Silas didn't pick it up.

"Means you have until midnight," Silas said. "It's only seven. You can eat."

"They said at orientation—"

Silas had forgotten; they all got orientation now. The expectations of generations. He'd been thrown into the pool feet first, fumbling his way for six months before someone told him that he could actually ask questions.

"—the longer you wait, the more they suffer."

Silas glanced at the paper. "If it's big, it's a surprise. They won't suffer. They'll just finish when you get there. That's all."

The boy bit his lip. "How do you know?"

Because he'd had big. He'd had grisly. He'd had disgusting. He'd overseen more deaths than the boy could imagine.

The headwaiter arrived, took Silas's order, and then turned to the boy.

"I don't got money," the boy said.

"You have one-hundred-and-twenty dollars," Silas said. "But I'm buying, so don't worry."

The boy opened the menu, saw the prices, and closed it again. He shook his head.

The waiter started to leave when Silas stopped him. "Give him what I'm having. Medium well."

Since the kid didn't look like he ate many steaks, he wouldn't like his rare. Rare was an acquired taste, just like burgundy wine and the cigar that Silas wished he could light up. Not everything in the modern era was an improvement.

"You don't have to keep paying for me," the kid said.

Silas waved the waiter away, then leaned back. The back of the booth, made of wood, was rigid against his spine. "After a while in this business," he said, "money is all you have."

The kid bit his lower lip. "Look at the paper. Make sure I'm not screwing up. Please."

But Silas didn't look.

"You're supposed to handle all of this on your own," Silas said gently.

"I know," the boy said. "I know. But this one, he's scary. And I don't think anything I do will make it right."

After he finished his steak and had his first sip of coffee, about the time he would have lit up his cigar, Silas picked up the paper. The boy had devoured the steak like he hadn't eaten in weeks. He ate all the bread and everything from his relish tray.

He was very, very new.

Silas wondered how someone that young had gotten into the death business, but he was determined not to ask. It would be some variation on his own story. Silas had begged for the life of his wife who should have died in the delivery of their second child. Begged, and begged, and begged, and somehow, in his befogged state, he actually saw the woman whom he then called the Angel of Death.

Now he knew better—none of them were angels, just working stiffs waiting for retirement—but then, she had seemed perfect and terrifying, all at the same time.

He'd asked for his wife, saying he didn't want to raise his daughters alone.

The angel had tilted her head. "Would you die for her?"

"Of course," Silas said.

"Leaving her to raise the children alone?" the angel asked.

His breath caught. "Is that my only choice?"

She shrugged, as if she didn't care. Later, when he reflected, he realized she didn't know.

"Yes," he said into her silence. "She would raise better people than I will. She's good. I'm . . . not."

He wasn't bad, he later realized, just lost, as so many were. His wife had been a God-fearing woman with strict ideas about morality. She had raised two marvelous girls, who became two strong women, mothers of large broods who all went on to do good works.

In that, he hadn't been wrong.

But his wife hadn't remarried either, and she had cried for him for the rest of her days.

They had lived in Texas. He had made his bargain, got assigned Nevada, and had to swear never to head east, not while his wife and children lived. His parents saw him, but they couldn't tell anyone. They thought he ran out on his wife and children, and oddly, they had supported him in it.

Remnants of his family still lived. Great-grandchildren generations removed. He still couldn't head east, and he no longer wanted to.

Silas touched the paper and it burned his fingers. A sign, a warning, a remembrance that he wasn't supposed to work these two days.

Two days out of an entire year.

He slid the paper back to the boy. "I can't open it. I'm not allowed. You tell me."

So the boy did.

And Silas, in wonderment that they had sent a rookie into a situation a veteran might not be able to handle, settled his tab, took the boy by the arm, and led him into the night.

Every city has pockets of evil. Vegas had fewer than most, despite the things the television lied about. So many people worked in law enforcement or security, so many others were bonded so that they could work in casinos or high-end jewelry stores or banks that Vegas's serious crime was lower than most comparable cities of its size.

Silas appreciated that. Most of the time, it meant that the deaths he attended in Vegas were natural or easy or just plain silly. He got a lot of silly deaths in that city. Some he even found time to laugh over.

But not this one.

As they drove from the very edge of town, past the rows and rows of similar houses, past the stink and desperation of complete poverty, he finally asked, "How long've you been doing this?"

"Six months," the boy said softly, as if that were forever.

Silas looked at him, looked at the young face reflecting the Christmas lights that filled the neighborhood, and shook his head. "All substitutes?"

The boy shrugged. "They didn't have any open routes."

"What about the guy you replaced?"

"He'd been subbing, waiting to retire. They say you could retire too, but you show no signs of it. Working too hard, even for a younger man."

He wasn't older. He was the same age he had been when his wife struggled with her labor—a breach birth that would be no problem in 2006, but had been deadly if not handled right in 1856. The midwife's hands hadn't been clean—not that anyone knew better in those days—and the infection had started even before the baby got turned.

He shuddered, that night alive in him. The night he'd made his bargain.

"I don't work hard," he said. "I work less than I did when I started."

The boy looked at him, surprised. "Why don't you retire?"

"And do what?" Silas asked. He hadn't planned to speak up. He normally shrugged off that question.

"I dunno," the boy said. "Relax. Live off your savings. Have a family again."

They could all have families again when they retired. Families and a good, rich life, albeit short. Silas would age when he retired. He would age and have no special powers. He would watch a new wife die in childbirth and not be able to see his former colleague sitting beside the bed. He would watch his children squirm after a car accident, blood on their faces, knowing that they would live poorly if they lived at all, and not be able to find out the future from the death dealer hovering near the scene.

Better to continue. Better to keep this half-life, this half-future, time without end.

"Families are overrated," Silas said. They look at you with betrayal and loss when you do what was right.

But the boy didn't know that yet. He didn't know a lot.

"You ever get scared?" the boy asked.

"Of what?" Silas asked. Then gave the standard answer. "They can't kill you. They can't harm you. You just move from place to place, doing your job. There's nothing to be scared of."

The boy grunted, sighed, and looked out the window.

Silas knew what he had asked, and hadn't answered it. Of course he got scared. All the time. And not of dying—even though he still wasn't sure what happened to the souls he freed. He wasn't scared of that, or of the people he occasionally faced down, the drug addicts with their knives, the gangsters with their guns, the wanna-be outlaws with blood all over their hands.

No, the boy had asked about the one thing to be afraid of, the one thing they couldn't change.

Was he scared of being alone? Of remaining alone, for the rest of his days? Was he scared of being unknown and nearly invisible, having no ties and no dreams?

It was too late to be scared of that.

He'd lived it. He lived it every single day.

The house was one of those square adobe things that filled Vegas. It was probably pink in the sunlight. In the half-light that passed for nighttime in this perpetually alive city, it looked gray and foreboding.

The bars on the windows—standard in this neighborhood—didn't help.

Places like this always astounded him. They seemed so normal, so incorruptible, just another building on another street, like all the other buildings on all the other streets. Sometimes he got to go into those buildings. Very few of them were different from what he expected. Oh, the art changed or the furniture. The smells differed—sometimes unwashed diapers, sometimes perfume, sometimes the heavy scent of meals eaten long ago—but the rest remained the same: the television in the main room, the kitchen with its square table (sometimes decorated with flowers, sometimes nothing but trash), the double bed in the second bedroom down the hall, the one with its own shower and toilet. The room across from the main bathroom was sometimes an office, sometimes a den, sometimes a child's bedroom. If it was a child's bedroom, there were pictures on the wall, studio portraits from the local mall, done up in cheap frames, showing the passing years. The pictures were never straight, and always dusty, except for the most recent, hung with pride in the only remaining empty space.

He had a hunch this house would have none of those things. If anything, it would have an overly neat interior. The television would be in the kitchen or the bedroom or both. The front room would have a sofa set designed for looks, not for comfort. And one of the rooms would be blocked off, maybe even marked private, and in it, he would find (if he looked) trophies of a kind that made even his cast-iron stomach turn.

These houses had no attic. Most didn't have a basement. So the scene would be the garage. The car would be parked outside of it, blocking the door, and the neighbors would assume that the garage was simply a workspace—not that far off, if the truth be told.

He'd been to places like this before. More times than he wanted to think about, especially in the smaller communities out in the desert, the communities that had no names, or once had a name and did no longer. The communities sometimes made up of cheap trailers and empty storefronts, with a whorehouse a few miles off the main highway, and a casino in the center of town, a casino so old it made the one that the boy found him in look like it had been built just the week before.

He hated these jobs. He wasn't sure what made him come with the boy. A moment of compassion? The prospect of yet another long Christmas Eve with nothing to punctuate it except the bong-bong of nearby slots?

He couldn't go to church any more. It didn't feel right, with as many lives as he had taken. He couldn't go to church or listen to the singing or look at the families and wonder which of them he'd be standing beside in thirty years.

Maybe he belonged here more than the boy did. Maybe he belonged here more than anyone else.

They parked a block away, not because anyone would see their car—if asked, hours later, the neighbors would deny seeing anything to do with Silas or the boy. Maybe they never saw, maybe their memories vanished. Silas had never been clear on that either.

As they got out, Silas asked, "What do you use?"

The boy reached into the breast pocket. For a moment, Silas

thought he'd remove the I-Pod, and Silas wasn't sure how a device that used headphones would work. Then the boy removed a harmonica—expensive, the kind sold at high-end music stores.

"You play that before all this?" Silas asked.

The boy nodded. "They got me a better one, though."

Silas's banjo had been all his own. They'd let him take it, and nothing else. The banjo, the clothes he wore that night, his hat.

He had different clothes now. He never wore a hat. But his banjo was the same as it had always been—new and pure with a sound that he still loved.

It was in the trunk. He doubted it could get stolen, but he took precautions just in case.

He couldn't bring it on this job. This wasn't his job. He'd learned the hard way that the banjo didn't work except in assigned cases. When he'd wanted to help, to put someone out of their misery, to step in where another death dealer had failed, he couldn't. He could only watch, like normal people did, and hope that things got better, even though he knew it wouldn't.

The boy clutched the harmonica in his right hand. The dry desert air was cold. Silas could see his breath. The tourists down on the Strip, with their short skirts and short sleeves, probably felt betrayed by the normal winter chill. He wished he were there with them, instead of walking through this quiet neighborhood, filled with dark houses, dirt-ridden yards, and silence.

So much silence. You'd think there'd be at least one barking dog.

When they reached the house, the boy headed to the garage, just like Silas expected. A car was parked on the road—a 1980s sedan that looked like it had seen better days. In the driveway, a brand-new van with tinted windows, custom-made for bad deeds.

In spite of himself, Silas shuddered.

The boy stopped outside and steeled himself, then he looked at Silas with sadness in his eyes. Silas nodded. The boy extended a hand—Silas couldn't get in without the boy's momentary magic —and then they were inside, near the stench of old gasoline, urine, and fear.

The kids sat in a dimly lit corner, chained together like the slaves on ships in the 19th century. The windows were covered with dirty cardboard, the concrete floor was empty except for stains as old as time. It felt bad in here, a recognizable bad, one Silas had encountered before.

The boy was shaking. He wasn't out of place here, his old wool jacket and his dirty jeans making him a cousin to the kids on the floor. Silas had a momentary flash: they were homeless. Runaways, lost, children without borders, without someone looking for them.

"You've been here before," Silas whispered to the boy and the boy's eyes filled with tears.

Been here, negotiated here, moved on here—didn't quite die, but no longer quite lived—and for who? A group of kids like this one? A group that had somehow escaped, but hadn't reported what had happened?

Then he felt the chill grow worse. Of course they hadn't reported it. Who would believe them? A neat homeowner kidnaps a group of homeless kids for his own personal playthings, and the cops believe the kids? Kids who steal and sell drugs and themselves just for survival.

People like the one who owned this house were cautious. They were smart. They rarely got caught unless they went public with letters or phone calls or both.

They had to prepare for contingencies like losing a plaything now and then. They probably had all the answers planned.

A side door opened. It was attached to the house. The man who came in was everything Silas had expected—white, thin, balding, a bit too intense.

What surprised Silas was the look the man gave him. Measuring, calculating.

Pleased.

The man wasn't supposed to see Silas or the boy. Not until the last moment.

Not until the end.

Silas had heard that some of these creatures could see the death dealers. A few of Silas's colleagues speculated that these men continued to kill so that they could continue to see death in all its forms, collecting images the way they collected trophies.

After seeing the momentary victory in that man's eyes, Silas believed it.

The man picked up the kid at the end of the chain. Too weak to stand, the kid staggered a bit, then had to lean into the man.

"You have to beat me," the man said to Silas. "I slice her first, and you have to leave."

The boy was still shivering. The man hadn't noticed him. The man thought Silas was here for him, not the boy. Silas had no powers, except the ones that humans normally had—not on this night, and not in this way.

If he were here alone, he'd start playing, and praying he'd get the right one. If there was a right one. He couldn't tell. They all seemed to have the mark of death over them.

No wonder the boy needed him.

It was a fluid situation, one that could go in any direction.

"Start playing," Silas said under his breath.

But the man heard him, not the boy. The man pulled the kid's head back, exposing a smooth white throat with the heartbeat visible in a vein.

"Play!" Silas shouted, and ran forward, shoving the man aside, hoping that would be enough.

It saved the girl's neck, for a moment anyway. She fell, and landed on the other kid next to her. The kid moved away, as if proximity to her would cause the kid to die.

The boy started blowing on his harmonica. The notes were faint, barely notes, more like bleats of terror.

The man laughed. He saw the boy now. "So you're back to rob me again," he said.

The boy's playing grew wispier.

"Ignore him," Silas said to the boy.

"Who're you? His coach?" The man approached him. "I know your rules. I destroy you, I get to take your place."

The steak rolled in Silas's stomach. The man was half right. He destroyed Silas, and he would get a chance to take the job. He destroyed both of them, and he would get the job, by old magic not new. Silas had forgotten this danger. No wonder these creatures liked to see death—what better for them than to be the facilitator for the hundreds of people who died in Nevada every day.

The man brandished his knife. "Lessee," he said. "What do I do? Destroy the instrument, deface the man. Right? And send him to hell."

Get him fired, Silas thought. It wasn't really hell, although it seemed like it. He became a ghost, existing forever, but not allowed to interact with anything. He was fired. He lost the right to die.

The man reached for the harmonica. Silas shoved again.

"Play!" Silas shouted.

And miraculously, the boy played. "Home on the Range," a silly song for these circumstances, but probably the first tune the boy had ever learned. He played it with spirit as he backed away from the fight.

But the kids weren't rebelling. They sat on the cold concrete floor, already half dead, probably tortured into submission. If they didn't rise up and kill this monster, no one would.

Silas looked at the boy. Tears streamed down his face, and he nodded toward the kids. Souls hovered above them, as if they couldn't decide whether or not to leave.

Damn the ones in charge: they'd sent the kid here as his final test. Could he take the kind of lives he had given his life for? Was he that strong?

The man reached for the harmonica again, and this time Silas grabbed his knife. It was heavier than Silas expected. He had never wielded a real instrument of death. His banjo eased people into forever. It didn't force them out of their lives a moment too early.

The boy kept playing and the man—the creature—laughed. One of the kids looked up, and Silas thought the kid was staring straight at the boy.

Only a moment, then. Only a moment to decide.

Silas shoved the knife into the man's belly. It went in deep, and the man let out an *oof* of pain. He stumbled, reached for the knife, and then glared at Silas.

Silas hadn't killed him, maybe hadn't even mortally wounded him. No soul appeared above him, and even these creatures had souls—dark and tainted as they were.

The boy's playing broke in places as if he were trying to catch his breath. The kid at the end of the chain, the girl, managed to get up. She looked at the knife, then at the man, then around the room. She couldn't see Silas or the boy.

Which was good.

The man was pulling on the knife. He would get it free in a moment. He would use it, would destroy these children, the ones no one cared about except the boy who was here to take their souls.

The girl kicked the kid beside her. "Stand up," she said.

The kid looked at her, bleary. Silas couldn't tell if these kids were male or female. He wasn't sure it mattered.

"Stand up," the girl said again.

In a rattle of chains, the kid did. The man didn't notice. He was working the knife, grunting as he tried to dislodge it. Silas stepped back, wondering if he had already interfered too much.

The music got louder, more intense, almost violent. The girl stood beside the man and stared at him for a moment.

He raised his head, saw her, and grinned.

Then she reached down with that chain, wrapped it around his neck and pulled. "Help me," she said to the others. "Help me."

The music became a live thing, wrapping them all, filling the smelly garage, and reaching deep, deep into the darkness. The soul did rise up—half a soul, broken and burned. It looked at Silas, then flared at the boy, who—bless him—didn't stop playing.

Then the soul floated toward the growing darkness in the corner, a blackness Silas had seen only a handful of times before, a blackness that felt as cold and dark as any empty desert night, and somehow much more permanent.

The music faded. The girl kept pulling, until another kid, farther down the line, convinced her to let go.

"We have to find the key," the other kid—a boy—said.

"On the wall," a third kid said. "Behind the electric box."

They shuffled as a group toward the box. They walked through Silas, and he felt them, alive and vibrant. For a moment, he worried that he had been fired, but he knew he had too many years for that. Too many years of perfect service—and he hadn't killed the man. He had just injured him, took away the threat to the boy.

That was allowed, just barely.

No wonder the boy had brought him. No wonder the boy had asked him if he was scared. Not of being alone or being lonely. But of certain jobs, of the things now asked of them as the no-longer-quite-human beings that they were.

Silas turned to the boy. His face was shiny with tears, but his eyes were clear. He stuffed the harmonica back into his breast pocket.

"You knew he'd beat you without me," Silas said.

The boy nodded.

"You knew this wasn't a substitution. You would have had this job, even without me."

"It's not cheating to bring in help," the boy said.

"But it's nearly impossible to find it," Silas said. "How did you find me?"

"It's Christmas Eve," the boy said. "Everyone knows where you'd be."

Everyone. His colleagues. People on the job. The only folks who even knew his name any more.

Silas sighed. The boy reached out with his stubby dirty hand. Silas took it, and then, suddenly, they were out of that fetid garage. They stood next to the van and watched as the cardboard came off one of the windows, as glass shattered outward.

Kids, homeless kids, injured and alone, poured out of that window like water.

"Thanks," the boy said. "I can't tell you how much it means."

But Silas knew. The boy didn't yet, but Silas did. When he retired—no longer if. When—this boy would see him again. This boy would take him, gently and with some kind of majestic harmonica music, to a beyond Silas could not imagine.

The boy waved at him, and joined the kids, heading into the dark Vegas night. Those kids couldn't see him, but they had to know he was there, like a guardian angel, saving them from horrors that would haunt their dreams for the rest of their lives.

Silas watched them go. Then he headed in the opposite direction, toward his car. What had those kids seen? The man—the creature—with his knife out, raving at nothing. Then stumbling backward, once, twice, the second time with a knife in his belly. They'd think that he tripped, that he stabbed himself. None of them had seen Silas or the boy.

They wouldn't for another sixty years.

If they were lucky.

The neighborhood remained dark, although a dog barked in the distance. His car was cold. Cold and empty.

He let himself in, started it, warmed his fingers against the still-hot air blowing out of the vents. Only a few minutes gone. A few minutes to take away a nasty, horrible lifetime. He wondered what was in the rest of these houses, and hoped he'd never have to find out.

The clock on the dash read 10:45. As he drove out of the neighborhood, he passed a small, adobe church. Outside, candles burned in candleholders made of baked sand. Almost like the churches of his childhood.

Almost, but not quite.

He watched the people thread inside. They wore fancy clothing —dresses on the women, suits on the men, the children dressing like their parents, faces alive with anticipation.

They believed in something.

They had hope.

He wondered if hope was something a man could recapture, if it came with time, relaxation, and the slow inevitable march toward death.

He wondered, if he retired, whether he could spend his Christmas Eves inside, smelling the mix of incense and candlewax, the evergreen bows, and the light dusting of ladies' perfume.

He wondered . . .

Then shook his head.

And drove back to the casino, to spend the rest of his time off in peace.

G-Men

"There's something addicting about a secret."
—J. Edgar Hoover

THE SQUALID LITTLE ALLEY SMELLED OF PISS.
Detective Seamus O'Reilly tugged his overcoat closed and
wished he'd worn boots. He could feel the chill of his metal flashlight through the worn glove on his right hand.

Two beat cops stood in front of the bodies, and the coroner
crouched over them. His assistant was already setting up the gur-
neys, body bags draped over his arm. The coroner's van had blocked
the alley's entrance, only a few yards away.

O'Reilly's partner, Joseph McKinnon, followed him. McKinnon
had trained his own flashlight on the fire escapes above, uninten-
tionally alerting any residents to the police presence.

But they probably already knew. Shootings in this part of the city
were common. The neighborhood teetered between swank and corrupt. Far enough from Central Park for degenerates and muggers to
use the alleys as corridors, and, conversely, close enough for new
money to want to live with a peek of the city's most famous expanse
of green.

The coroner, Thomas Brunner, had set up two expensive, bat-
tery-operated lights on garbage can lids placed on top of the dirty
ice, one at the top of the bodies, the other near the feet. O'Reilly
crouched so he wouldn't create any more shadows.

"What've we got?" he asked.

"Dunno yet." Brunner was using his gloved hands to part the hair on the back of the nearest corpse's skull. "It could be one of those nights."

O'Reilly had worked with Brunner for eighteen years now, since they both got back from the war, and he hated it when Brunner said it could be one of those nights. That meant the corpses would stack up, which was usually a summer thing, but almost never happened in the middle of winter.

"Why?" O'Reilly asked. "What else we got?"

"Some colored limo driver shot two blocks from here." Brunner was still parting the hair. It took O'Reilly a minute to realize it was matted with blood. "And two white guys pulled out of their cars and shot about four blocks from that."

O'Reilly felt a shiver run through him that had nothing to do with the cold. "You think the shootings are related?"

"Dunno," Brunner said. "But I think it's odd, don't you? Five dead in the space of an hour, all in a six-block radius."

O'Reilly closed his eyes for a moment. Two white guys pulled out of their cars, one Negro driver of a limo, and now two white guys in an alley. Maybe they were related, maybe they weren't.

He opened his eyes, then wished he hadn't. Brunner had his finger inside a bullet hole, a quick way to judge caliber.

"Same type of bullet," Brunner said.

"You handled the other shootings?"

"I was on scene with the driver when some fag called this one in."

O'Reilly looked at Brunner. Eighteen years, and he still wasn't used to the man's casual bigotry.

"How did you know the guy was queer?" O'Reilly asked. "You talk to him?"

"Didn't have to." Brunner nodded toward the building in front of them. "Weekly party for degenerates in the penthouse apartment every Thursday night. Thought you knew."

O'Reilly looked up. Now he understood why McKinnon had been shining his flashlight at the upper story windows. McKinnon had worked vice before he got promoted to homicide.

"Why would I know?" O'Reilly said.

McKinnon was the one who answered. "Because of the standing orders."

"I'm not playing twenty questions," O'Reilly said. "I don't know about a party in this building and I don't know about standing orders."

"The standing orders are," McKinnon said as if he were an elementary school teacher, "not to bust it, no matter what kind of lead you got. You see someone go in, you forget about it. You see someone come out, you avert your eyes. You complain, you get moved to a different shift, maybe a different precinct."

"Jesus." O'Reilly was too far below to see if there was any movement against the glass in the penthouse suite. But whoever lived there—whoever partied there—had learned to shut off the lights before the cops arrived.

"Shot in the back of the head," Brunner said before O'Reilly could process all of the information. "That's just damn strange."

O'Reilly looked at the corpses—really looked at them—for the first time. Two men, both rather heavy set. Their faces were gone, probably splattered all over the walls. Gloved hands, nice shoes, one of them wearing a white scarf that caught the light.

Brunner had to search for the wound in the back of the head, which made that the entry point. The exit wounds had destroyed the faces.

O'Reilly looked behind him. No door on that building, but there was one on the building where the party was held. If they'd been exiting the building and were surprised by a queer basher or a mugger, they'd've been shot in the front, not the back.

"How many times were they shot?" O'Reilly asked.

"Looks like just the once. Large caliber, close range. I'd say it was a purposeful headshot, designed to do maximum damage." Brunner felt the back of the closest corpse. "There doesn't seem to be anything on the torso."

"They still got their wallets?" McKinnon asked.

"Haven't checked yet." Brunner reached into the back pants pocket of the corpse he'd been searching and clearly found nothing. So he grabbed the front of the overcoat and reached inside.

He removed a long, thin wallet—old fashioned, the kind made for the larger bills of forty years before. Hand-tailored, beautifully made.

These men weren't hurting for money.

Brunner handed the wallet to O'Reilly, who opened it. And stopped when he saw the badge inside. His mouth went dry.

"We got a feebee," he said, his voice sounding strangled.

"What?" McKinnon asked.

"FBI," Brunner said dryly. McKinnon had only moved to homicide the year before. Vice rarely had to deal with FBI. Homicide did only on sensational cases. O'Reilly could count on one hand the number of times he'd spoken to agents in the New York bureau.

"Not just any feebee either," O'Reilly said. "The Associate Director. Clyde A. Tolson."

McKinnon whistled. "Who's the other guy?"

This time, O'Reilly did the search. The other corpse, the heavier of the two, also smelled faintly of perfume. This man had kept his wallet in the inner pocket of his suit coat, just like his companion had.

O'Reilly opened the wallet. Another badge, just like he expected. But he didn't expect the bulldog face glaring at him from the wallet's interior.

Nor had he expected the name.

"Jesus, Mary, and Joseph," he said.

"What've we got?" McKinnon asked.

O'Reilly handed him the wallet, opened to the slim paper identification.

"The Director of the FBI," he said, his voice shaking. "Public Hero Number One. J. Edgar Hoover."

Francis Xavier Bryce—Frank to his friends, what few of them he still had left—had just dropped off to sleep when the phone rang. He cursed, caught himself, apologized to Mary, and then remembered she wasn't there.

The phone rang again and he fumbled for the light, knocking over the highball glass he'd used to mix his mom's recipe for sleepless nights: hot milk, butter, and honey. It turned out that, at the tender age of thirty-six, hot milk and butter laced with honey wasn't a recipe for sleep; it was a recipe for heartburn.

And for a smelly carpet if he didn't clean the mess up.

He found the phone before he found the light.

"What?" he snapped.

"You live near Central Park, right?" A voice he didn't recognize, but one that was clearly official, asked the question without a hello or an introduction.

"More or less." Bryce rarely talked about his apartment. His parents had left it to him and, as his wife was fond of sniping, it was too fancy for a junior G-Man.

The voice rattled off an address. "How far is that from you?"

"About five minutes." If he didn't clean up the mess on the floor. If he spent thirty seconds pulling on the clothes he'd piled onto the chair beside the bed.

"Get there. Now. We got a situation."

"What about my partner?" Bryce's partner lived in Queens.

"You'll have back-up. You just have to get to the scene. The moment you get there, you shut it down."

"Um." Bryce hated sounding uncertain, but he had no choice. "First, sir, I need to know who I'm talking to. Then I need to know what I'll find."

"You'll find a double homicide. And you're talking to Eugene Hart, the Special Agent in Charge. I shouldn't have to identify myself to you."

Now that he had, Bryce recognized Hart's voice. "Sorry, sir. It's just procedure."

"Fuck procedure. Take over that scene. *Now.*"

"Yes, sir," Bryce said, but he was talking into an empty phone line. He hung up, hands shaking, wishing he had some Bromo-Seltzer.

He'd just come off a long, messy investigation of another agent. Walter Cain had been about to get married when he remembered he had to inform the Bureau of that fact and, as per regulation, get his bride vetted before walking down the aisle.

Bryce had been the one to investigate the future Mrs. Cain, and had been the one to find out about her rather seamy past—two vice convictions under a different name, and one hospitalization after a rather messy backstreet abortion. Turned out Cain knew about his future wife's past, but the Bureau hadn't liked it.

And two nights ago, Bryce had to be the one to tell Cain that he couldn't marry his now-reformed, somewhat religious, beloved. The soon-to-be Mrs. Cain had taken the news hard. She had gone to Bellevue this afternoon after slashing her wrists.

And Bryce had been the one to tell Cain what his former fiancé had done. Just a few hours ago.

Sometimes Bryce hated this job.

Despite his orders, he went into the bathroom, soaked one of Mary's precious company towels in water, and dropped the thing on the spilled milk. Then he pulled on his clothes, and finger-combed his hair.

He was a mess—certainly not the perfect representative of the Bureau. His white shirt was stained with marina from that night's take-out, and his tie wouldn't keep a crisp knot. The crease had long since left his trousers and his shoes hadn't been shined in weeks. Still, he grabbed his black overcoat, hoping it would hide everything.

He let himself out of the apartment before he remembered the required and much hated hat, went back inside, grabbed the hat as well as his gun and his identification. Jesus, he was tired. He hadn't slept since Mary walked out. Mary, who had been vetted by the FBI and who had passed with flying colors. Mary, who had turned out to be more of a liability than any former hooker ever could have been.

And now, because of her, he was heading toward something big, and he was one-tenth as sharp as usual.

All he could hope for was that the SAC had overreacted. And he had a hunch—a two in the morning, get-your-ass-over-there-now hunch—that the SAC hadn't overreacted at all.

Attorney General Robert F. Kennedy sat in his favorite chair near the fire in his library. The house was quiet even though his wife and eight children were asleep upstairs. Outside, the rolling landscape was covered in a light dusting of snow—rare for McLean, Virginia even at this time of year.

He held a book in his left hand, his finger marking the spot. The Greeks had comforted him in the few months since Jack died, but lately Kennedy had discovered Camus.

He had been about to copy a passage into his notebook when the phone rang. At first he sighed, feeling all of the exhaustion that had weighed on him since the assassination. He didn't want to answer the phone. He didn't want to be bothered—not now, not ever again.

But this was the direct line from the White House and if he didn't answer it, someone else in the house would.

He set the Camus book face down on his chair and crossed to the desk before the third ring. He answered with a curt, "Yes?"

"Attorney General Kennedy, sir?" The voice on the other end sounded urgent. The voice sounded familiar to him even though he couldn't place it.

"Yes?"

"This is Special Agent John Haskell. You asked me to contact you, sir, if I heard anything important about Director Hoover, no matter what the time."

Kennedy leaned against the desk. He had made that request back when his brother had been president, back when Kennedy had been the first attorney general since the 1920s who actually demanded accountability from Hoover.

Since Lyndon Johnson had taken over the presidency, accountability had gone by the wayside. These days Hoover rarely returned Kennedy's phone calls.

"Yes, I did tell you that," Kennedy said, resisting the urge to add, *but I don't care about that old man any longer.*

"Sir, there are rumors—credible ones—that Director Hoover has died in New York."

Kennedy froze. For a moment, he flashed back to that unseasonably warm afternoon when he'd sat just outside with the federal attorney for New York City, Robert Morganthau and the chief of Morganthau's criminal division, Silvio Mollo, talking about prosecuting various organized crime figures.

Kennedy could still remember the glint of the sunlight on the swimming pool, the taste of the tuna fish sandwich Ethel had brought him, the way the men—despite their topic—had seemed lighthearted.

Then the phone rang, and J. Edgar Hoover was on the line. Kennedy almost didn't take the call, but he did and Hoover's cold voice said, *I have news for you. The president's been shot.*

Kennedy had always disliked Hoover, but since that day, that awful day in the bright sunshine, he hated that fat bastard. Not once—not in that call, not in the subsequent calls—did Hoover express condolences or show a shred of human concern.

"Credible rumors?" Kennedy repeated, knowing he probably sounded as cold as Hoover had three months ago, and not caring. He'd chosen Haskell as his liaison precisely because the man didn't like Hoover either. Kennedy had needed someone inside Hoover's hierarchy, unbeknownst to Hoover, which was difficult since Hoover kept his hand in everything. Haskell was one of the few who fit the bill.

"Yes, sir, quite credible."

"Then why haven't I received official contact?"

"I'm not even sure the president knows, sir."

Kennedy leaned against the desk. "Why not, if the rumors are credible?"

"Um, because, sir, um, it seems Associate Director Tolson was also shot, and um, they were, um, in a rather suspect area."

Kennedy closed his eyes. All of Washington knew that Tolson was the closest thing Hoover had to a wife. The two old men had been lifelong companions. Even though they didn't live together, they had every meal together. Tolson had been Hoover's hatchet man until the last year or so, when Tolson's health hadn't permitted it.

Then a word Haskell used sank in. "You said shot."

"Yes, sir."

"Is Tolson dead too then?"

"And three other people in the neighborhood," Haskell said.

"My God." Kennedy ran a hand over his face. "But they think this is personal?"

"Yes, sir."

"Because of the location of the shooting?"

"Yes, sir. It seems there was an exclusive gathering in a nearby building. You know the type, sir."

Kennedy didn't know the type—at least not through personal experience. But he'd heard of places like that, where the rich, famous, and deviant could spend time with each other, and do whatever it was they liked to do in something approaching privacy.

"So," he said, "the Bureau's trying to figure out how to cover this up."

"Or at least contain it, sir."

Without Hoover or Tolson. No one in the Bureau was gong to know what to do.

Kennedy's hand started to shake. "What about the files?"

"Files, sir?"

"Hoover's confidential files. Has anyone secured them?"

"Not yet, sir. But I'm sure someone has called Miss Gandy."

Helen Gandy was Hoover's long-time secretary. She had been his right hand as long as Tolson had operated that hatchet.

"So procedure's being followed," Kennedy said, then frowned. If procedure were being followed, shouldn't the acting head of the Bureau be calling him?

"No, sir. But the director put some private instructions in place should he be killed or incapacitated. Private emergency instructions. And those involve letting Miss Gandy know before anyone else."

Even me, Kennedy thought. *Hoover's nominal boss.* "She's not there yet, right?"

"No, sir."

"Do you know where those files are?" Kennedy asked, trying not to let desperation into his voice.

"I've made it my business to know, sir." There was a pause and then Haskell lowered his voice. "They're in Miss Gandy's office, sir."

Not Hoover's like everyone thought. For the first time in months, Kennedy felt a glimmer of hope. "Secure those files."

"Sir?"

"Do whatever it takes. I want them out of there, and I want someone to secure Hoover's house too. I'm acting on the orders of the president. If anyone tells you that they are doing the same, they're mistaken. The president made his wishes clear on this point. He often said if anything happens to that old queer—" and here Kennedy deliberately used LBJ's favorite phrase for Hoover "—then we need those files before they can get into the wrong hands."

"I'm on it, sir."

"I can't stress to you the importance of this," Kennedy said. In fact, he couldn't talk about the importance at all. Those files could ruin his brother's legacy. The secrets in there could bring down Kennedy too, and his entire family.

"And if the rumors about the director's death are wrong, sir?"

Kennedy felt a shiver of fear. "Are they?"

"I seriously doubt it."

"Then let me worry about that."

And about what LBJ would do when he found out. Because the president upon whose orders Kennedy acted wasn't the current one. Kennedy was following the orders of the only man he believed should be president at the moment.

His brother, Jack.

The scene wasn't hard to find; a coroner's van blocked the entrance to the alley. Bryce walked quickly, already cold, his heartburn worse than it had been when he had gone to bed.

The neighborhood was in transition. An urban renewal project had knocked down some wonderful turn of the century buildings that had become eyesores. But so far, the buildings that had replaced them were the worst kind of modern—all planes and angles and white with few windows.

In the buildings closest to the park, the lights worked and the streets looked safe. But here, on a side street not far from the construction, the city's shady side showed. The dirty snow was piled against the curb, the streets were dark, and nothing seemed inhabited except that alley with the coroner's van blocking the entrance.

The coroner's van and at least one unmarked car. No press, which surprised him. He shoved his gloved hands in the pockets of his overcoat even though it was against FBI dress code, and slipped between the van and the wall of a grimy brick building.

The alley smelled of old urine and fresh blood. Two beat cops blocked his way until he showed identification. Then, like people usually did, they parted as if he could burn them.

The bodies had fallen side by side in the center of the alley. They looked posed, with their arms up, their legs in classic P position—one leg bent, the other straight. They looked like they could fit perfectly on the dead body diagrams the FBI used to put out in the 1930s. He wondered if they had fallen like this or if this had been the result of the coroner's tampering.

The coroner had messed with other parts of the crime scene—if, indeed, he had been the one who put the garbage can lids on the ice and set battery-powered lamps on them. The warmth of the lamps was melting the ice and sending runnels of water into a nearby grate.

"I hope to hell someone thought to photograph the scene before you melted it," he said.

The coroner and the two cops who had been crouching beside the bodies stood up guiltily. The coroner looked at the garbage can lids and closed his eyes. Then he took a deep breath, opened them, and snapped his fingers at the assistant who was waiting beside a gurney.

"Camera," he said.

"That's Crime Scene's—" the assistant began, then saw everyone looking at him. He glanced at the van. "Never mind."

He walked behind the bodies, further disturbing the scene. Bryce's mouth thinned in irritation. The cops who stood were in plain clothes.

"Detectives," Bryce said, holding his identification, "Special Agent Frank Bryce of the FBI. I've been told to secure this scene. More of my people will be here shortly."

He hoped that last was true. He had no idea who was coming or when they would arrive.

"Good," said the younger detective, a tall man with broad shoulders and an all-American jaw. "The sooner we get out of here the better."

Bryce had never gotten that reaction from a detective before. Usually the detectives were territorial, always reminding him that this was New York City and that the scene belonged to them.

The other detective, older, face grizzled by time and work, held out his gloved hand. "Forgive my partner's rudeness. I'm Seamus O'Reilly. He's Joseph McKinnon and we'll help you in any way we can."

"I appreciate it," Bryce said, taking O'Reilly's hand and shaking it. "I guess the first thing you can do is tell me what we've got."

"A hell of a mess, that's for sure," said McKinnon. "You'll understand when . . ."

His voice trailed off as his partner took out two long, old-fashioned wallets and handed them to Bryce.

Bryce took them, feeling confused. Then he opened the first, saw the familiar badge, and felt his breath catch. Two FBI agents, in this alley? Shot side-by-side? He looked up, saw the darkened windows.

There used to be rumors about this neighborhood. Some exclusive private sex parties used to be held here, and his old partner had always wanted to visit one just to see if it was a hotbed of communists like some of the agents had claimed. Bryce had begged off. He was an investigator, not a voyeur.

The two detectives were staring at him, as if they expected more from him. He still had the wallet open in his hand. If the dead men were New York agents, he would know them. He hated solving the deaths of people he knew.

But he steeled himself, looked at the identification, and felt the blood leave his face. His skin grew cold and for a moment he felt lightheaded.

"No," he said.

The detectives still stared at him.

He swallowed. "Have you done a visual I.D.?"

Hoover was recognizable. His picture was on everything. Sometimes Bryce thought Hoover was more famous than the president—any president. He'd certainly been in power longer.

"Faces are gone," O'Reilly said.

"Exit wounds," the coroner added from beside the bodies. His assistant had returned and was taking pictures, the flash showing just how much melt had happened since the coroner arrived.

"Shot in the back of the head?" Bryce blinked. He was tired and his brain was working slowly, but something about the shots didn't match with the body positions.

"If they came out that door," O'Reilly said as he indicated a dark metal door almost hidden in the side of the brick building, "then the shooters had to be waiting beside it."

"Your crime scene people haven't arrived yet, I take it?" Bryce asked.

"No," the coroner said. "They think it's a fag kill. They'll get here when they get here."

Bryce clenched his left fist and had to remind himself to let the fingers loose.

O'Reilly saw the reaction. "Sorry about that," he said, shooting a glare at the coroner. "I'm sure the director was here on business."

Funny business. But Bryce didn't say that. The rumors about Hoover had been around since Bryce joined the FBI just after the war. Hoover quashed them, like he quashed any criticism, but it seemed like the criticism got made, no matter what.

Bryce opened the other wallet, but he already had a guess as to who was beside Hoover, and his guess turned out to be right.

"You want to tell me why your crime scene people believe this is a homosexual killing?" Bryce asked, trying not to let what Mary called his FBI tone into his voice. If Hoover was still alive and this was some kind of plant, Hoover would want to crush the source of this assumption. Bryce would make sure that the source was worth pursuing before going any farther.

"Neighborhood, mostly," McKinnon said. "There're a couple of bars, mostly high-end. You have to know someone to get in. Then there's the party, held every week upstairs. Some of the most important men in the city show up at it, or so they used to say in vice when they told us to stay away."

Bryce nodded, letting it go at that.

"We need your crime scene people here ASAP, and a lot more cops so that we can protect what's left of this scene, in case these men turn out to be who their identification says they are. You search the bodies to see if this was the only identification on them?"

O'Reilly started. He clearly hadn't thought of that. Probably had been too shocked by the first wallets that he found.

The younger detective had already gone back to the bodies. The coroner put out a hand, and did the searching himself.

"You think this was a plant?" O'Reilly asked.

"I don't know what to think," Bryce said. "I'm not here to think. I'm here to make sure everything goes smoothly."

And to make sure the case goes to the FBI. Those words hung unspoken between the two of them. Not that O'Reilly objected, and now Bryce could understand why. This case would be a political nightmare, and no good detective wanted to be in the middle of it.

"How come there's no press?" Bryce asked O'Reilly. "You manage to get rid of them somehow?"

"Fag kill," the coroner said.

Bryce was getting tired of those words. His fist had clenched again, and he had to work at unclenching it.

"Ignore him," O'Reilly said softly. "He's an asshole and the best coroner in the city."

"I heard that," the coroner said affably. "There's no other identification on either of them."

O'Reilly's shoulders slumped, as if he'd been hoping for a different outcome. Bryce should have been hoping as well, but he hadn't been. He had known that Hoover was in town. The entire New York bureau knew, since Hoover always took it over when he arrived—breezing in, giving instructions, making sure everything was just the way he wanted it.

"Before this gets too complicated," O'Reilly said, "you want to see the other bodies?"

"Other bodies?" Bryce felt numb. He could use some caffeine now, but Hoover had ordered agents not to drink coffee on the job. Getting coffee now felt almost disrespectful.

"We got three more." O'Reilly took a deep breath. "And just before you arrived, I got word that they're agents too."

Special Agent John Haskell had just installed six of his best agents outside the director's suite of offices when a small woman showed up, key clutched in her gloved right hand. Helen Gandy, the director's secretary, looked up at Haskell with the coldest stare he'd ever seen outside of the director's.

"May I go into my office, Agent Haskell?" Her voice was just as cold. She didn't look upset, and if he hadn't known that she never stayed past five unless directed by Hoover himself, Haskell would have thought she was coming back from a prolonged work break.

"I'm sorry, ma'am," he said. "No one is allowed inside. President's orders."

"Really?" God, that voice was chilling. He remembered the first time he'd heard it, when he'd been brought to this suite of offices as a brand-new agent, after getting his "Meet the Boss" training before his introduction to the director. She'd frightened him more than Hoover had.

"Yes, ma'am. The president says no one can enter."

"Surely he didn't mean me."

Surely he did. But Haskell bit the comment back. "I'm sorry, ma'am."

"I have a few personal items that I'd like to get, if you don't mind. And the director instructed me that in the case of . . ." and for the first time she paused. Her voice didn't break nor did she clear her throat. But she seemed to need a moment to gather herself. "In case of emergency, I was to remove some of his personal items as well."

"If you could tell me what they are, ma'am, I'll get them."

Her eyes narrowed. "The director doesn't like others to touch his possessions."

"I'm sorry, ma'am," he said gently. "But I don't think that matters any longer."

Any other woman would have broken down. After all, she had worked for the old man for forty-five years, side-by-side, every day. Never marrying, not because they had a relationship—Helen Gandy, more than anyone, probably knew the truth behind the director's relationship with the associate director—but because for Helen Gandy, just like for the director himself, the FBI was her entire life.

"It matters," she said. "Now if you'll excuse me . . ."

She tried to wriggle past him. She was wiry and stronger than he expected. He had to put out an arm to block her.

"Ma'am," he said in the gentlest tone he could summon, "the president's orders supersede the director's."

How often had he wanted to say that over the years? How often had he wanted to remind everyone in the Bureau that the president led the Free World, not J. Edgar Hoover.

"In this instance," she snapped, "they do not."

"Ma'am, I'd hate to have some agents restrain you." Although he wasn't sure about that. She had never been nice to him or to anyone he knew. She'd always been sharp or rude. "You're distraught."

"I am not." She clipped each word.

"You are because I say you are, ma'am."

She raised her chin. For a moment, he thought she hadn't understood. But she finally did.

The balance of power had shifted. At the moment, it was on his side.

"Do I have to call the president then to get my personal effects?" she asked.

But they both knew she wasn't talking about her personal things. And the president was smart enough to know that as well. As hungry to get those files as the attorney general had seemed despite his Eastern reserve, the president would be utterly ravenous. He wouldn't let some old skirt, as he'd been known to call Miss Gandy, get in his way.

"Go ahead," Haskell said. "Feel free to use the phone in the office across the hall."

She glared at him, then turned on one foot and marched down the corridor. But she didn't head toward a phone—at least not one he could see.

He wondered who she would call. The president wouldn't listen. The attorney general had issued the order in the president's name. Maybe she would contact one of Hoover's assistant directors, the four or five men that Hoover had in his pocket.

Haskell had been waiting for them. But word still hadn't spread through the Bureau. The only reason he knew was because he'd received a call from the SAC of the New York office. New York hated the director, mostly because the old man went there so often and harassed them.

Someone had probably figured out that there was a crisis from the moment that Haskell had brought his people in to secure the director's suite. But no one would know that the director was dead until Miss Gandy made the calls or until someone in the Bureau started along the chain of command—the one designated in the book Hoover had written all those years ago.

Haskell crossed his arms. Sometimes he wished he hadn't let the A.G. know how he felt about the director. Sometimes he wished he were still a humble assistant, the man who had joined the FBI because he wanted to be a top cop like his hero J. Edgar Hoover.

A man who, it turned out, never made a real arrest or fired a gun or even understood investigation.

There was a lot to admire about the director—no matter what you said, he'd built a hell of an agency almost from scratch—but he wasn't the man his press made him out to be.

And that was the source of Haskell's disillusionment. He'd wanted to be a top cop. Instead, he snooped into homes and businesses and sometimes even investigated fairly blameless people, looking for a mistake in their past.

Since he'd been transferred to FBIHQ, he hadn't done any real investigating at all. His arrests had slowed, his cases dwindled.

And he'd found himself investigating his boss, trying to find out where the legend ended and the man began. Once he realized that the old man was just a bureaucrat who had learned where all the bodies were buried and used that to make everyone bow to his bidding, Haskell was ripe for the undercover work the A.G. had asked him to do.

Only now he wasn't undercover any more. Now he was standing in the open before the director's cache of secrets, on the president's orders, hoping that no one would call his bluff.

As O'Reilly led him to the limousine, Bryce surreptitiously checked his watch. He'd already been on scene for half an hour, and no back-up had arrived. If he was supposed to secure everything and chase off the NYPD, he'd need some manpower.

But for now, he wanted to see the extent of the problem. The night had gotten colder, and this street was even darker than the street he'd walked down. All of the streetlights were out. The only light came from some porch bulbs above a few entrances. He could barely make out the limousine at the end of the block, and then only because he could see the shadowy forms of the two beat cops standing at the scene, their squad cars parking the limo in.

As he got closer, he recognized the shape of the limo. It was thicker than most limos and rode lower to the ground because it was encased in an extra frame, making it bulletproof. Supposedly, the glass would all be bulletproof as well.

"You said the driver was shot inside the limo?" Bryce asked.

"That's what they told me," O'Reilly said. "I wasn't called to this scene. We were brought in because of the two men in the alley. Even then we were called late."

Bryce nodded. He remembered the coroner's bigotry. "Is that standard procedure for cases involving minorities?"

O'Reilly gave him a sideways glance. Bryce couldn't read O'Reilly's expression in the dark.

"We're overtaxed," O'Reilly said after a moment. "Some cases don't get the kind of treatment they deserve."

"Limo drivers," Bryce said.

"If he'd been killed in the parking garage under the Plaza maybe," O'Reilly said. "But not because of who he was. But because of where he was."

Bryce nodded. He knew how the world worked. He didn't like it. He spoke up against it too many times, which was why he was on shaky ground at the Bureau.

Then his already upset stomach clenched. Maybe he wasn't going to get back-up. Maybe they'd put him on his own here to claim he'd botched the investigation, so that they would be able to cover it up.

He couldn't concentrate on that now. What he had to do was

take good notes, make the best case he could, and keep a copy of every damn thing—maybe in more than one place.

"You were called in because of the possibility that the men in the alley could be important," Bryce said.

"That's my guess," O'Reilly said.

"What about the others down the block? Has anyone taken those cases?"

"Probably not," O'Reilly said. "Those bars, you know. It's department policy. The coroner checks bodies in the suspect area, and decides, based on . . . um . . . evidence of . . . um . . . activity . . . whether or not to bring in detectives."

Bryce frowned. He almost asked what the coroner was checking for when he figured out that it was evidence on the body itself, evidence not of the crime, but of certain kinds of sex acts. If that evidence was present, apparently no one thought it worthwhile to investigate the crime.

"You'd think the city would revise that," Bryce said. "A lot of people live dual lives—productive and interesting people."

"Yeah," O'Reilly said. "You'd think. Especially after tonight."

Bryce grinned. He was liking this grizzled cop more and more.

O'Reilly spoke to the beat cops, then motioned Bryce to the limo. As Bryce approached, O'Reilly trained his flashlight on the driver's side.

The window wasn't broken like Bryce had expected. It had been rolled down.

"You got here one James Crawford," said one of the beat cops. "He got identification says he's a feebee, but I ain't never heard of no colored feebee."

"There's only four," Bryce said dryly. And they all worked for Hoover as his personal housekeepers or drivers. "Can I see that identification?"

The beat cop handed him a wallet that matched the ones on Tolson and Hoover. Inside was a badge and identification for James Crawford as well as family photographs. Neither Tolson nor Hoover had had any photographs in their wallets.

Bryce motioned O'Reilly to move a little closer to the body. The head was tilted toward the window. The right side of the skull was gone, the hair glistening with drying blood. With one gloved finger, Bryce pushed the head upright. A single entrance wound above the left ear had caused the damage.

"Brunner says the shots are the same caliber," O'Reilly said.

It took Bryce a moment to realize that Brunner was the coroner.

Bryce carefully searched Crawford but didn't find the man's weapon. Nor could he found a holster or any way to carry a weapon.

"It looks like he wasn't carrying a weapon," Bryce said.

"Neither were the two in the alley," O'Reilly said, and Bryce appreciated his caution in not identifying the other two corpses. "You'd think they would have been."

Bryce shook his head. "They were known for not carrying weapons. But you'd think their driver would have one."

"Maybe they had protection," O'Reilly said.

And Bryce's mouth went dry. Of course they did. The office always joked about who would get HooverWatch on each trip. He'd had to do it a few times.

Agents on HooverWatch followed strict rules, like everything else with Hoover. Remain close enough to see the men entering and exiting an area, stop any suspicious characters, and yet somehow remain inconspicuous.

"You said there were two others shot?"

"Yeah. A block or so from here." O'Reilly waved a hand vaguely down the street.

"Pulled out of one car or two?"

"Not my case," O'Reilly said.

"Two," said the beat cop. "Black sedans. Could barely see them on this cruddy street."

HooverWatch. Bryce swallowed hard, that bile back. Of course. He probably knew the men who were shot.

"Let's look," he said. "You two, make sure the coroner's man photographs this scene before he leaves."

"Yessir," said the second beat cop. He hadn't spoken before.

"And don't let anyone near this scene unless I give the okay," Bryce said.

"How come this guy's in charge?" the talkative beat cop asked O'Reilly.

O'Reilly grinned. "Because he's a feebee."

"I'm sorry," the beat cop said automatically turning to Bryce. "I didn't know, sir."

Feebee was an insult—or at least some in the Bureau thought so. Bryce didn't mind it. Any more than he minded when some rookie said "Sack" when he meant "Ess-Ay-Cee." Shorthand worked, sometimes better than people wanted it to.

"Point me in the right direction," he said to the talkative cop.

The cop nodded south. "One block down, sir. You can't miss it. We got guys on those scenes too, but we weren't so sure it was important. You know. We coulda missed stuff."

In other words, they hadn't buttoned up the scene immediately. They'd waited for the coroner to make his verdict, and he probably hadn't, not with the three new corpses nearby.

Bryce took one last look at James Crawford. The man had rolled down his window, despite the cold, and in a bad section of town.

He leaned forward. Underneath the faint scent of cordite and mingled with the thicker smell of blood was the smell of a cigar.

He took the flashlight from O'Reilly and trained it on the dirty snow against the curb. It had been trampled by everyone coming to this crime scene.

He crouched, and poked just a little, finding three fairly fresh cigarette butts.

As he stood, he said to the beat cops, "When the scene of the crime guys get here, make sure they take everything from the curb."

O'Reilly was watching him. The beat cops were frowning, but they nodded.

Bryce handed O'Reilly back his flashlight and headed down the street.

"You think he was smoking and tossing the butts out the window?" O'Reilly asked.

"Either that," Bryce said, "or he rolled his window down to talk to someone. And if someone was pointing a gun at him, he wouldn't have done it. This vehicle was armored. He had a better chance starting it up and driving away than he did cooperating."

"If he wasn't smoking," O'Reilly said, "he knew his killer."

"Yeah," Bryce said. And he was pretty sure that was going to make his job a whole hell of a lot harder.

Kennedy took the elevator up to the fifth floor of the Justice Department. He probably should have stayed home, but he simply couldn't. He needed to get into those files and he needed to do so before anyone else.

As he strode into the corridor he shared with the Director of the FBI, he saw Helen Gandy hurry in the other direction. She looked like she had just come from the beauty salon. He had never seen her look anything less than completely put together but he was surprised by her perfect appearance on this night, after the news that her long-time boss was dead.

Kennedy tugged at the overcoat he'd put on over his favorite sweater. He hadn't taken the time to change or even comb his hair. He probably looked as tousled as he had in the days after Jack died.

Although, for the first time in three months, he felt like he had a purpose. He didn't know how long this feeling would last, or how long he wanted it to. But this death had given him an odd kind of hope that control was coming back into his world.

Haskell stood in front of the director's office suite, arms crossed. The director's suite was just down the corridor from the attorney general's offices. It felt odd to go toward Hoover's domain instead of his own.

Haskell looked relieved when he saw Kennedy.

"Was that the dragon lady I just saw?" Kennedy asked.

"She wanted to get some personal effects from her office," Haskell said.

"Did you let her?"

"You said the orders were to secure it, so I have."

"Excellent." Kennedy glanced in both directions and saw no one. "Make sure your staff continues to protect the doors. I'm going inside."

"Sir?" Haskell raised his eyebrows.

"This may not be the right place," Kennedy said. "I'm worried that he moved everything to his house."

The lie came easily. Kennedy would have heard if Hoover had moved files to his own home. But Haskell didn't know that.

Haskell moved away from the door. It was unlocked. Two more agents stood inside, guarding the interior doors.

"Give me a minute, please, gentlemen," Kennedy said.

The men nodded and went outside.

Kennedy stopped and took a deep breath. He had been in Miss Gandy's office countless times, but he had never really looked at it. He'd always been staring at the door to Hoover's inner sanctum, waiting for it to open and the old man to come out.

That office was interesting. In the antechamber, Hoover had memorabilia and photographs from his major cases. He even had the plaster-of-paris death mask of John Dellinger on display. It was a ghastly thing, which made Kennedy think of the way that English kings used to keep severed heads on the entrance to London Bridge to warn traitors of their potential fate.

But this office had always looked like a waiting room to him. Nothing very special. The woman behind the desk was the focal

point. Jack had been the one who nicknamed her the dragon lady
and had even called her that to her face once, only with his trade-
mark grin, so infectious that she hadn't made a sound or a grimace
in protest.

Of course, she hadn't smiled back either.

Her desk was clear except for a blotter, a telephone, and a jar of
pens. A typewriter sat on a credenza with paper stacked beside it.

But it wasn't the desk that interested him the most. It was the
floor-to-ceiling filing cabinets and storage bins. He walked to them.
Instead of the typical system—marked by letters of the alphabet—
this one had numbers that were clearly part of a code.

He pulled open the nearest drawer, and found row after row of
accordion files, each with its own number, and manila folders with
the first number set followed by another. He cursed softly under his
breath.

Of course the old dog wouldn't file his confidentials by name.
He'd use a secret code. The old man liked nothing more than his
secrets.

Still, Kennedy opened half a dozen drawers just to see if the system continued throughout. And it wasn't until he got to a bin near
the corner of the desk that he found a file labeled "Obscene."

His hand shook as he pulled it out. Jack, for all his brilliance,
had been sexually insatiable. Back when their brother Joe was still
alive and no one ever thought Jack would be running for president,
Jack had had an affair with a Danish émigré named Inga Arvad.
Inga Binga, as Jack used to call her, was married to a man with ties
to Hitler. She'd even met and liked Der Fuhrer, and had said so in
print.

She'd been the target of FBI surveillance as a possible spy, and
during that surveillance who should turn up in her bed but a young
naval lieutenant whose father had once been ambassador to
England. The Ambassador, as he preferred to be called even by his
sons, found out about the affair, told Jack in no uncertain terms
to end it, and then to make sure he did by getting him assigned to a
PT boat in the Pacific, as far from Inga Binga as possible.

Kennedy had always suspected that Hoover had leaked the information to the Ambassador, but he hadn't known for certain until
Jack became president when Hoover told them. Hoover had been
surveilling all of the Kennedy children at the Ambassador's request.
He'd given Kennedy a list of scandalous items as a sample, and
hoped that would control the president and his brother.

It might have controlled Jack, but Hoover hadn't known Kennedy very well. Kennedy had told Hoover that if any of this information made it into the press, then other things would appear in print as well, things like the strange FBI budget items for payments covering Hoover's visits to the track or the fact that Hoover made some interesting friends, mobster friends, when he was vacationing in Palm Beach.

It wasn't quite a Mexican stand-off—Jack was really afraid of the old man—but it gave Kennedy more power than any attorney general had had over Hoover since the beginnings of the Roosevelt administration.

But now Kennedy needed those files, and he had a hunch Hoover would label them obscene.

Kennedy opened the file, and was shocked to see Richard Nixon's name on the sheets inside. Kennedy thumbed through quickly, not caring what dirt they'd found on that loser. Nixon couldn't win an election after his defeat in 1960. He'd even told the press after he lost a California race that they wouldn't have him to kick around any more.

Yet Hoover had kept the files, just to be safe.

That old bastard really and truly had known where all the bodies were buried. And it wouldn't be easy to find them.

Kennedy took a deep breath. He stood, shoved his hands in his pockets, and surveyed the walls of files. It would take days to search each folder. He didn't have days. He probably didn't have hours.

But he was Hoover's immediate supervisor, whether the old man had recognized it or not. Hoover answered to him. Which meant that the files belonged to the Justice Department, of which the FBI was only one small part.

He glanced at his watch. No one pounded on the door. He probably had until dawn before someone tried to stop him. If he was really lucky, no one would think of the files until mid-morning.

He went to the door and beckoned Haskell inside.

"We're taking the files to my office," he said.

"All of them, sir?"

"All of them. These first, then whatever is in Hoover's office, and then any other confidential files you can find."

Haskell looked up the wall as if he couldn't believe the command. "That'll take some time, sir."

"Not if you get a lot of people to help."

"Sir, I thought you wanted to keep this secret."

He did. But it wouldn't remain secret for long. So he had to control when the information got out—just like he had to control the information itself.

"Get this done as quickly as possible," he said.

Haskell nodded and turned the doorknob, but Kennedy stopped him before he went out.

"These are filed by code," he said. "Do you know where the key is?"

"I was told that Miss Gandy had the keys to everything from codes to offices," Haskell said.

Kennedy felt a shiver run through him. Knowing Hoover, he would have made sure he had the key to the attorney general's office as well.

"Do you have any idea where she might have kept the code keys?" Kennedy asked.

"No," Haskell said. "I wasn't part of the need-to-know group. I already knew too much."

Kennedy nodded. He appreciated how much Haskell knew. It had gotten him this far.

"On your way out," Kennedy said, "call building maintenance and have them change all the locks in my office."

"Yes, sir." Haskell kept his hand on the doorknob. "Are you sure you want to do this, sir? Couldn't you just change the locks here? Wouldn't that secure everything for the president?"

"Everyone in Washington wants these files," Kennedy said. "They're going to come to this office suite. They won't think of mine."

"Until they heard that you moved everything."

Kennedy nodded. "And then they'll know how futile their quest really is."

The final crime scene was a mess. The bodies were already gone—probably inside the coroner's van that blocked the alley a few blocks back. It had taken Bryce nearly a half an hour to find someone who knew what the scene had looked like when the police had first arrived.

That someone was Officer Ralph Voight. He was tall and trim, with a pristine uniform despite the fact that he'd been on duty all night.

O'Reilly was the one who convinced him to talk with Bryce. Voight was the first to show the traditional animosity between the

NYPD and the FBI, but that was because Voight didn't know who had died only a few blocks away.

Bryce had Voight walk him through the crime scene. The buildings on this street were boarded up, and the lights burned out. Broken glass littered the sidewalk—and it hadn't come from this particular crime. Rusted beer cans, half buried in the ice piles, cluttered each stoop like passed-out drunks.

"Okay," Voight said, using his flashlight as a pointer, "we come up on these two cars first."

The two sedans were parked against the curb, one behind the other. The sedans were too nice for the neighborhood—new, black, without a dent. Bryce recognized them as FBI issue—he had access to a sedan like that himself when he needed it.

He patted his pocket, was disgusted to realize he'd left his notebook at the apartment, and turned to O'Reilly. "You got paper? I need those plates."

O'Reilly nodded. He pulled out a notebook and wrote down the plate numbers.

"They just looked wrong," Voight was saying. "So we stopped, figuring maybe someone needed assistance."

He pointed the flashlight across the street. The squad had stopped directly across from the two cars.

"That's when we seen the first body."

He walked them to the middle of the street. This part of the city hadn't been plowed regularly and a layer of ice had built over the pavement. A large pool of blood had melted through that ice, leaving its edges reddish black and revealing the pavement below.

"The guy was face down, hands out like he'd tried to catch himself."

"Face gone?" Bryce asked, thinking maybe it was a head shot like the others.

"No. Turns out he was shot in the back."

Bryce glanced at O'Reilly, whose lips had thinned. This one was different. Because it was the first? Or because it was unrelated?

"We pull our weapons, scan to see if we see anyone else, which we don't. The door's open on the first sedan, but we didn't see anyone in the dome light. And we didn't see anyone obvious on the street, but it's really dark here and the flashlights don't reach far." Voight turned his light toward the block with the parked limousine, but neither the car nor the sidewalk was visible from this distance.

"So we go to the cars, careful now, and find the other body right there."

He flashed his light on the curb beside the door to the first sedan.

"This one's on his back and the door is open. We figure he was getting out when he got plugged. Then the other guy—maybe he was outside his car trying to help this guy with I don't know what, some car trouble or something, then his buddy gets hit, so he runs for cover across the street and gets nailed. End of story."

"Did you check to see if the cars start?" O'Reilly asked. Bryce nodded that was going to be his next question as well.

"I'm not supposed to touch the scene, sir," Voight said with some resentment. "We secured the area, figured everything was okay, then called it in."

"Did you hear the other shots?"

"No," Voight said. "I know we got three more up there, and you'd think I'd've heard the shooting if something happened, but I didn't. And as you can tell, it's damn quiet around here at night."

Bryce could tell. He didn't like the silence in the middle of the city. Neighborhoods that got quiet like this so close to dawn were usually among the worst. The early morning maintenance workers, and the delivery drivers stayed away whenever they could.

He peered in the sedan, then pulled the door open. The interior light went on, and there was blood all over the front seat and steering wheel. There were Styrofoam coffee cups on both sides of the little rise between the seats. And the keys were in the ignition. Like all Bureau issue, the car was an automatic.

Carefully, so that he wouldn't disturb anything important in the scene, he turned the key. The sedan purred to life, sounding well-tuned just like it was supposed to.

"Check to see if there are other problems," Bryce said to O'Reilly. "A flat maybe."

Although Bryce knew there wouldn't be one. He shut off the ignition.

"You didn't see the interior light when you pulled up?" he asked Voight.

"Yeah, but it was dim," Voight said. "That's why I figured there was car problems. I figured they left the lights on so they could see."

Bryce nodded. He understood the assumption. He backed out of the sedan, then walked around it, shining his own flashlight at the hole in the ice, and then back at the first sedan.

Directly across.

He walked to the second sedan. Its interior was clean—no Styrofoam cups, no wadded up food containers, no notebooks. Not even some tools hastily pulled to help the other driver in need.

He let out a small sigh. He finally figured out what was bothering him.

"You find weapons on the two men?" he asked Voight.

"Yes, sir."

"Holstered?"

"The guy by the car. The other one had his in his right hand. We figured we just happened on the scene or someone would have taken the weapon."

Or not. People tended to hide for a while after shots were fired, particularly if they had nothing to do with the shootings but might get blamed anyway.

Bryce tried to open the passenger door on the second sedan, but it was locked. He walked around to the driver's door. Locked as well.

"No one looked inside this car?"

"No, sir. We figured crime scene would do it."

"But they haven't been here yet?" Bryce asked.

"It's the neighborhood, sir. Right there—" Voight aimed his flashlight at stairs heading down to a lower level "—is one of those men-only clubs, you know? The kind that you go to when you're . . . you know . . . looking for other men."

Bryce felt a flash of irritation. He'd been running into this all night. "Okay. What I'm hearing in a sideways way from every representative of the NYPD on this scene is that crimes in this neighborhood don't get investigated."

Voight sputtered. "They get investigated—"

"They get investigated," O'Reilly said, "enough to tell the families they probably want to back off. You heard Brunner. That's what most in the department call it. The rest of us, we call them lifestyle kills. And we get in trouble if we waste too many resources on them."

"Lovely," Bryce said dryly. His philosophy, which had gotten him in trouble with the Bureau more than once, was that all crimes deserved investigation, no matter how distasteful you found the victims. Which was why he kept getting moved, from communists to reviewing wire-taps to digging dirt on other agents.

And that was probably why he was here. He was expendable.

"Did you find car keys on either of the victims?" Bryce asked.

"No, sir," Voight said. "And I helped the coroner when he first arrived."

"Then start looking. See if they got dropped in the struggle."

Although Bryce doubted they had.

"I got something to jimmy the lock in my car," O'Reilly said.

Bryce nodded. Then he stood back, surveying the whole thing. He didn't like how he was thinking. It was making his heartburn grow worse.

But it was the only thing that made sense.

Agents worked HooverWatch in pairs. There were two dead agents and two cars. If the second sedan was back-up, there should have been four agents and two cars.

But it didn't look that way. It looked like someone had pulled up behind the HooverWatch vehicle, and got out, carefully locking the door.

Then he went to the door of the HooverWatch car. The driver had got out to talk to him, and the new guy shot him.

At that point, the second HooverWatch agent was an easy target. He scrambled out of the car, grabbed his own weapon, and headed across the street—maybe shooting as he went. The shooter got him, and then casually walked up the street to the limo, which he had to know was there even though he couldn't see it.

As he approached the limo, the limo driver lowered his window. He would have recognized the approaching man, and thought he was going to report on the danger.

Instead, the man shot him, then went to lie in wait for Hoover and Tolson.

Bryce shivered. It would have happened very fast, and long before the beat cops showed up.

The guy in the street had time to bleed out. The limo driver couldn't warn his boss. And the beat cops hadn't heard the shots in the alley, which they would have on such a quiet night.

O'Reilly brought the jimmy, shoved it into the space between the window and the lock, and flipped the lock up with a single movement. Then he opened the door.

No keys in the ignition.

Bryce flipped open the glove box. Nothing inside but the vehicle registration. Which, as he expected, identified it as an FBI vehicle.

The shooter had planned to come back. He'd planned to drive away in this car. But he got delayed. And by the time he got here, the two beat cops were on scene. He couldn't get his car.

He had to improvise. So he probably walked away or took the subway, hoping the cops would think the extra car belonged to one of the victims.

And that was his mistake.

"How come you guys were here in the middle of the night?" Bryce asked Voight.

Voight swallowed. It was the first sign of nervousness he'd shown. "This is part of our beat."

"But?" Bryce asked.

Voight looked away. "We're supposed to go up Central Park West."

"And you don't."

"Yeah, we do. Just not every time."

"Because?"

"Because I figure, you know, when the bars let out, we could, you know, let our presence be known."

"Prevent a lifestyle kill."

"Yes, sir."

"And you care about this because . . . ?"

"Everyone should," Voight snapped. "Serve and protect, right, sir?"

Voight was touchy. He thought Bryce was accusing him of protecting the lifestyle because he lived it.

"Does your partner like this drive?" Bryce asked.

"He complains, sir, but he lets me do it."

"Have you stopped any crimes?"

"Broken up a few fights," Voight said.

"But not something like this."

"No, sir."

"You don't patrol every night, do you, Voight?"

"No, sir. We get different regions different nights."

"Do you think our killer would have thought that this street was unprotected?"

"It usually is, sir."

O'Reilly was frowning, but not at Voight. At Bryce. "You think this was planned?" O'Reilly asked.

Bryce didn't answer. This was a Bureau matter, and he wasn't sure how the Bureau would handle it.

But he did think the killing was planned. And he had a hunch it would be easy to solve because of the abandoned sedan.

And that abandoned sedan bothered him more than he wanted

to admit. Because the presence of that sedan meant only one thing: that the person who had shot all five FBI agents was—almost without a doubt—an FBI agent himself.

Kennedy looked at the bins and the filing cabinets stacked around his office and allowed himself one moment to feel overwhelmed. People ribbed him about the office; he had taken the reception area and made it his, rather than use the standard size office in the back.

As a result, his office was as long as a football field, with stunning windows along the walls. The watercolors painted by his children had been covered by the cabinets. His furniture was pushed aside to make room for the bins, and for the first time, this space felt small.

He put his hands on his hips and wondered how to begin.

Since six agents began moving the filing cabinets across the corridor more than an hour ago, Kennedy had received five phone calls from LBJ's chief of staff. Kennedy hadn't taken one of them. The last had been a direct order to come to the Oval Office.

Kennedy ignored it.

He also ignored the ringing telephone—the White House line—and the messages his own assistant (called in after a short night's sleep) had been bringing to him.

Helen Gandy stood in the corridor, arms crossed, her purse hanging off her wrist, and watching with deep disapproval. Haskell was trying to find out if there were remaining files and where they were. But Kennedy had found the one thing he was looking for: the key.

It was in a large, innocuous index file box inside the lowest drawer of Helen Gandy's desk. Kennedy had brought it into his office and was thumbing through it, hoping to understand it before he got interrupted again.

A man from building maintenance had changed the lock on the door leading into the interior offices, and was working on the main doors now that the files were all inside. Kennedy figured he'd have his own office secure by seven A.M.

Then he heard a rustling in the hallway, a lot of startled, "Mr. President, sir!" followed by official, "Make way for the president," and instinctively he turned toward the door. The maintenance man was leaning out of it, the doorknob loose in his hand.

"Where the fuck is that bastard?" Lyndon Baines Johnson's voice echoed from the corridor. "Doesn't anyone in this building have balls enough to tell him that he works for me?"

Even though the question was rhetorical, someone tried to answer. Kennedy heard something about "your orders, sir."

"Horseshit!" Then LBJ stood in the doorway. Two secret service agents flanked him. He motioned with one hand at the maintenance man. "I suggest you get out."

The man didn't have to be told twice. He scurried away, still carrying the doorknob. LBJ came inside alone, pushed the door closed, then grimaced as it popped back open. He grabbed a chair and set it in front of the door, then glared at Kennedy.

The glare was effective in that hang-dog face, despite LBJ's attire. He wore a plaid silk pajama top stuffed into a pair of suit pants, finished with dress shoes and no socks. His hair—what remained of it—hadn't been Brylcreemd down like usual, and stood up on the sides and the back.

"I get a phone call from some weasel underling of that Old Cocksucker, informing me that he's dead, and you're stealing from his tomb. I try to contact you, find out that you are indeed removing files from the director's office, and that you won't take my calls. Now, I should've sent one of my boys over here, but I figured they're still walking on tip-toe around you because you're in fucking mourning, and this don't require tip-toe. Especially since you got to be wondering about now what the hell you did to deserve all of this."

"Deserve what?" Kennedy had expected LBJ's anger, but he hadn't expected it so soon. He also hadn't expected it here, in his office, instead of in the Oval Office a day or so later.

"Well, there's only two things that tie J. Edgar and your brother. The first is that someone was gunning for them and succeeded. The second is that they went after the mob on your bidding. There's a lot of shit running around here that says your brother's shooting was a mob hit, and I know personally that J. Edgar was doing his best to make it seem like that Oswald character acted alone. But now Edgar is dead and Jack is dead and the only tie they have is the way they kowtowed to your stupid prosecution of the men that got your brother elected."

Kennedy felt lightheaded. He hadn't even thought that the deaths of his brother and J. Edgar were connected. But LBJ had a point. Maybe there was a conspiracy to kill government officials. Maybe the mob was showing its power. He'd had warning.

Hell, he'd had suspicions. He hadn't let himself look at any of the evidence in his brother's assassination, not after he secured the body and prevented a disastrous autopsy in Texas. If those doctors at

Parkland had done their job, they would've seen just how advanced Jack's Addison's disease was. The best kept secret of the Kennedy Administration—an administration full of secrets—was how close Jack was to incapacitation and death.

Kennedy clutched the file box. But LBJ knew that. He knew a lot of the secrets—had even promised to keep a few of them. And he wanted the files as badly as Kennedy did.

There had to be a lot in here on LBJ too. Not just the women, which was something he had in common with Jack, but other things, from his days in Congress.

"From what I heard," Kennedy said, making certain his voice was calm even though he wasn't, "all they know is someone shot Hoover. Did you get more details than that? Something that mentions organized crime in particular?"

"I'm sure it'll come out," LBJ said.

"You're sure that saying such things would upset me," Kennedy said. "You're after the files."

"Damn straight," LBJ said. "I'm the head of this government. Those files are mine."

"You're the head of this government for another year. Next January, someone'll take the oath of office and it might not be you. Do you really want to claim these in the name of the presidency? Because you might be handing them over to Goldwater come January."

LBJ blanched.

Someone knocked on the door, and startled both men. Kennedy frowned. He couldn't think of anyone who would have enough nerve to interrupt him when he was getting shouted at by LBJ. But someone had.

LBJ pulled the door open. Helen Gandy stood there.

"You boys can be heard in the hallway," she said, sweeping in as if the leader of the free world wasn't holding the door for her. "And it's embarrassing. It was precisely this kind of thing the director hoped to avoid."

Then she nodded at LBJ. Kennedy watched her. The dragon lady. Jack, as usual, had been right with his jibes. Only the dragon lady would walk in here as if she were the most important person in the room.

"Mr. President," she said, "these files are the director's personal business. He wanted me to take care of them, and get them out of the office, where they do not belong."

"Personal files, Miss Gandy?" LBJ asked. "These are his secret files."

"If they were secret, Mr. President, then you wouldn't be here. Mr. Hoover kept his secrets."

Mr. Hoover used his secrets, Kennedy thought, but didn't say.

"These are just his confidential files," Miss Gandy was saying. "Let me take care of them and they won't be here to tempt anyone. That's what the director wanted."

"These are government property," LBJ said with a sly look at Kennedy. For the first time, Kennedy realized his Goldwater argument had gotten through. "They belong here. I do thank you for your time and concern, though, ma'am."

Then he gave her a courtly little bow, put his hand on the small of her back, and propelled her out of the room.

Despite himself Kennedy was impressed. He'd never seen anyone handle the dragon lady that efficiently before.

LBJ grabbed one of the cabinets and slid it in front of the door he had just closed. Kennedy had forgotten how strong the man was. He had invited Kennedy down to his Texas ranch before the election, trying to find out what Kennedy was made of, and instead, Kennedy had realized just what LBJ was made of—strength, not bluster, brains *and* brawn.

He'd do well to remember that.

"All right," LBJ said as he turned around. "Here's what I'm gonna offer. You can have your family's files. You can watch while we search for them and you can have everything. Just give me the rest."

Kennedy raised his eyebrows. He hadn't felt this alive since November. "No."

"I can fire your ass in five minutes, put someone else in this fancy office, and then you can't do a goddamn thing," LBJ said. "I'm being kind."

"There's historical precedent for a cabinet member barricading himself in his office after he got fired," Kennedy said. "Seems to me it happened to a previous president named Johnson. While I'm barricaded in, I'll just go through the files and find out everything I need to know."

LBJ crossed his arms.

It was a standoff and neither of them had a good play. They only had a guess as to what was in those files—not just theirs but all of the others as well. They did know that whatever was in those files had given Hoover enough power to last in the office for more than forty years.

The files had brought down presidents. They could bring down congressmen, supreme court justices, and maybe even the current president. In that way, Helen Gandy was right.

The best solution was to destroy everything.

Only Kennedy wouldn't. Just like he knew LBJ wouldn't. There was too much history here, too much knowledge.

And too much power.

"These are our files," Kennedy said after a moment, although the word "our" galled him, "yours and mine. Right now we control them."

LBJ nodded, almost imperceptivity. "What do you want?"

What did he want? To be left alone? To have his family left alone? At midnight, he might have said that. But now, his old self was reasserting itself. He felt like the man who had gone after the corrupt leaders of the Teamsters, not the man who had accidentally gotten his brother murdered.

Besides, there might be things in that file that could head off other problems in the future. Other murders. Other manipulations.

He needed a bulletproof position. LBJ was right: the attorney general could be fired. But there was one position, constitutionally, that the president couldn't touch.

"I want to be your vice president," Kennedy said. "And in 1972, when you can't run again, I want your endorsement. I want you to back me for the nomination."

LBJ swallowed hard. Color suffused his face and for a moment, Kennedy thought he was going to shout again.

But he didn't.

Instead he said, "And what happens if we don't win?"

"We move these to a location of our choosing. And we do it with trusted associates. We get this stuff out of here."

LBJ glanced at the door. He was clearly thinking of what Helen Gandy had said, how it was better to be rid of all of this than it was to have it corrupting the office, endangering everyone.

But if LBJ and Kennedy controlled the entire cache, they also controlled their own files. LBJ could destroy his and Kennedy could preserve his family's legacy.

If it weren't for the fact that LBJ hated him almost as much as Kennedy hated LBJ, the decision would be easy.

"You'd trust me to a gentleman's agreement?" LBJ asked, not disguising the sarcasm in his tone. He knew Kennedy thought he was too uncouth to ever be considered a gentleman.

"You know where your interests lie. Just like I do," Kennedy said. "If we don't let Miss Gandy have the files, then this is the only choice."

LBJ sighed. "I hoped to be rid of the Kennedys by inauguration day."

"And what if I planned to run against you?" Kennedy asked, even though he knew he wouldn't. Already the party stalwarts had been approaching him about a 1964 presidential bid, and he had put them off. He had been too shaky, too emotionally fragile.

He didn't feel fragile now.

LBJ didn't answer that question. Instead, he said, "You can be an incautious asshole. Why should I trust you?"

"Because I saved Jack's ass more times than you can count," Kennedy said. "I'm saving yours too."

"How do you figure?" LBJ asked.

"Your fear of those files brought you to me, Mr. President." Kennedy put an emphasis on the title, which he usually avoided using around LBJ. "If I barricade myself in here, I'll have the keys to the kingdom and no qualms about letting the information free when I go free. If you work with me, your secrets remain just secrets."

"You're a son of bitch, you know that?" LBJ asked.

Kennedy nodded. "The hell of it is you are too or you wouldn't've brought up Jack's death before we knew what really happened to Hoover. So let's control the presidency for the next sixteen years. By then the information in these files will probably be worthless."

LBJ stared at him. It took Kennedy a minute to realize that although he'd won the argument, he wouldn't get an agreement from LBJ, not if Kennedy didn't make the first move.

Kennedy held out his hand. "Deal?"

LBJ stared at Kennedy's extended hand for a long moment before taking it in his own big clammy one.

"You goddamn son of a bitch," LBJ said. "You've got a deal."

It took Bryce only one phone call. The guy who ran the motor pool told him who checked out the sedan without asking why Bryce want to know. And Bryce, as he leaned in the cold telephone booth half a block from the first crime scene, instantly understood what had happened and why.

The agent who checked out the sedan was Walter Cain. He should've been on extended leave. Bryce had recommended it after he had told Cain that his ex-fiancé had tried to commit suicide. On getting the news, Cain had just had that look, that blank, my-life-is-over look.

And it had scared Bryce. Scared him enough that he asked Cain be put on indefinite leave. How long ago had that been? Less than twelve hours.

More than enough time to get rid of the morals police—the one man who made all the rules at the FBI. The man who had no morals himself.

J. Edgar Hoover.

Bryce had spent the past week studying Cain's file. Cain had had HooverWatch off and on throughout the past year. Cain knew the procedure, and he knew how to thwart it.

He'd killed five agents.

Because no one would listen to Bryce about that vacant look in Cain's eye.

Bryce let himself out of the phone booth. He walked back to the coroner's van. If he didn't have back up by now, he'd call for some all over again. They couldn't leave him hanging on this. They had to let him know, if nothing else, what to do with the director's body.

But he needn't've worried. When he got back to the alley, he saw five more sedans, all FBI issue. And as he stepped into the alley proper, the first person he saw was his boss, crouching over Hoover's corpse.

"I thought I told you to secure the scene," said the SAC for the District of New York, Eugene Hart. "In fact, I ordered you to do it."

"The scene extends over six blocks. I'm just one guy," Bryce said.

Hart walked over to him. He looked tired.

"I need to speak to you," Bryce said. He walked Hart back to the two sedans, explained what he'd learned, and watched Hart's face.

The man flinched, then, to Bryce's surprise, put his hand on Bryce's shoulder. "It's good work."

Bryce didn't thank him. He was worried that Hart hadn't asked any questions. "I'd heard Cain bitch more than once about Hoover setting the moral values for the office. And with what happened this week—"

"I know." Hart squeezed his shoulder. "We'll take care of it."

Bryce turned so quickly that he made Hart lose his grip. "You're going to cover it up."

Hart closed his eyes.

"You weren't hanging me out to dry. You were trying to figure out how to handle this. Son of bitch. And you're going to let Cain walk."

"He won't walk," Hart said. "He'll just . . . be guilty of something else."

"You can't cover this up. It's too important. So soon after President Kennedy—"

"That's precisely why we're going to handle it," Hart said. "We don't want a panic."

"And you don't want anyone to know where Hoover and Tolson were found. What're you going to say? That they died of natural causes in their beds? Their *separate* beds?"

"It's not your concern," Hart said. "You've done well for us. You'll be rewarded."

"If I keep my mouth shut."

Hart sighed. He didn't seem to have the energy to glare. "I don't honestly care. I'm glad to have the old man gone. But I'm not in charge of this. We've got orders now, and everything'll get taken care of at a much higher level than either you or me. You should be grateful for that."

Bryce supposed he should be. It took the political pressure off him. It also took the personal pressure off.

But he couldn't help feeling if someone had listened to him before, if someone had paid attention, then none of this would have happened.

No one cared that an FBI agent was going to marry a former prostitute. If the Bureau knew—and it did, then not even the KGB could use that as blackmail.

It was all about appearances. It would always be about appearances. Hoover had designed a damn booklet about appearances, and it hadn't stopped him from getting shot in a back alley after a party he would never admit attending.

Hoover had been so worried about people using secrets against each other, he hadn't even realized how his own secrets could be used against him.

Bryce looked at Hart. They were both tired. It had been a long night. And it would be an even longer few weeks for Hart. Bryce would get some don't-tell promotion and he'd stay there for as long as he had to. He had to make sure that Cain got prosecuted for something, that he paid for five deaths.

Then Bryce would resign.

He didn't need the Bureau, any more than he had needed Mary, his own pre-approved wife. Maybe he'd talk to O'Reilly, see if he could put in a good word with the NYPD. At least the NYPD occasionally investigated cases.

If they happened in the right neighborhood.

To the right people.

Bryce shoved his hands in his pockets and walked back to his apartment. Hart didn't try to stop him. They both knew Bryce's work on this case was done. He wouldn't even have to write a report.

In fact, he didn't dare write a report, didn't dare put any of this on paper where someone else might discover it. The wrong someone. Someone who didn't care about handling and the proper information.

Someone who would use that information to his own benefit.

Like the director had.

For more than forty-five years.

Bryce shook the thought off. It wasn't his concern. He no longer had concerns. Except getting a good night's sleep.

And somehow he knew that he wouldn't get one of those for a long, long time.

The End of the World

Then

*T*HE AIR REEKED OF SMOKE.

The people ran, and the others chased them.

She kept tripping. Momma pulled her forward, but Momma's hand was slippery. Her hand slid out, and she fell, sprawling on the wooden sidewalk.

Momma reached for her, but the crowd swept Momma forward.

All she saw was Momma's face, panicked, her hands, grasping, and then Momma was gone.

Everyone ran around her, over her, on her. She put her hands over her head and cringed, curling herself into a little ball.

She made herself change color. Brown-gray like the sidewalk, with black lines running up and down.

Dress hems skimmed over her. Boots brushed her. Heels pinched the skin on her arms.

No spikes, Momma always said. *No spikes or they'll know.*

So she held her breath, hoping the spikes wouldn't break through her skin because she was so scared, and her side hurt where someone's boot hit it, and the wooden sidewalk bounced as more and more people ran past her.

Finally, she started squinching, like Daddy taught her before he left.

Slide, he said. *A little bit at a time. Slide. Squinch onto whatever surface you're on and cling.*

It was hard to squinch without spikes, but she did, her head tucked in her belly, her hair trailing to one side. More boots stomped on it, pulling it, but she bit her lower lip so that she wouldn't have to think about the pain.

She was almost to the bank door when the sidewalk stopped shaking. No one ran by her. She was alone.

She flattened herself against the brick and shuddered. Her skin smelled of chewing tobacco, spit, and beer from the saloon next door.

She had shut down her ears, but she finally rotated them outward. Men were shouting, women yelling. There was pounding and screaming and a high-pitched noise she didn't like.

If they found her flattened against the brick, they'd know. If they saw the spikes rise from her body, they'd know. If they saw her squinching, they'd know.

But she couldn't move.

She was shivering, and she didn't know what to do.

Now

The call didn't come through channels. It rang to Becca Keller's personal cell.

Chase Waterston hadn't even said hello.

"Got a problem at the End of the World," he'd said, his usually self-assured voice shaky. "Can you get here right away? Just you."

Normally, she would have told him to call the precinct or 911, but something stopped her. Probably that scared edge to his voice, a sound she'd never heard in all the years she'd known him.

She drove from the center of downtown Hope to the End of the World, a drive that, in the old days, would have taken five minutes. Now it took twenty, and the only thing that kept her from being annoyed at the traffic were the mountains, bleak and cold, rising up like goddesses at the edge of Hope.

Hope was a mountain city, but its terrain was high desert. Vast expanses of brown still marked the outskirts of town, although the interior had lost much of its desert feel. By the time she passed the latest ticky-tacky development, she hit the rolling dunes of her childhood. Even though she had on the air-conditioning, the smell of sagebrush blew in—full of promise.

If she kept going straight too much farther, she'd hit small, windy roads filled with switchbacks that led to now-trendy ski resorts. If she turned right, she'd follow the old stagecoach route over the edge of the mountains into the Willamette Valley where most of Oregon's population lived.

The End of the World was an ancient resort at the fork between the mountain roads and the old stagecoach route. At the turn of the previous century, some enterprising entrepreneur figured travelers who were taking the narrow road toward the Willamette Valley would welcome a place to rest and recover from the long, dusty trip.

Now bumper-to-bumper traffic filled that wagon route, which had expanded to a four-lane highway. Hope actually had a real rush hour, thanks to ex-patriate Californians, retired baby boomers, and ridiculously cheap housing.

Chase was rebuilding the resort for those baby boomers and Californians. For some reason, he thought they'd want to stay in a hundred-year-old hotel, with a view of the mountains and the river, even in the heat of the summer and the deep cold of the desert winter.

Becca steered the squad with her left hand and fiddled with the air-conditioner with her right, wishing her own car was out of the shop. No matter what she did, she couldn't get the squad car cooled. Nothing seemed to be working properly. Or maybe that was the effect of the heat.

It was a hundred and three degrees, and the third week without rain. The radio's most recent weather report promised the temperature would reach one hundred and eight by the time the day was over.

Finally, she reached the construction site.

Chase had set up the site so that it only blocked part of the ever-present wind and as a consequence, the dust billowed across the highway with the gusts.

The city had cited Chase twice for the hazard, and he'd promised to fix it just after the Fourth of July holiday. It looked like he'd been keeping his word, too. A huge plastic construction fence leaned against the old building. Graders and post-diggers were parked on the side of the road.

Nothing moved. Not the cats Chase had been using to dig out the old parking lot, not the crane he'd rented the week before, and not the crew, most of whom sat on the backs of pickup trucks, their faces blackened with dust and grime and too much sun. She could see their eyes, white against the darkness of their skins, watching her as she turned onto the dirt path that Chase had been using as an access road.

He was waiting for her in the doorway of what had once been a natatorium. Built over an old underground spring, the Natatorium had once boasted the largest swimming pool in Eastern Oregon. There was some kind of pipe system that pumped water into the pool, keeping it perpetually cold. In the Natatorium's heyday, the water had been replaced daily.

Behind the Natatorium was the old five-story brick hotel that still had the original fixtures. No vandals had ever attacked the place. Even the windows were intact.

Becca had gone inside more than once, first as an impressionable twelve-year-old, and ever since, part of her believed the rumors that the hotel was haunted.

She pulled up beside the Natatorium door, in a tiny patch of shade provided by the overhanging roof. She got out and the blast-furnace heat hit her, prickling sweat on her skin almost instantly. Apparently the air conditioner had been working in the piece-of-crap squad after all.

Chase watched her. His lips were chapped, his skin fried blackish red from the sun. He had weather-wrinkles around his eyes and narrow mouth. His hair was cropped short, and over it he wore a regulation hard hat. He clutched another one in his left hand, slapping it rhythmically against his thigh.

"Thanks for coming, Becca," he said, and he still sounded shaken.

The tone was unfamiliar, but the expression on his face wasn't. She'd seen it only once, after she'd told him she wanted out, that his values and hers were so different, she couldn't stomach a relationship any longer.

"What do you got, Chase?" she asked.

"Come with me." He handed her the hard hat he'd been holding.

She took it as a gust of wind caught her short hair and blew its clipped edges into her face. She slipped the hard hat on, and tucked her hair underneath it, then followed Chase inside the building.

It was hotter inside the Natatorium, and the air smelled of rot and mold. She usually thought of those as humidity smells, but the Natatorium's interior was so dry that it was crumbly.

The floor was shredded with age, the wood so brittle that she wondered if it would hold her weight. Most of the walls were gone, the remains of them piled in a corner. Chase had gutted the interior.

When she had been a girl, she had played in this place. Her parents had forbidden her to come, which made it all the more inviting. The rot and mold smells had been present even then. But the walls had still been up, and there had been some ancient furniture in here as well, made unusable by weather and critters chewing the interior.

She used to stand inside the entrance with the door open, the stream of sunlight carrying a spinning tunnel of dust motes. When she closed her eyes halfway, she could just imagine the people arriving here after a long day of travel, happy to be in a place of such elegance, such warmth.

But now even that sense of a long ago but lively past was gone, and all that remained was the shell of the building itself—a hazard, an eyesore, something to be torn down and replaced.

Chase's boots echoed on the wood floor. He led her along the edges, pointing at holes closer to the center. She wondered if any of his employees had caused the holes, walking imprudently across the floor, foot catching on the weak spot, and then slipping through.

He was taking her to the employees' staircase in the back. When they reached it, she saw why. It was made of metal. Rusted metal, but metal all the same. Someone had recently bolted the stairs into the wall, probably under Chase's orders. A metal hand railing had been reinforced as well.

Chase looked over his shoulder to make sure she was following. She caught a glimpse of something in his face—reluctance? Fear? She couldn't quite tell—and then, as suddenly as it appeared, it was gone.

He went down the steps two at a time. She followed. Even though the handrail had been rebolted, the metal still flaked under her hand. The bolts might hold if she suddenly fell through the stairs but she wasn't sure if the railing would.

The smell grew stronger here, as if the mold had somehow managed to survive the dry summers. The farther down she went, the cooler the air got. It was still hot, but no longer oppressive.

Chase stopped at the bottom of the stairs. He watched her come down the last few, his gaze holding hers. The intensity of his gaze startled her. It was vulnerable, in a way she hadn't seen since their first year together.

Then he stepped away so that she could stand on the floor below.

The smell was so strong that it overwhelmed her. Beneath the mold and rot, there was something else, something familiar, something foul. It made the hair rise on the back of her neck.

"That way," Chase said, and this time she wasn't mistaking it. His voice was shaking. "I'll wait here."

She frowned at him, and then kept going. The floor here was covered in ceramic tile, chipped and broken, but sturdy. She wondered what was beneath it. Ground? Old-fashioned concrete? Wood? She couldn't tell. But the floor didn't creak here, and it felt solid.

A long wall hid everything from view. A door stood open, sending in sunlight filled with dust motes, just like she remembered. Only there shouldn't be sunlight here. This was the basement, the miraculous swimming pool, the place that had helped make the End of the World famous.

She stepped through the door.

The light came from the back wall—or what had been the back. Chase's crew had destroyed this part of the building.

The basement of the End of the World was open to the air for the first time since it had been completed.

That strange feeling she'd had since she reached the bottom of the stairs grew. If the basement wasn't sealed, then the stench shouldn't have been so strong. The old air should have escaped, letting the freshness of the desert inside.

Some of the heat had trickled in, but not enough to dissipate the natural coolness. She stepped forward. The tile on the other side of the pool was hidden under mounds of dirt. The pool itself was half destroyed, but the cat which had done the damage wasn't anywhere near it. She could see the big tire tracks, scored deeply into the sandy earth, as if the cat itself had been stuck or if the operator had tried to escape in a hurry.

They had uncovered something. That much was clear. And she was beginning to get an idea as to what it was.

A body.

Given the smell, it had to have died here recently. Bodies didn't decay in the desert—not in the dry air and the sand. Inside a building like this, there might be standard decomposition, but considering how hot it had been, even that seemed unlikely.

She'd have to assume cause of death was suspicious because the body had been located here. And then she'd have to figure out a way to find out whose body it was.

She was already planning how she'd conduct her case when she stepped off the tile onto a mound of dirt, and peered into the gaping hole, and saw—

Bones. Piles of bones. Recognizable bones. Femurs, hipbones, pelvic bones, rib cages. Hundreds of human bones. And more skulls than she could count.

She rocked back on her heels, pressing her free hand to her face, the smell—the illogical and impossible smell—now turning her stomach.

A mass grave, of the kind she'd only seen in film or police academy photos.

A mass grave, anywhere from a hundred to seventy-five years old.

A mass grave, in Hope. She hadn't even heard rumors of it, and she had lived here all her life.

"Son of a bitch," she said.

"Yeah," Chase said from the stairs, "I couldn't agree more."

Then

The screaming sent ripples through her. She couldn't complete the change. She couldn't even assume the color and texture of the brick.

Tears pricked her eyes. Tears, as big a giveaway as her hair, her fingers, her ears. Somehow, when she stopped the spikes, she stopped all her abilities.

Or maybe it was just the fear.

A door squeaked open, then boots hit the sidewalk. Polished boots with only a layer of black dust along the edge. Men's boots, not the dainty things Momma tried to wear.

She tried to will the shivering away, but she couldn't.

She couldn't move at all.

Not that she had anywhere to go.

She could only pray that he wouldn't look down, that he wouldn't see her, that she would be safe for just a little longer.

Now

Becca stared at the hole. She couldn't even count all the skulls, rising like white stones out of the dirt. Not to mention the rib cages off to one side or the tiny bones lying in a corner, bones that probably belonged in a hand or a foot.

She couldn't do much on her own. But she could find out where that stink was coming from.

She turned around and headed for the stairs.

Chase tipped his hard hat back, revealing his dark eyes. "Where're you going?"

"To get some things from my evidence bag," Becca said.

"You're not going to call anyone, are you?" he asked.

She stopped in front of him. "I can't take care of this alone. You should know that."

He leaned against the railing, that assumed casual gesture, which meant he was the most distressed. "This'll ruin me, Becca. Half my capital is in this place."

"You told me no good businessman ever invests his own money," she snapped, mostly because she was surprised.

He shrugged. "Guess I'm not a good businessman."

But he was. He had restored three of the downtown's oldest buildings, making them into expensive condominiums with views of the mountains. Single-handedly, he'd revitalized Hope's downtown, by adding trendy stores that the locals claimed would never succeed (yet somehow they did, thanks to the "foreigners," as the Californians were called) and restaurants so upscale that Becca would have to spend half a week's pay just to eat lunch.

"You knew I'd go by the book when you called me here," she said, more sharply than she intended. He'd gotten to her. That was the problem; he always did.

"I thought maybe we could talk. They're old bones. If we can get someone to recover them and keep it quiet—"

"How many workers saw this?" she asked. "Do you think they'll keep it quiet?"

"If I pay them enough," he said. "And if we move the bones to a proper cemetery."

"Is that what you think this is?" she asked. "A graveyard?"

"Isn't it?" He seemed genuinely surprised. "It was so far out in the desert when this place was built that it's possible—no, it's probable—that the memory of the graveyard got lost."

"I saw at least two ribcages with shattered bones, and several skulls looked crushed."

His lips trembled, and it was a moment before he spoke. "The equipment could have done that."

But he didn't sound convinced.

"It could have," she said. "But we need to know."

"Why?" he asked.

She looked over her shoulder. That patch of sunlight still glinted through the hole in the wall. The dust motes still floated. If she didn't look down, the place would seem just as beautiful and interesting as it always had.

"Because someone loved them once. Someone probably wants to know what happened to them."

"Someone?" He snorted. "Becca, the pool was put over a tennis court that was built at the turn of the 20th century. No one remembers these people. Only historians would care."

He paused, and she felt her breath catch.

Then he said, "This is my life."

He used a tone and inflection she used to find particularly mesmerizing. Once she told their couples therapist that with that tone, he could convince her to do anything, and that was when the therapist told her that she had to get out.

"It's a crime scene," Becca said, knowing that the argument was weak.

"You don't know that for sure, and even if it is, it's a hundred years old," he said.

"Then what's the smell?"

He frowned, clearly not understanding her.

"This is a desert, Chase. Bodies buried in dirt in a dry climate don't decay. They mummify."

He blinked. He obviously hadn't thought of that.

"And," she said, "even if they had decayed because of some strange environmental reason particular to this basement, they wouldn't smell after a hundred years."

That guarded expression had returned to his face. Only his eyes moved now.

"Maybe it's something small," he said. "A mouse, someone's lost cat."

She shook her head. "Smell's too strong, and over the entire building. If it were something small, the smell would have faded back when you broke open that wall."

"Not when it was dug up?" he asked, seeming surprised.

"No," she said. "Is that when you first smelled it?"

"That's when they called me."

They, meaning his crew. She frowned at him, wondering if he was going to blame them.

But for what? A smell?

She'd have to find the source before she made assumptions.
And that, she knew, was going to be hard.

Then

A hand touched her shoulder. A human hand, warm and gentle.
Another shivery ripple ran through her. She still had a shoulder; she
hadn't gotten rid of that either. How silly she must look, plastered
against the brick wall like a half-formed younglin.

Screams still echoed. The shouts had died down, although
sometimes they rose up altogether, like a group got excited about
something.

"You're one of them, aren't you?"

Male voice, human, just as gentle as the hand. She couldn't stop
shivering.

"I won't hurt you."

She resisted the urge to rotate an eye upward, so that she could
see more than the boot.

"But you better come with me before they find you."

That did startle her. Her eye moved before she could stop it. It
formed above her shoulder. He jumped back slightly when her eye
appeared, but his hand never left her skin, even though it was finally
turning tannish-red like the brick.

She'd seen him before. Daddy had laughed with him in the
good days. He had slicked-back hair and a narrow face and kind
eyes.

He crouched beside her, and looked right at her eye, like it
didn't bother him, even though she knew it did. He wouldn't've
jumped like that if it didn't.

"Please," he said, "come with me. I don't know when they're
coming back. And someone might see us. Please."

She had to form a mouth. Her nose remained, tucked against
her stomach from when she'd formed a ball, but her mouth had
disappeared when she had tried to take on the appearance of the
wooden sidewalk.

It took all her strength to make the mouth come out near the
eye, and from the look of disgust that passed over his face, she still
didn't look right. Her hair was on the other side of her body, and her
eye was just above her shoulder. The mouth had probably come out
on what would have been her back if she put herself together right.

Right being human.

That's what Momma said.

Momma.

"Please," he said again, and this time, she heard panic in his voice.

"Stuck," she said.

"Oh, Christ." He looked up and down the street, then at the buildings across from it.

He seemed younger than she remembered, or maybe she was as bad at telling human ages like Momma was.

"How do we get you unstuck?" he asked.

She didn't know. She'd never been like this, not this scared, not all by herself.

She tried to shrug and felt her other shoulder form into the wood. A splinter dug into her skin, and her entire body turned red with pain.

"What a mess," he said, and she didn't know if he meant her or what was going on or how scared they both seemed to be.

She willed herself to let go, but she was attached to the brick, and she'd lost control of half her body functions. Daddy said fear would do that.

Whatever happens, baby, he'd say, *you have to trust us. You have to believe we'll get together again. Let that be your strength, so that you never, ever succumb to fear.*

But he'd been gone for a long time now. And Momma hadn't come back for her, even though people were screaming.

The man tried to pry a flat corner of her skin from the edge of the brick. She could feel the tug, saw his face scrunch up in disgust when he got to the sticky underneath part.

"How'd you get there?" he asked.

"Squinched," she said.

"Squinched." He didn't understand. And she spoke his language, she knew she did. She formed the right mouth, she'd been using the words for a long time now, and she knew how they felt inside her brain and out.

"Can you show me?" he asked. "Can you squinch onto my arm?"

She wasn't supposed to squinch to a human. Momma was strict about that. Like there was something bad about it, something awful would happen.

But something awful was happening now.

The screams . . .

"No," she said, even though that had to be a lie. Momma and Daddy wouldn't forbid something if she couldn't've done it in the first place.

"God," he said, then looked down the street where the screams had come from. Where the shouts had grown more and more angry every time they rose up.

Right now, it was quiet, and she hated that more.

She hated it all.

"Stay here," he said.

He stood up, letting go of her shoulder. The warm vanished, and the fear rose even worse. Her other shoulder disappeared, and she felt the spikes, threatening to appear.

She had to close both eyes and will the spikes away.

When she opened the eyes, he was gone.

She moved the eyes all over her skin, looking for him, and she didn't see him at all.

The street was still empty, and too quiet.

Then, faraway, someone laughed. A mean, nasty, brittle laugh.

She folded her ears inside her skin, and willed herself flat, hoping, this time, that it would work.

Now

Becca climbed the stairs, clinging to the handrail, the rust flaking against her palms. She had to call for help. At most, she needed a coroner, and probably a few officers just to search for the source of that smell.

But she felt guilty about calling. Chase used to talk about restoring the End of the World when she'd met him. He had brought her out here on their first date, even though she'd told him that she had explored the property repeatedly when she was a child.

Maybe they'd be able to keep this out of the paper, particularly if it turned out to be a graveyard or a dumping ground. But even that probably wouldn't happen.

The newspapers seemed to love this kind of story.

If she reported this, she would condemn Chase's project to a kind of limbo. With so much capital invested, he probably couldn't afford to wait until the legal issues were solved.

She almost turned around to ask him how much time he could give them, but then she'd be compromising the investigation. For all she knew, there was a recently killed human beneath that dirt, and someone (Chase?) was using the old bones to hide it.

Then she shook her head. Not Chase. He was manipulative and difficult, moody and untrustworthy, but he wasn't—nor had he ever been—violent.

She sighed and continued up the stairs. Much as she wanted to help him, she couldn't. She had an obligation to the entire community.

She had an obligation to herself.

The wind hit her the moment she stepped outside. Bits of sand stung her skin, sticking to the sweat. Even with the sun, it now felt cooler out here because of that wind.

The construction workers watched her. She didn't know most of them; the town had grown too big for her to know everyone by sight like she had when she was a child. Many of these workers were Hispanic, some of them probably illegal.

Hispanics expected her to check their papers. She was supposed to do that too, although she never did. She didn't object to people who worked hard and tried to improve their lives.

With one hand, she tipped her hard hat back and nodded toward the workers. Then she opened the squad's driver's door, and winced at the heat that poured out at her. She leaned inside, unwilling to go into that heat voluntarily, and grabbed the radio's handset.

She paused before turning it on, knowing that even that momentary hesitation was a victory for Chase.

Then she clicked the handset and asked the dispatch to send Jillian Mills.

Jillian Mills was the head coroner for Hope and the surrounding counties. She actually worked the job full time, but her assistants were dentists and veterinarians, and one retired doctor.

"You want the crime scene unit?" the dispatch asked. It was standard procedure for a crime scene unit to come with the coroner.

"Not yet," Becca said. "I'm not sure what exactly we have here, except that it's dead."

Which was technically true, if she ignored all the crushed and broken bones.

"Tell her to hurry," Becca added. "It's hot as hell out here and there's a construction crew waiting."

That usually worked to get any city official moving. Lately, the "foreigners" had taken to suing the city if their emergency or official personnel delayed money-making operations, even for a day.

Chase would never do that—he knew that getting along with the city helped his permits go through and his iffy projects get approved —but Becca still used the excuse.

She didn't want to be here any longer than she had to.

She stood, lifted her hard hat, and wiped the sweat off her forehead. Then she closed the door and leaned on it for a moment.

The End of the World.

She wondered if Chase had ever thought that the name might have been prophetic.

Then

She had shut down her ears, and didn't know he had come back until the sidewalk shook. She opened her eyes. He stood above her holding a long wooden box. His mouth was moving, but he kept looking down the street. A single bead of sweat ran down one side of his face.

She unfolded her ears, and said, "What?"

"This can hide you," he said, setting the box on the sidewalk. He glanced at her, then looked away. "Think maybe you can squinch into it?"

He set the box in front of her. It did cover her strangeness from anyone who didn't look too hard.

Her shivering stopped.

"Maybe," she said.

"Well," he said, wiping at that drop of sweat, "the sooner you squinch, the better chance I have of getting you out of here."

That brought a shiver. She looked at the box, saw it had some dirt inside. He had taken it from some kind of storage.

If she just thought about the box—not the screaming (which seemed to be gone? How come it was gone?)—not the way Momma's hand had slipped through hers, not the fall against the sidewalk, not the bruises that still radiated through her skin, maybe then she could squinch to it.

She'd have to stare at it like a younglin, think only of the box, only of the box and becoming part of it . . .

A long, drawn out scream sent ripples through her.

"Jesus," the man said and closed his eyes.

She squinched. She had to. The scream made her move. She squinched to the edge of the box, then cowered against the back, just a blob, as small as she could make herself.

"Mister?" she said and heard the terror in her voice. She wasn't sure why she was trusting him, but she didn't have a lot of choice.

That scream sounded like Momma.

He looked down, and his shoulders slumped.

"Thank God," he said, and picked up the box.

He tucked it under his arm like it weighed nothing, and hurried back through the door.

Now

Jillian drove the white coroner's van. Becca's breath caught as she scanned the windshield, looking for an assistant.

There was none. Either none was available, or dispatch conveyed the message about the stalled work crew.

Either way, Becca was grateful.

She finished the last of her water and tossed the bottle in a nearby recycling can. She had waited up here, unwilling to go back inside without Jillian.

Or maybe she had just been unwilling to talk to Chase again.

He had come out of the basement after about ten minutes. He saw her near the squad, shook his head slightly, and sat against one of the cats, his face half-hidden by shade.

She didn't go to talk to him and he didn't talk to her. They both knew the futility of these kinds of arguments. Once again, she and Chase were on opposite paths, and trying to influence each other would only end in misery.

Jillian got out of the van. Her hair was already pulled back and tucked in a net. She was small and delicate, with skin so pale that it almost looked translucent. She seemed fragile at first glance, but Becca had seen her split a corpse's ribcage open with her bare hands.

"What've we got?" Jillian asked.

"I'm not sure," Becca said. She grabbed the flashlight and gloves from her own kit, as well as the portable radio, and led Jillian inside.

Chase didn't come with them. Instead, he watched them go with the same wariness that his crew had.

Becca was relieved. She half-hoped that Jillian hadn't noticed him, standing in the shade.

They were on the steps to the basement before Jillian said, "This is Chase Waterston's project, isn't it?"

"Unfortunately," Becca said.

Jillian knew Becca's troubles with Chase. It had been no-nonsense Jillian who had listened to Becca's difficulties extricating herself from Chase's world.

I'm a cop, she used to say, it seemed, during every conversation. *I shouldn't be so easily influenced.*

We all have a hook that'll draw us in, Jillian would respond. *He knows how to find yours.*

He did too. There should have been a full team here, along with a crime scene unit.

Jillian probably knew it just from the smell.

She stopped at the bottom of the stairs and looked around. "Where's the body?"

Becca had thought about how to answer that one the entire time she waited for Jillian.

"I don't know where the smell is coming from," Becca said. "But it's not our only problem."

Jillian glanced at her sideways. Becca sighed and led her to the hole.

The sun had moved away from the gap in the wall, no longer sending rays filled with dust motes into the basement. But the light was still strong enough that she didn't need a flashlight to lead Jillian to the dig itself.

"Chase thinks this is an old cemetery," Becca said as she approached.

"You don't," Jillian said, slipping on her gloves. "So you brought me here to be the bad guy."

Maybe she had. Or maybe she just needed someone between her and Chase, someone sensible.

She didn't say any more. Instead, she turned on the flashlight and turned it to the ribcages and skulls.

"Mother of God," Jillian said, touching the tiny cross she wore around her neck even though her Catholicism had lapsed decades ago. "This is going to take an entire team."

"I know," Becca said softly.

They stared for a long moment. Becca didn't move the flashlight beam. Finally, Jillian grabbed it from her and swept the entire large hole. The light caught more bits of bone, scattered throughout the dirt.

"How'd you even get me here?" Jillian asked. "Chase has to know this will ruin him."

"He does." Becca didn't look at Jillian.

"So he called you." Jillian shook her head. "Bastard."

"Jillian, it's bad enough."

"It's bad enough that he thought you'd cover for him."

"He didn't ask that," Becca said. But he had, hadn't he? He asked that this be handled quickly and discreetly and with a minimum of fuss.

Although he stopped arguing when she explained about the smell.

God, she was still making excuses for him, and she was no longer married to him.

"He knows I'm going to do this right."

"He knows," Becca said.

"That'll mean the media'll get wind."

"Let's try to prevent that as long as possible."

"So Chase can save his ass?"

"So that we don't have weirdoes contaminating the crime scene."

"You didn't block it off. It could be contaminated now."

Becca pursed her lips. "I kept an eye on everyone."

"I hope so," Jillian said. "I'm going to call for back-up."

Becca nodded.

Jillian didn't move, even though she said she was going to. "You think maybe you should take yourself off this investigation?"

Becca'd been thinking about it. "I'm the only qualified investigator we have. Everyone else has been promoted through the ranks and most haven't even completed the crime lab courses."

Because they were only offered in the Willamette Valley, and that was more than two hours from here. The department couldn't afford to lose personnel for days on end just so that they could have classes in criminal justice, classes that the chief—a good ole boy who had worked his way through the ranks without a damn class, thank you—didn't believe anyone needed, not even his detectives.

Jillian sighed. "You've got a conflict."

"No kidding."

"What if Chase is behind the smell?"

Becca almost said, *He isn't*, but she stopped herself in time. "I'll treat him like anyone else."

Even though she knew that was a lie the moment she spoke it.

"No matter what you do, everyone'll think you're soft on him."

"Then everyone'll be supervising me, won't they?" Becca snapped.

Jillian put a hand on her shoulder. "Rethink this, Becca."

Becca sighed. "If this starts leading to Chase, maybe I will."

*　　*　　*

Then

He didn't take her very far. She managed to squinch part of herself to the edge of the box, away from his arm, and pop an eye forward.

They were inside the bank. No one else was. The afternoon sun filtered through the large windows, illuminating heavy wooden desks, the wide row of grills that people got money out of or put money into, the safe just behind the far door.

Momma and Daddy had brought her in here early, as part of her training in being "normal" and they explained how banks worked. She used to come with Daddy when he had money to deposit, but Momma didn't know how to get it when he went away.

Momma said maybe he got it, but she had that funny sound in her voice, the one that meant she really didn't believe it. She always sounded sad when she spoke of Daddy, and after a few weeks, she stopped speaking of him at all.

"We can't go far yet," the man said softly. "People'll wonder. They'll probably wonder why I was here, and not with them."

He said that last very, very softly. She almost didn't hear him.

He hurried to one of the desks near the back and set the box underneath it with one edge sticking out.

"If you can, stay low," he said. "It's safer."

She wondered how he knew. Maybe he could tell her what was going on. Because she didn't know at all.

Momma had smelled the smoke—they were burning Shanty-town, that's what Momma said. Then Momma grabbed her hand and pulled her to the safe place. She didn't know where that was either or what would happen there.

They had run to the middle of the town, right near the fanciest store where Momma liked to look through the windows sometimes, when people caught up to them. Running, just like they were, only the other people's running was different somehow.

Momma seemed really scared now. Some of the men smelled of kerosene, and one of them was laughing even though the edges of his hair were burned off.

Momma pulled and pulled and she was having trouble keeping up and people started looking at them and Momma tried to pick her up but didn't have the strength and she tried to keep running but she couldn't—she was getting so tired—and then she tripped and her hand slipped and she couldn't see Momma and she didn't know where Momma went or why she hadn't come back . . .

Except for the scream.

She closed her eyes and rolled up into a ball.

She wanted to forget the scream—and she couldn't, no matter how hard she tried.

Now

Jillian started to work in one corner of the hole. Becca took the far end of the basement, using her nose first to see where the smell was the strongest.

Jillian had contacted the crime scene investigators, asking for everyone not just the folks on duty, and another detective as well as some officers to handle the interviews. Becca should have done that. But Jillian was covering for her, getting her off the hook with Chase.

Both of them knew that Chase was their key. He could set up a lot of roadblocks to the investigation, and he might have already done so. Becca would try to find out by remaining close to him, buddying him, if she could.

Jillian wasn't sure that Becca could manipulate him. Hence the request for the second detective.

Becca wasn't going to argue with that. She wasn't going to argue with any of it. Not yet.

But she did know Chase well enough that if he had committed a crime, he wouldn't have done it in a way that would jeopardize his entire fortune. He would have covered it up creatively, hidden the body in the desert or taken it to Waloon Lake or maybe all the way to the ocean.

He was too smart to kill someone and call her. He knew that he could manipulate her, but he also knew that the manipulation didn't always work.

She took a breath. Olfactory nerves grew used to smells, but this one—the smell of rot and decay—never completely vanished. You could live with that smell for weeks, and still recognize it, unlike most other odors. It just wouldn't seem as strong to you as it did to others.

It was still new to her at the moment. And it wasn't coming from this part of the basement.

She walked the perimeter, sniffing the whole way, knowing she would regret this part of the investigation. Strong smells like this remained in the nose and in the memory. She would be able to recall it whenever she wanted.

As if she would want to.

After she finished, she walked the perimeter again, careful to use the same tracks.

Finally, she said, "It's coming from the hole."

"Of course," Jillian said. She had started in one corner as well.

When Becca spoke, Jillian leaned back on her knees, resting on her heels. She brushed her hands together, then surveyed the mess before them.

"This is beyond me," she said. "I don't know how to proceed. We're not trained for a disaster this big. I'm going to have to call in experts."

"Experts?" Becca asked.

"There are people who specialize in dealing with mass graves."

"So this is a graveyard."

Jillian looked at her, as if Becca had deliberately misunderstood her.

"Mass graves. Like the ones they found in Iraq or Bosnia or Nazi Germany."

Becca let out a small breath. The air felt thicker than desert air usually did. The odors seemed to be getting worse, not better.

"That's what this is? Some kind of massacre?"

"I don't know for sure. That's why I want experts. You want to protect Chase—"

Becca started to deny it, but then that was silly. She did want to protect Chase.

"—but I want to protect Hope."

It took her a moment to understand what Jillian had said.

"Protect Hope?"

"How much history do you know, Becca?" Jillian asked.

"I know enough to know that no large group of people has ever died in Hope. We still have our Chinatown, and we were one of the havens for blacks, even when the State of Oregon constitutionally banned them. We had that in school, Jillian, remember?"

"You think people talk about massacres?"

"I think people remember," Becca said. "I think massacres don't stay buried forever."

Jillian looked at the dirt before her. A snapped femur was only a few inches from her knees.

"You're right," Jillian said. "Nothing stays buried forever."

Then

"What's your name?" he asked after a little while.

The question startled her. The bank had been so quiet, even though she had kept one ear on top and an eye prepared. She could control the ears and the eyes and sometimes the mouth, she still hadn't got control over anything else. The shivers came less now, but they still came, rippling through her like water.

"It's okay," he said. "We're still alone."

Like that was the problem. Her family tried not to name anything. Names made items rigid.

Still, her parents had given her a human name, just so everyone had something to call her, and Momma said the name made it easier for her to keep her shape.

Maybe if she thought about it now . . .

He peered under the desk. "Are you all right?"

Another shiver ran through her and she couldn't find her mouth.

"They're not back yet."

If she had her human form, she'd nod. But she didn't. Then the mouth popped forward.

He moved away so fast, he hit his head on the underside of the desk.

"Sorry," he said. "You startled me."

"Sarah," she said.

"Hmm?" He frowned at her.

"I'm Sarah."

"Oh." He bit his upper lip, pulling it inward. "I'd thought maybe something more unusual. . . ."

He stopped talking, wiped a hand over his mouth, then smiled. "How about a last name?"

A second name. Momma had explained that too. The second name described your clan. The first name was just yours, special to you.

"Jones," she said.

"Jones," he repeated. "Earl Jones's daughter?"

Earl was what they decided to first-name Daddy.

"Yes," she said.

"Christ." He wiped his hand over his mouth again, then looked behind him. "I'm Jess Taylor. Your dad may have told you about me."

Daddy hadn't said anything about anybody, at least not to her. "Have you seen him lately? Your dad? I have some things for him."

Tears filled her eye, then her face—her human face—formed on top of her skin.

Jess Taylor's expression froze, then he smiled, even though the smile didn't look real.

She wanted to wipe the tear from her eye, but she didn't have hands. One started to form, and she willed it away. She had to stay small.

"You haven't seen him, have you?" Jess Taylor said.

"Not for a long time."

Jess nodded. Then he frowned. He slid out from under the desk, and sat up straight. She squinched to the edge of the box. He was looking at the windows, and now that he thought she couldn't see him, he looked scared.

"What's going on?" she asked.

"I think they're coming back," he said. "We have to move you. Can you stay quiet?"

She had stayed quiet until he asked questions. But she didn't say that. Instead, she said, "Yes."

"I'm going to cover the box. Don't do anything till I come for you. Okay?"

"Okay," she said, even though she was supposed to do two things. She was supposed to stay quiet, and she was supposed to hide.

Maybe when "they" came back, they would bring Momma. Maybe when "they" came back, she could finally go home.

Now

Becca and Jillian used police tape to rope off the Natatorium. The crime scene squad could handle the upper floors. Becca saw no point. She knew that the body—the body that was freshly dead— was in that dug-out pool.

Jillian was in the basement of the Nat, laying out a grid to work the scene. She knew that some of the work would come from the local team. Even though she had been on the phone with the state crime lab, she had no idea when the experts would show up.

The sooner the better, she had told them, but both she and Becca knew that would make no difference. Oregon was a low tax state, and rather than fund important services, Oregon cut them. The lab was now working two years out on important cases, and had no extra people to spare for a mass grave deep in the desert.

The lab certainly didn't have the funds to hire an expert. Becca would have to take the money from the police budget or she would have to get the Hopewell County District Attorney to pay for the expert before any charges were filed.

Jillian's office certainly didn't have the money either. She barely had enough funds for an assistant.

Even though other officers showed up, as well as two more detectives, Becca handled most of the interviews herself. She didn't want her colleagues scaring off the illegals. She needed them for the investigation.

Using a mixture of English and her high school Spanish, she managed to interview the work crew. She also learned that several employees had vanished when Chase stopped work and called her, even though he had told them that they'd be safe.

Of course, no one would give her their names. The handful of employees who'd even mentioned their friends seemed frightened by the slip.

Even the legal citizens—the ones who had citizenship, and the ones who were born in the United States—insisted on showing her their papers. A number of the men slapped the documents with their hands, and said, "Test them. Go see. Everything is in order."

When she finished, she went to her car, got some more bottled water, and took a long drink. Yes, the heat had drained her, as had the bodies and the destruction below, but the fear she'd encountered had stressed her as well.

People shouldn't be afraid to answer simple questions. Not in America.

She sighed, then drank half a bottle. She set the bottle inside, shielded her eyes, and looked at the sun.

It seemed to have a long way to go before it disappeared behind the mountains. Usually she liked the long days of summer. Today she didn't.

"Can I send everyone home now?" Chase asked from behind her.

"Yeah." She didn't turn around. She hated his habit of standing so close that she would have to bump into him if she made any movement at all. "Unfortunately, they're not going to be able to work here tomorrow."

"Or the next day or the next. What's this about experts?"

"Jillian can't handle the site," Becca said. "She thinks it's historical, and if she does something wrong . . ."

He sighed. She knew he understood historical red tape. He had to deal with a lot of it just to get this project off the ground.

"What else do you need from me?" he asked.

I need you to back up a little, she thought. But she said, "I need to see the rest of the buildings. Are any of them locked?"

"A few," he said. "Mostly the theater, which is where I've been storing supplies, and of course, the hotel."

He had stepped into her line of sight, apparently annoyed at the way she had been ignoring him. Since he was no longer so close, she could turn.

"The hotel?" she asked. "Why the hotel? We all went in it as kids."

"And had no idea how much the front desk or the doorknobs were worth. I've got a lot of subcontractors here, and it's a different time." He ran a hand through his hair. Sweat glistened on some of the strands. "I'm going to lose it all, aren't I?"

She felt a pull of empathy. "I don't know. You will be able to work here again. I'm just not sure when."

He gave her a bitter smile. "Yeah."

She wanted to ask him if he regretted calling her. She wanted to ask if he was going to blame her for the loss of time.

But she didn't. The old Becca would have asked those questions. The new Becca had to pretend she didn't care.

Then

Jess Taylor picked up the box and carried it under his arm. It bumped as he walked. She lost her mouth and one of the eyes as more shivers ran through her.

She wondered: If she thought of herself as Sarah, would she change into a little human girl?

She wasn't willing to try it. Not yet.

He set her next to a filing cabinet. The grained wood reminded her of her father. He'd turned into an expensive filing cabinet once, just to show her how to change into common business objects.

For an emergency, he had said. *For an emergency*.

Like this one. If she had thought it through, she should have turned into something freestanding like the filing cabinet, not something long and seemingly never-ending, like the sidewalk or the bricks.

It was different to become a permanent non-breathing object. Then she had to cling to it, and somehow sleep. But younglins couldn't do that. It was a skill they got when they grew older.

At her age, only a parent could help her make a sleep-change.

Jess Taylor dropped a towel over the box. The towel smelled of soap and sweat. It filtered the light.

She closed her remaining eye, and listened as voices filled the bank. Excited voices, male—

"What the hell were you thinking staying here?"

"You missed it all."

"You should've seen it. They didn't even look human by the end."

The voices mingled and tumbled and twisted into jumbles of words. But *they didn't even look human* got repeated over and over again.

They didn't look human, her people. Not when they were filing cabinets or chairs or wooden sidewalk planks. But they breathed and fought and *thought*. Wasn't that enough?

Daddy had said it would be, that day so long ago:

We have no choice, he'd said to the assembled. *We're stuck here, and Hope is better than the other cities I've seen. We're isolated. If we can work our way into their minds as laborers, maybe they'll accept us. They can't see how we live—we'll have to live as they do. But after a while, they'll get used to us. They'll see how similar we are. We breathe like them, fight like them, think like them. They'll understand. They'll accept. Given time.*

Time passed. And nothing changed. They had their own part of town, near the Chinese who also refused to talk to them.

And when one of their own got attacked outside of town and couldn't hold her shape—

Well, Momma wouldn't talk about it. And everyone expected Daddy to do something, but he didn't know what to do. He told Momma that. He didn't know.

Then he left. Looking for someplace new, Momma said. But she didn't believe it any more. Daddy would have come back long before now. And he hadn't.

And Jess Taylor looked sad when he learned her human name. Because of Daddy.

The voices continued:

"They scream real pretty though."

"One of them even begged."

"You shoulda been there."

And then Jess Taylor said, "Someone had to watch the bank."

"If I didn't know better," said a deep male voice, "I'd check the vault. What a perfect time to take something for yourself."

"Please do, sir," Jess Taylor said. "You won't find anything awry."

He sounded funny. Like they'd hurt his feelings. Humans did that to each other sometimes. But they always made up. Never with her people, but with each other.

Only no one apologized to Jess Taylor. Instead, the conversations changed. Someone walked past her and she heard a dial spin, then something metal click. She swiveled her good eye, but she couldn't see through that towel Jess Taylor had thrown over her box.

"Looks fine to me, sir," said another voice.

"Double-check," said the deep voice.

"I don't receive credit for staying, do I?" Jess Taylor asked in that low tone he'd used when he called his own people names.

"What's that?" the deep voice asked.

"Nothing, sir."

More clicking. The sound of boots against marble. Low voices, counting and comparing.

Then deep voice—"Looks like you did well, Taylor."

"Thank you, sir."

"Just don't act on your own again, all right? Makes people suspicious. Especially in these times."

"Do you think I'm one of them, sir?"

"If you were, you'd be dumb to stay," deep voice said.

"Besides," said another voice, "we seen you hurt. You don't change like those demons do."

"I suppose," Jess Taylor said in that low tone again.

"You don't approve," said the other voice.

"Of what?" Jess Taylor asked, louder this time.

"What we done."

For a long moment, Jess Taylor didn't answer. She held her breath, hoping he wouldn't make a mistake. If he made a mistake, they would find her.

Finally, he said, "I don't know what you did."

"We could show you," one of the men said, and everyone laughed.

"Thank you," Jess Taylor said without any warmth, "but I think I can figure it out for myself."

Now

The front door of the hotel was padlocked. The window shutters were closed and locked as well. When she was a child, this looked like an abandoned building, spooky but still alive. Now it seemed like an unloved place, a place that would fall apart if someone took the locks off.

Becca watched Chase remove the padlock and hook it onto his belt. Then he swung back the metal latch and pushed open the double mahogany doors.

Those Becca remembered. She remembered the way that the light filtered out through them, more dust motes than she thought possible dancing inside of it.

Small windows stood beside the door, but on the far side of the lobby, floor-to-ceiling windows opened onto the expanse of high desert and the mountains beyond. The glass was old and bubbled and clearly handmade. Such dramatic windows were rare a hundred years ago, and had been—in the hotel's heyday—one of its main drawing points.

She stepped inside, sneezed at the smells of mold and dust, and watched as more motes swirled because of her movements. Chase stood beside the door, watching her.

"We were going to revive it all," he said. The past tense saddened her. "Imagine that desk over there, polished, with employees behind it, computers on top, guests in front."

She looked at the registration desk, scratched and filthy, which wrapped around an entire corner of the room. Behind it were old-fashioned mail slots, some filled with stuffing from chairs—probably rats' or mice nests.

"People would look at the view, or go to the Natatorium for tennis or a swim. We were going to build a golf course alongside this, and build homes, just outside the line of sight for these windows." Chase stuck his hands in his back pockets. He stared at the view, still sending in light despite the dirty glass. "It would have been spectacular."

"It's not over yet, Chase," Becca said. It wasn't like him to give up so easily. In fact, this speech of his was making her suspicious. Had he run into financial difficulty? Had he put something recently dead among the bones as a way of notifying the authorities? Did he want the project to end for a reason she didn't understand yet?

"Half my crew probably ran away today."

"They aren't the people who will restore this building."

"Who's going to come once they find out there's a mass grave on the property?"

She didn't know the answer to that. "People go to battlefields all the time."

"Battlefields," he said, "are different."

"We went to Little Big Horn. They're still discovering bodies up there."

"From a hundred and forty years ago," he said.

"You have no idea how old these bodies are," she said.

He shrugged, then turned and gave her one of his "aw-what-the-hell" smiles. "You're right. I don't know anything yet. Except that this place was well named."

The End of the World. She sighed, and asked the question she'd suddenly started to dread. "Are you insured?"

"For what? Construction losses? Sure. Lost income and disability? Sure. Dead bodies on my construction site? Who the hell knows."

"Maybe you should find out," she said. "I'm sure this doesn't qualify as an act of God."

He inclined his head toward her, as if to say "Touché."

"I need to look," she said. "Alone."

He nodded, then walked to the door. "Find me when you're done."

"Yeah," she said, but he had already stepped outside. She sighed and looked at the floor. Dirt covered the old carpet. Footprints ran through it, some of them so old that they were buried under layers of sand. Broken chairs huddled in the corner, and the stairs to the second floor had rotted away.

But the hotel did have good bones. The brick on the outside had insulated it from harsh weather in the high desert—the hot, hot summers and the blisteringly cold winters. Even the floor-to-ceiling windows were double paned, something so unusual, she'd never seen it in a building this old.

The place didn't smell of death like the Natatorium. In fact, except for her prints and Chase's it didn't look like anyone had been here in a month or more.

She turned on her flashlight and aimed it at the dark corners. Something skittered away from the ornate gold leaf in front of the elevator. She scanned the steps—yep, rotted—and the scarred reception desk. A door was open behind it, leading to the offices. She'd been back there when she was a kid.

In fact, she'd been everywhere in this place as a child. The whole hotel had fascinated her, except for one part.

She steeled herself, then moved to the right, aiming the light at the far wall. When the beam hit it, the wallpaper shimmered like a heat mirage.

She swallowed. That, at least, hadn't changed. The shimmering wall and the building moans—probably from the way the wind whistled through it on dry desert days—gave rise to the stories of the hotel being haunted.

A shiver ran through her. She'd just seen a hole filled with long-dead bodies, her nose still carried the odor of decay (and her clothing probably did too), and it was the old hotel that scared her out of her wits.

Let someone else investigate it. Let the crime scene techs make sure nothing bad had happened here in the recent past. She'd done as much as she was going to.

She shut off her light, and tried not to listen to the rustling as she let herself out.

Then

After a long, long time, most of the voices stopped. A few continued. Deep Voice did. He gave orders and talked to some of the others.

Then he told Jess Taylor to leave.

She held her breath, wondering what would happen to her.

Then someone picked up the box. She bumped against the side.

"What've you got there?" Deep Voice asked.

"Just a box," Jess Taylor said. "I need to move a few things from my house. I thought I'd take this to pack them in. I'll bring it back in the morning."

"Check it, Dunnigan," Deep Voice said.

She shivered. She couldn't help herself. She squinched as far as she could into the corner of the box, turned her ear inward, and closed her remaining eye, hoping this Dunnigan couldn't see her—or if he did, he wouldn't know what he was looking at.

The box bounced, then the light changed. The towel must have come off. Tobacco and sweat filled the air. She held herself rigid, feeling a shiver start, and willing it away.

"It's empty, boss," said this Dunnigan, right above her.

The box bumped again, and the light dimmed.

"Satisfied?" Jess Taylor asked. His tone was bitter.

"You got to admit," Deep Voice said, "you've been acting odd today."

"I acted like a responsible employee," Jess Taylor said. "I stayed when everyone else left. No one thought to lock up in all the excitement. I made sure the drawers were closed and locked, the safe was closed, and the account registers were in the proper desks. I kept an eye on the place, and you treat me like a criminal."

"You'd do the same, Taylor," Deep Voice said.

"No, sir, I beg your pardon, but I wouldn't. I would acknowledge when an employee does well, not suspect him of thievery because he takes an initiative."

The silence went on forever. She was still holding her breath. She had to let it out, as quietly as she could. She could feel the box bounce with Jess Taylor's breathing—if he was the one holding it. She hoped he was.

He seemed like the only human—the only person—she could trust.

Finally, Deep Voice said, "You can keep the box."

"Thank you, sir." Such sarcasm in Jess Taylor's voice. She wondered if Deep Voice could hear it. "May I go now?"

"Of course," Deep Voice said.

The box bounced with each step. She heard a door screech open, then bang closed. The air grew warmer and the towel blew up ever so slightly.

"Stay still," Jess Taylor said in that undertone of his. "We're not out of this yet."

Now

When she came out of the hotel, the sky was a deep grayish blue. Twilight had fallen fast, like it always did on the high desert. The moment the sun dipped behind the mountain peaks, the light changed and the air had a suggestion of coolness.

Now if only the wind would stop. It rose for a half-hour or so at real twilight, sending sand pellets against her skin like tiny knives.

Chase's employees had already left. So had the police, except for two officers who had been assigned to guard the crime scene. Apparently the crime scene techs weren't going to work at night, which made sense, given the location and the questions still lingering about how to handle the scene.

Chase leaned against his Ford Bronco, a cell phone pressed

against his ear. His back was to her, but she could tell from the position of his shoulders how annoyed he was.

She walked toward him, then stopped when she heard what he was saying.

". . . I'm not sure what they're going to find here, Lester, but that's not the point. The point is that this project probably won't go forward for months. I need you to check our liability. I also need you to examine the insurance policies, and to somehow, without tipping our hand, talk to the few investors who came on board early. I'd promised them the chance of a return within two years. This project came alive because I thought we could fast track it."

He was talking to his lawyer. Usually such conversations had lawyer-client privilege, but she wasn't sure about that when he conducted it outside on a cell phone.

Still, she should let him know she was there.

She didn't move.

"That's not the point, Lester. The point is that I already have one point two million dollars in capital tied up in this place, and now everything's going to be on hold—"

One of the officers saw her. She nodded at him.

"That's why I want you to find out if we're insured for something like this. I'm not sure I can afford to have that much money tied up indefinitely."

She scraped her foot against the dirt as she walked forward again. He continued talking, so she coughed.

He turned, paused, and sighed. Then he said, "Listen, I'll call you in a few hours. Have some answers for me by then, will you?"

"How's Lester?" she asked.

"You heard that?"

"Enough to know who you were talking to." Lester had handled their divorce. He had been Chase's lawyer for more than two decades. She had no idea if he was any good, but Chase obviously had no complaints. He usually fired people who didn't perform their jobs well.

Chase stuck his phone into the front pocket of his shirt. Then he took the padlock off his belt. "I suppose this is the wrong time to ask you to dinner."

"It's always the wrong time, Chase," she said.

He shook his head ever so slightly. "What did I do, Becca? Was being married to me that bad?"

"I divorced you," she said. "That should be answer enough."

But it wasn't, because he asked her often. And he made it sound like she had been crazy to leave him. Which, her therapist said, was proof enough to her that she had done the right thing.

Becca waited until he'd padlocked the hotel before she walked to her squad. Even then, she stood with an arm resting on the open door as he walked back to his Bronco.

He looked defeated. Was Chase a good enough actor to play such a difficult emotion? She wasn't sure, but she doubted it.

And Jillian would say that she doubted it because she wanted to.

"Changed my mind," Becca said when he got close. "How's pizza sound to you?"

"Good if they had the real thing here."

He'd gone to school in Chicago; he thought the pizza out west was too mainstream or too California. Tasteless and low-fat, he'd once said.

She expected the response, just not the rote way he said it.

"Well, how about that thing we call pizza out here in the Wild, Wild West?"

He looked at her for the longest time as if he were sizing her up. She made sure her expression remained neutral.

"You going to interrogate me?" he asked.

"Should I?"

"I suppose you should." He opened the Bronco's door. "And you should know I'm ordering spaghetti."

"Spoilsport," she said, got into the squad, and followed Chase out of the lot.

Then

The box bounced for what seemed like forever. She heard boots tapping on the wooden sidewalk, boots scraping on dirt, boots going silent as they hit the grass. She heard voices, conversations far from her. She heard a motorized engine, one of those new-fangled automobiles that made humans think they had entered a technological age.

Daddy had always said they were backward. If they were just a bit farther along, if the Earth hadn't been so focused on oil and gas and coal, then maybe their people could have rebuilt the ship. But the materials hadn't been manufactured yet, and the energy sources were too heavy or too combustible. The people needed something more sophisticated, but didn't have the resources to make it themselves.

Nor did they have the ability to take what passed for technology in this place and modify it for their needs.

Occasionally one of the voices would greet Jess Taylor and ask him what he had in the box. He'd give the same reply—*Nothing*—and continue as if that were true.

He walked for a long time.

Then she heard boots on wood again, a few creaks, and the click of a doorknob. Another creak—this one different, like a door opening—and the light filtering through the towel seemed dimmer.

Finally, Jess Taylor set the box down.

"Just a minute," he said.

She heard a door close, then a swish that she recognized—curtains being closed. This place was hot. The windows should've been open instead of covered. The air smelled faintly of grease and unwashed sheets.

Then the towel came off. She swiveled her eye upward. Jess Taylor was looking down at her.

"This is my house," he said. "I live alone, so no one'll bother us. I don't have to be anywhere until tomorrow."

She wasn't sure why he was telling her all that.

He scooted a chair closer to the table, sat down, then asked, "Do you have any idea what we should do next?"

Now

Becca didn't have to tell him where they were going because there was only one pizza parlor in all of Hope that he would step into. It was in a beat-up old building on the southeast side, about as far from the End of the World as they could go.

The pizza parlor—called Reuben's of all things—was actually owned by a displaced New York Italian who missed his grandmother's cooking. He made pizza because teenagers loved it and because it was a cheap, easy meal for families, but his heart was in the Italian dishes, from lasagna to a special homemade sausage marinara whose recipe he kept secret.

Chase came out of the bathroom as she went into the ladies room. When she came out, Chase was sitting toward the back, in a red vinyl booth, his hands folded on the checked tablecloth. The edges of his hair were wet as was one side of his face.

Washing up hadn't entirely gotten rid of the smell of rot that had permeated her nose, but it got knocked back a degree. The rich odor of garlic and baking bread helped.

By the time she got to the table, Chase was sipping a glass of wine. An iced tea waited for her. Irritation flooded through her—how did he know what she wanted? Had he asked? No, of course not—and then she shook it off.

He had always done this, and until she left him, she had let him. She hadn't told him in any way that he no longer had the right to make decisions for her, and now didn't seem the time.

"I ordered the family-sized spaghetti with the sausage marinara," he said.

She sighed. She was going to have to confront him after all.

But he held up his hand, as if to forestall anything she had to say.

"Then I realized I was being a jerk, so I ordered a small pepperoni pizza and a basket of garlic bread."

As he said that, the garlic bread arrived, looking crisp and greasy and delicious.

"Sorry. I know I should know better."

Becca wasn't sure if that was a real apology or not. She wasn't even sure she should be annoyed or not. Sometimes she wished her therapist was on speed-dial, so she could ask a simple question: What was the appropriate response to this particular Chase action? Should she be flattered or insulted? Should she set him in his place? Or should she do her breathing exercises while she reminded herself that they were no longer married?

"We could, I think, change the topping on the pizza." He actually sounded worried. "I don't think it went into the oven yet."

"No, that's fine," she said. "A hundred-thousand fat-filled calories actually sound good right now."

So she had opted onto a response, and it was passive/aggressive. Bully for her. How non-constructive.

Chase blinked, looking a little stunned, then shrugged. "Sounds like you're in the mood to interrogate me."

Becca grabbed a slice of garlic bread. The butter welled against her fingers, and she realized she was hungry.

"How much do you stand to lose if the End of the World folds?"

"Folds?" he asked. "Or gets put on hold?"

"It's the same thing, isn't it? Didn't you tell me you needed to finish this quick?"

He swirled his wine glass, then took a huge swig, something she'd never seen him do.

"Let me explain the End of the World, can I, before we get into the details you think important?"

She wasn't the only one capable of being passive/aggressive, but she let the comment slide. She had baited him, after all.

"Shoot," she said.

He flagged the waiter down, got them both water, and drank his so quickly that he looked like a man dying of thirst. Then he pushed his other glass toward the back of the table, as if saving the wine for later.

"The End of the World," he said, the words rolling off his tongue like a lover's. "Remember how much we loved it?"

How much he had loved it. But she didn't correct him. She nodded instead.

"Remember when I used to talk about restoring it, about making the End of the World *the* destination resort in Oregon, and you'd laugh, and you'd say who would want to come to Hope?"

"That was before the boom," she said, surprised that she wasn't feeling defensive.

"Before Hollywood discovered how cheap the land was, before they filmed half the Western films up here, before the Californians bought everything in sight."

And tried to change the town into a mini-California, with its strip malls and coffee bars and upscale shops that people like Becca couldn't set foot into unless there was a police emergency.

"Hollywood's left," she said. "They've gone to Canada."

"But they vacation here. They ski, they hunt, they fish. They look at the pretty views. They want to play golf and lacrosse and polo and soccer, if we could only accommodate them. The town doesn't have everything yet, and if we did, even more would come."

"Is this the speech you gave to prospective investors?" she asked. "Because I know the drill."

He'd practiced much of it on her over the years. She hadn't agreed with all of it, but she had encouraged some of it. She too wanted Hope to grow. When she'd been a girl, the town was dying, and the name seemed like the way the town planned for its future.

"Historic resorts are the next travel boom," he said. "People want to visit the past, so long as it has all the amenities of the present."

The waiter set down the pizza. The cheese was still popping because the tomato sauce was bubbling underneath.

Becca took a piece. To her surprise, Chase did too.

"So tell me," she said, "how come your money's in this instead of other people's?"

He sighed. "It costs more to refurbish the old hotel and the

Natatorium than it would to tear the place down, and build comparable modern buildings from scratch."

"And your investors didn't like that?"

"They like everything else. They like the resort, the golf
courses—"

"Courses?" Becca asked.

"Four," he said, "along with residential housing, riding trails,
and a possible dude ranch near the edge of the mountains."

"How much property did you buy?"

"Just the End of the World," he said. "Turns out that the property
runs from the highway all the way to the mountains."

"My god," Becca said.

"It was all scrub and desert, not even good enough for ranching,
although the End of the World's original owners did rent it out for
that."

"Who did you buy it from?" she asked.

"The heirs. They don't live in Oregon any longer. They remembered it from their childhoods, figured the land wasn't worth much,
and sold it for a song. The land wasn't the problem. The hotel and
resort were."

"The investors wanted you to build new, and you refused." Her
voice rose just a bit at the end of the statement, mostly because she
was surprised. Chase did what he wanted within reason, but he
never turned down money like this. "You really had your heart set
on rebuilding the place."

"I had documents and itineraries and research and projections
that showed just how much people would love it here. They go to
historic lodges now. Hell, Timberline Resort is the number two destination in Oregon."

"Number one being?"

He looked down. "Spirit Mountain Casino."

Which had no historic hotel. Nothing except a rather cheap
looking lodge and a large casino at the entrance to the Van Duzer
Corridor in the coastal mountain range.

"But that land was considered worthless forty years ago," he said.

"Because it was tribal land in the middle of nowhere," she said.

"You don't have to side with them," he snapped.

The reaction shocked her. He never snapped. He got angry or
frustrated and occasionally raised his voice, but usually he manipulated, twisting the conversation until she was surprised that she was
agreeing with him, even when she knew she shouldn't.

"So I repeat," she said, "how deep are you into this?"

"Ninety percent of the resort funding is from me." He took another swig of the wine, leaving the glass nearly empty. How many times had he told her wine was meant to be sipped not guzzled? He probably hadn't even tasted this one.

"That's a lot of money."

"More than you realize."

"So you go bankrupt if this place never gets off the ground."

He finished the wine, then set the glass at the edge of the table, an obvious signal for more. "You're awful damn pessimistic."

"I'm not pessimistic, and I'm not here to judge you." Even though that was a lie. At this moment, it was her job to judge him. "I am trying to figure out what happened in that Natatorium."

"You think someone murdered a lot of people and buried them beneath the swimming pool. A long, long time ago. I think it shouldn't interfere with my project."

She sighed. "I'm not talking about the old bodies. I'm talking about the smell."

He froze. The waiter returned, grabbed the wine glass, and left without asking what he was supposed to do about Chase's beverage. Maybe the look on Chase's face scared him off.

"I told you," Chase said. "It was an animal."

"We haven't found it yet. We're operating on the assumption that the recent body is human."

"And you think I what? Sabotaged my own project? Why the hell would I do that?"

"I don't know." Becca raised her voice enough to drown his out. "Maybe you don't have enough funding. Maybe you want out now."

"And you think that destroying the project is the way to leave? If I want to lose several million dollars, I'd put it on the roulette table. If I want to shut down the project, I'll do that."

"So why didn't you?"

"I didn't want to." He grabbed the edge of the table. For a moment, she thought he was going to leverage himself out of it.

But he didn't. He ran a hand through his hair, took a deep breath, and forced himself to lean back.

"You don't want to?" she asked. "Or you see this as a win-win situation?"

He looked at her as if she was crazy. "Excuse me?"

"Once you found the bodies below the pool, you knew that might stall the project. But you wanted out without losing any money. So you found a way that the insurance might cover it. Something guaranteed, not an ancient burial ground like you thought, but a police investigation—"

"You think I planted a body there for the *insurance money?*"

"I don't know," she said. "Did you?"

His mouth was open. He stared at her like the day she told him she was leaving. If she had to, she would wager that he was telling the truth. But those kind of experiences, that kind of hunch, didn't hold up in court.

Besides, she knew that her reactions to him weren't always the right ones.

"Do you really think that little of me?" he asked softly.

"What I think doesn't matter," she said. "This *is* a police investigation, and I have to—"

"Oh, bullshit," he said. "You don't have to explore every goddamn angle. You think I'm capable of killing someone and planting him in the Natatorium for the fucking insurance money."

The waiter hovered near the kitchen door. In his hand, he held another glass of wine. He watched them with a wary expression.

She had to get Chase to calm down. She needed him to think clearly.

"Do you want me to investigate this or someone from Portland? Because that's the way it's heading."

"Even if I turn out to be right and it's a goddamn coyote down there?"

"Even if," she said. "We have something big now, and there's no covering it up. Jillian called the state crime lab. We're going to have reporters. You want them to write about how we had a screaming fight in our favorite Italian restaurant?"

"Fuck you, Becca," he said. "You planned this."

"Your anger?"

"With a fucking audience. Do you hate me that much?"

She swallowed. She was getting angry now. "You ask me that a lot. So here's the answer, Chase. I don't hate you. If anything, I'm still in love with your sorry ass, and that's a problem for me. It's also a problem for this investigation, since I'm the only trained detective on Hope's police force. I'm holding off the Valley investigative team for the moment, but that won't last if we keep this up."

He slammed his hands on the booth so hard that the fake wood tabletop attached to the wall actually bounced. Then he stood up and stalked to the men's room.

Becca took a deep breath, let it out, and then took another. And another, and another, still wishing for the therapist on speed-dial. Did she keep breathing until she was light-headed or did she just leave?

She was handling this all wrong, and pretty soon word would get out. The chief would relieve her, and the investigation would become a state thing instead of a local thing. And that kind of publicity would hurt the new Hope, the place that actually had a future.

The waiter came to the table. He was still cradling the wine glass. "You think he's gonna want this? Because—"

"Yeah," she said. "He'll want that and more. Bring the whole bottle."

She ate her piece of pizza slowly, drank the iced tea, and waited, keeping an eye on the men's room door. The three other tables, filled with young families, kept an eye on her, as if she had been the problem, not Chase.

The men's room door opened as she finished her third piece. The waiter had been back twice—once with the wine bottle and once with a heaping bowl of spaghetti in sausage marina sauce. As stressed as Becca was, she could probably eat the entire thing without Chase's help.

To her relief, he came back to the booth and slid in.

"Okay," he said, "since you're going all official on me, here's what you need to know. I have six million dollars into this thing. That's real money. I also have outstanding loans of ten million, and that's not nearly enough to get everything done. I'm hoping when the hotel and Nat are finished, the investors will pour in. If they don't, I'll be in debt until I die, even if the place is a success."

Becca set down the pizza crust she'd been clinging too. She resisted the urge to slide the plate of spaghetti toward her.

"Does my insurance cover this? How the hell would I know? I'm sure my agent doesn't know. I'm sure the insurance company has no real idea, and its legal department will be haggling over the policy language and the politics of the entire thing for months. That's what I was talking to Lester about. I'm hoping that he can find a few answers, or at least an argument, so that some of the back and forth gets forestalled if and when you people actually decide to shut me down."

"We already shut you down, Chase," she said. "The question now is for how long."

"I know." He picked up the glass and then set it down again.

"But you know what I mean. This could be a two-day inconvenience or it could be a year-long nightmare. And since it's all one property, I'm pretty sure that you could tie me up for a long time."

"If those bodies are Native American, you could be right," she said.

He let out a long sigh. Then he moved the wine glass closer to her plate than his.

"So," he said, "do I have a motive to get insurance money? No. I'd be a fool to try this plan. If I wanted insurance money, I'd find another way to go about it. And I'd be smart, Becca. This is damn dumb. It jeopardizes everything without giving me any benefit at all. I'll be in the news forever, I won't be able to save face, and I'm going to go broke. Hell, I'd be better off disappearing and starting all over again than doing that. I'm not damn dumb, Becca."

"I know," she said.

"I have no reason to plant something there."

"Does anyone else?" she asked.

"Yeah," he said, reaching for the plate of spaghetti. "Yeah, I'm afraid a lot of people do."

Then

Why would he ask her what to do next? Wasn't he the grown one, the one in charge? She was just a baby, really, younger than anyone else in their group.

But he wasn't part of their group. She wasn't even sure there was a group any more. Where had everyone gone?

When the shanties burned, the remaining people fled. Momma had grabbed her. They were just a little behind the group.

And she never knew what happened to any of them.

"What about my Momma?" she asked Jess Taylor.

He closed his eyes, turned his head, and wiped the sweat off his forehead. Then he glanced at the window, like he wanted to open it. He stood, and she thought he was going to, but all he did was get another towel and clean off his fingers.

When he sat back down, his face had a different look to it. His eyes were open, but sadder, if that was possible.

Sometimes she wondered how these humans could think themselves so different from the people. These humans changed too, just not as much. And sometimes these humans changed by force of will, just like the people did.

Just like Jess Taylor had done a moment ago.

"You're going to keep asking, aren't you?" he said.

She blinked at him. She didn't know how to answer, except maybe to say of course she would. She loved her momma and her momma left her on the sidewalk.

Bad things happened this afternoon, and she heard some of them. One of them sounded like Momma.

"I don't know what happened," he said. "I'll find out as best I can. I promise. But it might take days."

Days. She wanted to fold her ears in, close her eyes, and huddle into a little ball. What would happen to her for those days?

"I've seen this before," he said. "Not this, exactly, but the same kind of thing. Folks get riled up about the strangest things, and you have to admit, your people are strange."

She didn't think so. But she didn't answer that either, just kept watching him.

"I mean, I think I finally understand where this violence comes from, this impulse. Not because of you."

He held up a hand, as if to reassure her. She wasn't sure what he was reassuring her about.

"It comes about because of the differences. They're startling. And sometimes—I don't mean to offend you—but sometimes, they're revolting. Humans don't handle revulsion well. We . . ."

He shook his head and stood up, walking to the window, and peeking through the curtain. Sweat stained the back of his shirt, leaving a V-shaped wet spot in the fabric.

"I can't believe I'm defending them."

He shook his head again. Then he let the curtain drop close, and he came back to the chair.

"The chances are—I'm so sorry, but the chances are that your mother didn't make it. Just like your father. She probably—they probably—I mean, you heard it this afternoon. You're lucky to be here. And if your mother is alive—"

He stopped, wiped a hand over his mouth, then shook his head yet again.

He didn't say any more.

She was holding her breath. She finally let it out. Her other eye had appeared. Apparently she needed to see him. Her body was starting to make changes on its own.

"You think she's still alive?" she asked.

"No," he said.

"But you said—"

"I know what I said." He sighed. "Look, Sarah, if your mother is still alive, it probably won't be for long."

"Then we have to find her."

"That's not what I mean."

She felt her skin tighten. Another shiver ran through her. The spikes started to form and she willed them away. She didn't want him to know she suddenly felt threatened.

"What do you mean?" she asked.

"I mean they're probably not done."

"But I heard the men, they came into the bank, they said it was over, they said it was . . . fun. . . . They said—"

"I know what they said." He ran his fingers along his forehead. "I know. And I know a few of them will go back. Some probably haven't left. And they'll finish. Do you understand me? They'll finish."

"Can't we get her before they do?"

He stared at her, and that sadness returned to his eyes. His whole face looked sad, and she wondered for a minute if he even saw her, if he was looking at her or something else—someone else—like a memory, maybe, like those ghostly shapes that the people sometimes made when they thought of a relative long dead.

"If we try to get her," he said, "they'll kill us too."

"Not you," she said.

He let out half a laugh, like she'd startled the sound out of him.

"Sarah, honey," he said, "if your people hadn't come, they'd've gotten to me eventually. They always do."

Now

"You know who doesn't like me." Chase used tongs to dish up his spaghetti. Somehow he managed to do so without getting sauce on his shirt. "You used to put up with the phone calls."

Becca remembered. The calls came in late at night. Sometimes they were just hang-ups. Sometimes they were more serious than that. A few even included threats.

In those days, Hope's telephone system was too unsophisticated to provide services like Caller I.D., so Becca had had to put a trace on the line. She had gone to every single one of the callers, warning them that their behavior was illegal and should Chase's businesses go under or should he get hurt, they would be the first suspects she went to.

Most seemed to listen. A few grumbled that Chase had only married her because he wanted police protection. Not even Becca was insecure enough to believe that.

She took a small portion of the spaghetti, barely enough to fill a corner of the plate provided, and then only because she loved the sauce. Mostly, she focused on the pizza, her iced tea, and Chase.

"What about this project?" she asked. "Anyone new surface?"

He used his spoon as a counterweight to keep the spaghetti he was winding from falling off his fork. He worked at it as if it were a particularly difficult puzzle.

"Obviously, you never went to the city council meetings."

"Not for this, no," she said. She avoided city business as much as possible.

"Half the town hated it. Some I didn't expect, folks who had supported me when I wanted to redo Beiker's Department Store downtown."

"The preservationists went against you?"

"Yeah." He ate the forkful, swallowed, and then drank some water. "They think the End of the World is a bad idea, a dangerous place, and the last straw in turning Hope into a replica of California."

"Wow," Becca said. "I'd've thought they would've loved it."

"Me, too," he said. "I was stunned. A few actually threatened me."

"You're kidding."

He shook his head. "Ray McGuillicuty, remember him? He told me I'd regret buying the End of the World."

"You think that was a threat, coming from a 90-year-old man?"

Chase shrugged. "I thought it was idle talk at the time. But he has money, connections, and a shady reputation. He made his money running illegal speakeasies in the late thirties, and gambling dens in the forties. Word around town was that if there was an illegal business—an abortionist, a fight ring, drug smuggling—McGuillicuty would rent space or manpower to that business for a cut, of course."

She had heard the rumors, but she also knew Old Man McGuillicuty had been an upstanding citizen since the 1960s.

"You think he's still got that kind of pull?"

"I think if anyone in Hope is smart enough to stop my project by burying a body on the property, it's Ray McGuillicuty."

"That's giving him a lot of power."

"If you're right," Chase said, "and someone is trying to shut me down, Ray's my first choice."

Becca tried not to laugh. She couldn't imagine that old man caring so much about the future of Hope. But she wasn't going to ignore this.

"Who else?" she asked as she finished her iced tea. She waved the glass at the waiter, and he nodded.

"Oh, Christ," Chase said. "Damn near the entire preservation society. All the matrons and their husbands too. Most of the old money in Hope—what there is of it—warned me away."

"Like Old Man McGuillicuty did?" Becca asked. The waiter showed up with a pitcher and set it on the table. He didn't even bother to pour. He still seemed a bit nervous about Chase's earlier outburst.

"Not that blatant," Chase said. "But they all took time to tell me that the End of the World is the most unlucky place in Hope and that everyone connected to it has been harmed by that connection."

"Lovely," Becca said. "Superstition still alive and well."

"And apparently they thought I should make business decisions based on it."

"You didn't, though," she said.

"I think some of my investors did," he said. "The preservation committee knew who my usual investors were. A number of them were contacted and a few backed out. One even told me that old properties that had bad luck rumors usually had a reason for them."

"Turns out he was right," Becca said.

"She," he said. "And I guess she was."

"Which means . . ." Becca tapped a finger against her chin. ". . . that someone knew about those bodies."

"How do you figure?" Chase asked.

She smiled at him. "Bad luck rumors have to start somewhere."

"You think that's tied to the smell?" he asked.

"Probably not, but right now, those old bodies are the only crime I have to investigate. I'll start there."

"After you finish harassing the local businessman."

"After I finish dinner with my former husband, who has had a hell of a day."

Then

She didn't know what Jess Taylor meant by the humans getting to him, and he wouldn't say. He paced around the front part of the cabin, poured some water from a pitcher into a glass, and drank.

Then he stared at her.

She wondered if he was sorry he'd helped her. Maybe he would turn her in.

Maybe she would scream.

She wanted to beg him to keep her, beg him to help her. But she didn't. Daddy used to say that people who begged didn't deserve help. They had to help themselves.

Only she couldn't do that, not without knowing what had happened. The answers weren't simple. Her home was gone—she knew that much. When the shanties burned, hers would've burned with it. Daddy always kept water near the candles. He used to say, *This place is so primitive and so badly built that we're going to die here in a stupid fire because we couldn't get to it in time.*

He'd been wrong about them dying. None of them had died in that cabin, although she wasn't sure about the others, the people who lived in the shanties where the fires started.

She wished Daddy were here now. She wished he would talk to Jess Taylor, grown one to grown one. They would understand each other. They would know what had happened and what would happen next.

"Do you eat?" Jess Taylor asked. He swished the water around in his glass. He was still looking at her that funny way.

She had to form a mouth. She had lost it while he'd been pacing. Her body wasn't sure what form to take so it was taking several at once, which made her dizzy.

"I eat," she said.

"I mean, do you eat what we eat?"

"When I look like you," she said. Her people's food had gone away when she was really, really little. They had to become like the humans just so that they could take in human nourishment.

"When you look like me," Jess Taylor repeated. "How about the way you look now?"

"I'm not anything now," she said. "I need to be something to take in food."

Something she understood. Something whose systems were somewhat compatible. Daddy and the other scientists had to work for a while to make their systems work like a human's. They still had to make changes—changes she didn't understand.

Daddy said she was lucky. She started changing into human form really young, so it would be engrained. If she had to hide, she could hide as one of them forever because her body was used to their strangeness.

His never would be. Some of the older people got really sick in the first years.

Some of the older people died.

"How often do you have to eat?" Jess Taylor asked.

"I don't know," she said. "Whenever you do, I guess."

Because she always ate when Momma did. She was too young to pick her own times to eat. Eating had to be trained like everything else.

"Wonderful," he said in that low voice of his, the one no one else was supposed to hear. Then he raised it a little. "How about water? Do you need that too?"

"If I look like you," she said, "I act like you. My needs are like yours."

That's the beauty of it, Daddy said to Momma once. *And the curse. If we stay here too long, we lose our identity. We become someone else. Then they'll never find us.*

Why would they look for us? Momma asked. *For all they know, we missed our settlement location and made do.*

They trace new colonies. They have to, Daddy said. *We don't just move there because of population growth. These places are carefully chosen for raw material wealth as well.*

She wasn't sure what "raw material wealth" was, but Momma had known. Momma had looked at Daddy disapprovingly. Daddy had shrugged, because he wore his human all the time now, and then he had smiled at her.

They'll track us down, if only to see what kind of wealth we discovered here.

And if we don't find any? Momma said.

That's not the concern, Daddy said. *The concern is whether or not they'll find us before we lose ourselves.*

"So you're going to have to pick a shape sometime tonight, aren't you?" Jess Taylor said. He had moved closer to her. She hadn't noticed before. Had she been so lost in her memories that she hadn't seen him walk?

"I guess," she said.

"Can you be something else for a while? A table, maybe or the box?"

"I'm too little," she said. "I can't do it by myself, not for long. That's why I couldn't be brick. I tried, but I'm not good yet. And I can't stay long anyway. I don't know the sleep-change. I need to move and breathe and feed myself like you."

He sighed. He sank into the chair next to the table. "I was afraid of that."

He took another sip of the water, studied his hand, then studied the small cabin. Then he got up and went to the window again, peering out the curtain.

"No one," he said. "We're okay for now."

"I know," she said, even though she didn't. She wanted him to figure out how to help her. She was becoming more and more afraid he would just throw her out now that he knew most of her secrets.

He put his hand in the box, near her skin but not touching it. "You turned the color of the brick this afternoon," he said. "Can you turn the same color as me?"

She looked at him as hard as he had looked at her. Then she let out a little sigh.

"Yes," she said.

"You sounded hesitant," he said.

"I can't do blue eyes," she said. "Yours aren't."

He smiled suddenly, as if he hadn't expected that. "You're right. Mine aren't. Anything else human you can't do?"

"I can't be a grown one," she said. "I have to 'roughly correspond.' "

She said those last two words carefully. They were Daddy's words. Before she had only known the concept, not how to express it. She used to point to things, things she wanted to be for more than an hour, more than a day.

He would shake his head. Sometimes he would laugh. She loved it when her Daddy laughed.

Younglin, he'd say, *they have to roughly correspond.*

Mostly she wanted to be a grown one. Humans, more than the people, treated their young ones very differently. But she didn't have enough years to be a grown one. She couldn't pretend it, couldn't even get the size right.

That problem translated to other living things as well. She could be a sapling, but not a tree. A kitten, but not a cat.

Someday, she would roughly correspond. But she wouldn't know when until she changed to human form, and that form was grown one.

"You're a girl," Jess Taylor said, "or they wouldn't call you Sarah. What age do you roughly correspond to?"

"Ten," she said because that's what Momma said when she took her to the school two years before. Even though her learning had grown and her grades had advanced, she hadn't changed, not like her classmates.

So she'd asked Daddy about that, and he'd said, *Roughly, younglin. Roughly correspond. We age differently than they do. Slower, I think.*

But he didn't know. There was so much they didn't know. So much that they didn't understand.

Then he left and no one knew, and Momma hated the questions.

"Ten," Jess Taylor said, and nodded, almost pleased. "Ten might work."

"For what?" she asked, the words catching in her newly formed mouth.

"For keeping you alive, child," he said, and tapped the edge of the box as he stood. "For keeping you alive."

Now

By the time Becca got home, she was too tired to chase rumors. She took a shower, which didn't get that smell out of her nose. Her tiny house was an oven, despite the heat pump she'd wasted the last of her divorce settlement money on, and she actually had to turn on the good, old-fashioned swamp cooler she couldn't bring herself to get rid of.

Theoretically, the desert cooled at night, but lately the coolness had come without benefit of a breeze. She started with the air-conditioner, which was nearly as old as she was, and by midnight, shut it down, shoved a fan in the window, and hoped for the best.

She couldn't sleep. Worries about herself, about Chase, about the appropriateness of the investigation had her pacing. The mentions Chase had made over dinner about rumors concerning the End of the World had her worried as well.

Hope had once been called the Hope of the West. Founded just after the Civil War by philanthropists and political idealists, Hope was supposed to be a refuge for displaced former slaves as well as immigrants who weren't wanted in larger cities, and even Chinese families, so long as they remained in their own enclave at the edge of town.

The founders of Hope put ads in all the major newspapers, promising land and jobs to people no one else wanted. Hope also promised full equality to blacks and immigrants, although "immigrants" did not include the Chinese, who wouldn't be allowed to vote or hold office. Hope was notable in its Chinese relations, though, for allowing entire families to live there, so long as they kept to themselves. Most states only tolerated Chinese males.

The experiment didn't last. The United States barred Chinese immigration in the early part of the 20th century, and then the State of Oregon itself started enforcing the discrimination built into its constitution, attempting to bodily throw Hope's blacks out of the state. The entire town prevented that, letting the blacks stay so long as the city (and county) promised not to let them hold elected office or take state jobs.

Still, Hope was something of a legend in the state, a place where people could be perceived as nothing more than a set of skills. Where, in the words of Martin Luther King Jr., people could be judged by the content of their character instead of the color of their skin.

That was Hope's legacy, and the reason for its name. Hope's children got spoon-fed this history from the moment they walked into Hope Elementary, and heard about it all the way to graduation from Hope High.

So the idea of a massacre, any massacre, particularly one that someone remembered and tried to hide, went against everything Hope stood for. People didn't die here, not in large groups. Hell, they didn't die in small ones.

Becca got out of bed, grabbed her lightest robe—which Chase had bought her for one of their anniversaries—and headed for the couch, the television, and late-night talk shows. Maybe some blathering would shut down her brain.

Because all this thinking about a possible massacre—even one nearly a hundred years old—upset her more than she wanted to admit.

Then

They waited until it was full dark before she grew herself back to human. It took a long time.

Jess Taylor's cabin had three rooms and a windowless room he called a storage room. It scared her. It was like the box, only bigger, and it was in the middle of all three rooms—like it took a part off the corners of them and made its own little space.

She had never seen anything like that. He said he kept things in there, but there wasn't much, a few boxes pushed against a corner, and some jars filled with jam.

All three walls had hangers for lanterns. He hung one before he brought her into the room. He kept it on low, so it wouldn't burn too much kerosene and stink up the place—or start a fire. (At least, she hoped it wouldn't start a fire; she'd seen too much fire this day.)

He took the box off the table, talking to her the whole time, mostly nonsense stuff like humans did with babies, stuff about how it would be okay, and the room might be close, but it would do, no one could see in, they would be safe.

She wasn't sure about safe. She wasn't sure about trusting Jess Taylor any more, but she had to. She didn't know what other choice she had.

He set her box on top of the other boxes, then propped the door partly open with one of the jars.

"I'll let you just change now," he said, like she was going to put on a dress. "Let me know when you're done."

"No!" she said, as loud as she could, which wasn't very loud, considering. She didn't have the body behind the sound, and she didn't know she needed it until just now.

That scared her too.

She finally realized how truly helpless she was.

"You have to stay," she said.

He sighed, keeping one hand on the door. "I'm sure it's private. We—folks like me—we let each other be private."

"I got to see you," she said.

"I'll be just outside the door," he said.

"To change," she said. "I got to see you to change. I can't do it without an example."

He frowned. "I can't . . . change . . . like you. I can't show you how."

She shook her head. "To look at. I need to see what I'm changing into."

And even then it might not work.

His head bowed, and his arm dropped. "I'm not sure I want to be here for that."

She wasn't sure she could do it without him. In the past, Momma or Daddy had always helped her. They had always found a way to get her through the difficult parts, like making the fingers different lengths or remembering to grow hair.

"How about I stand just outside the door with my back to you?" he asked. "Would that help?"

"Can you tell me if I get it wrong?" she asked.

He bowed his head even more, but he finally said, "I guess I could. Wait one moment, all right?"

She was scared. She knew that just as he left the room. If he hadn't propped open the door, she would've been even more scared. She couldn't see him at all.

Then he came back, carrying a sheet. "I don't have girl clothes. We'll have to find some for you. Can you put this on?"

Modesty, Daddy called it.

Silly, Momma called it, especially when it got really hot. But they learned how to wear things, and taught her about it too.

The clothes she'd been wearing when she was running probably got absorbed into her skin as fuel when she became the sidewalk. She'd been so scared, she hadn't noticed.

She'd most likely be sick later.

"If I put that on, how will you know if I get things right?" she asked.

"I'm sure no one'll notice and you'll do just fine," he said, running the words together like he couldn't breathe.

"I never got everything right before on the first try," she said.

"You'll do fine," he repeated and eased out the door, leaving the sheet on one of the shelves.

It took her a long time to squinch to the edge of the box. By then, she'd formed fingers (probably because she'd been thinking of them) and they were the wrong lengths. But they were good for grabbing onto stuff, especially when she was squinching, so she didn't pay attention to right or wrong.

When she reached the edge of the box, she either had to get all the way to the floor or she had to make legs. She couldn't quite remember the details of legs. The knees she knew and the ankles—they were the bendy parts—and the feet, but there was other stuff she'd forgotten about and she knew they'd look funny.

And she also knew if she hooked the legs up wrong, they'd be impossible to move. So she made hips too.

In fact, everything would be better if she did the bendy parts first. She just finished elbows when Jess Taylor leaned partway in the door, keeping his face averted.

"You all right?"

"Yeah," she said because she didn't know how else to answer.

"Will you be a lot longer?"

"I don't know." She didn't know how long she'd already been. She didn't really care. It took a lot of concentration to make herself all over again, and because she'd been so scared earlier, it was going to be harder.

Just him asking the question knocked her off for a little while. She put one of the elbows just above the hip, and she had to reform, trying to remember exactly how arms bend.

Finally, she had a guess at the human shape she used to wear—just that morning even though it seemed like forever ago—she grabbed the sheet and held it in front of her.

"Is this all right?" she asked.

Jess Taylor turned very slowly. And then he looked at her.

He was trying not to show how he felt, but she could see it in his eyes. Confused, sickened, surprised, all at the same time.

"Close," he said after a minute. "You're really close."

But it took most of the night just to get the general shape right—collarbones, she always forgot about collarbones—and somewhere along the way, he forgot about the sheet, telling her to make a belly button—which she'd never heard of—and explaining dimples in the knees.

By the time they got done, she had a hunch she was more human looking up close than any of her other people had ever been, and the thought made her sad.

But she didn't have long for sad. Because Jess Taylor gave her some bread and some water and an apple that he'd kept in the root cellar since last fall, and told her he needed just a little sleep before going to work.

"You're going to leave me?" she said.

"I have to," he said. "You'll be safe if you don't let anybody see you. They can't know you're here. I'll be back late afternoon. Maybe with some answers."

Maybe. She wanted him to promise her. But he couldn't promise her.

He couldn't promise her anything. Anything at all.

Now

If this were a normal investigation regarding a murder that involved the town's history, Becca would go to the Blue Diamond Café. The

Blue Diamond was in the exact center of town, in a building that had housed it since the 1930s. Tourists occasionally wandered into the Blue Diamond, saw the ripped booths and dirty windows, and wandered right out.

Becca looked at the Blue Diamond with longing as she walked past. Even though all the city old-timers would be long gone by now—it was the very late hour of 9 A.M.—she'd still find someone to welcome her and give her a free omelet that, in her private moments, she called a heart attack on a plate.

But she had to go two buildings down, to the Hope Historical Society, housed rent-free in one of Chase's renovations, the Hope Bankers Building and Trust.

The money people had long moved away from the Bankers Building, but they'd left behind one of the most solid brick buildings in all of Eastern Oregon. Chase had turned the lower floor into shops and restaurants, the second and third floors into offices, and the upper three floors into condos that sold for four times what Becca paid for her house just two years ago.

There was a diner in the Bankers Building, a 1950s wannabe called the Rock and Remember, and it was usually crammed with transplanted Californians or tourists or both. But the omelets, while large here, were made with egg-whites only, and the chefs—if you could call them that—used only "the good oils"—no butter or lard —which gave the food a cardboard aftertaste. Even the coffee wasn't coffee: it was a mochaccino or a cappuccino or an espresso, something that required a language all its own to order.

Still, she went inside, grabbed a double-tall latte with sprinkles and a "cuppa plain Joe," and then went to the elevator.

The only way she could get Gladys Conyers to talk to her, after that last disastrous interview, was to ply her with her favorite beverage, while making the bribe seem entirely accidental.

Gladys Conyers was forty-five and earnest, a California transplant herself who desperately wanted to convince the entire town of Hope that she was a local. She had some claim. Her grandparents were born here, her parents were raised here, and she spent every summer here from the day she was born.

Her grandfather, Jack Conyers, started the Hope Historical Society as a labor of love in the 1950s, after he came back from the war. He thought every small American town should have its history engraved on its downtown so Americans knew what a wonderful place they came from.

In addition to keeping all of Hope's newspapers, as well as any clippings that pertained to the city from any other periodical—even the flashy *New York Times* article forty years ago that put Hope's ski resorts on the map—he also managed to acquire important items from Hope's history.

He used to run a small museum from the back of the Historical Society, but lately, he'd been involved in a fund-raising drive to give Hope its own historical museum.

Becca knew she wouldn't find Jack at the Historical Society. He had become understandably hard to reach these last few years, ever since his eighty-fifth birthday. He figured he only had a good ten years left, and he wanted to spend them preserving Hope's history, not talking to people who had questions they could easily answer on their own.

So Gladys had taken over the society. She had a lot of knowledge about Hope—more than most long-time residents, but nothing like her grandfather. Still, anyone who wanted to see Jack had to go through Gladys. If she could answer the questions, then she would and Jack wouldn't lose precious time talking about the past he supposedly loved.

The society had an office on the first floor because it sold items from various ski tournaments and rodeos as well as Hope memorabilia.

Becca tried to ignore the memorabilia, just as she tried to ignore the weird, milky scent of the latte she carried in its cardboard holder. She headed to the back, past the teenager manning the sales desk, to the office where Gladys held court.

"Don't think a latte's gonna get me to do you any favors," Gladys said from behind the slatted door. The woman had to have a nose like a Great Dane.

Becca pushed the door open, set the latte on Gladys's specially made cup holder in the center of her desk, then grabbed her own cuppa plain Joe and sat in the easy chair.

"I'm not asking for a favor," Becca said.

"I hear you stopped the work at the Natatorium," Gladys was slender, tanned, and overdressed for Hope. She wore a designer suit—pastel, of course, since it was summer—sandal pumps, and too much makeup. "We have pictures down at the museum of the Nat being built, being used, and being abandoned. I have a computer list already prepared for you, not that I think it'll do any good."

"Why'd you think I'd be here?" Becca asked.

"You always come here, even when you have a current case.

Besides, there's so much opposition to Chase's project, I figured you'd want to know if there's any historical reason for it."

Becca hid her smile behind her paper coffee cup. Gladys would be useful after all.

"Is there any historical reason?" Becca asked.

Gladys made a *pfumph* sound that she had to have learned from her curmudgeonly grandfather. "Besides the rumors of ghosts, of hauntings, of strange sounds in the night?"

"I know about those," Becca said.

"Wow," Gladys said, pealing the lid off her latte and adding even more sugar, "you actually admit you know something."

Becca sighed, and bit back her response. She knew she'd be in for some of this. Twice she had bypassed Gladys and gone to Jack directly, and neither of them let her forget it. For nearly a year, she had to send another officer to ask historical questions. Just recently, Becca had heard through the grapevine that she was welcome at the Historical Society again, so long as she respected its director.

She did respect its director, but she respected its director's grandfather more. Jack could answer her questions quickly and with a minimum of fuss. Gladys had to be babied, which Becca proceeded to do.

"I'm sorry about that," Becca said.

Gladys waved a beringed right hand. "Water under the bridge."

They continued that game until Gladys finished sugaring her latte and put the lid back on. Then she took a sip, eyed Becca, and said, "I hear there are some serious problems at the site."

Becca nodded. One more game, but a quick one. "You know I can't talk about the details, but there is a case."

"Murder?" Gladys asked.

"Sure looks that way," Becca said.

Gladys's eyes glinted. She loved crime and punishment so long as it didn't involve her family.

"Right now, I'm waiting for the crime lab," Becca said, "and while I'm stalled, I thought I'd ask you about a few other things I saw at the Nat."

Gladys tapped the lid of her latte. "Chase already had us run the history of the place. Aside from the usual drownings and accidental deaths that any long-running sports facility would have, we found nothing."

Becca nodded. She would take this one slow. "What about the ghost rumors?"

"Those are mostly from the hotel," Gladys said. "Apparently quite a few shady characters stayed there, as well as some famous folk. President Coolidge was the most famous, I would say. He loved the fishing up here. There are rumors that Hoover stayed there too, but I haven't been able to track them down. People weren't so proud of him, by the end."

Becca didn't need that kind of history lesson. "I'm more concerned with the Nat. Do you know what kind of laborers built it?"

"Of course I do." Gladys opened a drawer in her desk and pulled out a thick file. In it were computer reprints of the society's photos, articles on the construction of the End of the World, and the list that Gladys had mentioned right up front.

She put a lacquered nail on top of one of the photographs. A group of men stood on an empty patch of desert. Some leaned on shovels. Others held pickaxes. A few had rifles.

"These are the men who built the Nat," Gladys said. "We found all sorts of historical photographs for Chase. He loves the authenticity."

Gladys lingered over Chase's name. She'd had a crush on him for years, which bothered Chase a lot more than it bothered Becca.

"What're the rifles for?" Becca asked.

"Chase asked the same thing." Gladys spun the photograph so that she could look at it before spinning it back to Becca. "My grandfather says that the End of the World was so far out of town that the workers brought their guns, hoping that that night's dinner would lope past while they were working. This was jackrabbit country, back in the day, and from what I hear, you could find—and shoot—a rabbit as easily as a fly. The men got their paycheck and that night's supper."

"Was there labor trouble then?"

"In the 20s? In Oregon?" Gladys raised her voice just enough so that the teenager manning the sales desk could hear how stupid Becca was. "I'm sure in Portland, but not in Hope. And the End of the World was built around 1910, not the 20s. It became the premiere resort in this part of the country by 1918, with war vets bringing their brides here for a honeymoon. And I hear rumors that there was quite a speakeasy run out of the hotel's basement. The owners stocked up when it became clear that the dries were going to win."

Becca set the idea of the speakeasy aside for the moment. "What about among the crew? Troubles? Firings?"

"Do they look troubled?" Gladys tapped that nail on the photo again. "Take a close look. What do you see?"

Becca repressed a sigh and leaned forward. Gladys always made these visits seem like an oral exam. "A group of very rough-looking men."

"Well, they'd take any of our modern men and pound them into the ground, that's for sure," Gladys said, a trace of the Valley Girl she'd pretended to be still lingering in her speech. "But I mean their racial mix. Several black men standing side-by-side with several whites. Not even the Chinese are segregated in this photograph, and usually the old photographs kept all the minorities separate—or even more common, out of the picture altogether."

Becca peered at it. The men were touching shoulders, which wasn't something a racially mixed group did in those days.

"There are a few Native Americans as well," Gladys said. "I learned that from their names. These men are so grimy, it's hard to tell much else."

Becca nodded, then frowned. "So the building of the Nat went smoothly, then."

"And the building of the hotel. The rumors about the End of the World started after it opened for business," Gladys said.

"You mean the haunting."

"And the bad dreams. Those were the worst. People would stay at the End of the World, and wake up screaming. The interesting thing is that they all had the same complaint."

Becca swirled the coffee in her cup. She'd have to listen to this even though it wasn't what she had asked. She didn't care about the hauntings. All old hotels had ghost stories. She wanted to hear about the Nat.

"Which was?"

"That they'd had nightmares, and in the nightmares, they saw their long-dead relatives, begging for help." Gladys added a spooky tone to her voice, as if she actually believed this nonsense.

"Wow," Becca said, trying not to sound sarcastic. "Scary."

"No kidding. I've never heard of this kind of haunting."

"But nothing from the Nat?"

"Why do you ask? What did you find?"

"Evidence that something awful happened there as the place was being built," Becca said.

"What kind of awful?" Gladys asked.

"I was hoping you could tell me."

Gladys frowned at her, and Becca had to hide a smile again. For once Gladys had to be feeling as if she was taking a quiz.

"I've never heard a thing, and you'd think in this town, I would." She slid the picture back and studied it as if it held the answers. Then she put it in the file, and closed it.

For a moment, Becca thought the interview was over, and then Gladys said, "Here's what I know. I know the Natatorium was initially supposed to be an indoor tennis court, which was, in its day, a revolutionary idea. That was about 1905 or so, when tennis was very popular, particularly out west."

"You're kidding," Becca said.

Gladys actually smiled at her. "Think of all those photographs of women in their long gowns, holding tennis rackets. These women played, and some played very well, despite the handicap."

Becca shook her head. "I thought it was an East Coast thing."

"Every small western town had courts, if they had respectable women. Most of the women were barred from the saloons and the clubs, so they had to have something to do or they might form a temperance society, or a ladies aide society or do something to take away the men's fun."

"Aren't we always that way?" Becca asked, and smiled.

Gladys smiled back. "It didn't work. They didn't build the tennis court for some reason, I never could find out why. The pool came later. It used the tennis court's foundation as the part of the pool itself, and then got built from there."

"Isn't that unusual?" Becca asked.

Gladys shrugged. "Construction in those days was haphazard. I don't know what was usual and what wasn't. I mean, a place could be as sturdy as the hotel or it could be some boards knocked together to be called a house. Really, though, they were just shanties."

"I thought Hope didn't have a shanty town."

"Oh, we did, but it burned," Gladys said. "No one bothered to rebuild it. Folks didn't like to talk about that day. The entire city could've gone up in flames. Somehow it didn't happen, though."

This was one of the things Becca hated about seeing either Conyers about Hope history—their tendency to digress.

"But nothing else about the Nat? Nothing unusual?"

"No, not even the Nat was unusual. They had Natatoriums all over Oregon. They started as playgrounds for the rich—mostly pools and tennis—and then as they fell apart, they became the community pools and playgrounds for the poorer kids. Most of them got shut down in the polio scares of the late 1940s and early 1950s. I think ours is the last one standing, which makes it eligible for historical preservation."

"Which Chase has begged you not to apply for until he's done with the work, right?"

Gladys nodded. "Nothing wrong with that. He doesn't want the extra inspectors. He does the work better than the national preservation standards ask for, so we have no objections here."

"We" being Gladys and her grandfather.

"I hesitate to ask this," Becca said, mostly because she was afraid of Gladys's reaction, "but could you ask your grandfather about the Nat? It's important."

"I'm sure he doesn't know more than I do. It predates him, you know."

"I know," Becca said. "I'm not looking for the official history. I'm looking for rumors or strange comments or stories that he gives no credence to."

"Grandfather ignores anything that can't be proven," Gladys said with something like pride. "If you want innuendo, go see Abigail Browning. She knows every old story about Hope—and most of them are just plain lies."

Becca had forgotten about Abigail Browning. She had been Jack Conyers's assistant—and first major resource—until they had some sort of falling out in the 1950s. For a while, she tried to run the "real" Hope Historical Society, but no one would give her funding, which she said was because she was a woman. Jack Conyers always claimed it was because she knew nothing about history.

She had become one of the town's characters until the transplanted Californian who started Hope's weekly "alternative" paper printed a story about an affair Abigail Browning and Jack Conyers had. The story was supposed to be sympathetic to Abigail—see how poorly this married man treated this sad spinster lady—but it had the opposite effect. Abigail lost any support she had among the locals for trying to steal Jack Conyers from his still-living, still-popular wife.

Becca would talk to Abigail Browning. But Becca also wanted to talk to Jack Conyers.

She stood. "Please do ask him."

"Oh, I will," Gladys said. "But I'm sure he won't know more than I do."

And with that, Becca knew she had no hope of seeing the town's official historian. So she'd see the unofficial one, and hope for the best.

Then

The cabin got really hot that day and she wanted to open a window, but she was scared to. Mostly she slept and she hoped Jess Taylor would come back for her. She had to keep reminding herself that it was his cabin, he'd be back, but he didn't seem to have many things there, and Daddy had run away from more, so maybe Jess Taylor would too.

Finally, Jess Taylor came back, looking tired and even more scared than when he'd left. His shirt was covered with sweat and some dirt ran along the side of his face. He had one of those overcoats—the short ones Daddy called a suit coat—and he hung it on a chair.

She stood beside the table, and waited for him to tell her to leave.

He looked at her, his big eyes sad. "I have bad news."

She held her breath. She wasn't sure what she'd do when he let her out of here. She hadn't eaten anything since that apple, and even though she took some water because she couldn't help herself—it was so hot inside—she would tell him and offer to repay him. Somehow. Maybe then he wouldn't turn her over to those people.

"Your mother," he said—and she let out a bit of that breath— "Your mother and the other . . . people? . . . they're gone."

Her stomach clenched. "Gone?"

"That's what we say when we mean they died, honey."

Her cheeks heated. Everyone had told her Daddy was gone too. "I thought it just meant they went away," she said.

"It's a euphemism."

She'd never heard the word.

He shook his head tiredly. "A word we use when we don't want to be blunt. There are a lot of euphemisms in our language."

She nodded, even though she wasn't sure she understood.

"You're sure she's . . . gone?" she asked.

"Oh, I'm sure," he said, and shuddered. "You wouldn't ask if you knew the day I had today."

"What did you do?" she asked.

"Work white men wouldn't do," he said. "They consider what I did the dirty work."

She frowned. "What did you do?"

"I'm supposed to sit in a bank," he said. "But they said, *If you want to keep your job, you'll—*"

He stopped. Studied her like he wasn't sure what to say. Then sighed.

"I helped bury them, Sarah."

"Bury?" She knew what that was, at least. She'd seen it—the wooden boxes, the holes in the ground, the markers. "If they had the boxes and stuff, how did you know my mother was there?"

It seemed to take him a minute to understand her. Then he nodded, once. "There were no boxes, honey," he said gently. "They were just placed in the ground."

Barbaric, that's what it is, her daddy said. *How can they do that to their own?*

It's a religious custom, her mother said. *We used to have them too.*

"And they were dead?" she asked, her voice small.

"Oh, yeah," he said, and shuddered. "They were dead."

"Where are they?" she asked. "Where did you bury them?"

He studied her for a long time, as if he thought about whether or not to answer her.

Then he sighed again.

"It's a place they call the End of the World."

Now

Abigail Browning lived in a fairytale cottage at the end of one of Hope's oldest streets. Large trees, which somehow thrived despite the desert air, surrounded the place, making it look even more like something out of Hansel and Gretel. Blooming plants lined the walk, plants which Becca knew took more water than summer water rationing allowed. She decided to ignore them as she stood on the brick steps and rapped on the solid oak door.

A latch slammed back and then the door pulled open, sending a wave of lavender scent outside. The woman who stood before Becca was short and hunched, not the tall powerhouse that Becca remembered from her childhood.

"Abigail Browning?" Becca asked.

"Don't you recognize me, Rebecca Keller? I practically raised you."

That wasn't quite true. Abigail Browning did baby-sit when Becca's parents couldn't find anyone else, but otherwise she had little to do with Becca's childhood.

"Sure I do, Mrs. Browning," Becca said, falling back on her childhood name for this woman, even though Abigail Browning had never married. "I was wondering if you could help me with a case."

Abigail Browning smiled and stepped away from the door. "Of course, my dear. Would you like some tea?"

"I'd love some," Becca said as she walked inside. The house smelled the same—lavender and baking bread with the faint undertone of cat.

Now Becca was old enough to appreciate the mahogany staircase, built Craftsman-style, and the matching bookcases that graced the living room. The entire house had mahogany trim as well as built-in shelving, a feature Becca knew that Chase would love—particularly since no one had painted over the original wood.

Mrs. Browning led her into the kitchen. A coffeecake sat in a glass case in the center of the table, almost as if Mrs. Browning had expected her. Mrs. Browning filled a kettle and put it on the stove, then climbed on a stool to remove large mugs from the shiny mahogany cupboards.

"I'm not as tall as I used to be," she said. "Time crushes all of us."

Becca nodded, uncertain what to say. "The kitchen looks just the same."

"Which negates the ten thousand dollar remodel I did two years ago," Mrs. Browning said.

Becca looked at her in surprise.

"I had to update everything. I had dry rot. Or the house did. Your husband helped me."

Becca opened her mouth to correct Mrs. Browning, then thought the better of it. Abigail Browning often made misstatements to see how other people stood on things.

"He's a good man," Mrs. Browning said. "Maybe the best in town, and you let him get away."

"I didn't let—"

"You confused him with your father, who was a horrid, manipulative man, and you forgot that men can be strong without being horrid."

Becca felt her cheeks heat. "Would you like to hear about the case?"

"More than you'd like to hear how you threw away a good man because a bad one raised you," Mrs. Browning said, taking down two plates.

Becca did not offer to help her. Instead, Becca stood near the table, hands crossed in front of her, feeling ten years old again.

"So tell me," Mrs. Browning said, putting the plates on the table. The kettle whistled, and she removed it from the heat. She grabbed a teapot from a shelf that looked old, but had to be new because Becca didn't remember it.

"I was wondering what you know about the Natatorium."

"I can tell you how awful it smelled when I was a child, but that's not what you're asking, is it? Be specific, girl. Didn't I teach you anything?"

"What happened when it was built?"

"Which time?" Mrs. Browning set a beautiful wood trivet on the table, then placed the teapot on top of it.

"Which time?" Becca repeated. "Things are only built once, aren't they?"

Mrs. Browning stood near a chair near the teapot shelf, a chair that Becca remembered had always been Mrs. Browning's favorite. Becca had sat there once as a child, and had found it uncomfortable, molded to the elderly woman's body. Only then Mrs. Browning hadn't been elderly. She had only seemed that way.

"The foundation for the Natatorium was laid at the same time as the hotel, around 1908. It was abandoned that same year."

"Abandoned?" Becca asked. "I heard that the work stopped."

"Probably from that horrible Gladys Conyers. She really knows only the textbook history of this town which, I'm sorry to say, is wrong. People are never saints, you know. You always have to look for the darkness to balance the light."

Mrs. Browning peered at her. Mrs. Browning's eyes, buried under layers of wrinkles, were the same piercing blue they had always been.

Becca remembered Mrs. Browning trying to tell her that before. *You're the light, Rebecca. Remember that. Good things can come from dark places.*

She shook the memory away.

"Sit down, child, you're making me nervous."

Becca slid into her usual chair. Odd to think she had a usual chair, when she hadn't been to this house in more than twenty years.

"Do you still remember how to pour?"

Becca smiled. She did remember those lessons. Mrs. Browning had trained her in "company" manners, including how to set a table, how to dress for dinner, and how to pour for guests.

"I do," Becca said. She picked up the teapot, handling it as if Mrs. Browning had pulled down her silver service instead of her everyday.

Mrs. Browning watched her every move as if she were still being judged on perfection. Becca remembered everything, including when to ask if Mrs. Browning wanted sugar and cream, and to hold the top of the pot so that it wouldn't fall unceremoniously into Mrs. Browning's plate.

Mrs. Browning smiled, as if Becca's behavior was confirmation of the work she'd down bringing her up.

"So," Mrs. Browning said when Becca finished pouring, "which part of the Natatorium are you interested in? The first building or the second?"

"I'm interested in the pool, whenever it was laid."

"The pool." Mrs. Browning pursed her lips. "So your Chase finally found the bodies, did he?"

Becca felt her breath catch. Whatever she'd expected Mrs. Browning to say, it wasn't that.

"You knew?"

"Child, half the town knew. Why do you think that no one was allowed near that old wreck?"

"But you swam there as a child."

"All of us did," Mrs. Browning said. "And some of us brought our own children there, until the place shut down. It was just a rumor, after all. Except for the hotel."

Becca frowned. "We're talking about the Nat."

"We can't talk about the Nat without talking about the hotel. Have you ever been inside?"

"Just last night, as a matter of fact."

"Did you look at the walls?"

Becca's frown grew deeper. "Yes."

"Then you understand why I told your Chase not to tear them down."

"No," Becca said. "I don't."

Mrs. Browning touched her hand with dry fingers. "Rebecca, you've never been slow. Haven't you wondered why those walls move?"

"They don't move," Becca said. "They have heat shimmers. It piles up and—"

"Heat shimmers occur on pavement in sunlight," Mrs. Browning said. "Not in a dark, dusty hotel in the middle of a summer evening."

Becca licked her lips. When she was fourteen, she'd run from that hotel. She'd gone there to neck with Zack Wheeler, and when he'd pressed her against one of the walls, it was squishy. She turned to look at the wood, saw it shimmer, change, and shimmer again, and she couldn't help it.

She screamed.

Zack saw it too, grabbed her hand, and pulled her out of there. They'd run all the way to his car, and even told his father, who had looked at them with contempt. That was the first time Becca had heard the heat shimmer idea, but it wasn't the last.

"So what causes it?" Becca asked.

"Aliens," Mrs. Browning said. "The aliens haunting the End of the World."

Then

She couldn't go to the End of the World. She couldn't even leave the house. Jess Taylor didn't want her to. He was afraid for her. She was hot and sad and lonely, and she spent her days crying sometimes.

But she didn't practice changing. Instead, she worked on getting every detail right. Jess Taylor had to tell her sometimes that she was using masculine details—he'd actually laughed the time she put bits of hair on her own chin—but mostly, he said, she was looking solid.

Whatever that meant.

He wanted the town to think no one had survived. He didn't want them to question her or him.

It took him days and days to figure out how to do that.

Then one day he told her. She was going to take a train.

Now

Aliens? Of all the things Becca had expected from Mrs. Browning, a popular crazy notion wasn't one of them. Hope had been the talk of the alien conspiracy community since 2001, when one of her colleagues had discovered some metal in Lake Waloon. The lake had receded during one of the driest years on record, leaving all sorts of artifacts in its cracked and much-abused bed.

The experts, called in by the Historical Society, claimed it was part of an experimental airplane or maybe even one of the early do-it-yourself models from the 1920s.

UFO groupies looked at the pictures on the internet, and descended *en masse* to Hope, believing they'd found another ship like the one the government supposedly hid in Roswell, New Mexico.

Ever since, Hope had to endure annual pilgrimages from the UFO faithful. Becca tried to ignore them, just like she used to ignore the Deadheads when they came through on their way to Eugene to see the Grateful Dead in its natural habitat.

"Aliens," Becca said. "Surely you don't believe that hype from a few years ago—"

"Yes," Mrs. Browning said as she cut Becca a piece of coffee-cake. "Of course I do. I grew up knowing that we'd been invaded. The fact that the ship was found simply confirmed it."

"The ship wasn't found," Becca said, and then caught herself. She'd learned in a few, short months not to argue with the True Believers. Only she'd never taken Mrs. Browning to be one of them.

Mrs. Browning cut another piece of coffeecake and slid it onto her own plate. "If you do not believe that twisted hunk of metal was an alien spacecraft, then you won't believe anything I have to tell you about the Natatorium."

Becca sighed. "I saw the so-called ship. It's just a crumpled aircraft."

"No," Mrs. Browning said. "It was molded to look like an aircraft. It's a space ship."

Becca had heard this argument countless times as well. She took a deep breath, and then thought the better of all of it.

"All right," she said. "Let's pretend that you and I agree. Let's pretend that is a spaceship, and the squirming wall in the End of the World is made by alien ghosts. What else can you tell me?"

Mrs. Browning delicately cut her piece of coffee cake with her fork, her little finger extended. She had the same manners she always had. She seemed as sharp as she had thirty years ago.

But Becca knew that sometimes elderly people who lived alone developed "peculiarities." Now she was going to have to overlook Mrs. Browning's just to get to the heart of the story.

And maybe, just maybe, she was going to have to accept that she was wasting her time.

"Eat," Mrs. Browning said, "and I'll tell you what I know."

Then

She hadn't been that frightened since Jess Taylor found her. She thought he was going to make her leave by train.

She didn't know where he'd send her or what she'd do or who she'd meet. But by now, she knew she could trust him. He brought her clothes. He fed her. He helped her.

They had long talks when he got home from the bank, and one night, he told her his family had died just like hers.

"In Hope?" she asked.

He shook his head. "Far away from Hope in a place called Mississippi."

"How come you didn't get killed?" she asked. She already knew he couldn't change, so she wanted to know how he got away.

"I was in the North," he said. "Ohio. Going to school in Antioch. Then the money stopped—my whole family was supporting me, giving me an education, and I sent letters to find out why, and some-one sent me a postcard back. It was a drawing of the day—of the killings—like people were proud of it, and they said *Don't bother to come*, but I did anyway and . . ."

His voice trailed away. He didn't look at her. He was quiet a long time.

"What happened?" she asked because she couldn't take it any more.

"I ran, and ended up in Hope."

Now

Becca took a bite of her coffeecake. It was as good and rich as ever, a taste of her childhood.

Mrs. Browning watched her eat that bite, then leaned back in her own chair. Becca wondered if that position was even comfort-able, given Mrs. Browning's pronounced dowager's hump.

"In the summer of Aught Eight, the shanty town just outside of Hope burned to the ground," Mrs. Browning began in her teacherly voice. "Most of the histories do not mention the shanty town. Those that do claim the fire threatened Hope itself. It didn't threaten the buildings that comprised Hope. It threatened the vision of Hope."

Very dramatic, Becca thought. She took another bite of cake, then followed it with a sip of tea, straining to keep her expression interested and credulous.

"The fire was as controlled a burn as the people of Hope could manage in those bygone days."

The ease with which Mrs. Browning told this story made Becca believe that Mrs. Browning used to recite as part of the history project.

"The townspeople had gotten together and decided to rid themselves of the strangers once and for all."

Mrs. Browning shook her fork—still holding coffeecake—at Becca.

"If you look in the papers of the time, you'll see references to the strangers. They arrived in 1900, claiming to have lost their wagon several miles back. They had no luggage, few belongings, and they spoke a strange version of English. The locals thought they were ignorant immigrants who'd been tricked by their guide, and gave them some land just outside of town."

"Where the End of the World is?" Becca asked.

Mrs. Browning raised her eyebrows. "Am I telling this or are you?"

"Sorry," Becca said.

"Where that 1970s mall is. It's now near the center of town. But then, it was just outside, on land no one wanted. The strangers built their own little cabins—poorly. They looked like they didn't know what to do, and of course, no one was going to help them much more than provide a meal or some supplies. They got a bit of work too."

Becca nodded, wishing Mrs. Browning would get on with it.

"I don't know what happened. The reference in various letters I've seen is that the strangers confirmed their demonic qualities. I have no idea what that means or how they confirmed demonic qualities, but the upshot is that the town fathers asked them to leave. The strangers said they wouldn't. The fight went on for some months, when finally the shanty town burned."

"A controlled burn," Becca said. "Started by?"

"Anyone who's everyone," Mrs. Browning said. "I never asked. Besides, everyone would've told me they had nothing to do with it. But you'll notice—well, of course you won't, they're all dead—but I noticed when I was young just how many of the older generation carried some burn marks on their hands. Except for that controlled burn, and the loss of a building here and there, Hope was one of the few western communities that didn't have a serious fire. And not all of these men worked for the Hope Volunteer Fire Department."

Becca finished her coffeecake. Then she picked up her tea mug and cradled it. "So they burned the shanty town. What has that to do with the Natatorium?"

"It was being built. The hotel was just a shell—it wasn't nearly done yet—and the Nat was dug, but not poured. It was going to be a tennis court. In those days, I believe the courts were clay. Not that it matters. It never got finished."

"Because . . . ?" Becca was trying to keep the frustration from her voice.

"Because the town hated the place. It reminded them that they hadn't lived up to that promise we all learned about."

Becca gripped the mug tightly. "I still don't see the connection."

Mrs. Browning sighed, as if Becca were a particularly slow student. "They used the fire to round up the strangers and herd them to the Nat. Do I need to spell it out for you?"

"You're saying the town killed these strangers?" Becca asked. "And buried them under the Nat?"

"Yes." Mrs. Browning sounded exasperated.

"How many?"

"I don't know. No one kept records. I heard that they tried to bury them under the hotel, and when that didn't work, they went to the Nat. That's why the ghosts haunt the hotel."

"You'd think they'd haunt the Nat," Becca said.

"Hauntings aren't logical," Mrs. Browning said.

None of this was, Becca thought. "How do you know that these strangers were aliens, not just a group of Eastern Europeans who ran into some people who didn't understand them?"

"Because of the stories," Mrs. Browning said. "They had glowing eyes. They talked gibberish. They could seem taller than they were. And they came from nowhere. There were no wagon tracks. There was no wagon. And these people had no idea how people behaved. Not how Americans behaved, but how human beings behaved. They had to learn it all."

Becca shook her head. "I'm sorry, Mrs. Browning. But humans differ greatly. And if this group had been from a very different culture, the residents of Hope could have made the same charge. Aliens is as farfetched as it came."

Mrs. Browning smiled sadly. "I believe it was aliens."

"Why?" Becca asked.

"Because I met one," Mrs. Browning said.

Then

The train was big and dirty and smelly. Ash fell everywhere. It made an awful noise and she wanted to run away from it.

Jess Taylor stood beside her, holding her hand. He'd borrowed his neighbor's wagon, and they'd come to the small town of Brothers, which was two stops away from Hope.

"Remember," he said. "Tomorrow, you come here, and give the nice man this paper, and then you get on the train going that direction."

He pointed. He'd already shown her the engine, and how you could tell what direction a train was going in.

"I'll meet you at the station, and we'll pretend that we haven't seen each other in years. Okay?"

He'd told her all this before, and then it sounded easy, but now, it just sounded terrifying. She wanted to get back in the wagon, get back in his house, and hide there forever.

But he said, now that her people were gone, she needed to have a life.

Where will I have this life? She asked him.

In Hope, he said. *With me.*

Momma and Daddy said humans didn't do these things, they didn't make that kind of commitment, they didn't understand permanence and obligation and responsibility, which made them dangerous.

But Jess Taylor wasn't dangerous. And he seemed to understand all those words. He seemed to live them.

Only they came back now that she was standing on the platform with him, staring at the train.

"It's only one night," he said. "I already paid for the room. You'll be safe."

She wanted to believe him. But she was scared. What if she changed by accident? What if she said something wrong? Would they make her scream? Would they bury her without a box?

Who would tell Jess Taylor?

How would he ever know?

Now

"I was just a little girl," Mrs. Browning said, "and she was very old. Older than anyone I'd ever seen. She came to the Natatorium when I was swimming there. She cried."

"She cried?" Becca asked.

Mrs. Browning nodded. "She stood back from the pool, and she cried as she looked at it. My mother was there with me, and she just stared. Then she told me to get my towel. It was time to go."

"I don't understand," Becca said. "How do you know the old woman was an alien?"

"There'd always been stories about her," Mrs. Browning said. "She came to town to see her uncle, and she never left. At least that was the story, and some people claimed they saw her get off the train. But a few said the luggage she carried was her uncle's, and that he'd brought her there that very afternoon."

"So?" Becca asked.

"So that was right after the massacre. It was strange that he had a niece no one had ever heard of."

Becca shrugged. "I'm so sorry to be skeptical, Mrs. Browning, but I still don't understand how that translates to alien."

"I saw her once, all by myself. She was sitting at a bus stop near the old bank, and she put her hand on the bench. Her hand slid right through it."

Becca sighed. "You're not going to convince me. Not without some kind of real proof."

"What about those bodies, young lady?" Mrs. Browning said, bringing herself up as close to her old height as she could. "Are those good enough for you? They're not human, are they?"

Becca flashed on the broken femurs, so recognizable. "Of course they are."

Mrs. Browning's cheeks flushed. "You're just saying that."

"Actually," Becca said, "I'm not."

Then

That night, she slept on a single bed behind the kitchen of Mrs. Mother's Brothers Boarding House. Colored people—which was her and Jess Taylor, apparently—didn't get their own rooms. They couldn't even really stay at the boarding house, but Jess Taylor knew the cook, who volunteered to share her room. Mrs. Mother, the old lady who ran the place, had frowned in that mean way some humans had, but all she said was, "Make sure it doesn't get into the food."

She didn't understand for the longest time that the "it" Mrs. Mother referred to was her.

Maybe that's why Daddy said this was a dangerous place, why humans were scary people. She hadn't even known they cared about differences, and now she was finding out that the differences were everything.

No wonder they'd gone after her people. She hadn't noticed Jess Taylor's differences from the men at the bank and as time went on, she began to understand how badly her own people had mimicked the humans. No knee dimples, too smooth skin, eyes that didn't blink.

If the dark skin or the long braid of hair running down the back or the upswept eye angle scared them, they must've been really terrified by a whole group of people whose skin had no wrinkles, whose ankles didn't stick out, and whose expressions never changed.

No wonder.

Then she remembered Jess Taylor: *I can't believe I'm defending them* and she knew just how he felt.

The bed in the kitchen had bugs. They bit her during the night. Upstairs people laughed, and the place smelled like grease, and she wanted some water, just so she could wash the bugs off, but she didn't.

She picked them off and squished them between her fingers, and finally she got out of that bed and sat in a rocking chair, and watched out the window until the sun came up.

Then she picked up her little bag, and walked to the train station, just like Jess Taylor had told her to do, and she sat on the far edge of the platform so no one but the man who worked there saw her, and she waited for the train.

Now

Becca was happy to leave. Mrs. Browning did tell her other stories about the Natatorium—stories about its first few days as a recreation center, stories about the celebrities who used it—but both Becca and Mrs. Browning knew that the stories were merely Mrs. Browning's way of saving face.

As Becca made her good-byes, holding a piece of that delicious coffeecake in a napkin, both she and Mrs. Browning knew that she would never really trust Mrs. Browning again.

All the way to her car, Becca tried not to let sadness overwhelm her. She had lost more than a source for Hope's history. She'd lost an icon of her youth.

She had always believed that Abigail Browning was a woman of unassailable intellect and integrity. Even through the Conyers's scandal, Becca's opinion did not change. She still nodded at Abigail Browning on the street when others hadn't, and she still revered the woman she had once known.

If anything, the scandal had clarified something for her: Becca finally understood why Mrs. Browning, who had always seemed more knowledgeable than Mr. Conyers, had stopped working at the Hope Historical Society.

Now Becca wasn't so sure. Now she wondered if Mrs. Browning was fired because she believed the strange stories—the ones that had always been part of Hope. Stories of ghosts and aliens and things that went bump in the night.

Becca got into the squad and turned the ignition. The crappy air conditioning felt worse than the heat in Mrs. Browning's garden. Maybe if Becca believed in fairy tales, she would actually believe that Mrs. Browning had some sort of magic that kept the heat and the desert at bay.

But Becca only believed in reality. And only the reality she could see, Chase used to say. She could never envision his projects, not even when she looked at the architectural renderings.

She always had to wait until he was done to understand how perfect his vision had been.

What had Mrs. Browning said about Chase? *You confused him with your father, who was a horrid, manipulative man, and you forgot that men can be strong without being horrid.*

That's what Becca should have asked about. She should have asked what Mrs. Browning meant by that statement—not about Chase: women who hadn't married Chase loved him. (Hell, *Becca* still loved him)—but about her father.

Tell me about your father, her therapist said once.

He was a good man, Becca said.

But he didn't like your job.

Becca had smiled. *He was old-fashioned. He believed women didn't belong outside the home.*

What about in a police car?

Becca had laughed. *Are you kidding? He stopped paying for my school when he heard what I wanted to do.*

Is Chase like him?

Of course not, Becca said.

But your father's action sounds manipulative. You say Chase is manipulative.

Not like that, Becca said. *He respects women.*

Does he respect you?

Becca sighed and leaned back against the seat of the squad. Did he respect her? Yesterday, she would have said no, and she would have said that his secretive call about the Nat proved it.

But couldn't it also be viewed the other way? Couldn't his call be a sign of trust, of faith in her abilities instead of faith in his own ability to control her?

Could Mrs. Browning be right?

Becca shook her head. A headache was forming between her eyes. She put the squad in gear just as her cell rang.

She unhooked it from her belt and looked at the display. Jillian Mills. Becca took the call.

"Can you come down here?" Jillian asked.

"Is this about the Nat?" Becca asked.

"Yeah," Jillian said. "I have the weirdest results."

Then

They took her ticket just like Jess Taylor said they would, but they wouldn't let her sit in a chair like everybody else. They put her on one of the platforms in the back. The ash and the dirt and the stink were awful there, and as the train started to pull away, she could see the rails move.

She tried the door to get inside, but someone had locked it. She pounded on it, and the men in the nearby chairs—the men with white skin—laughed at her and pointed and she moved away from the blackened window so that they couldn't see her any more.

She was afraid they'd come out and hurt her.

Like they hurt her Momma.

Like they hurt Jess Taylor's family.

She was scared now, and she tried not to let that change her. Because if she changed, she'd lose this chance. She'd spend her life—what was left of it—as a railing or a board or a doorknob. And then, because she couldn't sleep-change, she'd starve and fall off,

all decayed, and they'd toss her aside—*what is that dried up thing?*
—and she'd die, probably in the nearby sagebrush, all alone.

Just like her Daddy.

The whole trip, she stared straight ahead and clung to her bag
and thought about Jess Taylor waiting for her. Thought about shoulders and backs and legs and human forms so that the spikes
wouldn't come out of her spine or her eyes wouldn't shift to a different part of her head.

She thought and thought and was surprised when she realized
she could hardly wait to get back to Hope.

Now

Becca's stomach clenched the entire way to the coroner's office. She
wished she hadn't eaten that coffeecake now. She wished she hadn't
gone to Mrs. Browning's. She didn't want the thoughts that were
crowding her brain. She didn't want to think the weird results were
because some aliens were massacred in Hope.

And yet she was thinking just that.

The coroner's office was on a side street behind the Hope's main
police station. The office wasn't an office at all, more like a science
lab, morgue, and training area rolled into one.

The college student who ran the front desk in exchange for rent
in the studio apartment above was reading Dostoevsky. He barely
looked up as Becca entered.

"She's expecting you," he said.

Becca nodded and continued to the small room that served as
Jillian's office. The smell of decay and formaldehyde seemed less
here than it did near the door, and wasn't nearly as strong as it was in
the basement where the autopsies actually took place.

Jillian was standing behind her desk, sorting paper files. She
wore a clean, white smock over her clothes—a sure sign that she
had just finished an autopsy—and had her hair pulled back with a
copper barrette.

"Your life just got easier," Jillian said without preamble.

"How's that?" Becca asked.

"Close the door."

Becca did.

"I did some preliminary work before calling the state crime lab,"
Jillian said. "Those bodies down there, they're not human."

Becca felt a shiver run down her back.

"I'm not sure what they are. I'm not even sure they are bodies."

Becca gripped the back of the nearest chair. She didn't want Mrs. Browning to be right.

"What are they then? Aliens?"

Jillian laughed. "Of course not. Whatever gave you that idea?"

"Abigail Browning," Becca said.

"Oh, our local UFOlogist," Jillian said. "You know she's been making her living these last few years providing historical tours of Lake Waloon?"

How could Becca have missed that? So Abigail Browning had a stake in keeping the alien story alive. And what could be better than a tale of alien massacre?

Hell, that would even give her a measure of revenge against Jack Conyers, showing that the story of racial unity in Hope was really just a myth.

"Just wondering," Becca said, trying to make light of it.

"Well, we all are. From what I can tell, these are very old bones —if they are bones as we know them. The material is something else, and it's hollow."

"But they looked human."

"So do a lot of things. Mammalian bones tend to look alike. I've had new trainees mistake cat spines and ribcages for human babies."

Becca swallowed. "What about the smell?"

"Well, that's the odd part," Jillian said. "It's coming from the— whatever they are—bones."

"Huh?"

Jillian shrugged. "Let me show you."

She grabbed an evidence bag from a table beside her desk. Inside was what looked to Becca to be an adult human rib bone. It even had the proper curvature.

"Break it," Jillian said.

"Isn't this destroying evidence?"

"Of what? Alien massacre? Just break it."

Becca grabbed a pair of medical gloves from the box beside Jillian's desk, then opened the evidence bag. She took out the rib bone, and immediately felt a sense of wrongness. It was too squishy. Even bones that had been in damp ground for a long period of time never felt like this—almost like a rubber chew toy that had been well loved.

Becca turned it over in her fingers, feeling a gag reflex, and swallowing hard against it.

Jillian nodded. "Kinda gross, huh?"

Becca didn't answer. Instead, she grabbed both ends of the bone and bent.

If it had been made of rubber—even old rubber—the bone should've bent with her hands. But it didn't bend. It snapped, and a waft of rot filled Becca's nose, almost as if she had put her face in the middle of a decaying corpse.

"Jesus Christ," she said, dropping both pieces into the evidence bag. "You could've warned me."

The gag reflex had gotten worse. Her eyes watered and she resisted the urge to wipe at them. She'd learned that lesson long ago, when she'd been a rookie: *Don't touch your own skin after touching a corpse.*

But that wasn't a corpse. It wasn't even a real bone, at least not of a kind she was familiar with.

"C'mon." Jillian took the sealed evidence bag from her, and led Becca to the back room where cleaning solutions and sharp-scented nostril-clearing substance that Jillian preferred waited.

Becca inhaled the substance, feeling her nose clear as if she'd sniffed smelling salts, and then she grabbed a clean washcloth, wiped her face, and leaned against a metal filing cabinet.

"So what the hell is it?" she asked.

"I wish I knew. I'm going to be calling not just the state, but some anthropologists to see if they've seen anything like it."

"Then why did you tell me my job got easier?"

"Because," Jillian said. "There's no recent body. There aren't even old bodies. There's a mystery, yes, but it's an archeological one. There's probably some plant or root or something that does this, and maybe it's extinct or something, which is why we're not familiar with it."

"You mean like that death plant?" Becca asked.

"The corpse flower?" Jillian nodded. "I forgot about that. I'll look it up on line. Maybe it used to grow around here."

Becca's fingers tingled. The bone—or whatever it was—had felt alive, but the way that plant roots did. She could believe that Chase had discovered the remains of a very old plant much easier than believing that an alien massacre happened in Hope.

"You want to tell Chase?" Jillian asked. "Or should I?"

Becca felt her breath catch. Chase's dream project was still on. It would still happen.

One day, the End of the World would become the premiere resort in Eastern Oregon.

"He's not going to be able to work for a while. If they think this thing is unusual, they'll do some excavation," Jillian said. "But it's not like a major dig, and it's not a crime scene. He should be thrilled."

Becca smiled in spite of her stinging nose. "Thrilled probably isn't the word I'd use. But he'll be relieved, once he's past the immediate inconvenience."

Jillian crossed her arms, looking amused. "So am I telling him?"

"No," Becca said. "I will."

Then

The train passed it.

Jess Taylor hadn't warned her.

But there was a big hand-carved sign saying, *Future Home of the End of the World Resort.* And there was a finished building right at the edge, with the word *Hotel* on it. And a big, brown patch where somebody had dug a hole and then covered it up.

Her momma was in there.

She went to the edge of the platform and stared at it until it got tiny in the distance.

And then she remembered: Her daddy, days before he left, telling Momma —

If anything happens, we go to the End of the World. We burrow into the walls or slide against the frames. We become other. We hibernate until our own people return.

She never learned how. Grown ones could do it. And they could coax their children into it, but no child could do it on her own.

She'd only seen the shimmers a few times, back when she was really little, in the ship before it crashed. Lots and lots of her people, people she didn't see until Daddy woke them, shimmered in the back compartment.

Sometimes they'd have dreams and you'd see their ghostly selves, wandering through the ship. She got scared by that, but Momma said it was normal. It was a way to check how time was passing, and when it was safe to wake up.

She didn't see any shimmers as she passed the End of the World.

She didn't see anyone she knew. It was quiet and empty and lonely.

Her people were really and truly gone, and now she was the only one left to wait for the others. The ones who were supposed to rescue them.

If they ever came.

Now

Becca and Chase stood at the End of the World, staring at the hole dug into the floor of the Natatorium. It was early evening, little more than twenty-four hours since Chase called Becca to the scene.

The area was quiet—as quiet as the desert got. A high-pitched whine from a bug Becca could not identify came from just outside the broken wall. The wind rustled a tarp that covered some of the wood Chase had bought, and not too far away, a bird peeped, probably as it hunted the whining bugs.

The sounds of workers waiting for instructions, the low buzz-growl of her radio unit, the crunch of vans on gravel were in the recent past. Right now, it was just her, Chase, and the plantlike, bonelike things half buried in the ground.

The smell wasn't as bad as it had been the day before. The bone-like things weren't freshly broken. The scent was fading, just like the smell of a dead body faded to an annoyance when the body was removed from the scene.

She and Chase stood side-by-side in the patch of sunlight that filtered through the hole in the Natatorium wall. She had brought him down here to tell him the news, and when she finished, he didn't say a word.

He swallowed once, stared at the ground, and then closed his eyes. His entire body trembled. She thought he was going to cry.

Then he took a deep breath, pushed his hard hat back, and frowned. "No one died."

"That's right," Becca said.

"And these aren't bodies."

Not human ones anyway, she almost said, but then felt the joke was in poor taste. For all she knew, Chase could have talked to Mrs. Browning too. He might have heard the alien rumors as well.

"Jillian thinks they're the remains of plants."

"*Thinks?*" Chase asked.

Becca shrugged. "All she knows is that they're not bone, not from humans or from animals. And they're the source of the smell."

"Weird," Chase said.

"You won't be able to work in the Nat for a while," Becca said. "People are coming from U of O and OSU's science and archeological departments to see what they can learn. Jillian thinks they might contact the Smithsonian or someplace like that. She made a ballpark estimate of eight months, but it could be more than that. It could be less."

Chase nodded. He still wasn't looking at her. "I can finish the hotel, though."

"The hotel, the golf course, the houses, you can do all of it."

"Golf courses," he reminded her.

"Golf courses," she said.

They stood in silence for a moment longer. Chase had his head bowed, as if he were looking at a grave.

Then he asked, "They'll clear this away?"

"Probably," Becca said. "Or you might have to find a way to build over it. You certainly don't want one of those things to break while guests are using the pool."

He shuddered, then nodded. He took off his hard hat and twisted it between his hands.

"Mrs. Browning says you're keeping the walls of the hotel," Becca said.

He looked at her sideways. "You spoke to Abigail?"

Becca nodded. "You know she used to baby-sit me, way back when."

"That's what she said. She also said I should give you time."

Becca felt her cheeks flush. That old woman meddled. "For what?"

He shrugged and looked away. "I still love you, Becca."

She wondered if that was manipulation. Or if it was just truth. Had she always mistaken truth for manipulation, and manipulation for truth?

Had she thrown away the most important thing in her life because she hadn't recognized it, because she hadn't been prepared for it, because nothing in her life taught her how to understand it?

She had had set ideas on the way that men were, on the ways they treated their wives, on the way they lived their lives.

We all have prejudices, her therapist had once told her, early in their sessions. *The key is recognizing them, and going around them. Because if we don't, we never see what's in front of us.*

Becca looked at the plantlike things. She had initially seen bone because of the smell, but they weren't bone. They just looked like bone. They were harmless and old and a curiosity, but not evidence of a horrible past.

She had misunderstood. Chase had misunderstood. And the End of the World had nearly died once again.

"You really love this place, don't you?" she said to Chase.

"It's the first place I recognized Hope's potential," he said. "It just took me fifteen years to get enough money and clout to bring my dream to reality."

"And this almost ruined it. What would you have done if Mrs. Browning had been right? If this was the site of a massacre?"

He put his hard hat on, then gave her a rueful look. "She told you that? About the aliens? Is that why you asked about the walls?"

"If there are alien ghosts, then you'll have some troubles when the End of the World opens."

"If there are alien ghosts, I'll get a lot of free publicity from the *Sci-Fi Channel* and the *Travel Channel*."

This time, she understood his tone. For all its lightness, it had some tension. He had thought about this. "It worried you, didn't it, when you dug this up?"

He nodded.

"Did you think she might be telling the truth?"

"Her version of it," he said. "Weren't you the one who told me that rumors hid real events? Maybe something bad had happened in Hope, and people made up the other story to cover it up."

"Not that anyone thought of aliens in 1908," Becca said.

He grinned, and slipped an arm around her. "Ever practical, aren't you, Becca?"

"Not ever," she said. Not during the drive from Mrs. Browning's to the coroner's office. Not when she remembered how that wall felt, squishy against her back.

"You never told me," she said. "Are you keeping the walls?"

"Why do you care?" he asked.

"They bother me," she said.

He looked at her. "You saw the alien ghosts."

She shook her head. "I didn't see anything. I just got scared as a teenager, is all."

He pulled her close. She didn't move away.

"Sometimes in old buildings," he said, "I feel like I can touch the past."

He wasn't looking at the ground any more. He was looking past the sunlight, into the desert itself.

"That's what you think that is?" Becca asked. "The past?"

"Or something," he said. "A bit of memory. A slice of time. Who knows? I always try to preserve that part of the old buildings, though."

"Why?" Becca asked.

"Because otherwise they're not worth saving. They're just wood or brick or marble. Ingredients. Buildings are living things, just like people."

She'd never heard mystical talk from him. Maybe she'd never listened.

"It's not about the money?" she asked.

"Becca, if it were about the money, I'd build cookie-cutter developments all over Hope and make millions." He shook his head. "It's about finding the surprises, whatever they might be. Good or bad."

"Or both," Becca said, moving some dirt at the edge of the hole.

"Or both," he said. "Sometimes I like both."

"Me too," she said. Then she studied him.

They were good together, but sometimes they were bad. She felt that longing for speed dial, then wondered if therapists were good and bad—good for some people, bad for others.

Maybe she should just trust herself.

She slid her hand into his.

He looked at her, surprised.

They stayed at the End of the World until the sun set—and waited for answers that might never ever come.

Then

The train had stopped in Hope for a long time before Jess Taylor found her. Her hand had molded to the railing near the door, and she couldn't remember how to set it free.

Besides, no one had unlocked the door for her. Apparently they thought it would be funny for her to climb over the edge to get off the train.

When he saw her, stuck there, her arm ending not in a hand but in a railing that went around the back of the train, he didn't say anything. Instead, he came up beside her. He hugged her, and she leaned into him.

He'd never hugged her before.

Then he set his own arm right next to hers, placing his hand right next to the place hers should be. And he watched as she shifted, slowly—fingers were so hard—and his body shielded hers from the platform, and all those other people meeting their families.

When she finished, and her arm fell at her side—complete with perfectly formed hand—he said, very softly, "They locked you out here, huh?"

She nodded and felt tears for the second time that day.

"I'm sorry. I didn't think they'd do that to a child."

And she thought of the End of the World, and all the children—the older children who had been her friends—and how they hadn't been locked out, they'd been *killed* and he'd helped bury them to keep his job, and she wondered how he could say something like that.

But she kept quiet. She was learning it was best to keep quiet sometimes.

"From now on," he was saying softly—she almost couldn't hear him over the engine, clanging as it cooled, "everyone'll think you're my niece from Mississippi. Try to talk like I do, and don't answer a lot of questions about back home. All right?"

"All right." She already knew this anyway. He'd told her before they went to Brothers.

"If we do this right," he said, pulling her close, "no one will ever know."

She swallowed, just like he did when he was nervous. No one would ever know. About her, about her family, about her people. No one would understand that for a while, her people waited and hoped.

Maybe she'd live to see the rescue ship come.

She wondered if she would recognize it.

She wondered if she would care.

Jess Taylor took her little bag with one hand, and with the other, he took her newly made hand.

"Chin up, Sarah," he said using the name she would hear from now on. In time, it would become her, just like the two arms and two legs and the permanent form and the dark skin would become her. Her self. Her identity.

She straightened her shoulders like he had taught her. She held her head high.

And then, clinging to Jess Taylor for support, she took her final steps away from the world she'd always known.

She took her first real steps into Hope.

June Sixteenth at Anna's

*J*UNE SIXTEENTH AT ANNA'S. TO A CONVERSA-
tion connoisseur, those words evoke the most pivotal afternoon
in early 21st century historical entertainment. No one knows why
these conversations have elevated themselves against the thousands of
others found and catalogued.

Theories abound. Some speculate that variety of conversational
types makes this one afternoon special. Others believe this perfor-
mance is the conversational equivalent of early jazz jam sessions—the
points and counterpoints have a beauty unrelated to the words. Still
others hypothesize that it is the presence of the single empty chair,
which allows the visitor to join the proceedings without feeling like an
intruder. . . .

—liner notes from *June Sixteenth at Anna's,*
Special six-hour edition

On the night after his wife's funeral, Mac pulled a chair in front of
the special bookcase, the one he'd built for Leta over forty years ago,
and flicked on the light attached to the top shelf. Two copies of
every edition ever produced of *June Sixteenth at Anna's*—one
opened and one permanently in its wrapper—winked back at him
as if they shared a joke.

Scattered between them, copies of the books, the e-jackets, the

DVDs, the out-dated Palms, all carrying analysis, all holding maybe a mention of Leta and what she once called the most important day of her life.

A whiff of lilacs, a jangle of gold bracelets, and then a bejeweled hand reached across his line of sight and turned the light off.

"Don't torture yourself, Dad," his daughter Cherie said. She was older than the shelf, her face softening with age, just like her mother's had. With another jangle of bracelets, she clicked on a table lamp, then sat on the couch across from him, a couch she used to flounce into when she was a teenager—which seemed to him, in his current state, just weeks ago. "Mom wouldn't have wanted it."

Mac threaded his fingers together, rested his elbows on his thighs and stared at the floor so that his daughter wouldn't see the flash of anger in his eyes. Leta didn't want anything any more. She was dead, and he was alone, with her memories taunting him from a homemade shelf.

"I'll be all right," he said.

"I'm a little worried to leave you here," Cherie said. "Why don't you come to my place for a few days? I'll fix you dinner, you can sleep in the guest room, have a look at the park. We can talk."

He had talked to Cherie. To Cherie, her soon-to-be second husband, her grown son, all of Leta's sisters and cousins, and friends, Lord knew how many friends they'd had. And reporters. Strange that one woman's death, one woman's relatively insignificant life, had drawn so many reporters.

"I want to sleep in my own bed," he said.

"Fine." Cherie stood as if she hadn't heard him. "We'll get you a cab when it's time to come home. Dad—"

"Cherie." He looked up at her, eyes puffy from her own tears, hair slightly mussed. "I won't stop missing her just because I'm at your place. The mourning doesn't go away once the funeral's over."

Her nose got red, like it always had when someone hit a nerve. "I just thought it might be easier, that's all."

Easier for whom, baby? he wanted to ask, but knew better. "I'll be all right," he said again, and left it at that.

The first time travel break-throughs came slowly. The break-throughs built on each other, though, and in the early thirties, scientists predicted that human beings would be visiting their own pasts by the end of the decade.

It turns out these scientists were right, but not in the way they expected. Human beings could not interact with time. They could only open a window into the time-space continuum, and make a record—an expensive record—of past events.

Historians valued the opportunity, but no one else did until Susan Yashimoto combined time recordings with virtual reality technology, and holography, added a few augmentations of her own, and began marketing holocordings.

Her first choices were brilliant. By using a list of historic events voted most likely to be visited should a time machine be invented, she created 'cordings of the birth of Christ, Mohammed's triumphal return to Mecca, the assassination of Abraham Lincoln, and dozens of others.

Soon, other companies entered the fray. Finding their choices limited by copyrights placed on a time period by worried historians afraid of losing their jobs, these companies began opening portals into daily life. . . .

—From *A History of Conversation*
J. Booth Centuri, 2066.
Download Reference Number:
ConverXGC112445
at Library of Congress [loc.org]

Mac had lied to Cherie. He would not sleep in his own bed. The bedroom was still filled with Leta—the blue and black bedspread they'd compromised on fifteen years before, the matching but frayed sheets she wanted to die on, the tiny strands of long, gray hairs that—no matter how much he cleaned—still covered her favorite pillow.

He'd thrown out her treatment bottles, taken the Kleenex off the nightstand, put the old-fashioned hardcover of *Gulliver's Travels* that she would now never finish on their collectibles bookshelf, but he couldn't get rid of her scent—faintly musky, slightly apricot, and always, no matter how sick she got, making him think of youth.

He carried a blanket and pillow to the couch, like he had for the last six months of Leta's life, pulled down the shade of the large picture window overlooking the George Washington Bridge—the view the reason he'd taken the apartment in that first week of the new millennium, when he'd been filled with hopes and dreams as yet unspoiled.

He wandered toward the small kitchen for a glass of something—water, beer, he wasn't certain—stopping instead by the Leta's shelf and flicking on the light, a small act of rebellion against his own daughter.

The 'cordings glinted again, like diamonds in a jewelry store window, tempting, teasing. He'd walked past this shelf a thousand times, laughed at Leta for her vanity—*sometimes I think you're the only reason the* June Sixteenth at Anna's *'cordings make any money,* he used to say to her—and derided her for attaching so much significance to that one day in her past.

You didn't even think it important until some holographer guy decided it was, he'd say, and she'd nod in acknowledgement.

Sometimes, she said to him once, *we don't know what's important until it's too late.*

He found himself holding the deluxe retrospective edition—six hours long, with the Latest Updates and Innovations!—the only set of *June Sixteenth at Anna's* with both copies still in their wrappers. It had arrived days before Leta died.

He'd carried the package in to her, brought her newest player out, the one he'd bought her that final Christmas, and placed them both on the edge of the bed.

"I'll set you up if you want," he'd said.

She had been leaning against nearly a dozen pillows, a cocoon he'd built for her when he realized that nothing would stop her inevitable march to the end. Her eyes were just slightly glazed as she took his hand.

"I've been there before," she said, her voice raspy and nearly gone.

"But not this one," he said. "You don't know the changes they've made. Maybe they have all five senses this time—"

"Mac," she whispered. "This time, I want to stay here with you."

In New York's second Guilded Age, Anna's was considered the premier spot for conversation. Like the cafes of the French Revolution or Hemingway's Movable Feast, Anna's became a pivotal place to sit, converse, and exchange ideas.

Director Hiram Goldman remembered Anna's. He applied for a time recording permit, and scanned appropriate days, finally settling on June 16, 2001 for its mix of customers, its wide-ranging conversational high points, and the empty chair that rests against a far wall, allowing the viewer to feel a part of the scene before him. . . .

—liner notes from *June Sixteenth at Anna's,*
original edition

Mac had never used a holocording, never saw the need to go back in time, especially to a period he'd already lived through. He'd said so to Leta right from the start, and after she picked up her fifth copy of *June Sixteenth*, she'd stopped asking him to join her.

He always glanced politely at the interviews, nodded at the crowds who gathered at the retrospectives, and never really listened to the speeches or the long, involved discussions of the fans.

Leta collected everything associated with that day, enjoying her minor celebrity, pleased that it had come to her after she had raised Cherie and, Leta would tell him, already had a chance to live a real life.

It was a shame she'd never opened the last 'cording. It was a sign of how ill she had been toward the end. Any other time, she might have read the liner notes — or had the box read them to her — looked at the still holos, and giggled over the inevitable analysis which, she said, was always pretentious and always wrong.

Mac opened the wrapping, felt it crinkle beneath his fingers as he tossed it in the trash. The plastic surface of the case had been engineered to feel like high-end leather. Someone had even added the faint odor of calfskin to add verisimilitude.

He opened the case, saw the shiny silver disk on the right side, and all his other choices on the left: analysis at the touch of a finger, in any form he wanted — hard-copy, audio, e-copy (format of his choice), holographic discussion; history of the 'cording; a biography of the participants, including but not limited to what happened to them after June 16, 2001; and half a dozen other things including plug-ins (for an extra charge) that would enhance the experience.

Leta used to spend hours over each piece, reviewing it as if she were going to be quizzed on it, carrying parts of it to him and sharing it with him against his will.

He was no longer certain why he was so against participating. Perhaps because he felt that life moved forward, not backward, and someone else's perspective on the past was as valid as a stranger's opinion of a book no one had ever read.

Or perhaps it was his way of dealing with minor celebrity, being Leta Thayer's husband, having his life scratched and pawned at without ever really being understood.

Mac left the case open on the shelf, next to all the other *June Sixteenth*'s, and stuck his finger through the hole in the center of the silver 'cording, carrying it with him.

The player was still in the hall closet where he'd left it two weeks before. He dragged it out, knocking over one of Leta's boots, still marked by last winter's slush, and felt a wave of such sadness he thought he wouldn't be able to stand upright.

He tried anyway, and thought it a small victory that he succeeded.

Then he carried the player, and the 'cording into the bedroom, and placed them on the foot of the bed.

Two-hundred-and-fifty people crossed the threshold at Anna's that afternoon, and although they were ethnically and culturally diverse, the sample was too small to provide a representative cross-section of the Manhattan population of that period. The restaurant was too obscure to appeal to the famous, too small to attract people from outside the neighborhood, and too new to have caché. The appeal of June Sixteenth *is the ordinariness of the patrons, the fact that on June 16, 2001 not one of them is known outside their small circle of friends and family. Their very obscurity raises their conversations to new heights.*

From A History of *June Sixteenth at Anna's*
Erik Reese, University of Idaho Press, 2051

Maybe it was the trace of her still left in the room. Maybe it was a hedge against the loneliness that threatened to overwhelm him. Maybe it was simply his only way to banish those final images—her skin yellowish and so thin that it revealed the bones in her face, the drool on the side of her mouth, and the complete lack of recognition in her eyes.

Whatever the reason, he put the 'cording in the player, sat the requisite distance from the wireless technology—so new and different when he was young, not even remarked on now—and flicked on the machine.

It didn't take him away like he expected it to. Instead it surrounded him in words and pictures and names. He didn't know how to jump past the opening credits, so he sat very still and waited for the actual 'cording to begin.

Because June Sixteenth at Anna's *is a conversation piece, its packagers never wasted their resources on sensual reconstructions. Sound is present and near perfect. Even the rattle of pans in the kitchen resonates in the dining room. The vision is also perfect—colors rich and lifelike, light and shadow so accurate that if you step into the sunlight you can almost feel the heat.*

But almost is the key word here. Except for fundamentals like making certain that solid objects are indeed solid, required of all successful holocordings, June Sixteenth at Anna's *lacks the essentials of a true historical projection. We cannot smell the garlic, the frying meat, the strawberries that look so fresh and ripe on the table nearest our chair.*

Purists claim this is so that we can concentrate on the conversation. But somehow the lack of sensation limits the spoken word. When Rufolio Field lights his illegal cigar three hours into our afternoon and management rebuffs him, we see the offense but do not take it. We are reminded that we are observers—part of the scene, but in no way of the scene.

Once the illusion is shattered, June Sixteenth at Anna's *is reduced to its component parts. It becomes a flat screen documentary remixed for the holocorders, both lifeless and old-fashioned, when what we long for is the kind of attention to detail given to truly historic moments, like* The Gettysburg Address (Weekend Edition) *or the newly released* Assassination of Archduke Ferdinand. . . .

—Review of *June Sixteenth at Anna's, Special Six Hour Edition*
in *The Essential Holographer*
February 22, 2050

The restaurant comes into view very slowly. Out of the post-credits darkness, he hears laughter, the gentle flow of voices, the clink of silverware. Then pieces appear—the maitre d's station, a simple podium flanked by two small indoor trees, the doorway leading into the restaurant proper, the couple—whom he would have termed elderly in 2001—slipping past him toward a table in the back.

Mac stands in the doorway, feeling a sense of déjà vu that would have been ridiculous if it weren't so accurate. He has been here before. Of course. A hundred times before the restaurant closed in 2021. Only he never saw the early décor—the round bistro tables covered with red checked cloths; the padded sweetheart chairs that didn't look comfortable; the floor-to-ceiling windows on the street level, an indulgence that went away only a few months later, shattered by ash and falling debris.

The restaurant is almost full. A busboy removes a sweetheart chair from the table closest to the window, holding the chair by its wire frame. He carries the chair to the wall closest to Mac, sets it down, and nods at the maitre d', who leads a young couple into the dining room.

Mac needs no more than the sway of her long, black hair to recognize Leta. His heart leaps, and for a moment, he thinks: she isn't dead. She's right here, trapped in a temporal loop, and if he frees her, she'll come home again.

Instead, he sits in the empty chair.

A speaker above him plays Charlie Burnet's "Skyliner," a CD from its poor quality, remixed from the original tapes. Pans rattle in the kitchen, and voices murmur around him, talking about the best place to eat foie gras, the history of graveyards in Manhattan, new ways to celebrate Juneteenth.

He cannot hear Leta. She is all the way across the room from him, several famous conversations away, her hand outstretched as if waiting for him to take it.

He has a good view of her face, illuminated by the thin light filtering through the windows—the canyons of the city blocking any real sun. She is smiling, nodding at something her companion says, her eyes twinkling in that way she had when she thought everything she heard was bullshit but she was too polite to say so.

Mac hadn't known her when she was here—they met in October, during that seemingly endless round of funerals, and he remembered telling her he felt guilty for feeling that spark of attraction, for beginning something new when everything else was ending.

She had put her hand on his, the skin on her palms dry and rough from all the assistance she'd been giving friends: dishes, packing, child-care. Her eyes had had shadows so deep he could barely see their shape. It wasn't until their second date that he realized her eyes had a slightly almond cast, and they were an impossible shade of blue.

There are no shadows under her eyes here, in Anna's. Leta is smiling, looking incredibly young. Mac never knew her this young, this carefree. Her skin has no lines, and that single, white strand that appeared above her right temple—the one she'd plucked on their first date and looked at in horror—isn't visible at all.

She wears a white summer dress that accents her sun-darkened skin, and as she talks, she takes a white sweater from the suitcase she used to call a purse. He recognizes the shudder, the gestures, as she puts the sweater over her shoulder.

She is clearly complaining about the cold, about air-conditioning he cannot feel. The air here is the same as the air in his bedroom, a little too warm. So much is missing, things his memory is supplying—the garlic and wine scent of Anna's, the mixture of perfumes that always seemed to linger in front of the door. He isn't hungry, and he should be. He always got hungry after a few moments in here, the rich fragrances of spiced pork in red sauce and beef sautéed in garlic and wine—Anna's specialties—making him wish that the restaurant hurried its service instead of priding itself on its European pace.

But Anna's had been a favorite of Leta's long before Mac ate there. She had been the one who showed it to him, at the grand reopening in that December, filled with survivors and firefighters and local heroes, all trying to celebrate a Christmas that had more melancholy than joy.

Six months away for this Leta. Six months and an entire lifetime away.

A waiter walks past with a full tray—polenta with a mushroom sauce, several side dishes of pasta, and breadsticks so warm their steam floats past Mac. He cannot smell them, although he wants to. He reaches for one and his fingers find bread so hard and crusty it feels stale. He cannot pull the breadstick off, of course. This is a construct, a group memory—the solidity added to make the scene feel real.

He's not confined to the chair—he knows that much about 'cordings. He can walk from table to table, listen to each conversation, maybe even go into the kitchen, depending on how deluxe this edition is.

He is not tempted to move around. He wants to stay here, where he can see the young woman who would someday become his wife flirting with a man whom she decides, one week later, to never see again after he gives her the only black eye she will ever have.

One of the many stories, she used to say, that never made it into the analysis.

Leta tucks a strand of hair behind her ear, laughs, sips some white wine. Mac watches her, enthralled. There is a carefreeness to her he has never seen before, a lightness that had vanished by the time he met her.

He isn't sure he would be interested in this Leta. She has beauty and style, but the substance, the caring that so touched him the day of his uncle's funeral, isn't present at all.

Maybe the substance is in the conversation. The famous conversation. After a moment's hesitation, he decides to listen after all.

June Sixteenth at Anna's *has often been compared with jazz—the lively, free-flowing jazz of the 1950s and 60s, recorded on vinyl with all the scratches and nicks, recorded live so that each cough and smattering of early applause adds to the sense of a past so close that it's almost tangible.*

Yet June Sixteenth at Anna's has more than that. It has community, a feeling that all the observer has to do is pull his chair to the closest table, and he will belong.

Perhaps it is the setting—very few holocordings take place in restaurants because of the ambient noise—or perhaps it is the palpable sense of enjoyment, the feeling that everyone in the room participates fully in their lives, leaving no moment unobserved. . . .

—"The Longevity of *June Sixteenth at Anna's,*"
by Michael Meller, first given as a speech
at the June Sixteenth Retrospective held
at the Museum of Conversational Arts
June 16, 2076

The cheap CD is playing "Sentimental Journey," Doris Day's melancholy voice at odds with the laughter in this well lit place. Mac walks past table after table, bumping one. The water glasses do not shake, the table doesn't even move, and although he reflexively apologizes, no one hears him.

He feels like a ghost in a room full of strangers.

The conversations float around him, intense, serious, sincere. He's not sure what makes these discussions famous. Is it the unintentional irony of incorrect predictions, like the group of businessmen discussing October's annual stock market decline? Or the poignancy of plans that would never come about, lives with less than three months left, all the obvious changes ahead?

He does not know. The conversations don't seem special to him. They seem like regular discussions, the kind people still have in restaurants all over the city. Perhaps that's the appeal, the link that sends the conversation collector from the present to the past.

His link still sits at her table, flipping her hair off her shoulder with a casual gesture. As he gets closer, he can almost smell her perfume. Right about now she should acknowledge him, that small turn in his direction, the slight raise of her eyebrows, the secret smile that they'd shared from the first instance they'd met.

But she doesn't turn. She doesn't see him. Instead, she's discussing the importance of heroes with a man who has no idea what heroism truly is.

Her fingers tap nervously against the table, a sign—a week before she throws Frank Dannen out of her life—that she doesn't like him at all. It always took time for Leta's brain to acknowledge her emotions. Too bad she hadn't realized before he hit her that Frank wasn't the man for her.

Mac stops next to the table, glances once at Frank. This is the first time Mac has seen the man outside of photographs. Curly black hair, a strong jaw, the thick neck of a former football player which, of course, he was. Frank died long before the first *June Sixteenth at Anna's* appeared, in a bar fight fifteen years after this meal.

Mac remembers because Leta showed him the story in the *Daily News*, and said with no pity in her voice, *I always knew he would come to a bad end.*

But here, in this timeless place, Frank is alive and handsome in a way that glosses over the details: the way his lower lip sets in a hard line, the bruised knuckles on his right hand, which he keeps carefully hidden from Leta, the two bottles of beer that have disappeared in the short forty-five minutes they've been at the table. Frank is barely listening to Leta; instead he checks out the other women in the room, short glances that are imperceptible to anyone who isn't paying attention.

Mac is, but he has wasted enough time on this man. Instead Mac stares at the woman who would become his wife. She stops speaking mid-thought, and leans back in her chair. Mac smiles, recognizing this ploy.

He can predict her next words: *Do you want me to continue talking to myself or would you prefer the radio for background noise?*

But she says nothing, merely watches Frank with a quizzical expression on her face, one that looks—to someone who doesn't know her—like affection, but is really a test to see when Frank will notice that she's done.

He doesn't, at least not while Mac is watching. Leta sighs, picks at the green salad before her, then glances out the window. Mac glances too, but sees nothing. Whoever recorded this scene, whoever touched it up, hadn't bothered with the outdoors, only with the restaurant and the small dramas occurring inside it.

Dramas whose endings were already known.

Because he can't help himself, Mac touches her shoulder. The flesh is warm and soft to the touch, but it is not Leta's flesh. It feels like someone else's. Leta's skin had a satiny quality that remained with her during her whole life. First, the expense of new satin, and later, the comforting patina of old satin, showing how much it was loved.

She does not look at him, and he pulls his hand away. Leta always looked at him when he touched her, always acknowledged their connection, their bond—sometimes with annoyance, when she was too busy to focus on them, yet always with love.

This isn't his Leta. This is a mannequin in a wax works, animated to go through its small part for someone else's amusement.

Mac can't take any more. He stands up, says, "Voice command: stop."

And the restaurant fades to blackness a piece at a time—the tables and patrons first, then the ambient noise, and finally the voices, fading, fading, until their words are nothing but a memory of whispers in the dark.

June Sixteenth at Anna's should not be a famous conversation piece. The fact that it is says more about our generation's search for meaning than it does about June 16, 2001.

We believe that our grandparents lived fuller lives because they endured so much more. Yet all that June Sixteenth at Anna's shows us is that each life is filled with countless moments, memorable and unmemorable—and the only meaning that these moments have are the meanings with which we imbue them at various points in our lives.

—From *June Sixteenth at Anna's Revisited,*
Mia Oppel, Harvard University Press, 2071.

Mac ended up standing beside the bed, only a foot from the player. The 'cording whirred as it wound down, the sound aggressive, as if resenting being shut off mid-program, before all the conversations had been played.

The scent of Leta lingered, and Mac realized that it had been the only real thing in his entire trip. The scent and the temperature of his bedroom had accompanied him into Anna's, bringing even more of the present into his glimpse of the past.

He took the 'cording out of the player, and carried it to the living room, placing the silver disk in its expensive case. Then he returned to the bedroom, put the player away, and lay down on the bed for the first time since Leta left it, almost a week ago.

If he closed his eyes, he could imagine her warmth, the way he used to roll into it mornings after she had gotten up. It was like being cradled in her arms, and often he would fall back to sleep until she would wake him in exasperation, reminding him that he had a job just like everyone else on the planet and it was time he went off to do it.

But the bed wasn't really warm, and if he fell asleep, she wasn't going to wake him, not now, not ever. The 'cording had left him feeling hollow, almost as if he'd done something dirty, forbidden, seeking out his wife where he knew she couldn't have been.

He had no idea why she watched all of the *June Sixteenths*. Read the commentary, yes, he understood that. And he understood the interviews, the way she accepted a fan's fawning over something she never got paid for, never even got acknowledged for. Some of the *June Sixteenth* participants sued for their percentage of the profits—and lost, since 'cordings were as much about packaging as the historical moment—but Leta had never joined them.

Instead, she went back to that single day in her life over and over again, watching her younger self from the outside, seeing—what? Looking for—what?

It certainly wasn't Frank. Mac knew her well enough for that. Had she been looking for a kind of perspective on herself, on her life? Or trying to figure out, perhaps, what her world would have been like if she had made different choices, tried other things?

He didn't know. And now, he would never know. He had teased her, listened to her talk about the ancillary materials, even bought her the latest copies of *June Sixteenth*, but he had never once heard her speak about the experience of walking around as an outsider in her own past.

A mystery of Leta—like all the other mysteries of Leta, including but not limited to why she had loved him—would remain forever unsolved.

He couldn't find the answers in *June Sixteenth*, just like he couldn't find Leta there. All that remained of Leta were bits and pieces—a scent, slowly fading; a voice, half remembered; the brush of her skin against his own.

Leta's life had an ending now, her existence as finite as *June Sixteenth at Anna's*, her essence as impossible to reproduce.

Mac hugged her favorite pillow to himself. Leta would never reappear again—not whole, breathing, surprising him with her depth.

The realization had finally come home to him, and settled in his heart: She was gone, and all he had left of her were her ghosts.

Craters

WHAT THEY DON'T TELL YOU WHEN YOU SIGN up is that the work takes a certain amount of trust. The driver, head covered by a half-assed turban, smiles a little too much, and when he yes-ma'ams you and no-ma'ams you, you can be lulled into thinking he actually works for you.

Then he opens the side door of his rusted jeep and nods at the dirt-covered seat. You don't even hesitate as you slide in, backpack filled with water bottles and purifying pills, vitamins, and six-days dry rations.

You sit in that jeep, and you're grateful, because you never allow yourself to think that he could be one of them, taking you to some roadside bunker, getting paid an advance cut of the ransom they anticipate. Or worse, getting paid to leave you there so that they can all take turns until you're bleeding and catatonic and don't care when they put the fifty-year-old pistol to your head.

You can't think about the risks, not as you're getting in that jeep, or letting some so-called civilian lead you down sunlight streets that have seen war for centuries almost non-stop.

You trust, because if you don't you can't do your job.

You trust, and hope you get away from this place before your luck runs out.

✧   ✧   ✧

I still have luck. I know it because today we pull into the camp. This camp's just like all the others I've seen in my twenty-year career. The ass-end of nowhere, damn near unbearable heat. Barbed wire, older than God, fences in everything, and at the front, soldiers with some kind of high tech rifle, some sort of programmable thing I don't understand.

My driver pulls into a long line of oil-burning cars, their engines only partly modified to hydrogen. The air stinks of gasoline, a smell I associate with my childhood, not with now.

We sit in the heat. Sweat pours down my face. I nurse the bottle of water I brought from the Green Zone—a misnomer we've applied to the American base in every "war" since Iraq. The Green Zone doesn't have a lick of green in it. It just has buildings that are theoretically protected from bombs and suicide attacks.

Finally, we pull up to the checkpoint. I clutch my bag against my lap, even though the canvas is heavy and hot.

My driver knows the soldiers. "Reporter lady," he tells them in English. The English is for my benefit, to prove once again that he is my friend. I haven't let him know that I know parts (the dirty parts mostly) of two dozen languages. "Very famous. She blog, she do vid, you see her on CNN, no?"

The soldiers lean in. They have young faces covered in sand and mud and three-day-old beards. The same faces I've been seeing for years—skin an indeterminate color, thanks to the sun and the dirt, eyes black or brown or covered with shades, expressions flat—the youth visible only in the body shape, the lack of wrinkles and sun lines, the leftover curiosity undimmed by too much death over too much time.

I lean forward so they can see my face. They don't recognize me. CNN pays me, just like the *New York Times News Service*, just like the Voice of the European Union. But none of them broadcast or replicate my image.

The woman everyone thinks of as me is a hired face, whose features get digitized over mine before anything goes out into public. Too many murdered journalists. Too many famous targets.

The military brass, they know to scan my wrist, send the code into the Reporter Registry, and get the retinal download that they can double-check against my eye. But foot soldiers, here on crap duty, they don't know for nothing.

So they eyeball me, expecting a pretty face—all the studio hires are skinny and gorgeous—and instead, getting my shoe-leather skin, my dishwater blond going on steel gray hair, and my seen-too-much eyes. They take in the sweat and the khakis and the pinkie jacks that look like plastic fingernails.

I wait.

They don't even confer. The guy in charge waves the jeep forward, figuring, I guess, that I clean up startlingly well. Before I can say anything, the jeep roars through the barbed wire into a wide, flat street filled with people.

Most cultures call them refugees, but I think of them as the dregs—unwanted and unlucky, thrown from country to country, or locked away in undesirable land, waiting for a bit of charity, a change of political fortune, waiting for an understanding that will never, ever come.

The smell hits you first: raw sewage combined with vomit and dysentery. Then the bugs, bugs like you've never seen, moving in swarms, sensing fresh meat.

After your first time with those swarms, you slather illegal bug spray on your arms, not caring that developed countries banned DDT as a poison/nerve toxin long ago. Anything to keep those creatures off you, anything to keep yourself alive.

You get out of your jeep, and immediately, the children who aren't dying surround you. They don't want sweets—what a quaint, old idea that is—they want to know what kind of tech you have, what's buried in your skin, what you carry under your eyes, what you record from that hollow under your chin. You give them short answers, wrong answers, answers you'll regret in the quiet of your hotel room days later, after you know you've made it out to report once more. You remember them, wonder how they'll do, hope that they won't become the ones you see farther into the camp, sprawled outside thin, government-issue tents, those bug-swarms covering their faces, their stomachs distended, their limbs pieces of scrap so thin that they don't even look like useful sticks.

Then you set the memories—the knowledge—aside. You're good at setting things aside. That's a skill you acquire in this job, if you didn't already have it when you came in. The I'll-think-about-it-later skill, a promise to the self that is never fulfilled.

Because if you do think about it later, you get overwhelmed. You figure out pretty damn quickly that if you do think about all the things you've seen—all the broken bodies, all the dying children—you'll break, and if you break you won't be able to work, and if you can't work, you can no longer be.

After a while, work is all that's left to you. Between the misplaced trust and the sights no human should have to bear, you stand, reporting, because you believe someone will care, someone stronger will Do Something.

Even though, deep down, you know, there is no one stronger, and nothing ever gets done.

5:15 Upload: **Suicide Squadron Part I** by Martha Trumante

General Amanda Pedersen tells the story as if it happened two days ago instead of twenty years ago. She's sitting in one of the many cafeterias in the Louvre, this one just beneath the glass pyramid where the tourists enter. She's an American soldier on leave, spending a week with her student boyfriend at the Sorbonne. He has classes. She's seeing the sights.

She's just resting her feet, propping them up—American-style— on the plastic chair across from her. From her vantage, she can't see the first round of security in the pyramid itself, but she can see the second set of metal detectors, the ones installed after the simultaneous attacks of '19 that leveled half the Prado in Madrid and the Tate in London.

She likes watching security systems—that's what got her to enlist in the first place, guaranteeing a sense of security in an insecure world—and she likes watching people go through them.

The little boy and his mother are alone on the escalator coming down. They reach the security desk, the woman opening her palm to reveal the number embedded under the skin, her son—maybe four, maybe five—bouncing with excitement beside her.

A guard approaches him, says something, and the boy extends his arms—European, clearly, used to high levels of security. The guard runs his wand up the boy's legs, over his crotch, in front of his chest—

And the world collapses.

That's how she describes it. The world collapses. The air smells of blood and smoke and falling plaster. Her skin is covered in dust and goo and she has to pull some kind of stone off her legs. Miraculously, they're not broken, but as the day progresses, part of her wishes they were, so she wouldn't be carrying dead through the ruins of the Roman area, up the back stairs, and into the thin Paris sunlight.

She can't go to the rebuilt pyramid, even now, nor to the Touleries Garden or even look at the Seine without thinking of that little boy, the smile on his face as he bounces, anticipating a day in the museum, a day with his mother, a day without cares, like five-year-olds are supposed to have.

Were supposed to have.
Before everything changed.

The driver has left me. He will be back in two days, he says, waiting for me near the checkpoint, but I do not believe him. My trust only goes so far, and I will not pay him in advance for the privilege of ferrying me out of this place. So he will forget, or die, or think I have forgotten, or died, whatever eases his conscience if a shred of his conscience still remains.

I walk deep into the camp, my pack slung over my shoulder. My easy walk, my relatively clean clothing, and my pack mark me as a newcomer, as someone who doesn't belong.

The heat is oppressive. There's no place out of the sun except the tents the Red Cross and its relative out here, the Red Crescent, have put up. People sit outside those tents, some clutching babies, other supervising children who dig in the dirt.

Rivulets of mud run across the path. Judging by the flies and the smell, the mud isn't made by water. It's overflowing sewage, or maybe it's urine from the lack of a good latrine system or maybe it's blood.

There's a lot of blood here.

I do no filming, record no images. The Western world has seen these places before, countless times. When I was a child, late-night television had infomercials featuring cheerful men who walked through such places with a single, well-dressed child, selling some religious charity that purported to help people.

Charities don't help people here. They merely stem the tide, stop the preventable deaths, keep the worst diseases at bay. But they don't find real homes for these people, don't do job training, don't offer language lessons, and more importantly, don't settle the political crises or the wars that cause the problems in the first place.

The aid worker has a harder job than I do, because the aid worker—the real aid worker—goes from country to country from camp to camp from crisis to crisis, knowing that for each life saved a thousand more will be lost.

I prefer my work, focused as it can be.

I have been on this assignment for six months now. Writing side pieces. Blogging about the bigger events. Uploading pieces that give no hint of my actual purpose.

My editors fear it will make me a target.

I know that I already am.

*   *   *

Whoever called these places camps had a gift for euphemism. These are villages, small towns with a complete and evolved social system.

You learn that early, in your first camp, when you ask the wrong person the wrong question. Yes, violence is common here—it's common in any human enclave—but it is also a means of crowd control.

Usually you have nothing to do with the extended social system. Usually you speak to the camp leaders—not the official leaders, assigned by the occupying power (whoever that may be), but the de facto leaders, the ones who ask for extra water, who discipline the teenagers who steal hydrogen from truck tanks, who kill the occasional criminal (as an example, always as an example).

You speak to these leaders, and then you leave, returning to the dumpy hotel in the dumpy (and often bombed-out) city, and lie on the shallow mattress behind the thin, wooden door, and thank whatever god you know that you have a job, that your employer pays the maximum amount to ensure your safety, that you are not the people you visited that afternoon.

But sometimes, you must venture deep into the enclave, negotiate the social strata without any kind of assistance. You guess which tents are the tents of the privileged (the ones up front, nearest the food?), which tents are the tents of the hopelessly impoverished (in the middle, where the mud runs deep and the smells overwhelm?), and which tents belong to the outcasts, the ones no one speaks to, the ones that make you unclean when you speak to them.

Never assume they're the tents farthest away from the entrance. Never assume they're the ones nearest the collapsing latrines.

Never assume.

Watch, instead. Watch to see which areas the adults avoid, which parts the parents grab their children away from in complete and utter panic.

Watch.

It is the only way you'll survive.

The people I have come to see live in a row near the back of the medical tent. The medical tent has open sides to welcome easy cases, and a smaller, air-conditioned tent farther inside the main one for difficult cases. There is no marking on the main tent—no garish red cross or scythe-like red crescent. No initials for Doctors

Without Borders, no flag from some sympathetic and neutral country.

Just a medical tent, which leads me to believe this camp is so unimportant that only representatives from the various charitable organizations come here. Only a few people even know how bad things are here, are willing to see what I can see.

Even though I will not report it.

I'm here for this group within the camp, an enclave within the enclave. I must visit them and leave. I have, maybe, eight hours here—seven hours of talk, and one hour to get away.

I'm aware that when I'm through, I may not be able to find a ride close to the camp. I must trust again or I must walk.

Neither is a good option.

The tents in this enclave are surprisingly clean. I suspect these people take what they need and no one argues with them. No children lay outside the flaps covered in bugs. No children have distended stomachs or too thin limbs.

But the parents have that hollow-eyed look. The one that comes when the illusions are gone, the one that comes to people who have decided their god has either asked too much of them or has abandoned them.

I stand outside the tent, my questions suddenly gone. I haven't felt real fear for twenty years. It takes a moment to recognize it.

Once I go inside one of these tents, I cannot go back. My interest—my story—gets revealed.

Once revealed, I am through here. I cannot stay in this camp, in this country, in this region. I might even have to go stateside—some place I haven't been in years—and even then I might not be safe.

When I came here, I was hoping to speak a truth.

Now I'm not even sure I can.

6:15 Upload: **Suicide Squadron Part 2** by Martha Trumante

Two other devastating explosions occurred in Paris that day: one hundred fifty people died as the elevator going up the Eiffel Tower exploded; and another twenty died when a bomb went off in one of the spires near the top of Notre Dame Cathedral.

France went into an unofficial panic. The country had just updated all its security systems in all public buildings. The systems, required by the European Union, were state-of-the-art. No explosives could get into any building undetected—or so the creators of the various systems claimed.

Armand de Monteverde had supervised the tests. He is a systems analyst and security expert with fifteen years experience in the most volatile areas—Iraq, Russia, and Saudi Arabia. The United States hired him to establish security at its borders with Mexico and Canada, as well as oversea security at the various harbors along the East, West, and Gulf Coasts.

He consulted with the French, went in as a spoiler—someone who tried to break the system—and declared the new process temporarily flawless.

"Why temporarily?" some British tabloid reporter asked him.

"Because," Monteverde said, "systems can always be beat."

But not usually so quickly, and not without detection. What bothered Monteverde as he poured over the data from all three Paris explosions was that he couldn't find, even then, the holes in the system.

He couldn't find who had brought the explosives in, how they'd been set off, or even what type they were.

No one else had those answers either, and they should have.

Until the Paris bombings, explosives left traces—some kind of fingerprints or signature. Until the Paris bombings, explosives were easy to understand.

I slip into the third tent to my left. It's cool inside, not just from the lack of sun, but also because some tiny, computerized system runs air-conditioning out of mesh covering the canvas. It's a rich person's tent, installed at great expense.

The tent has furniture, which surprises me. Chairs, blanket-covered beds, two small tables, for meals. A woman, sitting cross-legged on a rug near the back, wears western clothing—a thin, black blouse and black pants—her black hair cut in a stylish wedge. An eleven-year-old boy, clearly her son, sits beside her. He glances at me, his eyes dark and empty, then goes back to staring straight ahead.

I know he has no internal downloads. The camp doesn't allow any kind of net coverage, even if he has the personal chips. There's some kind of blocking technology that surrounds everything including the medical tent. International agreements allow medical facilities to have net links at all times, but these camps often exist outside an established international perimeter. Even though it straddles the borders of three separate countries, it is in none or all of them, depending on which international law the people in charge of the camp are trying to avoid.

I introduce myself. The woman gives me the look of disbelief that the soldiers should have given me. I slid her my plastic ID, since we have no systems to log onto here.

She stares at it, then turns it over, sees the hologram of the woman who plays me on the vids, and sighs.

"They warned me," she says, and I do not ask who they are. They are the people who arranged our meeting, the ones who use dozens of intermediaries, and who probably, even now, believe they are using me for some nefarious purpose. "They warned me you would not be what I expect."

A shiver runs through me. Even though I am impersonated on purpose so that the "bad guys," as our president calls them, do not know who I am, someone out there does. Maybe many someones. Maybe many someones connected to the "bad guys."

We go through preliminaries, she and I. I sit across from her, slightly out of range of her child's empty eyes. She offers tea, which I take but do not intend to drink. The cup is small and dainty, trimmed with gold. She has not yet had to trade it for a meal.

Then she slides a chip to me. I press it. A smiling man wearing a western business suit, his head uncovered, his hair as stylishly cut as the woman's is, grins at me. He holds the hand of a young girl, maybe five, who is the image of her mother. The girl laughs, one of those floaty childish laughs that some people never outgrow. The sound fills the tent, and the boy, sitting across from me, flinches.

"That's her?" I ask.

"Them," she says. "He died too."

I made it a point to know the case. There are so many cases that sometimes the details are irrelevant to all except the people involved. He had just parked his car outside a café in Cairo. He had told his wife he was taking his daughter to a special class—and indeed, an English-language class for the children of businessmen who had dealings with the West, was meeting just a block away.

He opened his door and the car exploded, killing him, his daughter, and three people on the sidewalk. If they had made it to class as was the plan, over fifty children would have died.

"She's so beautiful," I say. Hard to believe, even now, that a child like that can carry a bomb inside her. Hard to believe she exists only to kill others, at a specified place, at her own designated time.

I have promised myself I will not ask the standard question— *How can you do this? How can you do this to your own child?*

Instead, I say, "Did you know?"

"None of us knew." Her gaze meets mine. It is fierce, defiant. She has answered this question a hundred times, and her answer has never varied. Like so many survivors, she cannot believe her husband doomed his own child.

But I have promised myself I will get the real story, the story no one else has told. I want to know what it's like to be part of a society where children are tools, not people to be loved. I want to know how these people believe so much in a cause—any cause—that it is worth not only their own lives, but their child's as well.

So I must take her initial answers at face value. Perhaps I will challenge them later, but for now, I will see where they lead.

"If neither you nor your husband knew," I say.

"My son didn't know either." Just as fierce. Maybe fiercer. She puts her hand on her son's head. He closes his eyes, but doesn't acknowledge her in any other way.

"If none of you knew," I say, trying hard not to let my disbelief into my voice, "then how did this happen?"

"Like it always does," she snaps. "They put the chips in at the hospital. On the day she was born."

The job is strange. It cannot be work because you cannot leave at the end of the day. It becomes part of you and you become part of it. That's why you and your colleagues label it a calling, put it on par with other religions, other callings that deal with ethics.

You sit across from murderers and ask, *What made you decide to kill?* as if that's a valid question. You sit across from mass murderers and ask, *What is it about your political philosophy that makes your methods so attractive to others?* as if you care about the answer.

You think: we need to know, as if knowing's enough to make the problem go away. As if you did the right thing when you were granted the only meeting ever with some charismatic leader—this generation's Vlad the Impaler or Hitler or Osama bin Laden—and interviewed him as if he were a reasonable person. As if you did the right thing when you failed to grab a guard's old-fashioned pistol, and blow the charismatic leader away.

Later you discuss ethics as if they are an important concept.

You say: your job prevents you from judging other people.

You say: other reporters could not get interviews if we take such lethal sides.

You do not say: I lacked the courage to die for my beliefs.

And that is the bottom line. Behind the talk of ethics and jobs and callings lies a simple truth.

You can look. You can see.

But you cannot feel.

If you feel, you will see that your calling is simply a job, a dirty often disgusting one at that, and you realize there were times when you should have acted. When you could have saved one life or a dozen or maybe even a hundred, but you chose not to.

You chose not to—you say—for the greater good.

7:15 Upload: **Suicide Squadron Part 3** by Martha Trumante

Investigations always seem to hinge on luck. The Paris investigations are no different.

Three months into sorting the Louvre wreckage, the authorities find a chip, its information largely undamaged. Curiously, its technology was five years old, a detail that stumped the investigators more than anything else.

But not General Pedersen.

"I was watching the news that day," she says. "I don't know why. It's not something I normally do. I usually scan the relevant feeds. But that day, I was watching, and it hit me. I had seen the bomb come into the museum. I'd seen him laugh and rock back and forth and smile in anticipation. I'd thought he was looking forward to his day when really, he was looking forward to his death."

At first, other security experts would not listen to Pedersen. In a world where suicide bombers had become commonplace—when child suicide bombers packed with explosives were part of the norm—no one could believe that a child could have had a chip implanted years before with enough high density explosives to destroy an entire building.

People could not plan ahead that far, the common wisdom went. People could not be that cruel.

But they were. That was the new truth—or maybe it was an old truth.

They were.

She shows me the documents the hospital had her sign. She shows me the diagrams, the little marking some doctor made on a chart of a newborn baby, showing where the chips would be—"chips that will enable her to live in the modern world," the doctors told her.

She shows me computer downloads, bank accounts her husband set up in her daughter's name, the college enrollment forms— required for a wealthy child of age four to get into some of Cairo's best private schools—the plans she and her husband had for her daughter's future, her son's future, *their* future.

The authorities, she tells me, believe her husband created all these accounts and family documents to protect her, to prove that she and her son had nothing to do with the family's patriotic explosion.

Only he is not political, she tells me. He never was, and no one believes her.

They believe her enough to send her here instead of kill her as so many other families have been killed in the past. They don't even try or imprison her. They just disown her, her and her son, make them people without a country, refugees in a world filled with refugees.

She can afford this tent on this sandy piece of land. She pays for the space closest to the medical tent. She hoped that someone would befriend her, that the medical personnel—the aid workers— would help her and her unjustly accused son.

Instead, they shun her like everyone else does. They shun her for failing to protect her daughter. They shun her for failing to participate in her husband's crime. They shun her for being naïve, for forcing the so-called patriots to ignore her husband and daughter's martyrdom, for failing to die with her family.

They shun her because they cannot understand her.

Or because they do not want to.

8:15 Upload: **Suicide Squadron Part 4** by Martha Trumante
Experts spend their entire career studying this new bombing phenomenon. Some experts who specialized in suicide bombing have moved to this new area of research.

One, Miguel Franq, wanted to know how three families decided to murder their five-year-olds in well-known Paris landmarks on the same day. Initially, he believed he would find a link that would lead him to a terror cell.

When he did not find the link, he worked with some of the scientists to see if the bomb-chips were set to activate on a certain day, then detonate when they were hit with X-rays, laser beams, or sonar equipment—all three being the main items used in security scans.

The intact chip revealed nothing like that. Only a detonator that was set to go off on a particular time on a particular day.

After much research, many hours of survivor interviews, and that inevitable lucky break, Franq found the link. Someone gave the fami-

lies free tickets to each site. That all three children did not end up at the same tourist attraction is another matter of luck, although what kind of luck no one can say.

Would it have been better to lose more of the Louvre? Or the Eiffel Tower? Or Notre Dame?

Would it have been better to lose one monument instead of damage three? Would more lives have been saved? Lost? Would more people have noticed? Or would less?

I speak to all the parents in this part of the enclave. All of them survivors—some male, some female—of a once-intact family. All of them claiming to be non-political, claiming they did not know—nor did their spouse—that their child was programmed to die.

I ask for proof. They give me similar documents. They give me bank accounts. But, tellingly—at least to me—the names of the hospitals vary, the names of the doctors vary.

"It is the nursing staff," one man says to me.

"It is an out-patient procedure," says another woman.

"Anyone could do it," says a second man. "Even you."

The rules of journalism have tightened in the past forty years. The scandals of fifty years ago, the tales of made-up sources, or badly researched material or political bias—true or not—nearly destroyed the profession.

When you were hired, you were reminded of those past scandals, told that any story with less than three *verifiable* sources (sources that have proof of their claims, sources that can be reinterviewed by the fact-checker—no listening to vids [which can be manipulated], no scanning of notes), any story with less than three will not be run. Any such stories appearing in blogs or personal writings will be considered the same as a published or viewed newspiece.

Hire an editor for your own work, you're told. You will be watched.

We're all watched.

So you become an observer and a detective, a recorder of your facts and a disbeliever in someone else's. You need to verify and if you cannot, you risk losing your job.

You risk damaging the profession.

You risk losing your calling—because you might believe.

✻   ✻   ✻

Finally, they take me to the person I had hoped to see. They take me into the medical tent to see a six-year-old girl.

She has her own air-conditioned section. It has a hospital bed, a holo-vid player (nothing new; only old downloads), several comfortable chairs, and a table covered with playing cards. Someone is teaching her poker, the international game.

An aid worker accompanies me. He whispers, "No one outside the family visits her. We're not supposed to say she's here."

Until now, she has existed primarily as a rumor.

You know, right, of the little girl? The one who lived?

Permanently blind, she is . . .

They pay her millions of Euros just to remain quiet . . .

She lives in a palace in Switzerland . . .

. . . in Baghdad . . .

. . . in Singapore . . .

She lives in a corner of a medical tent in a refugee camp. Her face is crisscrossed with scars and the shiny tissue of a dozen different plastic surgeries. She has only one arm. You don't realize until you come close, that half her torso is a kind of clear plastic, one designed for the medical interns to monitor the fake parts inside her, the miracles that keep her alive.

As I say hello, her eyes move toward me. She can see, then. She says hello in return, her accent upper-class British with a touch of India in it. She looks wary.

I don't blame her.

No parent watches over her. Her mother committed suicide—the real kind, the kind that's personal, and lonely, and takes no one else with it—when she heard the news. The blast killed her father.

She was an only child.

I sit next to her, on her right side so that I don't have to see that clear torso, the workings of her rebuilt interior, that missing—and soon-to-be-replaced—arm.

She is being rebuilt as if she were a machine. Someone is paying for this, real money that keeps this medical tent, and hence the people in the camp, alive.

Someone who, no matter how hard I investigate, manages to remain anonymous.

"Do you know who I am?" I ask.

"Reporter-lady," she says, just like my driver, which makes me nervous. I will not stay here two days. I will leave tonight, maybe even on foot. There are too many connections, too many people who know what I'm doing. Not enough ways to make me safe.

"That's right," I say. "Reporter-lady. Can I talk to you about your accident?"

She makes a face, but half of her skin does not move. "Not an accident," she says. "I sploded."

The words, said so flatly, as if it is a fact of life. And, if I think about it, it is. A fact of her life.

A fact of all the lives I've touched here today. Every single one of them knew someone who became a bomb.

"Do you know why you exploded?" I ask.

She nods, runs her remaining hand over her stomach. "Someone put something in me."

So flat. Like a child discussing rape.

"Did your Daddy know about this?" I ask. Her father took her to an open-air market that day almost one year ago.

She shakes her head. Those bright, inquisitive eyes have moved away from me. Despite the flat tone, she hates talking about this. Or maybe hates talking about her father, the man who decided she was going to be a weapon.

"What did he say when he took you to the market?" I ask.

"Mommy wasn't feeling so good," she says. "We had to get her some medicine and a flower."

"Nothing else?" I ask.

She shrugs.

"Nothing about going to a better place?" I don't know what euphemism to use. I don't know enough about her or her past, being unable to research much of it. I don't know if she was raised Christian or Muslim or Jewish, since that open-air market catered to all three. I don't even know what nationality she is, something these camps like to keep as quiet as they can.

"No," she says.

"He didn't hug you extra hard? Tell you he loved you? Act strange in any way?"

"No," she says.

"Did your mom?"

"No!"

"Did they ever tell you that you were special?" I ask.

She looks at me again. A frown creases her brow, creating a line between the scars. "Yes."

My heart starts to pound. "What did they say?"

She shrugs.

"It's all right to tell me," I say.

She bites her lower lip. This is a question she clearly hasn't been asked much. "Special," she says, "because I'm the only one."

"The only one what?" I ask.

"The only one they ever wanted." Her voice shakes. "Everyone else, they have two, three, four."

I blink for a moment, trying to find the context.

She sees my confusion. Color runs up her cheeks, and I wonder if I've made her angry.

That fear returns—that odd sensation. Afraid twice in one day, after years without it. Afraid, of a damaged six-year-old girl.

"My daddy said I was so perfect, they only wanted me. Only me." Her voice rises, and she squeezes something in her hand.

The aid worker appears at the door. He looks sadly at me. I stand. My time is up.

As I walk out, he says, "She was an only child, in a culture that frowns on it. Her parents were trying to make her feel good about that."

"Is that what you think?" I ask.

"You're not the first she's told that to," he says. "Investigators, officials, everyone tries to find the two, three, and four others. You people never seem to remember that she's a lonely little girl, in a lot of pain, who can't understand why everyone thinks she's evil."

I look over my shoulder at her. Her lower lip trembles, but her eyes are dry.

I want to go back, ask her different questions, but the aid worker doesn't let me.

I am done here. I had hoped I would find my proof. Instead, I found a child whose parents told her she was special—because she was an only child? Or because they had planted a time-release bomb-chip in her?

Or both?

9:15 Upload: **Suicide Squadron Part 5** by Martha Trumante

The Paris bombings were the first and last time more than one child detonated in the same city on the same day. Ever since, these explosions have occurred at all times of the day, at hundreds of locations across the globe, at thousands of targets—some large, like the Eiffel Tower, and some small, like a deceptively normal home in a tiny suburban neighborhood.

The small bombings lend credence to the rumors that have

plagued this weapon from the beginning: that these children and their parents are innocent victims of fanatics who have wormed their way into the medical establishment, that the true bombers aren't suicidal at all. Instead they are nurses, doctors, interns, who piggyback the detonator chip onto a relatively normal chipping procedure—giving a child an identity chip, for example, or the standard parental notification chip that must now be inserted into every newborn—a procedure that's a law in more than 120 countries.

Hospitals insist that medical personal are screened. Each chip brought into the building is scanned for foreign technology. Each chip has its own identification number so that it can be traced to its source.

None of the chips found at the thousands of bomb sites since the Paris bombings have had hospital identification. Yet the rumors persist.

Perhaps it is wishful thinking on the part of all involved. How much easier it is to blame a nameless, faceless person hidden in the impersonal medical system than a parent who knowingly pays someone to place a bomb inside a child—a bomb that will not go off in days or even weeks, but years later, after that parent spends time feeding, clothing, and raising that child.

Bonding with that child.

Treating her as if she's normal.

Treating her as if she's loved.

One of the soldiers gives you a ride back to the Green Zone. You lean your head against the back of his modern, hydrogen powered, air-conditioned behemoth—too big to even call a truck—and close your eyes.

The little girl has shaken you. Some stories do that—some interviews do that—and the key is to hold onto your professionalism, to remember what you can prove.

But in that space between wakefulness and sleep, you find yourself thinking that you live your life in three distinct ways: You have your everyday experiences, which are so different from most people's. How many people travel from war zone to war zone, from danger spot to danger spot, running toward the crisis instead of away from it? Such behavior is now second nature to you. You think of it only at odd moments, like this one, when you should be asleep.

You also live through your articles, your "live" reports, your blogs. People who see/read/hear those things believe they know the real you. They believe they have walked with you into the valley of the shadow of death, and they believe that they, like you, have survived some kind of evil.

Really, however, you live inside your head, in the things you're afraid to write down, afraid to record, afraid to even feel. You lied when you implied that fear hasn't been in your life in decades. Fear is in your every movement. But you speak truth when you say you haven't *felt* fear.

You haven't felt anything in a long, long time.

That's the most important thing they fail to tell you when you sign up for this job. Not that it could kill you or that you might even want it to kill you.

But that you can look at a little girl who has lost everything— her health, her family, her belief that someone once loved her—and you think she does not measure up to the rumor. She isn't the story that will save you, the news that will make you even more famous than you already are.

She doesn't even merit a mention in your long piece on suicide squads because she doesn't change anything. She is, to you, another body—another item—another fact in a lifetime of useless facts.

She is not a child, any more than you are a woman.

She is a weapon, and you are a reporter.

And that's all you'll ever be.

Diving into the Wreck

*W*E APPROACH THE WRECK IN STEALTH MODE:
lights and communications array off, sensors on alert for
any other working ship in the vicinity. I'm the only one in the cockpit of the *Nobody's Business*. I'm the only one with the exact coordinates.

The rest of the team sits in the lounge, their gear in cargo. I personally searched each one of them before sticking them to their
chairs. No one, but no one, knows where the wreck is except me.
That was our agreement.

They hold to it or else.

We're six days from Longbow Station, but it took us ten to get
here. Misdirection again, although I'd only planned on two days
working my way through an asteroid belt around Beta Six. I ended
up taking three, trying to get rid of a bottom-feeder that tracked us,
hoping to learn where we're diving.

Hoping for loot.

I'm not hoping for loot. I doubt there's something space-valuable
on a wreck as old as this one looks. But there's history value, and
curiosity value, and just plain old we-done-it value. I picked my
team with that in mind.

The team: six of us, all deep-space experienced. I've worked with
two before—Turtle and Squishy, both skinny space-raised women

who have a sense of history that most out here lack. We used to do a lot of women-only dives together, back in the beginning, back when we believed that sisterhood was important. We got over that pretty fast.

Karl comes with more recommendations than God; I wouldn't've let him aboard with those rankings except that we needed him—not just for the varied dives he's gone on, but also for his survival skills. He's saved at least two diving-gone-wrong trips that I know of.

The last two—Jypé and Junior—are a father-and-son team that seem more like halves of the same whole. I've never wreck dived with them, though I took them out twice before telling them about this trip. They move in synch, think in synch, and have more money than the rest of us combined.

Yep, they're recreationists, but recreationists with a handle: their hobby is history, their desires—at least according to all I could find on them—to recover knowledge of the human past, not to get rich off of it.

It's me that's out to make money, but I do it my way, and only enough to survive to the next deep space trip. I don't thrive out here, but I'm addicted to it.

The process gets its name from the dangers: in olden days, wreck diving was called space diving to differentiate it from the planet-side practice of diving into the oceans.

We don't face water here—we don't have its weight or its unusual properties, particularly at huge depths. We have other elements to concern us: No gravity, no oxygen, extreme cold.

And greed.

My biggest problem is that I'm land-born, something I don't confess to often. I spent the first forty years of my life trying to forget that my feet were once stuck to a planet's surface by real gravity. I even came to space late: fifteen years old, already land-locked. My first instructors told me I'd never unlearn the thinking real atmosphere ingrains into the body.

They were mostly right; land pollutes me, takes out an edge that the space-raised come to naturally. I gotta consciously choose to go into the deep and dark; the space-raised glide in like it's mother's milk. But if I compare myself to the land-locked, I'm a spacer of the first order, someone who understands vacuum like most understand air.

Old timers, all space-raised, tell me my interest in the past comes from being land-locked. Spacers move on, forget what's behind them. The land-born always search for ties, thinking they'll understand better what's before them if they understand what's behind them.

I don't think it's that simple. I've met history-oriented spacers, just like I've met land-born who're always looking forward.

It's what you do with the knowledge you collect that matters and me, I'm always spinning mine into gold.

So, the wreck.

I came on it nearly a year before, traveling back from a bust I'd got suckered into with promise of glory. I was manually guiding my single-ship, doing a little mapping to pick up some extra money. They say there aren't any undiscovered places anymore in this part of our galaxy, just forgotten ones, and I think that's true.

An eye blink is all I'd've needed to miss the wreck. I caught the faint energy signal on a sensor I kept tuned to deep space around me. The sensor blipped once and was gone, that fast. But I had been around enough to know that something was there. The energy signal was too far out, too faint to be anything but lost.

As fast as I could, I dropped out of FTL, cutting my sublight speed to nothing in the drop. It still took me two jumps and a half day of searching before I found the blip again and matched its speed and direction.

I had been right. It was a ship. A black lump against the blackness of space.

My single-ship is modified—I don't have automatic anythings in it, which can make it dangerous (the reason single-ships are completely automatic is so that the sole inhabitant is protected), but which also makes it completely mine. I've modified engines and the computers and the communications equipment, so that nothing happens without my permission.

The ship isn't even linked to me, although it is set to monitor my heart rate, my respiration rate, and my eyes. Should my heart slow, my breathing even, or my eyes close for longer than a minute, the automatic controls take over the entire ship. Unconsciousness isn't as much of a danger as it would be if the ship was one-hundred-percent manual, but consciousness isn't a danger either. No one can monitor my thoughts or my movements simply by tapping the ship's computer.

Which turned out to be a blessing because now there are no

records of what I had found in the ship's functions. Only that I had stopped.

My internal computer attached to the eyelink told me what my brain had already figured out. The wreck had been abandoned long ago. The faint energy signal was no more than a still running current inside the wreck.

My internal computer hypothesized that the wreck was Old Earth make, five thousand years old, maybe older. But I was convinced that estimation was wrong.

In no way could Earthers have made it this far from their own system in a ship like that. Even if the ship had managed to survive all this time floating like a derelict, even if there had been a reason for it to be here, the fact remained: no Earthers had been anywhere near this region five thousand years ago.

So I ignored the computerized hypothesis, and moved my single-ship as close as I could get it to the wreck without compromising safety measures.

Pitted and space-scored, the wreck had some kind of corrosion on the outside and occasional holes in the hull. The thing clearly was old. And it had been floating for a very long time. Nothing lived in it, and nothing seemed to function in it either besides that one faint energy signature, which was another sign of age.

Any other spacer would've scanned the thing, but other spacers didn't have my priorities. I was happy my equipment wasn't storing information. I needed to keep this wreck and its whereabouts my secret, at least until I could explore it.

I made careful private notes to myself as to location and speed of the wreck, then went home, thinking of nothing but what I had found the entire trip.

In the silence of my free-floating apartment, eighteen stories up on the scattered space-station wheel that orbited Hector One Prime, I compared my eyeball scan to my extensive back-up files.

And got a jolt: The ship was not only Old Earth based, its type had a name:

It was a Dignity Vessel, designed as a stealth warship.

But no Dignity Vessel had made it out of the fifty light year radius of Earth—they weren't designed to travel huge distances, at least by current standards, and they weren't manufactured outside of Earth's solar system. Even drifting at the speed it was moving, it couldn't have made it to its location in five thousand years, or even fifty thousand.

A Dignity Vessel.

Impossible, right?

And yet . . .

There it was. Drifting. Filled with mystery.

Filled with time.

Waiting for someone like me to figure it out.

The team hates my secrecy, but they understand it. They know one person's space debris is another's treasure. And they know treasures vanish in deep space. The wrong word to the wrong person and my little discovery would disappear as if it hadn't existed at all.

Which was why I did the second and third scans myself, all on the way to other missions, all without a word to a soul. Granted, I was taking a chance that someone would notice my drops out of FTL and wonder what I was doing, but I doubted even I was being watched that closely.

When I put this team together, I told them only I had a mystery vessel, one that would tax their knowledge, their beliefs, and their wreck-recovery skills.

Not a soul knows it's a Dignity Vessel. I don't want to prejudice them, don't want to force them along one line of thinking.

Don't want to be wrong.

The whats, hows, and whys I'll worry about later. The ship's here.

That's the only fact I need.

After I was sure I had lost every chance of being tracked, I let the *Business* slide into a position out of normal scanner and visual range. I matched the speed of the wreck. If my ship's energy signals were caught on someone else's scans, they automatically wouldn't pick up the faint energy signal of the wreck. I had a half dozen cover stories ready, depending on who might spot us. I hoped no one did.

But taking this precaution meant we needed transport to and from the wreck. That was the only drawback of this kind of secrecy.

First mission out, I'm ferry captain—a role I hate, but one I have to play. We're using the skip instead of the *Business*. The skip is designed for short trips, no more than four bodies on board at one time.

This trip, there's only three of us—me, Turtle, and Karl. Usually we team-dive wrecks, but this deep and so early, I need two different kinds of players. Turtle can dive anything, and Karl can kill anything. I can fly anything.

We're set.

I'm flying the skip with the portals unshielded. It looks like we're inside a piece of black glass moving through open space. Turtle paces most of the way, walking back to front to back again, peering through the portals, hoping to be the first to see the wreck.

Karl monitors the instruments as if he's flying the thing instead of me. If I hadn't worked with him before, I'd be freaked. I'm not; I know he's watching for unusuals, whatever comes our way.

The wreck looms ahead of us—a megaship, from the days when size equaled power. Still, it seems small in the vastness, barely a blip on the front of my sensors.

Turtle bounces in. She's fighting the grav that I left on for me—that landlocked thing again—and she's so nervous, someone who doesn't know her would think she's on something. She's too thin, like most divers, but muscular. Strong. I like that. Almost as much as I like her brain.

"What the hell is it?" she asks. "Old Empire?"

"Older." Karl is bent at the waist, looking courtly as he studies the instruments. He prefers readouts to eyeballing things; he trusts equipment more than he trusts himself.

"There can't be anything older out here," Turtle says.

"Can't is relative," Karl says.

I let them tough it out. I'm not telling them what I know. The skip slows, shuts down, and bobs with its own momentum. I'm easing in, leaving no trail.

"It's gonna take more than six of us to dive that puppy," Turtle says. "Either that, or we'll spend the rest of our lives here."

"As old as that thing is," Karl says, "it's probably been plundered and replundered."

"We're not here for the loot." I speak softly, reminding them it's a historical mission.

Karl turns his angular face toward me. In the dim light of the instrument panel, his gray eyes look silver, his skin unnaturally pale. "You know what this is?"

I don't answer. I'm not going to lie about something as important as this, so I can't make a denial. But I'm not going to confirm either. Confirming will only lead to more questions, which is something I don't want just yet. I need them to make their own minds up about this find.

"Huge, old." Turtle shakes her head. "Dangerous. You know what's inside?"

"Nothing, for all I know."

"Didn't check it out first?"

Some of dive team leaders head into a wreck the moment they find one. Anyone working salvage knows it's not worth your time to come back to a place that's been plundered before.

"No." I pick a spot not far from the main doors, and set the skip to hold position with the monster wreck. With no trail, I hoped no one was gonna notice the tiny energy emanation the skip gives off.

"Too dangerous?" Turtle asks. "That why you didn't go in?"

"I have no idea," I say.

"There's a reason you brought us here." She sounds annoyed. "You gonna share it?"

I shake my head. "Not yet. I just want to see what you find."

She glares, but the look has no teeth. She knows my methods and even approves of them sometimes. And she should know that I'm not good enough to dive alone.

She peels off her clothes—no modesty in this woman—and slides on her suit. The suit adheres to her like it's a part of her. She wraps five extra breathers around her hips—just-in-case emergency stuff, barely enough to get her out if her suit's internal oxygen system fails. Her suit is minimal—it has no back-up for environmental protection. If her primary and secondary units fail, she's a little block of ice in a matter of seconds.

She likes the risk; Karl doesn't. His suit is bulkier, not as form-fitting, but it has external environmental back-ups. He's had environmental failures and barely survived them. I've heard that lecture half a dozen times. So has Turtle, even though she always ignores it.

He doesn't go starkers under the suit either, leaving some clothes in case he has to peel quickly. Different divers, different situations. He only carries two extra breathers, both so small that they fit on his hips without expanding his width. He uses the extra loops for weapons, mostly lasers, although he's got a knife stashed somewhere in all that preparedness.

The knife has saved his life twice that I know of—once against a claim-jumper, and once as a pick that opened a hole big enough to squeeze his arm through.

They don't put on the headpieces until I give them the plan. One hour only: twenty minutes to get in, twenty minutes to explore, twenty minutes to return. Work the buddy system. We just want an idea of what's in there.

One hour gives them enough time on their breathers for some margin of error. One hour also prevents them from getting too involved in the dive and forgetting the time. They have to stay on schedule.

They get the drill. They've done it before, with me anyway. I have no idea how other team leaders run their ships. I have strict rules about everything, and expect my teams to follow.

Headpieces on—Turtle's is as thin as her face, tight enough to make her look like some kind of cybernetic human. Karl goes for the full protection—seven layers, each with a different function; double night vision, extra cameras on all sides; computerized monitors layered throughout the external cover. He gives me the hand-held, which records everything he "sees." It's not as good as the camera eyeview they'll bring back, but at least it'll let me know my team is still alive.

Not that I can do anything if they're in trouble. My job is to stay in the skip. Theirs is to come back to it in one piece.

They move through the airlock—Turtle bouncing around like she always does, Karl moving with caution—and then wait the required two minutes. The suits adjust, then Turtle presses the hatch, and Karl sends the lead to the other ship.

We don't tether, exactly, but we run a line from one point of entry to the other. It's cautionary. A lot of divers get wreck blindness—hit the wrong button, expose themselves to too much light, look directly into a laser, or the suit malfunctions in ways I don't even want to discuss—and they need the tactical hold to get back to safety.

I don't deal with wreck blindness either, but Squishy does. She knows eyes, and can replace a lens in less than fifteen minutes. She's saved more than one of my crew in the intervening years. And after overseeing the first repair—the one in which she got her nickname—I don't watch.

Turtle heads out first, followed by Karl. They look fragile out there, small shapes against the blackness. They follow the guideline, one hand resting lightly on it as they propel themselves toward the wreck.

This is the easy part: should they let go or miss by a few meters, they use tiny air chips in the hands and feet of their suits to push them in the right direction. The suits have even more chips than that. Should the diver get too far away from the wreck, they can use little propellants installed throughout their suits.

I haven't lost a diver going or coming from a wreck.

It's inside that matters.

My hands are slick with sweat. I nearly drop the handheld. It's not providing much at the moment—just the echo of Karl's breathing, punctuated by an occasional "fuck" as he bumps something or moves slightly off-line.

I don't look at the images he's sending back either. I know what they are—the gloved hand on the lead, the vastness beyond, the bits of the wreck in the distance.

Instead, I walk back to the cockpit, sink into my chair, and turn all monitors on full. I have cameras on both of them and read-outs running on another monitor watching their heart and breathing patterns. I plug the handheld into one small screen, but don't watch it until Karl approaches the wreck.

The main door is scored and dented. Actual rivets still remain on one side. I haven't worked a ship old enough for rivets; I've only seen them in museums and histories. I stare at the bad image Karl's sending back, entranced. How have those tiny metal pieces remained after centuries? For the first time, I wish I'm out there myself. I want to run the thin edge of my glove against the metal surface.

Karl does just that, but he doesn't seem interested in the rivets. His fingers search for a door release, something that will open the thing easily.

After centuries, I doubt there is any easy here. Finally, Turtle pings him.

"Got something over here," she says.

She's on the far side of the wreck from me, working a section I hadn't examined that closely in my three trips out. Karl keeps his hands on the wreck itself, sidewalking toward her.

My breath catches. This is the part I hate: the beginning of the actual dive, the place where the trouble starts.

Most wrecks are filled with space, inside and out, but a few still maintain their original environments, and then it gets really dicey—extreme heat or a gaseous atmosphere that interacts badly with the suits.

Sometimes the hazards are even simpler: a jagged metal edge that punctures even the strongest suits; a tiny corridor that seems big enough until it narrows, trapping the diver inside.

Every wreck has its surprises, and surprise is the thing that leads to the most damage—a diver shoving backward to avoid a floating object, a diver slamming his head into a wall jarring the suit's delicate internal mechanisms, and a host of other problems, all of them documented by survivors, and none of them the same.

The handheld shows a rip in the exterior of the wreck, not like any other caused by debris. Turtle puts a fisted hand in the center, then activates her knuckle lights. From my vantage, the hole looks large enough for two humans to go through side-by-side.

"Send a probe before you even think of going in there," I say into her headset.

"Think it's deep enough?" Turtle asks, her voice tinny as it comes through the speakers.

"Let's try the door first," Karl says. "I don't want surprises if we can at all avoid them."

Good man. His small form appears like a spider attached to the ship's side. He returns to the exit hatch, still scanning it.

I look at the timer, running at the bottom of my main screen.

17:32

Not a lot of time to get in.

I know Karl's headpiece has a digital readout at the base. He's conscious of the time, too, and as cautious about that as he is about following procedure.

Turtle scuttles across the ship's side to reach him, slips a hand under a metal awning, and grunts.

"How come I didn't see that?" Karl asks.

"Looking in the wrong place," she says. "This is real old. I'll wager the metal's so brittle we could punch through the thing."

"We're not here to destroy it." There's disapproval in Karl's voice.

"I *know*."

19:01. I'll come on the line and demand they return if they go much over twenty minutes.

Turtle grabs something that I can't see, braces her feet on the side of the ship, and tugs. I wince. If she loses her grip, she propels, spinning, far and fast into space.

"Crap," she says. "Stuck."

"I could've told you that. These things are designed to remain closed."

"We have to go in the hole."

"Not without a probe," Karl says.

"We're running out of time."

21:22

They are out of time.

I'm about to come on and remind them, when Karl says, "We have a choice. We either try to blast this door open or we probe that hole."

Turtle doesn't answer him. She tugs. Her frame looks small on my main screen, all bunched up as she uses her muscles to pry open something that may have been closed for centuries.

On the handheld screen, enlarged versions of her hands disappear under that awning, but the exquisite detail of her suit shows the ripple of her flesh as she struggles.

"Let go, Turtle," Karl says.

"I don't want to damage it," Turtle says. "God knows what's just inside there."

"Let go."

She does. The hands reappear, one still braced on the ship's side.

"We're probing," he says. "Then we're leaving."

"Who put you in charge?" she grumbles, but she follows him to that hidden side of the ship. I see only their limbs as they move along the exterior—the human limbs against the pits and the dents and the small holes punched by space debris. Shards of protruding metal near rounded gashes beside pristine swatches that still shine in the thin light from Turtle's headgear.

I want to be with them, clinging to the wreck, looking at each mark, trying to figure out when it came, how it happened, what it means.

But all I can do is watch.

The probe makes it through sixteen meters of stuff before it doesn't move any farther. Karl tries to tug it out, but the probe is stuck, just like my team would've been if they'd gone in without it.

They return, forty-two minutes into the mission, feeling defeated.

I'm elated. They've gotten farther than I ever expected.

We take the probe readouts back to the *Business*, over the protests of the team. They want to recharge and clean out the breathers and dive again, but I won't let them. That's another rule I have to remind them of—only one dive per twenty-four hour period. There are too many unknowns in our work; it's essential that we have time to rest.

All of us get too enthusiastic about our dives—we take chances we shouldn't. Sleep, relaxation, downtime all prevent the kind of haste that gets divers killed.

Once we're in the *Business*, I download the probe readouts, along with the readings from the suits, the gloves, and the handheld. Everyone gathers in the lounge. I have three-D holotech in there, which'll allow us all to get a sense of the wreck.

As I'm sorting through the material, thinking of how to present it (handheld first? Overview? A short lecture?), the entire group arrives. Turtle's taken a shower. Her hair's wet, and she looks tired. She'd sworn to me she hadn't been stressed out there, but her eyes tell me otherwise. She's exhausted.

Squishy follows, looking somber. Jypé and Junior are already there, in the best seats. They've been watching me set up. Only Karl is late. When he arrives—also looking tired—Squishy stops him at the door.

"Turtle says it's old."

Turtle shoots Squishy an angry look.

"She won't say anything else." Squishy glances at me as if it's my fault. Only I didn't swear the first team to secrecy about the run. That was their choice.

"It's old," Karl says, and squeezes by her.

"She's says it's weird-old."

Karl looks at me now. His angular face seems even bonier. He seems to be asking me silently if he can talk.

I continue setting up.

Karl sighs, then says, "I've never seen anything like it."

No one else asks a question. They wait for me. I start with the images the skip's computer downloaded, then add the handheld material. I've finally decided to save the suit readouts for last. I might be the only one who cares about the metal composition, the exterior hull temperature, and the number of rivets lining the hatch.

The group watches in silence as the wreck appears, watches intently as the skip's images show a tiny Turtle and Karl sliding across the guideline.

The group listens to the arguments, and Jypé nods when Karl makes his unilateral decision to use the probe. The nod reassures me. Jypé is as practical as I'd hoped he'd be.

I move to the probe footage next. I haven't previewed it. We've all seen probe footage before, so we ignore the grainy picture, the thin light, and the darkness beyond.

The probe doesn't examine so much as explore: its job is to go as far inside as possible, to see if that hole provides an easy entrance into the wreck.

It looks so easy for ten meters—nothing along the edges, just light and darkness and weird particles getting disturbed by our movements.

Then the hole narrows and we can see the walls as large shapes all around the probe. The hole narrows more, and the walls become visible in the light—a shinier metal, one less damaged by space debris. The particles thin out too.

Finally a wall looms ahead. The hole continues, so small that it seems like the probe can continue. The probe actually sends a laser pulse, and gets back a measurement: the hole is six centimeters in diameter, more than enough for the equipment to go through.

But when the probe reaches that narrow point, it slams into a barrier. The barrier isn't visible. The probe runs several more readouts, all of them denying that the barrier is there.

Then there's a registered tug on the line: Karl trying to get the probe out. Several more tugs later, Karl and Turtle decide the probe's stuck. They take even more readouts, and then shut it down, planning to use it later.

The readouts tell us nothing except that the hole continues, six centimeters in diameter, for another two meters.

"What the hell do you think that is?" Junior asks. His voice hasn't finished its change yet, even though both Jypé and Junior swear he's over eighteen.

"Could be some kind of forcefield," Squishy says.

"In a vessel that old?" Turtle asks. "Not likely."

"How old is that?" Squishy's entire body is tense. It's clear now that she and Turtle have been fighting.

"How old is that, boss?" Turtle asks me.

They all look at me. They know I have an idea. They know age is one of the reasons they're here.

I shrug. "That's one of the things we're going to confirm."

"Confirm." Karl catches the word. "Confirm what? What do you know that we don't?"

"Let's run the readouts before I answer that," I say.

"No." Squishy crosses her arms. "Tell us."

Turtle gets up. She pushes two icons on the console beside me, and the suits' technical readouts come up. She flashes forward, through numbers and diagrams and chemical symbols to the conclusions.

"Over five thousand years old." Turtle doesn't look at Squishy.

"That's what the boss isn't telling us. This wreck is human-made, and it's been here longer than humans have been in this section of space."

Karl stares at it.

Squishy shakes her head. "Not possible. Nothing human made would've survived to make it this far out. Too many gravity wells, too much debris."

"Five thousand years," Jypé says.

I let them talk. In their voices, in their argument, I hear the same argument that went through my head when I got my first readouts about the wreck.

It's Junior that stops the discussion. In his half-tenor, half-baritone way, he says, "C'mon, gang, think a little. That's why the boss brought us out here. To confirm her suspicions."

"Or not," I say.

Everyone looks at me as if they've just remembered I'm there.

"Wouldn't it be better if we knew your suspicions?" Squishy asks.

Karl is watching me, eyes slitted. It's as if he's seeing me for the first time.

"No, it wouldn't be better." I speak softly. I make sure to have eye contact with each of them before I continue. "I don't want you to use my scholarship—or lack thereof—as the basis for your assumptions."

"So should we discuss this with each other?" Squishy's using that snide tone with me now. I don't know what has her so upset, but I'm going to have to find out. If she doesn't calm, she's not going near the wreck.

"Sure," I say.

"All right." She leans back, staring at the readouts still floating before us. "If this thing is five thousand years old, human made, and somehow it came to this spot at this time, then it can't have a force-field."

"Or fake readouts like the probe found," Jypé says.

"Hell," Turtle says. "It shouldn't be here at all. Space debris should've pulverized it. That's too much time. Too much distance."

"So what's it doing here?" Karl asked.

I shrug for the third and last time. "Let's see if we can find out."

They don't rest. They're as obsessed with the readouts as I've been. They study time and distance and drift, forgetting the weirdness inside the hole. I'm the one who focuses on that.

I don't learn much. We need more information—we revisit the

probe twice while looking for another way into the ship—and even then, we don't get a lot of new information.

Either the barrier is new technology or it is very old technology, technology that has been lost. So much technology has been lost in the thousands of years since this ship was built.

It seems like humans constantly have to reinvent everything.

Six dives later and we still haven't found a way inside the ship. Six dives, and no new information. Six dives, and my biggest problem is Squishy.

She has become angrier and angrier as the dives continue. I've brought her along on the seventh dive to man the skip with me, so that we can talk.

Junior and Jypé are the divers. They're exploring what I consider to be the top of the ship, even though I'm only guessing. They're going over the surface centimeter by centimeter, exploring each part of it, looking for a weakness that we can exploit.

I monitor their equipment using the skip's computer, and I monitor them with my eyes, watching the tiny figures move along the narrow blackness of the skip itself.

Squishy stands beside me, at military attention, her hands folded behind her back.

She knows she's been brought for conversation only; she's punishing me by refusing to speak until I broach the subject first.

Finally, when J&J are past the dangerous links between two sections of the ship, I mimic Squishy's posture—hands behind my back, shoulders straight, legs slightly spread.

"What's making you so angry?" I ask.

She stares at the team on top of the wreck. Her face is a smooth reproach to my lack of attention; the monitor on board the skip should always pay attention to the divers.

I taught her that. I believe that. Yet here I am, reproaching another person while the divers work the wreck.

"Squishy?" I ask.

She isn't answering me. Just watching, with that implacable expression.

"You've had as many dives as everyone else," I say. "I've never questioned your work, yet your mood has been foul, and it seems to be directed at me. Do we have an issue I don't know about?"

Finally she turns, and the move is as military as the stance was. Her eyes narrow.

"You could've told us this was a Dignity Vessel," she says.

My breath catches. She agrees with my research. I don't under-stand why that makes her angry.

"I could've," I say. "But I feel better that you came to your own conclusion."

"I've known it since the first dive," she says. "I wanted you to tell them. You didn't. They're still wasting time trying to figure out what they have here."

"What they have here is an anomaly," I say, "something that makes no sense and can't be here."

"Something dangerous." She crosses her arms. "Dignity Vessels were used in wartime."

"I know the legends." I glance at the wreck, then at the handheld readout. J&J are working something that might be a hatch.

"A lot of wartimes," she says, "over many centuries, from what historians have found out."

"But never out here," I say.

And she concedes. "Never out here."

"So what are you so concerned about?"

"By not telling us what it is, we can't prepare," she says. "What if there're weapons or explosives or something else—"

"Like that barrier?" I ask.

Her lips thin.

"We've worked unknown wrecks before, you and me, together."

She shrugs. "But they're of a type. We know the history, we know the vessels, we know the capabilities. We don't know this at all. No one really knows what these ancient ships were capable of. It's some-thing that shouldn't be here."

"A mystery," I say.

"A dangerous one."

"Hey!" Junior's voice is tinny and small. "We got it open! We're going in."

Squishy and I turn toward the sound. I can't see either man on the wreck itself. The handheld's imagery is shaky.

I press the comm, hoping they can still hear me. "Probe first. Remember that barrier."

But they don't answer, and I know why not. I wouldn't either in their situation. They're pretending they don't hear. They want to be the first inside, the first to learn the secrets of the wreck.

The handheld moves inside the darkness. I see four tiny lights— Jypé's glovelights—and I see the same particles I saw before, on the first images from the earliest probe.

Then the handheld goes dark. We were going to have to adjust it to transmit through the metal of the wreck.

"I don't like this," Squishy says.

I've never liked any time I was out of sight and communication with the team.

We stare at the wreck as if it can give us answers. It's big and dark, a blob against our screen. Squishy actually goes to the portals and looks, as if she can see more through them than she can through the miracle of science.

But she doesn't. And the handheld doesn't wink on.

On my screen, the counter ticks away the minutes.

Our argument isn't forgotten, but it's on hold as the first members of our little unit vanish inside.

After thirty-five minutes—fifteen of them inside (Jypé has rigorously stuck to the schedule on each of his dives, something which has impressed me)—I start to get nervous.

I hate the last five minutes of waiting. I hate it even more when the waiting goes on too long, when someone doesn't follow the timetable I've devised.

Squishy, who's never been in the skip with me, is pacing. She doesn't say any more—not about danger, not about the way I'm running this little trip, not about the wreck itself.

I watch her as she moves, all grace and form, just like she's always been. She's never been on a real mystery run. She's done dangerous ones—maybe two hundred deep space dives into wrecks that a lot of divers, even the most greedy, would never touch.

But she's always known what she's diving into, and why it's where it is.

Not only are we uncertain as to whether or not this is an authentic Dignity Vessel (and really, how can it be?), we also don't know why it's here, how it came here, or what its cargo was. We have no idea what its mission was either—if, indeed, it had a mission at all.

37:49

Squishy's stopped pacing. She looks out the portals again, as if the view has changed. It hasn't.

"You're afraid, aren't you?" I ask. "That's the bottom line, isn't it? This is the first time in years that you've been afraid."

She stops, stares at me as if I'm a creature she's never seen before, and then frowns.

"Aren't you?" she asks.

I shake my head.

The handheld springs to life, images bouncy and grainy on the corner of my screen. My stomach unclenches. I've been breathing shallowly and not even realizing it.

Maybe I am afraid, just a little.

But not of the wreck. The wreck is a curiosity, a project, a conundrum no one else has faced before.

I'm afraid of deep space itself, of the vastness of it. It's inexplicable to me, filled with not just one mystery, but millions, and all of them waiting to be solved.

A crackle, then a voice—Jypé's.

"We got a lot of shit." He sounds gleeful. He sounds almost giddy with relief.

Squishy lets out the breath she's obviously been holding.

"We're coming in," Junior says.

It's 40:29.

The wreck's a Dignity Vessel, all right. It's got a DV number etched inside the hatch, just like the materials say it should. We mark the number down to research later.

Instead, we're gathered in the lounge, watching the images J&J have brought back.

They have the best equipment. Their suits don't just have sensors and readouts, but they have chips that store a lot of imagery woven into the suits' surfaces. Most suits can't handle the extra weight, light as it is, or the protections to ensure that the chips don't get damaged by the environmental changes—the costs are too high, and if the prices stay in line, then either the suits' human protections are compromised, or the imagery is.

Two suits, two vids, so much information.

The computer cobbles it together into two different information streams—one from Jypé's suit's prospective, the other from Junior's. The computer cleans and enhances the images, clarifies edges if it can read them and leaves them fuzzy if it can't.

Not much is fuzzy here. Most of it is firm, black-and-white only because of the purity of the glovelights and the darkness that surrounds them.

Here's what we see:

From Junior's point-of-view, Jypé going into the hatch. The edge is up, rounded, like it's been opened a thousand times a day instead of once in thousands of years. Then the image switches to Jypé's leg-cams and at that moment, I stop keeping track of which images belong to which diver.

The hatch itself is round, and so is the tunnel it leads down. Metal rungs are built into the wall. I've seen these before: they're an ancient form of ladder, ineffective and dangerous. Jypé clings to one rung, then turns and pushes off gently, drifting slowly deep into a darkness that seems profound.

Numbers are etched on the walls, all of them following the letters DV, done in ancient script. The numbers are repeated over and over again—the same ones—and it's Karl who figures out why: each piece of the vessel has the numbers etched into it, in case the vessel was destroyed. Its parts could always be identified then.

Other scratches marked the metal, but we can't read them in the darkness. Some of them aren't that visible, even in the glovelights. It takes Jypé a while to remember he has lights on the soles of his feet as well—a sign, to me, of his inexperience.

Ten meters down, another hatch. It opens easily, and ten meters beneath it is another.

That one reveals a nest of corridors leading in a dozen different directions. A beep resounds in the silence and we all glance at our watches before we realize it's on the recording.

The reminder that half the dive time is up.

Junior argues that a few more meters won't hurt. Maybe see if there are items off those corridors, something they can remove, take back to the *Business* and examine.

But Jypé keeps to the schedule. He merely shakes his head, and his son listens.

Together they ascend, floating easily along the tunnel as they entered it, leaving the interior hatches open, and only closing the exterior one, as we'd all learned in dive training.

The imagery ends, and the screen fills with numbers, facts, figures, and readouts which I momentarily ignore. The people in the room are more important. We can sift through the numbers later.

There's energy here—a palpable excitement—dampened only by Squishy's fear. She stands with her arms wrapped around herself, as far from Turtle as she can get.

"A Dignity Vessel," Karl says, his cheeks flushed. "Who'd've thought?"

"You knew," Turtle says to me.

I shrug. "I hoped."

"It's impossible," Jypé says, "and yet I was inside it."

"That's the neat part," Junior says. "It's impossible and it's here."

Squishy is the only one who doesn't speak. She stares at the read-outs as if she can see more in them than I ever will.

"We have so much work to do," says Karl. "I think we should go back home, research as much as we can, and then come back to the wreck."

"And let others dive her?" Turtle says. "People are going to ghost us, track our research, look at what we're doing. They'll find the wreck and claim it as their own."

"You can't claim this deep," Junior says, then looks at me. "Can you?"

"Sure you can," I say. "But a claim's an announcement that the wreck's here. Something like this, we'll get jumpers for sure."

"Karl's right." Squishy's voice is the only one not tinged with excitement. "We should go back."

"What's wrong with you?" Turtle says. "You used to love wreck diving."

"Have you read about early period stealth technology?" Squishy asks. "Do you have any idea what damage it can do?"

Everyone is looking at her now. She still has her back to us, her arms wrapped around herself so tightly her shirt pulls. The screen's readout lights her face, but all we can see are parts of it, illuminating her hair like an inverse nimbus.

"Why would you have studied stealth tech?" Karl asks.

"She was military," Turtle says. "Long, long ago, before she realized she hates rules. Where'd you think she learned field medicine?"

"Still," Karl says, "I was military too —"

Which explained a lot.

"— and no one ever taught me about stealth tech. It's the stuff of legends and kid's tales."

"It was banned." Squishy's voice is soft, but has power. "It was banned five hundred years ago, and every few generations, we try to revive it or modify it or improve it. Doesn't work."

"What doesn't work?" Junior asks.

The tension is rising. I can't let it get too far out of control, but I want to hear what Squishy has to say.

"The tech shadows the ships, makes them impossible to see, even with the naked eye," Squishy says.

"Bullshit," Turtle says. "Stealth just masks instruments, makes it impossible to read the ships on equipment. That's all."

Squishy turns, lets her arms drop. "You know all about this now?

Did you spend three years studying stealth? Did you spend two years of post-doc trying to recreate it?"

Turtle is staring at her like she's never seen her before. "Of course not."

"You have?" Karl asks.

Squishy nods. "Why do you think I find things? Why do you think I *like* finding things that are lost?"

Junior shakes his head. I'm not following the connection either.

"Why?" Jypé asks. Apparently he's not following it as well.

"Because," Squishy says, "I've accidentally lost so many things."

"Things?" Karl's voice is low. His face seems pale in the lounge's dim lighting.

"Ships, people, materiel. You name it, I lost it trying to make it invisible to sensors. Trying to recreate the tech you just found on that ship."

My breath catches. "How do you know it's there?"

"We've been looking at it from the beginning," Squishy says. "That damn probe is stuck like half my experiments got stuck, between one dimension and another. There's only one way in and no way out. And the last thing you want—the very last thing—is for one of us to get stuck like that."

"I don't believe it." Turtle says with such force that I know she and Squishy have been having this argument from the moment we first saw the wreck.

"Believe it." Squishy says that to me, not Turtle. "Believe it with all that you are. Get us out of here, and if you're truly humane, blow that wreck up, so no one else can find it."

"Blow it up?" Junior whispers.

The action is so opposite anything I know that I feel a surge of anger. We don't blow up the past. We may search it, loot it, and try to understand it, but we don't destroy it.

"Get rid of it." Squishy's eyes are filled with tears. She's looking at me, speaking only to me. "Boss, please. It's the only sane thing to do."

Sane or not, I'm torn.

If Squishy's right, then I have a duel dilemma: the technology is lost, new research on it banned, even though the military keeps conducting research anyway, trying, if I'm understanding Squishy right, to rediscover something we knew thousands of years before.

Which makes this wreck so very valuable that I could more than retire with the money we'd get for selling it. I would—we would—be rich for the rest of our very long lives.

Is the tech dangerous because the experiments to rediscover it are dangerous? Or is it dangerous because there's something inherent about it that makes it unfeasible now and forever?

Karl is right: to do this properly, we have to go back and research Dignity Vessels, stealth tech, and the last few thousand years.

But Turtle's also right: we'll take a huge chance of losing the wreck if we do that. We'll be like countless other divers who sit around bars throughout this sector and bemoan the treasures they lost because they didn't guard them well enough.

We can't leave. We can't even let Squishy leave. We have to stay until we make a decision.

Until I make a decision.

On my own.

First, I look up Squishy's records. Not her dive histories, not her arrest records, not her disease manifolds—the stuff any dive captain would examine—but her personal history, who she is, what she's done, who she's become.

I haven't done that on any of my crew before. I've always thought it an invasion of privacy. All we need to know, I'd say to other dive captains, is whether they can handle the equipment, whether they'll steal from their team members, and if their health is good enough to handle the rigors.

And I believed it until now, until I found myself digging through layers of personal history that are threaded into the databases filling the *Business*'s onboard computer.

Fortunately for me and my nervous stomach, the more sensitive databases are linked only to me—no one else even knows they exist (although anyone with brains would guess that they do)—and even if someone finds the databases, no one can't access them without my codes, my retinal scan, and, in many cases, a sample of my DNA.

Still, I'm skittish as I work this—sound off, screen on dim. I'm in the cockpit, which is my domain, and I have the doors to the main cabin locked. I feel like everyone on the *Business* knows I'm betraying Squishy. And I feel like they all hate me for it.

Squishy's real name is Rosealma Quintinia. She was born forty years ago in a multinational cargo vessel called *The Bounty*. Her parents insisted she spend half her day in artificial gravity so she wouldn't develop spacer's limbs—truncated, fragile—and she didn't. But she gained a grace that enabled her to go from zero-G to Earth Normal and back again without much transition at all, a skill few ever gain.

Her family wanted her to cargo, maybe even pirate, but she rebelled. She had a scientific mind, and without asking anyone's permission, took the boards—scoring a perfect 100, something no cargo monkey had ever done before.

A hundred schools all over the known systems wanted her. They offered her room, board, and tuition, but only one offered her all expenses paid both coming and going from the school, covering the only cost that really mattered to a spacer's kid—the cost of travel.

She went, of course, and vanished into the system, only to emerge twelve years later—too thin, too poor, and too bitter to ever be considered a success. She signed on with a cargo vessel as a medic, and soon became one of its best and most fearless divers.

She met Turtle in a bar, and they became lovers. Turtle showed her that private divers make more money, and brought her to me.

And that was when our partnership began.

I sigh, rub my eyes with my thumb and forefinger, and lean my head against the screen.

Much as I regret it, it's time for questions now.

Of course, she's waiting for me.

She's brought down the privacy wall in the room she initially shared with Turtle, making their rift permanent. Her bed is covered with folded clothes. Her personal trunk is open at the foot. She's already packed her nightclothes and underwear inside.

"You're leaving?" I ask.

"I can't stay. I don't believe in the mission. You've preached forever the importance of unity, and I believe you, Boss. I'm going to jeopardize everything."

"You're acting like I've already made a decision about the future of this mission."

"Haven't you?" She sits on the edge of the bed, hands folded primly in her lap, her back straight. Her bearing *is* military—something I've always seen, but never really noticed until now.

"Tell me about stealth tech," I say.

She raises her chin slight. "It's classified."

"That's fucking obvious."

She glances at me, clearly startled. "You tried to research it?"

I nod. I tried to research it when I was researching Dignity Vessels. I tried again from the *Business*. I couldn't find much, but I didn't have to tell her that.

That was fucking obvious too.

"You've broken rules before," I say. "You can break them again."

She looks away, staring at that opaque privacy wall—so representative of what she'd become. The solid backbone of my crew suddenly doesn't support any of us anymore. She's opaque and difficult, setting up a divider between herself and the rest of us.

"I swore an oath."

"Well, let me help you break it," I snap. "If I try to enter that barrier, what'll happen to me?"

"Don't." She whispers the word. "Just leave, Boss."

"Convince me."

"If I tell you, you gotta swear you'll say nothing about this."

"I swear." I'm not sure I believe me. My voice is shaky, my tone something that sounds strange to even me.

But the oath—however weak it is—is what Squishy wants.

Squishy takes a deep breath, but she doesn't change her posture. In fact, she speaks directly to the wall, not turning toward me at all.

"I became a medic after my time in Stealth," she says. "I decided I had to save lives after taking so many of them. It was the only way to balance the score . . ."

Experts believe stealth tech was deliberately lost. Too dangerous, too risky. The original stealth scientists all died under mysterious circumstances, all much too young and without recording any part of their most important discoveries.

Through the ages, their names were even lost, only to be rediscovered by a major researcher, visiting Old Earth in the latter part of the past century.

Squishy tells me all this in a flat voice. She sounds like she's reciting a lecture from very long ago. Still, I listen, word for word, not asking any questions, afraid to break her train of thought.

Afraid she'll never return to any of it.

Earth-owned Dignity Vessels had all been stripped centuries before, used as cargo ships, used as junk. An attempt to reassemble one about five hundred years ago failed because the Dignity Vessels' main components and their guidance systems were never, ever found, either in junk or in blueprint form.

A few documents, smuggled to the colonies on Earth's Moon,

suggested that stealth tech was based on interdimensional science—that the ships didn't vanish off radar because of a "cloak" but because they traveled, briefly, into another world—a parallel universe that's similar to our own.

I recognized the theory—it's the one on which time travel is based, even though we've never discovered time travel, at least not in any useful way, and researchers all over the universe discourage experimentation in it. They prefer the other theory of time travel, the one that says time is not linear, that we only perceive it as linear, and to actually time travel would be to alter the human brain.

But what Squishy is telling me is that it's possible to time travel, it's possible to open small windows in other dimensions, and bend them to our will.

Only, she says, those windows don't bend as nicely as we like, and for every successful trip, there are two that don't function as well.

I ask for explanation, but she shakes her head.

"You can get stuck," she says, "like that probe. Forever and ever."

"You think this is what the Dignity Vessels did?"

She shakes her head. "I think their stealth tech is based on some form of this multi-dimensional travel, but not in any way we've been able to reproduce."

"And this ship we have here? Why are you so afraid of it?" I ask.

"Because you're right." She finally looks at me. There are shadows under her eyes. Her face is skeletal, the lower lip trembling. "The ship shouldn't be here. No Dignity Vessel ever left the sector of space around Earth. They weren't designed to travel vast distances, let alone halfway across our known universe."

I nod. She's not telling me something I don't already know. "So?"

"So," she says. "Dozens and dozens of those ships never returned to port."

"Shot down, destroyed. They were battleships, after all."

"Shot down, destroyed, or lost," she says. "I vote for lost. Or used for something, some mission now lost in time."

I shrug. "So?"

"So you wondered why no one's seen this before, why no one's found it, why the ship itself has drifted so very far from home."

I nod.

"Maybe it didn't drift."

"You think it was purposely sent here?"

She shakes her head. "What if it stealthed on a mission to the outer regions of Old Earth's area of space?"

My stomach clenches.

"What if," she says, "the crew tried to destealth—and ended up here?"

"Five thousand years ago?"

She shakes her head. "A few generations ago. Maybe more, maybe less. But not very long. And you were just the lucky one who found it."

I spend the entire night listening to her theories.

I hear about the experiments, the forty-five deaths, the losses she suffered in a program that started the research from scratch.

After she left R&D and went into medicine, she used her high security clearance to explore older files. She found pockets of research dating back nearly five centuries, the pertinent stuff gutted, all but the assumptions gone.

Stealth tech. Lost, just like I assumed. And no one'd been able to recreate it.

I listen and evaluate, and realize, somewhere in the dead of night, that I'm not a scientist.

But I am a pragmatist, and I know, from my own research, that Dignity Vessels, with their stealth tech, existed for more than two hundred years. Certainly not something that would have happened had the stealth technology been as flawed as Squishy said.

So many variables, so much for me to weigh.

And beneath it all, a greed pulses, one that—until tonight—I thought I didn't have.

For the last five centuries, our military has researched stealth tech and failed.

Failed.

I might have all the answers only a short distance away, in a wreck no one else has noticed, a wreck that is—for the moment anyway—completely my own.

I leave Squishy to sleep. I tell her to clear her bed, that she has to remain with the group, no matter what I decide.

She nods as if she's expecting that, and maybe she is. She grabs her nightclothes as I let myself out of the room, and into the much cooler, more dimly lit corridor.

As I walk to my own quarters, Jypé finds me.

"She tell you anything worthwhile?" His eyes are a little too bright. Is greed eating at him like it's eating at me? I'm almost afraid to ask.

"No," I say. "She didn't. The work she did doesn't seem all that relevant to me."

I'm lying. I really do want to sleep on this. I make better decisions when I'm rested.

"There isn't much history on the Dignity Vessels—at least that's specific," he says. "And your database has nothing on this one, no serial number listing, nothing. I wish you'd let us link up with an outside system."

"You want someone else to know where we are and what we're doing?" I ask.

He grins. "It'd be easier."

"And dumber."

He nods. I take a step forward and he catches my arm.

"I did check one other thing," he says.

I am tired. I want sleep more than I can say. "What?"

"I learned long ago that if you can't find something in history, you look in legends. There're truths there. You just have to dig more for them."

I wait. The sparkle in his eyes grows.

"There's an old spacer's story that has gotten repeated through various cultures for centuries as governments have come and gone. A spacer's story about a fleet of Dignity Vessels."

"What?" I asked. "Of course there was a fleet of them. Hundreds, if the old records are right."

He waves me off. "More than that. Some say the fleet's a thousand strong, some say it's a hundred strong. Some don't give a number. But all the legends talk about the vessels being on a mission to save the worlds beyond the stars, and how the ships moved from port to port, with parts cobbled together so that they could move beyond their design structures."

I'm awake again, just like he knew I would be. "There are a lot of these stories?"

"And they follow a trajectory—one that would work if you were, say, leading a fleet of ships out of your area of space."

"We're far away from the Old Earth area of space. We're so far away, humans from that period couldn't even imagine getting to where we are now."

"So we say. But think how many years this would take, how much work it would take."

"Dignity Vessels didn't have FTL," I say.

"Maybe not at first." He's fairly bouncing from his discovery. I'm feeling a little more hopeful as well. "But in that cobbling, what if someone gave them FTL?"

"Gave them," I muse. No one in the worlds I know gives anyone anything.

"Or sold it to them. Can you imagine? One legend calls them a fleet of ships for hire, out to save worlds they've never seen."

"Sounds like a complete myth."

"Yeah," he says, "it's only a legend. But I think sometimes these legends become a little more concrete."

"Why?"

"We have an actual Dignity Vessel out there, that got here somehow."

"Did you see evidence of cobbling?" I ask.

"How would I know?" he asks. "Have you checked the readouts? Do they give different dates for different parts of the ship?"

I hadn't looked at the dating. I had no idea if it was different. But I don't say that.

"Download the exact specs for a Dignity Vessel," I say. "The materials, where everything should be, all of that."

"Didn't you do that before you came here?" he asks.

"Yes, but not in the detail of the ship's composition. Most people rebuild ships exactly as they were before they got damaged, so the shape would remain the same. Only the components would differ. I meant to check our readouts against what I'd brought, but I haven't yet. I've been diverted by the stealth tech thing, and now I'm going to get a little sleep. So you do it."

He grins. "Aye, aye, captain."

"Boss," I mutter as I stagger down the corridor to my bed. "I can't tell you how much I prefer boss."

I sleep, but not long. My brain's too busy. I'm sure those specs are different which confirms nothing. It just means that someone repaired the vessel at one point or another. But what if the materials are the kind that weren't available in the area of space around Earth when Dignity Vessels were built? That disproves Squishy's worry about the tech of that thing.

I'm at my hardwired terminal when Squishy comes to my door. I've gone through five or six layers of security to get to some very old data, data that isn't accessible from any other part of my ship's networked computer system.

Squishy waits. I'm hoping she'll leave, but of course she doesn't. After a few minutes, she coughs.

I sigh audibly. "We talked last night."

"I have one more thing to ask."

She stepped inside, unbidden, and closed the door. My quarters felt claustrophobic with another person inside them. I'd always been alone here—always—even when I had a liaison with one of the crew. I'd go to his quarters, never bring him into my own.

The habits of privacy are long engrained, and the habits of secrecy even longer. It's how I've protected my turf for so many years, and how I've managed to first-dive so many wrecks.

I dim the screen and turn to her. "Ask."

Her eyes are haunted. She looks like she's gotten even less sleep than I have.

"I'm going to try one last time," she says. "Please blow the wreck up. Make it go away. Don't let anyone else inside. Forget it was here."

I fold my hands on my lap. Yesterday I hadn't had an answer for that request. Today I do. I'd thought about it off and on all night, just like I'd thought about the differing stories I'd heard from her and from Jypé, and how, I realized fifteen minutes before my alarm, neither of them had to be true.

"Please," she says.

"I'm not a scientist," I say, which should warn her right off, but of course it doesn't. Her gaze doesn't change. Nothing about her posture changes. "I've been thinking about this. If this stealth tech is as powerful as you claim, then we might be making things even worse. What if the explosion triggers the tech? What if we blow a hole between dimensions? Or maybe destroy something else, something we can't see?"

Her cheeks flush slightly.

"Or maybe the explosion'll double-back on us. I recall something about Dignity Vessels being unfightable, that anything that hit them rebounded to the other ship. What if that's part of the stealth tech?"

"It was a feature of the shields," she says with a bit of sarcasm. "They were unknown in that era."

"Still," I say. "You understand stealth tech more than I do, but you don't really *understand* it or you'd be able to replicate it, right?"

"I think there's a flaw in that argument—"

"But you don't really grasp it, right? So you don't know if blowing up the wreck will create a situation here, something worse than anything we've seen."

"I'm willing to risk it." Her voice is flat. So are her eyes. It's as if she's a person I don't know, a person I've never met before. And something in those eyes, something cold and terrified, tells me that if I met her this morning, I wouldn't want to know her.

"I like risks," I say. "I just don't like that one. It seems to me that the odds are against us."

"You and me, maybe," she says. "But there's a lot more to 'us' than just this little band of people. You let that wreck remain and you bring something dangerous back into our lives, our culture."

"I could leave it for someone else," I say. "But I really don't want to."

"You think I'm making this up. You think I'm worrying over nothing." She sounds bitter.

"No," I say. "But you already told me that the military is trying to recreate this thing, over and over again. You tell me that people die doing it. My research tells me these ships worked for hundreds of years, and I think, maybe your methodology was flawed. Maybe getting the real stealth tech into the hands of people who can do something with it will *save* lives."

She stares at me, and I recognize the expression. It must have been the one I'd had when I looked at her just a few moments ago.

I'd always known that greed and morals and beliefs destroyed friendships. I also knew they influenced more dives than I cared to think about.

But I'd always tried to keep them out of my ship and out of my dives. That's why I pick my crews so carefully; why I call the ship *Nobody's Business.*

Somehow, I never expected Squishy to start the conflict.

Somehow, I never expected the conflict to be with me.

"No matter what I say, you're going to dive that wreck, aren't you?" she asks.

I nod.

Her sigh is as audible as mine was, and just as staged. She wants me to understand that her disapproval is deep, that she will hold me accountable if all the terrible things she imagines somehow come to pass.

We stare at each other in silence. It feels like we're having some kind of argument, an argument without words. I'm loathe to break eye contact.

Finally, she's the one who looks away.

"You want me to stay," she says. "Fine. I'll stay. But I have some conditions of my own."

I expected that. In fact, I'd expected that earlier, when she'd first come to my quarters, not this prolonged discussion about destroying the wreck.

"Name them."

"I'm done diving," she says. "I'm not going near that thing, not even to save lives."

"All right."

"But I'll man the skip, if you let me bring some of my medical supplies."

So far, I see no problems. "All right."

"And if something goes wrong—and it will—I reserve the right to give my notes, both audio and digital, to any necessary authorities. I reserve the right to tell them what we found and how I warned you. I reserve the right to tell them that you're the one responsible for everything that happens."

"I *am* the one responsible," I say. "But the entire group has signed off on the hazards of wreck diving. Death is one of the risks."

A lopsided smile fills her face, but doesn't reach her eyes. The smile itself seems like sarcasm.

"Yeah," she says as if she's never heard me make that speech before. "I suppose it is."

I tell the others that Squishy has some concerns about the stealth tech and wants to operate as our medic instead of as a main diver. No one questions that. Such things happen on long dives—someone gets squeamish about the wreck; or terrified of the dark; or nearly dies and decides to give up wreck-diving then and there.

We're a superstitious bunch when it gets down to it. We put on our gear in the same order each and every time; we all have one piece of equipment we shouldn't but we feel we need just to survive; and we like to think there's something watching over us, even if it's just a pile of luck and an ancient diving belt.

The upside of Squishy's decision is that I get to dive the wreck. I have a good pilot, although not a great one, manning the skip, and I know that she'll make sensible decisions. She'll never impulsively come in to save a team member. She's said so, and I know she means it.

The downside is that she's a better diver than I am. She'd find things I never would; she'd see things I'll never see; she'd avoid things I don't even know are dangerous.

Which is why, on my first dive to that wreck, I set myself up with Turtle, the most experienced member of the dive team after Squishy.

The skip ride over is tense: those two have gone beyond not talking into painful and outspoken silence. I spend most of my time going over and over my equipment looking for flaws. Much as I want to dive this wreck—and I have since the first moment I saw her—I'm scared of the deep and the dark and the unknown. Those first few instances of weightlessness always catch me by surprise, always remind me that what I do is somehow unnatural.

Still, we get to our normal spot, I suit up, and somehow I make it through those first few minutes, zip along the tether with Turtle just a few meters ahead of me, and make my way to the hatch.

Turtle's gonna take care of the recording and the tracking for this trip. She knows the wreck is new to me. She's been inside once now, and so has Karl. Junior and Jypé had the dive before this one.

I've assigned three corridors: one to Karl, one to J&J, and one to Turtle. Once we discover what's at the end of those babies, we'll take a few more. I'm floating; I'll take the corridor of the person I dive with.

Descending into the hatch is trickier than it looks on the recordings. The edges are sharper; I have to be careful about where I put my hands.

Gravity isn't there to pull at me. I can hear my own breathing, harsh and insistent, and I wonder if I shouldn't have taken Squishy's advice: a ten/ten/ten split on my first dive instead of a twenty/twenty/twenty. It takes less time to reach the wreck now; we get inside in nine minutes flat. I would've had time to do a bit of acclimatizing and to have a productive dive the next time.

But I hadn't been thinking that clearly, obviously. I'd been more interested in our corridor, hoping it led to the control room, whatever that was.

Squishy had been thinking, though. Before I left, she tanked me up with one more emergency bottle. She remembered how on my first dives after a long lay-off, I used too much oxygen.

She remembered that I sometimes panic.

I'm not panicked now, just excited. I have all my exterior suit lights on, trying to catch the various nooks and crannies of the hatch tube that leads into the ship.

Turtle's not far behind. Because I'm lit up like a tourist station, she's not using her boot lights. She's letting me set the pace, and I'm probably setting it a little too fast.

We reach the corridors in at 11:59. Turtle shows me our corridor at 12:03. We take off down the notched hallway at 12:06, and I'm giddy as a child on her first space walk.

Giddy we have to watch. Giddy can be the first sign of oxygen deprivation, followed by a healthy disregard for safety.

But I don't mention this giddy. I've had it since Squishy bowed off the teams, and the giddy's grown worse as my dive day got closer. I'm a little concerned—extreme emotion adds to the heavy breathing—but I'm going to trust my suit. I'm hoping it'll tell me if the oxygen's too low, the pressure's off or the environmental controls are about to fail.

The corridor is human-sized and built for full gravity. Apparently no one thought of adding rungs along the side or the ceiling in case the environmental controls fail.

To me, that shows an astonishing trust in technology, one I've always read about but have never seen. No ship designed in the last three hundred years lacks clingholds. No ship lacks emergency oxygen supplies spaced every ten meters or so. No ship lacks communications equipment near each door.

The past feels even farther away than I thought it would. I thought once I stepped inside the wreck—even though I couldn't smell the environment or hear what's going on around me—I'd get a sense of what it would be like to spend part of my career in this place.

But I have no sense. I'm in a dark, dreary hallway that lacks the emergency supplies I'm used to. Turtle's moving slower than my giddy self wants, although my cautious, experienced boss self knows that slow is best.

She's finding handholds, and signaling me for them, like we're climbing the outside of an alien vessel. We're working on an ancient system—the lead person touches a place, deems it safe, uses it to push off, and the rest of the team follows.

There aren't as many doors as I would have expected. A corridor, it seems to me, needs doors funneling off it, with the occasional side corridor bisecting it.

But there are no bisections, and every time I think we're in a tunnel not a corridor, a door does appear. The doors are regulation height, even now, but recessed farther than I'm used to.

Turtle tries each door. They're all jammed or locked. At the moment, we're just trying to map the wreck. We'll pry open the difficult places once the map is finished.

But I'd love to go inside one of those closed off spaces, probably as much as she would.

Finally, she makes a small scratch on the side of the wall, and nods at me.

The giddy fades. We're done. We go back now—my rule—and if you get back early so be it. I check my readout: 29:01. We have ten minutes to make it back to the hatch.

I almost argue for a few more minutes, even though I know better. Sure, it didn't take us as long to get here as it had in the past, but that doesn't mean the return trip is going to be easy. I've lost four divers over the years because they made the mistake I wanted to make now.

I let Turtle pass me. She goes back, using the same push-off points as before. As she does that, I realize she's marked them somehow, probably with something her suit can pick up. My equipment's not that sophisticated, but I'm glad hers is. We need that kind of expertise inside this wreck. It might take us weeks just to map the space, and we can expect each other to remember each and every safe touch spot because of it.

When we get back to the skip and I drop my helmet, Squishy glares at me.

"You had the gids," she says.

"Normal excitement," I say.

She shakes her head. "I see this coming back the next time, and you're grounded."

I nod, but know she can't ground me without my permission. It's my ship, my wreck, my job. I'll do what I want.

I take off the suit, indulge in some relaxation while Squishy pilots. We didn't get much, Turtle and I, just a few more meters of corridor mapped, but it feels like we'd discovered a whole new world.

Maybe that is the gids, I don't know. But I don't think so. I think it's just the reaction of an addict who returns to her addiction—an elation so great that she needs to do something with it besides acknowledge it.

And this wreck. This wreck has so many possibilities.

Only I can't discuss them on the skip, not with Squishy at the helm and Turtle across from me. Squishy hates this project, and Turtle's starting to. Her enthusiasm is waning, and I don't know if it's because of her personal war with Squishy or because Squishy has convinced her the wreck is even more dangerous than usual.

I stare out a portal, watching the wreck grow tinier and tinier in the distance. It's ironic. Even though I'm surrounded by tension, I finally feel content.

Half a dozen more dives, maybe sixty more meters, mostly corridor. One potential storage compartment, which we'd initially hoped was a stateroom or quarters, and a mechanic's corridor, filled with equipment we haven't even begun to catalogue.

I spend my off-hours analyzing the materials. So far, nothing conclusive. Lots of evidence of cobbling, but that's pretty common for any ship—with FTL or not—that's made it on a long journey.

What there's no evidence of are bodies. We haven't found a one, and that's even more unusual. Sometimes there're skeletons floating—or pieces of them at least—and sometimes we get the full-blown corpse, suited and intact. A handful aren't suited. Those're the worst. They always make me grateful we can't smell the ship around us.

The lack of bodies is beginning to creep out Karl. He's even talked to me in private about skipping the next few dives.

I'm not sure what's best. If he skips them, the attitudes might become engrained, and he might not dive again. If he goes, the fears might grow worse and paralyze him in the worst possible place.

I move him to the end of the rotation, and warn Squishy she might have to suit up after all.

She just looks at me and grins. "Too many of the team quit on you, you'll just have to go home."

"I'll dive it myself, and you all can wait," I say, but it's bravado and we both know it.

That wreck isn't going to defeat me, not with the perfect treasure hidden in its bulk.

That's what's fueling my greed. The perfect treasure: *my* perfect treasure. Something that answers previously unasked historical questions—previously unknown historical questions; something that will reveal facts about our history, our humanity, that no one has suspected before; and something that, even though it does all that, is worth a small—physical—fortune.

I love the history part. I get paid a lot of money to ferry people to other wrecks, teach them to dive old historical sites. Then I save up my funds and do this: find new sites that no one else knows about, and mine them for history.

I never expected to mine them for real gold as well.

I shake every time I think about it, and before each dive, I do feel the gids. Only now I report them to Squishy. I tell her that I'm a tad too excited, and she offers me a tranq which I always refuse. Never go into the unknown with senses dulled, that's my motto, even though I know countless people who do it.

We're on a long diving mission, longer than some of these folks have ever been on, and we're not even halfway through. We'll have gids and jitters and too many superstitions. We'll have fears and near-emergencies, and God forbid, real emergencies as well.

We'll get through it, and we'll have our prize, and no one, not any one person, will be able to take that away from us.

It turned this afternoon.

I'm captaining the skip. Squishy's back at the *Business*, taking a boss-ordered rest. I'm tired of her complaints and her constant negative attitude. At first, I thought she'd turn Turtle, but Turtle finally got pissed, and decided she'd enjoy this run.

I caught Squishy ragging on J&J, my strong links, asking them if they really want to be mining a death ship. They didn't listen to her, not really—although Jypé argued with her just a little—but that kind of talk can depress an entire mission, sabotage it in subtle little ways, ways that I don't even want to contemplate.

So I'm manning the skip alone, while J&J are running their dive, and I'm listening to the commentary, not looking at the grainy, nearly worthless images from the handheld. Mostly I'm thinking about Squishy and how to send her back without sending information too and I can't come to any conclusions at all when I hear:

". . . yeah, it opens." Junior.

"Wow." Jypé.

"Jackpot, eh?" Junior again.

And then a long silence. Much too long for my tastes, not because I'm afraid for J&J, but because a long silence doesn't tell me one goddamn thing.

I punch up the digital readout, see we're at 25:33—plenty of time. They got to the new section faster than they ever have before.

The silence runs from 25:33 to 28:46, and I'm about to chew my fist off, wondering what they're doing. The handheld shows me grainy walls and more grainy walls. Or maybe it's just grainy nothing. I can't tell.

For the first time in weeks, I want someone else in the skip with me just so that I can talk to somebody.

"Almost time," Jypé says.

"Dad, you gotta see this." Junior has a touch of breathlessness in his voice. Excitement—at least that's what I'm hoping.

And then there's more silence . . . thirty-five seconds of it, followed by a loud and emphatic "Fuck!"

I can't tell if that's an angry "fuck," a scared "fuck" or an awed "fuck." I can't tell much about it at all.

Now I'm literally chewing on my thumbnail, something I haven't done in years, and I'm watching the digital, which has crept past thirty-one minutes.

"Move your arm," Jypé says, and I know then that wasn't a good fuck at all.

Something happened.

Something bad.

"Just a little to the left," Jypé says again, his voice oddly calm. I'm wondering why Junior isn't answering him, hoping that the only reason is he's in a section where the communications relay isn't reaching the skip.

Because I can think of a thousand other reasons, none of them good, that Junior's communication equipment isn't working.

"We're five minutes past departure," Jypé says, and in that, I'm hearing the beginning of panic.

More silence.

I'm actually holding my breath. I look out a portal, see nothing except the wreck, looking like it always does. The handheld has been showing the same grainy image for a while now.

37:24

If they're not careful, they'll run out of air. Or worse.

I try to remember how much extra they took. I didn't really watch them suit up this time. I've seen their ritual so many times that I'm not sure what I think I saw is what I actually saw. I'm not sure what they have with them, and what they don't.

"Great," Jypé says, and I finally recognize his tone. It's controlled parental panic. Sound calm so that the kid doesn't know the situation is bad. "Keep going."

I'm holding my breath, even though I don't have to. I'm holding my breath and looking back and forth between the portal and the handheld image. All I see is the damn wreck and that same grainy image.

"We got it," Jypé says. "Now careful. Careful—son of a bitch! Move, move, move—ah, hell."

I stare at the wreck, even though I can't see inside it. My own breath sounds as ragged as it did inside the wreck. I glance at the digital:

44:11

They'll never get out in time. They'll never make it, and I can't go in for them. I'm not even sure where they are.

"C'mon." Jypé is whispering now. "C'mon son, just one more, c'mon, help me, c'mon."

The "help me" wasn't a request to a hearing person. It was a comment. And I suddenly know.

Junior's trapped. He's unconscious. His suit might even be ripped. It's over for Junior.

Jypé has to know it on some deep level.

Only he also has to know it on the surface, in order to get out.

I reach for my own communicator before I realize there's no talking to them inside the wreck. We'd already established that the skip doesn't have the power to send, for reasons I don't entirely understand. We've tried boosting power through the skip's diagnostic, and even with the *Business*'s diagnostic, and we don't get anything.

I judged we didn't need it, because what can someone inside the skip do besides encourage?

"C'mon, son." Jypé grunts. I don't like that sound.

The silence that follows lasts thirty seconds, but it seems like forever. I move away from the portal, stare at the digital, and watch the numbers change. They seem to change in slow-motion:

45:24 to

. . . 25 to

. . . 2 . . . 6 . . .

    to

. . . 2 . . . . 7 . . .

until I can't even see them change anymore.

Another grunt, and then a sob, half-muffled, and another, followed by—

"Is there any way to send for help? Boss?"

I snap to when I hear my name. It's Jypé and I can't answer him. I can't answer him, dammit.

I can call for help, and I do. Squishy tells me that the best thing I can do is get the survivor—her word, not mine, even though I know it's obvious too—back to the *Business* as quickly as possible.

"No sense passing midway, is there?" she asks, and I suppose she's right.

But I'm cursing her—after I get off the line—for not being here, for failing us, even though there's not much she can do, even if she's here, in the skip. We don't have a lot of equipment, medical equipment, back at the *Business*, and we have even less here, not that it mattered, because most of the things that happen are survivable if you make it back to the skip.

Still, I suit up. I promise myself I'm not going to the wreck, I'm not going help with Junior, but I can get Jypé along the guideline if he needs me too.

"Boss. Call for help. We need Squishy and some divers and oh, shit, I don't know."

His voice sounds too breathy. I glance at the digital.

56:24

Where has the time gone? I thought he was moving quicker than that. I thought I was too.

But it takes me a while to suit up, and I talked to Squishy, and everything is fucked up.

What'll they say when we get back? The mission's already filled with superstitions and fears of weird technology that none of us really understand.

And only me and Jypé are obsessed with this thing.

Me and Jypé.

Probably just me now.

"I left him some oxygen. I dunno if it's enough . . ."

So breathy. Has Jypé left all his extra? What's happening to Junior? If he's unconscious, he won't use as much, and if his suit is fucked, then he won't need any.

"Coming through the hatch . . ."

I see Jypé, a tiny shape on top of the wreck. And he's moving slowly, much too slowly for a man trying to save his own life.

My rules are clear: let him make his own way back.

But I've never been able to watch someone else die.

I send to the *Business*: "Jypé's out. I'm heading down the line."

I don't use the word help on purpose, but anyone listening knows what I'm doing. They'll probably never listen to me again, but what the hell.

I don't want to lose two on my watch.

When I reach him six minutes later, he's pulling himself along the guideline, hand over hand, so slowly that he barely seems human. A red light flashes at the base of his helmet—the out of oxygen light, dammit. He did use all of his extra for his son.

I grab one small container, hook it to the side of his suit, press the "on" only halfway, knowing too much is as bad as too little.

His look isn't grateful: it's startled. He's so far gone, he hasn't even realized that I'm here.

I brought a grappler as well, a technology I always said was more dangerous than helpful, and here's the first test of my theory. I wrap Jypé against me, tell him to relax, I got him, and we'll be just fine.

He doesn't. Even though I pry him from the line, his hands still move, one over the other, trying to pull himself forward.

Instead, I yank us toward the skip, moving as fast as I've ever moved. I'm burning oxygen at three times my usual rate according to my suit and I don't really care. I want him inside, I want him safe, I want him *alive*, goddammit.

I pull open the door to the skip. I unhook him in the airlock, and he falls to the floor like an empty suit. I make sure the back door is sealed, open the main door, and drag Jypé inside.

His skin is a grayish blue. Capillaries have burst in his eyes. I wonder what else has burst, what else has gone wrong.

There's blood around his mouth.

I yank off the helmet, his suit protesting my every move.

"I gotta tell you," he says. "I gotta tell you."

I nod. I'm doing triage, just like I've been taught, just like I've done half a dozen times before.

"Set up something," he says. "Record."

So I do, mostly to shut him up. I don't want him wasting more energy. I'm wasting enough for both of us, trying to save him, and cursing Squishy for not getting here, cursing everyone for leaving me on the skip, alone, with a man who can't live, and somehow has to.

"He's in the cockpit," Jypé says.

I nod. He's talking about Junior, but I really don't want to hear it. Junior is the last of my worries.

"Wedged under some cabinet. Looks like—battlefield in there."

That catches me. Battlefield how? Because there are bodies? Or because it's a mess?

I don't ask. I want him to wait, to save his strength, to *survive*.

"You gotta get him out. He's only got an hour's worth, maybe less. Get him out."

Wedged beneath something, stuck against a wall, trapped in the belly of the wreck. Yeah, like I'll get him out. Like it's worth it.

All those sharp edges.

If his suit's not punctured now, it would be by the time I'm done getting the stuff off him. Things have to piled pretty high to get them stuck in zero-G.

I'll wager the *Business* that Junior's not stuck, not in the literal, gravitational sense. His suit's hung up on an edge. He's losing—he's lost—environment and oxygen, and he's probably been dead longer than his father's been on the skip.

"Get him out." Jypé's voice is so hoarse it sounds like a whisper. I look at his face. More blood.

"I'll get him," I say.

Jypé smiles. Or tries to. And then he closes his eyes, and I fight the urge to slam my fist against his chest. He's dead and I know it, but some small part of me won't believe it until Squishy declares him.

"I'll get him," I say again, and this time, it's not a lie.

Squishy declared him the moment she arrived on the skip. Not that it was hard. He'd already sunken in on himself, and the blood—it wasn't something I wanted to think about.

She flew us back. Turtle was in the other skip, and she never came in, just flew back on her own.

I stayed on the floor, expecting Jypé to rise up and curse me for not going back to the wreck, for not trying, even though we all knew—even though he probably had known—that Junior was dead.

When we got back to the *Business*, Squishy took his body to her little medical suite. She's going to make sure he died from suit failure or lack of oxygen or something that keeps the regulators away from us.

Who knows what the hell he actually died of. Panic? Fear? Stupidity?—or maybe that's what I'm doomed for. Hell, I let a man dive with his son, even though I'd ordered all of my teams to abandon a downed man.

Who can abandon his own kid anyway?

And who listens to me?

Not even me.

My quarters seem too small, the *Business* seems too big, and I don't want to go anywhere because everyone'll look at me, with an I-told-you-so followed by a let's-hang-it-up.

And I don't really blame them. Death's the hardest part. It's what we flirt with in deep-dives.

We claim that flirting is partly love.

I close my eyes and lean back on my bunk but all I see are digital readouts. Seconds moving so slowly they seem like days. The spaces between time. If only we can capture that—the space between moments.

If only.

I shake my head, wondering how I can pretend I have no regrets.

When I come out of my quarters, Turtle and Karl are already watching the vids from Jypé's suit. They're sitting in the lounge, their faces serious.

As I step inside, Turtle says, "They found the heart."

It takes me a minute to understand her, then I remember what Jypé said. They were in the cockpit, the heart, the place we might find the stealth tech.

He was stuck there. Like the probe?

I shudder in spite of myself.

"Is the event on the vid?" I ask.

"Haven't got that far." Turtle shuts off the screens. "Squishy's gone."

"Gone?" I shake my head just a little. Words aren't processing well. I'm having a reaction. I recognize it: I've had it before when I've lost crew.

"She took the second skip, and left. We didn't even notice until I went to find her." Turtle sighs. "She's gone."

"Jypé too?" I ask.

She nods.

I close my eyes. The mission ends, then. Squishy'll go to the authorities and report us. She's gonna tell them about the wreck and the accident and Junior's death. She's gonna show them Jypé, whom I haven't reported yet because I didn't want anyone to find our position, and the authorities'll come here—whatever authorities have jurisdiction over this area—and confiscate the wreck.

At best, we'll get a slap, and I'll have a citation on my record.

At worst, I'll—maybe we'll—face charges for some form of reckless homicide.

"We can leave," Karl says.

I nod. "She'll report the *Business*. They'll know who to look for."

"If you sell the ship—"

"And what?" I ask. "Not buy another? That'll keep us ahead of them for a while, but not long enough. And when we get caught, we get nailed for the full count, whatever it is, because we acted guilty and ran."

"So, maybe she won't say anything," Karl says, but he doesn't sound hopeful.

"If she was gonna do that, she woulda left Jypé," I say.

Turtle closes her eyes, rests her head on the seat back. "I don't know her any more."

"I think maybe we never did," I say.

"I didn't think she got scared," Turtle says. "I yelled at her—I told her to get over it, that diving's the thing. And she said it's not the thing. Surviving's the thing. She never used to be like that."

I think of the woman sitting on her bunk, staring at her opaque wall—a wall you think you can see through, but you really can't—and wonder. Maybe she always used to be like that. Maybe surviving was always her thing. Maybe diving was how she proved she was alive, until the past caught up with her all over again.

The stealth tech.

She thinks it killed Junior.

I nod toward the screen. "Let's see it," I say to Karl.

He gives me a tight glance, almost—but not quite—expressionless. He's trying to rein himself in, but his fears are getting the best of him.

I'm amazed mine haven't got the best of me.

He starts it up. The voices of men so recently dead, just passing information—"Push off here." "Watch the edge there."—makes Turtle open her eyes.

I lean against the wall, arms crossed. The conversation is familiar to me. I heard it just a few hours ago, and I'd been too preoccupied to give it much attention, thinking of my own problems, thinking of the future of this mission, which I thought was going to go on for months.

Amazing how much your perspective changes in the space of a few minutes.

The corridors look the same. It takes a lot so that I don't zone—I've been in that wreck, I've watched similar vids, and in those I haven't learned much. But I resist the urge to tell Karl to speed it up—there can be something, some wrong movement, piece of the wreck that gloms onto one of my guys—my former guys—before they even get to the heart.

But I don't see anything like that, and since Turtle and Karl are quiet, I assume they don't see anything like that either.

Then J&J find the holy grail. They say something, real casual—which I'd missed the first time—a simple "shit, man" in a tone of such awe that if I'd been paying attention, I would've known.

I bite back the emotion. If I took responsibility for each lost life, I'd never dive again. Of course, I might not after this anyway—one of the many options the authorities have is to take my pilot's license away.

The vids don't show the cockpit ahead. They show the same old grainy walls, the same old dark and shadowed corridor. It's not until Jypé turns his suit vid toward the front that the pit's even visible, and then it's a black mass filled with lighter squares, covering the screen.

"What the hell's that?" Karl asks. I'm not even sure he knows he's spoken.

Turtle leans forward and shakes her head. "Never seen anything like it."

Me either. As Jypé gets closer, the images become clearer. It looks like every piece of furniture in the place has become dislodged, and has shifted to one part of the cockpit.

Were the designers so confident of their artificial gravity that they didn't bolt down the permanent pieces? Could any ship's designers be that stupid?

Jypé's vid doesn't show me the floor, so I can't see if these pieces have been ripped free. If they have, then that place is a minefield for a diver, more sharp edges than smooth ones.

My arms tighten in their cross, my fingers forming fists. I feel a tension I don't want—as if I can save both men by speaking out now.

"You got this before Squishy took off, right?" I ask Turtle.

She understands what I'm asking. She gives me a disapproving sideways look. "I took the vids before she even had the suit off."

Technically, that's what I want to hear, and yet it's not what I want to hear. I want something to be tampered with, something to be slightly off because then, maybe then, Jypé would still be alive.

"Look," Karl says, nodding toward the screen.

I have to force myself to see it. The eyes don't want to focus. I know what happens next—or at least, how it ends up. I don't need the visual confirmation.

Yet I do. The vid can save us, if the authorities come back. Turtle, Karl, even Squishy can testify to my rules. And my rules state that an obviously dangerous site should be avoided. Probes get to map places like this first.

Only I know J&J didn't send in a probe. They might not have because we lost the other so easily, but most likely, it was that greed, the same one which has been effecting me. The tantalizing idea that somehow, this wreck, with its ancient secrets, is the dive of a lifetime—the discovery of a lifetime.

And the hell of it is, beneath the fear and the panic and the anger—more at myself than at Squishy for breaking our pact—that greed remains.

I'm thinking, if we can just get the stealth tech before the authorities arrive, it'll all be worth it. We'll have a chip, something to bargain with.

Something to sell to save our own skins.

Junior goes in. His father doesn't tell him not to. Junior's blurry on the vid—a human form in an environmental suit, darker than the pile of things in the center of the room, but grayer than the black around them.

And it's Junior who says, "It's open," and Junior who mutters "Wow" and Junior who says, "Jackpot, huh?" when I thought all of that had been a dialogue between them.

He points at a hole in the pile, then heads toward it, but his father moves forward quickly, grabbing his arm. They don't talk— apparently that was the way they worked, such an understanding they didn't need to say much, which makes my heart twist—and together they head around the pile.

The cockpit shifts. It has large screens that appear to be un-retractable. They're off, big blank canvases against dark walls. No windows in the cockpit at all, which is another one of those techno-logically arrogant things—what happens if the screen technology fails?

The pile is truly in the middle of the room, a big lump of things. Why Jypé called it a battlefield, I don't know. Because of the pile? Because everything is ripped up and moved around?

My arms get even tighter, my fists clenched so hard my knuckles hurt.

On the vid, Junior breaks away from his father, and moves toward the front (if you can call it that) of the pile. He's looking at what the pile's attached to.

He mimes removing pieces, and the cameras shake. Apparently Jypé is shaking his head.

Yet Junior reaches in there anyway. He examines each piece before he touches it, then pushes at it, which seems to move the entire pile. He moves in closer, the pile beside him, something I can't see on his other side. He's floating, head first, exactly like we're not supposed to go into one of these spaces—he'd have trouble backing out if there's a problem—

And of course there is.

Was.

"Ah, hell," I whisper.

Karl nods. Turtle puts her head in her hands.

On screen nothing moves.

Nothing at all.

Seconds go by, maybe a minute—I forgot to look at the digital readout from earlier, so I don't exactly know—and then, finally, Jypé moves forward.

He reaches Junior's side, but doesn't touch him. Instead the cameras peer in, so I'm thinking maybe Jypé does too.

And then the monologue begins.

I've only heard it once, but I have it memorized.

Almost time.

Dad, you've gotta see this.

Jypé's suit shows us something—a wave? A blackness? A table?—something barely visible just beyond Junior. Junior reaches for it, and then—

Fuck!

The word sounds distorted here. I don't remember it being distorted, but I do remember being unable to understand the emotion behind it. Was that from the distortion? Or my lack of attention?

Jypé has forgotten to use his cameras. He's moved so close to the objects in the pile that all we can see now are rounded corners and broken metal (apparently these did break off then) and sharp, sharp edges.

Move your arm.

But I see no corresponding movement. The visuals remain the same, just like they did when I was watching from the skip.

Just a little to the left.

And then:

We're five minutes past departure.

That was panic. I had missed it the first time, but the panic began right there. Right at that moment.

Karl covers his mouth.

On screen, Jypé turns slightly. His hands grasp boots and I'm assuming he's tugging.

Great. But I see nothing to feel great about. Nothing has moved.

Keep going.

Going where? Nothing is changing. Jypé can see that, can't he?

The hands seem to tighten their grip on the boots, or maybe I'm imagining that because that's what my hands would do.

We got it.

Is that a slight movement? I step away from the wall, move closer to the vid, as if I can actually help.

Now careful.

This is almost worse because I know what's coming, I know Junior doesn't get out, Jypé doesn't survive. I know—*Careful—son of a bitch!*

The hands slid off the boot, only to grasp back on. And there's desperation in that movement, and lack of caution, no checking for edges nearby, no standard rescue procedures.

Move, move, move—ah, hell.

This time, the hands stay. And tug—clearly tug—sliding off.

C'mon.

Sliding again.

C'mon son,

And again.

just one more,

And again.

c'mon, help me, c'mon.

Until, finally, in despair, the hands fall off. The feet are motionless, and, to my untrained eye, appear to be in the same position they were in before.

Now Jypé's breathing dominates the sound—which I don't remember at all—maybe that kind of hiss doesn't make it through our patchwork system—and then the vid whirls. He's reaching, grabbing, trying to pull things off the pile, and there's no pulling, everything goes back like it's magnetized.

He staggers backward—all except his hand, which seems attached—sharp edges? No, his suit wasn't compromised—and then, at the last moment, eases away.

Away, backing away, the visuals are still of those boots sticking out of that pile, and I squint, and I wonder—am I seeing other boots? Ones that are less familiar?—and finally he's bumping against walls, losing track of himself.

He turns, moves away, coming for help even though he has to know I won't help (although I did) and panicked—so clearly panicked. He gets to the end of the corridor, and I wave my hand.

"Turn it off." I know how this plays out. I don't need any more.

None of us do. Besides, I'm the only one watching. Turtle still has her face in her hands, and Karl's eyes are squinched shut, as if he can keep out the horrible experience just by blocking the images.

I grab the controls and shut the damn thing off myself.

Then I slide onto the floor and bow my head. Squishy was right, dammit. She was so right. This ship has stealth tech. It's the only thing still working, that one faint energy signature that attracted me in the first place, and it has killed Junior.

And Jypé.

And if I'd gone in, it would've killed me.

No wonder she left. No wonder she ran. This is some kind of flashback for her, something she feels we can never ever win.

And I'm beginning to think she's right, when a thought flits across my brain.

I frown, flick the screen back on, and search for Jypé's map. He had the system on automatic, so the map goes clear to the cockpit.

I superimpose that map on the exterior, accounting for movement, accounting for change —

And there it is, clear as anything.

The probe, our stuck probe, is pressing against whatever's near Junior's faceplate.

I'm worried about what'll happen if the stealth tech is open to space, and it always has been — at least since I stumbled on the wreck.

Open to space and open for the taking.

Karl's watching me. "What're you gonna do?"

Only that doesn't sound like his voice. It's the greed. It's the greed talking, that emotion I so blithely assumed I didn't have.

Everyone can be snared, just in different ways.

"I don't know what to do," I say. "I have no idea at all."

I go back to my room, sit on the bed, stare at the portal, which, mercifully, doesn't show the distant wreck.

I'm out of ideas, out of energy, and out of time.

Squishy and the calvary'll be here soon, to take the wreck from me, confiscate it, and send it into governmental oblivion.

And then my career is over. No more dives, no more space travel.

No more nothing.

I think I doze once because suddenly I'm staring at Junior's face inside his helmet. His eyes move, ever so slowly, and I realize—in the space of a heartbeat—that he's alive in there: his body's in our dimension, his head on the way to another.

And I know, as plainly as I know that he's alive, that he'll suffer a long and hideous death if I don't help him, so I grab one of the sharp edges—with my bare hands (such an obvious dream)—and slice the side of his suit.

Saving him.

Damning him.

Condemning him to an even uglier slow death than the one he would otherwise experience.

I jerk awake, nearly hitting my head on the wall. My breath is coming in short gasps. What if the dream is true? What if he is still alive? No one understands interdimensional travel, so he could be, but even if he is, I can do nothing.

Absolutely nothing, without condemning myself.

If I go in and try to free him, I will get caught as surely as he is. So will anyone else.

I close my eyes, but don't lean back to my pillow. I don't want to fall asleep again. I don't want to dream again, not with these thoughts on my mind. The nightmares I'd have, all because stealth tech exists are terrifying, worse than any I'd had as a child—

And then my breath catches. I open my eyes, rub the sleep from them, think:

This is a Dignity Vessel. Dignity Vessels have stealth tech, unless they've been stripped of them. Squishy described stealth tech to me —and this vessel, this *wreck* has an original version.

Stealth tech has value.

Real value, unlike any wreck I've found before.

I can stake a claim. The time to worry about pirates and privacy is long gone, now.

I get out of bed, pace around the small room. Staking a claim is so foreign to wreck-divers. We keep our favorite wrecks hidden, our best dives secret from pirates and wreck divers and the government.

But I'm not going to dive this wreck. I'm not going in again— none of my people are—and so it doesn't matter that the entire universe knows what I have here.

Except that other divers will come, gold-diggers will try to rob me of my claim—and I can collect fees from anyone willing to mine this, anyone willing to risk losing their life in a long and hideous way.

Or I can salvage the wreck and sell it. The government buys salvage.

If I file a claim, I'm not vulnerable to citations, not even to reckless homicide charges, because everyone knows that mining exacts a price. It doesn't matter what kind of claim you mine, you could still lose some, or all, of your crew.

But best of all, if I stake a claim on that wreck, I can quarantine it—and prosecute anyone who violates the quarantine. I can stop people from getting near the stealth tech if I so chose.

Or I can demand that whoever tries to retrieve it, retrieve Junior's body.

His face rises, unbidden, not the boy I'd known, but the boy I'd dreamed of, half-alive, waiting to die.

I know there are horrible deaths in space. I know that wreck-divers suffer some of the worst.

I carry these images with me, and now, it seems, I'll carry Junior's.

Is that why Jypé made me promise to go in? Had he had the same vision of his son?

I sit down at the network, and call up the claim form. It's so simple. The key is giving up accurate coordinates. The system'll do a quick double-check to see if anyone else has filed a claim, and if so, an automatic arbitrator will ask if I care to withdraw. If I do not, then the entire thing will go to the nearest court.

My hands itch. This is so contrary to my training.

I start to file—and then stop.

I close my eyes—and he's there again, barely moving, but alive.

If I do this, Junior will haunt me until the end of my life. If I do this, I'll always wonder.

Wreck-divers take silly, unnecessary risks, by definition.

The only thing that's stopping me from taking this one is Squishy and her urge for caution.

Wreck-divers flirt with death.

I stand. It's time for a rendezvous.

Turtle won't go in. She's stressed, terrified, and blinded by Squishy's betrayal. She'd be useless on a dive anyway, not clear-headed enough, and probably too reckless.

Karl has no qualms. His fears have left. When I propose a dive to see what happened in there, he actually grins at me.

"Thought you weren't gonna come around," he says.

But I have.

Turtle mans the skip. Karl and I have gone in. We've decided on 30/40/30, because we're going to investigate that cockpit. Karl theorizes that there's some kind of off switch for the stealth tech, and of course he's right. But the wreck has no real power, and since the designers had too much faith in their technology to build redundant safety systems, I'm assuming they had too much faith to design an off switch for their most dangerous technology, a dead-man's switch that'll allow the stealth tech to go off even if the wreck has no power.

I mention that to Karl and he gives me a startled look.

"You ever wonder what's keeping the stealth tech on then?" he asks.

I've wondered, but I have no answer. Maybe when Squishy comes back with the government ships, maybe then I'll ask her. What my non-scientific mind is wondering is this: Can the stealth tech operate from both dimensions? Is something on the other side powering it?

Is part of the wreck—that hole we found in the hull on the first day, maybe—still in that other dimension?

Karl and I suit up, take extra oxygen, and double-check our suit's environmental controls. I'm not giddy this trip—I'm not sure I'll be giddy again—but I'm not scared either.

Just coldly determined.

I promised Jypé I was going back for Junior, and now I am.

No matter what the risk.

The trip across is simple, quick, and familiar. Going down the entrance no longer seems like an adventure. We hit the corridors with fifteen minutes to spare.

Jypé's map is accurate to the millimeter. His push-off points are marked on the map and with some corresponding glove grip. We make record time as we head toward that cockpit.

Record time, though, is still slow. I find myself wishing for all my senses: sound, smell, taste. I want to know if the effects of the stealth tech have made it out here, if something is off in the air—a bit of a burnt smell, something foreign that raises the small hairs on the back of my neck. I want to know if Junior is already decomposing, if he's part of a group (the crew?) pushed up against the stealth tech, never to go free again.

But the wreck doesn't cough up those kind of details. This corridor looks the same as the other corridor I pulled my way through.

Karl moves as quickly as I do, although his suit lights are on so full that looking at him almost blinds me. That's what I did to Turtle on our trip, and it's a sign of nervousness.

It doesn't surprise me that Karl, who claimed not to be afraid, is nervous. He's the one who had doubts about this trip once he'd been inside the wreck. He's the one I thought wouldn't make it through all of his scheduled dives.

The cockpit looms in front of us, the doors stuck open. It does look like a battlefield from this vantage: the broken furniture, the destruction all cobbled together on one side of the room, like a barricade.

The odd part about it is, though, that the barricade runs from floor to ceiling, and unlike most things in zero-G, seem stuck in place.

Neither Karl nor I give the barricade much time. We've vowed to explore the rest of the cockpit first, looking for the elusive deadman switch. We have to be careful; the sharp edges are everywhere.

Before we left, we used the visuals from Jypé's suit, and his half-finished map, to assign each other areas of the cockpit to explore. I'm going deep, mostly because this is my idea, and deep—we both feel—is the most dangerous place. It's closest to the probe, closest to that corner of the cockpit where Junior still hangs, horizontal, his boots kicking out into the open.

I go in the center, heading toward the back, not using handholds. I've pushed off the wall, so I have some momentum, a technique that isn't really my strong suit. But I volunteered for this, knowing the edges in the front would slow me down, knowing that the walls would raise my fears to an almost incalculable height.

Instead, I float over the middle of the room, see the uprooted metal of chairs and the ripped shreds of consoles. There are actual wires protruding from the middle of that mess, wires and stripped bolts—something I haven't seen in space before, only in old colonies—and my stomach churns as I move forward.

The back wall is dark, with its distended screen. The cockpit feels like a cave instead of the hub of the Dignity Vessel. I wonder how so many people could have trusted their lives to this place.

Just before I reach the wall, I spin so that I hit it with the soles of my boots. The soles have the toughest material on my suit. The wall is mostly smooth, but there are a few edges here, too—more stripped bolts, a few twisted metal pieces that I have no idea what they once were part of.

This entire place feels useless and dead.

It takes all of my strength not to look at the barricade, not to search for the bottoms of Junior's boots, not to go there first. But I force myself to shine a spot on the wall before me, then on the floor, and the ceiling, looking for something—anything—that might control part of this vessel.

But whatever had, whatever machinery there'd been, whatever computerized equipment, is either gone or part of that barricade. My work in the back is over quickly, although I take an extra few minutes to record it all, just in case the camera sees something I don't.

It takes Karl a bit longer. He has to pick his way through a tiny debris field. He's closer to a possible site: there's still a console or two stuck to his near wall. He examines them, runs his suit-cam over them as well, but shakes his head.

Even before he tells me he's found nothing, I know.

I know.

I join him at a two-pronged handhold, where his wall and mine meet. The handhold was actually designed for this space, the first such design I've seen on the entire Dignity Vessel.

Maybe the engineers felt that only the cockpit crew had to survive uninjured should the artificial gravity go off. More likely, the lack of grab bars was simply an oversight in the other areas, or a cost-saving measure.

"You see a way into that barricade?" Karl asks.

"We're not going in," I say. "We're going to satisfy my curiosity first."

He knows about the dream; I told him when we were suiting up. I have no idea if Turtle heard—if she did, then she knows too. I don't know how she feels about the superstitious part of this mission, but I know that Karl understands.

"I think we should work off a tether," he says. "We can hook up to this handhold. That way, if one of us gets stuck—"

I shake my head. There are clearly other bodies in that barricade, and I would wager that some of them have tethers and bits of equipment attached.

If the stealth tech is as powerful as I think it is, then these people had no safeguard against it. A handhold won't defend us either, even though, I believe, the stealth tech is running at a small percentage of capacity.

"I'm going first," I say. "You wait. If I pull in, you go back. You and Turtle get out."

We've discussed this drill. They don't like it. They believe leaving me behind will give them two ghosts instead of one.

Maybe so, but at least they'll still be alive to experience those ghosts.

I push off the handhold, softer this time than I did from the corridor, and let the drift take me to the barricade. I turn the front suit-cams on high. I also use zoom on all but a few of them. I want to see as much as I can through that barricade.

My suit lights are also on full. I must look like a child's floaty toy heading in for a landing.

I stop near the spot where Junior went in. His boots are there, floating, like expected. I back as far from him as I can, hoping to catch a reflection in his visor, but I get nothing.

I have to move to the initial spot, that hole in the barricade that Junior initially wanted to go through.

I'm more afraid of that than I am of the rest of the wreck, but I do it. I grasp a spot marked on Jypé's map, and pull myself toward that hole.

Then I train the zoom inside, but I don't need it.

I see the side of Junior's face, illuminated by my lights. The helmet is what tells me that it's him. I recognize the modern design, the little logos he glued to its side.

His helmet has bumped against the only intact console in the entire place. His face is pointed downward, the helmet on clear. And through it, I see something I don't expect: the opposite of my fears.

He isn't alive. He hasn't been alive in a long, long time.

As I said, no one understands interdimensional travel, but we suspect it manipulates time. And what I see in front of me makes me realize my hypothesis is wrong:

Time sped up for him. Sped to such a rate that he isn't even recognizable. He's been mummified for so long that the skin looks petrified, and I bet, if we were to somehow free him and take him back to the *Business*, that none of our normal medical tools could cut through the surface of his face.

There are no currents and eddies here, nothing to pull me forward. Still, I scurry back to what I consider a safe spot, not wanting to experience the same fate as the youngest member of our team.

"What is it?" Karl asks me.

"He's gone," I say. "No sense cutting him loose."

Even though cutting isn't the right term. We'd have to free him from that stealth tech, and I'm not getting near it. No matter how rich it could make me, no matter how many questions it answers, I no longer want anything to do with it.

I'm done—with this dive, this wreck—and with my brief encounter with greed.

We do have answers, though, and visuals to present to the government ships when they arrive. There are ten of them—a convoy—unwilling to trust something as precious as stealth tech to a single ship.

Squishy didn't come back with them. I don't know why I thought she would. She dropped off Jypé, reported us and the wreck, and vanished into Longbow Station, not even willing to collect a finder's fee that the government gives whenever it locates unusual technologies.

Squishy's gone, and I doubt she'll ever come back.

Turtle's not speaking to me now, except to say that she's relieved we're not being charged with anything. Our vids showed the government we cared enough to go back for our team member, and also that we had no idea about the stealth tech until we saw it function.

We hadn't gone into the site to raid it, just to explore it—as the earlier vids showed. Which confirmed my claim—I'm a wreck-diver, not a pirate, not a scavenger—and that allowed me to pick up the reward that Squishy abandoned.

I'd've left it too, except that I needed to fund the expedition, and I'm not going to be able to do it the way I'd initially planned—by taking tourists to the Dignity Vessel so far from home.

The wreck got moved to some storehouse or warehouse or way station where the government claims it's safe. Turtle thinks we should've blown it up; Karl's just glad it's out of our way.

Me, I just wished I had more answers to all the puzzles.

That vessel'd been in service awhile, that much was clear from how it had been refitted. When someone activated the stealth, something went wrong. I doubt even the government scientists would find out exactly what in that mess.

Then there's the question of how it got to the place I found it. There's no way to tell if it traveled in stealth mode or over those thousands of years, although that doesn't explain how the ship avoided gravity wells and other perils that lie in wait in a cold and difficult universe. Or maybe it had been installed with an updated FTL. Again, I doubted I would ever know.

As for the crew—I have no idea, except that I suspect the cockpit crew died right off. We could see them in that pile of debris. But the rest—there were no bodies scattered throughout the ship, and there could've been, given that the vessel is still intact after all this time.

I'm wondering if they were running tests with minimal crew or if the real crew looked at that carnage in the cockpit and decided, like we did, that it wasn't worth the risk to go in.

I never looked for escape pods, but such things existed on Dignity Vessels. Maybe the rest of the crew bailed, got rescued, and blended into cultures somewhere far from home.

Maybe that's where Jypé's legends come from.

Or so I like to believe.

Longbow Station has never seemed so much like home. It'll be nice to shed the silent Turtle, and Karl, who claims his diving days are behind him.

Mine are too, only in not quite the same way. The *Business* and I'll still ferry tourists to various wrecks, promising scary dives and providing none.

But I've had enough of undiscovered wrecks and danger for no real reason. Curiosity sent me all over this part of space, looking for hidden pockets, places where no one has been in a long time.

Now that I've found the ultimate hidden pocket—and I've seen what it can do—I'm not looking anymore. I'm hanging up my suit and reclaiming my land legs.

Less danger there, on land, in normal gravity. Not that I'm afraid of wrecks now. I'm not, no more than the average spacer.

I'm more afraid of that feeling, the greed, which came on me hard and fast, and made me tone-deaf to my best diver's concerns, my old friend's fears, and my own giddy response to the deep.

I'm getting out before I turn pirate or scavenger, before my greed—which I thought I didn't have—draws me as inexorably as the stealth tech drew Junior, pulling me in and holding me in place, before I even realize I'm in trouble.

Before I even know how impossible it'll be to escape.

Afterword

Kristine Kathryn Rusch

*A*S I SAT DOWN TO WRITE THE INTRODUCTION TO this collection of short stories, I realized that most of what I wanted to say had to do with the stories themselves—the inspiration for them, the writing of them, and sometimes the reaction to them.

At the same time, I realized that most of you would come to these stories cold, having never seen them before. The last thing I wanted to do was spoil the reading experience by accidentally talking about an element of a story that should have remained secret until the story was over.

So I decided to put the little pieces about the stories at the end of the book, as an afterword, which you can chose to read or not. As a reader, I've always loved this kind of material. In fact, I was recently disappointed in a short story collection by one of my favorite writers because it lacked even the most basic information about the stories, from the initial copyright dates to where the stories were first published. There was no introduction, and certainly no discussion of the stories.

The purists can skip all of this. For those of you who want a tiny insight into the writer's (warped) mind, read on:

Recovering Apollo 8: For years, I kept asking scientists and other science fiction writers what would have happened if astronauts had died while orbiting the Moon. Initially, I was trying to write a story set in the future space program—a high adventure piece about an attempt to rescue those astronauts as their oxygen ran out, sort of an *Apollo 13* meets *Armageddon*.

One day, one of the writers claimed he didn't understand what I wanted. So I said, "What if NASA miscalculated and the Apollo 8 crew never made it back from the Moon? What if . . . ?"

My voice trailed off at the point, because I suddenly realized where the germ of my high-adventure story had come from. It had come from my eight-year-old self, who worried as she watched the news reports about Apollo 8. My father took me aside, just like Richard's father did in the story, and explained to me what might go wrong, trying to protect me from bad news by preparing me for it.

In that discussion with my fellow writer, I found the story I wanted to tell, but I wasn't sure my skills were up for it. I brain-stormed the idea with my writer friends at our weekly lunch, and after months of this, I think they grew tired of my strange questions. But that group helped immensely.

Because the story was so difficult for me to write, I wasn't sure what the reader response would be. My husband, who is my first reader, loved the story, but he had helped brainstorm it, so I worried that he wasn't objective. Then Sheila Williams at *Asimov's* had a similar reaction, making it the cover story of the February 2007 issue. The *Asimov's* readers gave me the best vote of all, by choosing "Recovering Apollo 8" as the best novella of the year. (It was also a Hugo nominee.)

One odd coda: When the story was nominated for the Sidewise Award for Best Alternate History Story (Long Form), I was stunned. I had worked so hard on getting the science right and on actually finding the science fiction story I wanted to tell, that I had never consciously realized I was writing an alternate history story. Usually I look at alternate histories as soft science stories at best. Most of my alternate histories have no science at all (look at "G-Men" later in this volume). "Recovering Apollo 8" went on to win the Sidewise award, proving to me yet again that the writer never knows exactly what she has written.

A Taste of Miracles: I wrote "A Taste of Miracles" nearly ten years before I wrote "Recovering Apollo 8," even though they appeared in the same calendar year. "A Taste of Miracles" was the first short story

I wrote after I quit editing *The Magazine of Fantasy and Science Fiction*, and I was suffering from a problem that I call "critical brain." I finished the story, decided it was "slight" and shelved it.

Years later, I found a copy, reread it, and loved it. It wouldn't win any awards, but it did exactly what I wanted it to do—it talked about an imagined future for outer space while harking back to the past. I immediately mailed the story to *Analog*, which published it the month before *Asimov's* published "Recovering Apollo 8." You can see that I was dealing with my Apollo 8 obsession even then.

The Strangeness of the Day: Martin H. Greenberg invited me into an anthology called *Battle Magic*. The title says it all: the story had to have a battle and there had to be magic.

I love writing for Greenberg anthologies because they stretch me. My first reaction is often "I don't want to write about that," but eventually I do. I also analyze the anthology before I start. I figured most people would have giant wizard battles in made-up fantasy universes or unicorns facing off against dragons or that kind of thing.

I decided to do something different. How I ended up with Prince Charming fighting the Evil Stepmother for Sleeping Beauty's body, I'll never know. What I do know is that this story became the impetus for my Kristine Grayson romance novels. The fantasy world first introduced here appeared in all six Grayson novels. The first, *Utterly Charming*, is an expansion of the short story itself.

By the way, the short story went pretty much unnoticed in the United States, but the French gave it their prestigious *Le Prix Imaginales* in 2003.

Substitutions: I have been writing about Silas, who deals in Death, since the early 1990s. In fact, I started "Substitutions" on December 20, 1996. I wrote the first three paragraphs and stopped, uncertain where the story was going to go.

Fast forward eight years. During that time, I would open the file, read my three paragraphs, and decide not to finish the story. Then Brittiany A. Koren asked me into an anthology she was editing with Martin H. Greenberg about assassins, called *Places to Be, People to Kill*. I realized at that moment that Silas could be considered an assassin. I opened the story again and this time, I finished it.

Soon after it was published, I received an e-mail from Ed

Gorman, a fine writer who edits an annual year's best mystery volume. He wanted "Substitutions" for his mystery anthology.

I was surprised. I hadn't thought of the story as a mystery. Once again, I learned that a story isn't what the writer thinks it is.

G-Men: "G-Men" is what I think of when I think of alternate history stories. It has no science at all. It simply takes SF's basic proposition "what if?" and applies it to history. What if Germany had won World War II? What if Christ had not been crucified?

In this case, the what-if is simple: What if J. Edgar Hoover was murdered three months after John F. Kennedy was assassinated? I'd love to have credit for that idea, but it came from my husband, Dean Wesley Smith, in the middle of lunch. I was whining about an alternate history story I had to write for an alternate history *mystery* anthology edited by Lou Anders. All of my ideas either had no alternate history or no mystery.

So Dean, probably to shut me up, suggested the Hoover idea. And it worked. I shut up, started researching, and by my deadline had this novelette—which has been getting great acclaim. It is the first story (that we can find) to appear in both a mystery best of the year collection (*The Best American Mysteries 2009*) and a science fiction best of the year collection (*The Year's Best Science Fiction 26*).

The End of the World: "The End of the World" is another story that took years to finish. I began the story in the late 1990s, and all that existed for years was the first section marked "Now." I knew I was dealing with aliens. I knew I had a story based half in Oregon's past and half in the present. But I was afraid of the subject matter for two reasons—it was going to be dark and it was going to be long.

It wasn't until 2005, when Mike Resnick asked me to participate in an anthology of science fiction crime novellas, that I decided to finish this story.

While the story didn't get much attention in the United States, the story did win a Special Mention (essentially second place) in the UPC contest, a prestigious international novella competition run out of Spain every year.

June Sixteenth at Anna's: I wrote this story days after the 9/11 tragedy. Those events so shocked me that I worried I might never write again. After all, what was fiction when compared to the hardship of real life? Gradually I came back from that position, but it took some effort.

I had a lot of trouble in those days after the attack, as most Americans did. I found comfort in the music of World War II. My mother, who was in her twenties during WWII, once told me that the music of her generation was better than the music of mine "because of the war."

I didn't understand what she meant until 9/11, when the loss and heartache hidden beneath the lovely words of songs like "Sentimental Journey" and "White Christmas" became clear to me.

Her words, that music, and the attacks themselves inspired this story.

Craters: I wrote "Craters" in three days, just after I finished a devastatingly difficult mystery novel. I was exhausted, but I had promised this story to yet another anthology, this one for my friend and mentor Joe Haldeman, about a topic I didn't much like, *Future Weapons of War*.

I was burned out. I was also disillusioned with the direction our country was taking and with many of the things happening in the world.

This story came out fast partially because I knew that if I had set the story aside I never would have finished it. The story disturbs me to this day—which is exactly what it's supposed to do.

Diving into the Wreck: "Diving into the Wreck" is another comeback story for me. I got very ill from 2001-2003. I also had some serious problems with my writing business. I lost confidence and lacked the energy to write.

But I kept imagining the hulk of the wreck from this story, and I had to put it on paper. The story went slowly, partly because of my state of mind. After I finished it, Dean had to convince me to mail it. Even then, I sat on it for some time.

Within a week of mailing, Sheila Williams at *Asimov's* bought the story and told me she wanted it to be the first cover story that she had chosen as the new editor of the magazine. Reader response was tremendous, winning me a Reader's Choice Award. "Diving" also won the UPC contest in Spain.

By the time all that good stuff had happened, I was already deep into plotting the novel. *Diving into the Wreck* the novel appeared from Pyr in November of 2009.

*   *   *

I have a very strange writing process. Short stories often spawn novels for me. Three of the stories in this volume have become novels: "Strangeness of the Day" has become *Utterly Charming,* "G-Men" is an (as yet unsold) novel titled *The Enemy Within,* and "Diving into the Wreck" is the first section of a novel of the same name.

Someday the Silas stories will be a novel, and who knows what'll happen to the characters in "The End of the World."

Short stories are my first love and often the genesis of my most important work. Thanks for sharing the collection with me. I hope you enjoyed it.

Two thousand copies of this book have been printed by the MapleVail Book Manufacturing Group, Binghamton, NY, for Golden Gryphon Press, Urbana, IL. The typeset is Electra with Palette display on 55# Sebago. The binding cloth is Roxite A. Typesetting by The Composing Room, Inc., Kimberly, WI.